FAST FORWARD

FAST ▶▶ FORWARD 1

FUTURE FICTION from the CUTTING EDGE

Edited by LOU ANDERS

To Cindi:
The Future begins first in
imagination,
then in will,
then in reality.
Thank you for nurturing
our son's imagination.
We are grateful
for all you
do,

Lou
Anders

an imprint of **Prometheus Books**
Amherst, NY

Published 2007 by Pyr®, an imprint of Prometheus Books

Inquiries should be addressed to
Pyr
59 John Glenn Drive
Amherst, New York 14228–2197
VOICE: 716–691–0133, ext. 207
FAX: 716–564–2711
WWW.PYRSF.COM

11 10 09 08 07   5 4 3 2 1

Library of Congress Cataloging-in-Publication Data

Fast forward 1 : future fiction from the cutting edge / edited by Lou Anders.
　　p. cm.
　ISBN 978–1–59102–486–6 (alk. paper)
　　1. Science fiction, American. 2. Science fiction, English. I. Anders, Lou. II. Title :
Fast forward one.

PS648.S3F39 2007
813'.0876608—dc22

2006035269

Printed in the United States of America on acid-free paper

For my son, Arthur
Our Once and Future King

ACKNOWLEDGMENTS

Every time I produce an anthology, there are a host of people, beyond the writers themselves and my publisher, to whom I am immensely grateful. This time out, foremost among them are my wife Xin Anders for her infinite patience and support; Stephenson Crossley, who read it first; Gordon Van Gelder, for introducing me to Paolo and making sure I paid attention; Deanna Hoak, our marvelous copyeditor; John Picacio, for talent beyond imagination; Frederik Pohl, for the use of his superb definition of SF as well as providing the initial inspiration for a new anthology series; Robert J. Sawyer, for friendship and a shared point of view; Eric Spitznagel, for assigning me the article that circuitously led to Robyn Hitchcock's involvement; Hitchcock himself, for willingness to be drawn into SFnal waters; and Jonathan Strahan, for early and much-appreciated enthusiasms. You are all wonderful people, and you have my heartfelt thanks. Even you, Eric.

CONTENTS

CONTENTS

Does the story tell me something worth knowing, that I had not known before, about the relationship between man and technology? Does it enlighten me on some area of science where I had been in the dark? Does it open a new horizon for my thinking? Does it lead me to think new kinds of thoughts, that I would not otherwise perhaps have thought at all? Does it suggest possibilities about the alternative possible future courses my world can take? Does it illuminate events and trends of today, by showing me where they may lead tomorrow? Does it give me a fresh and objective point of view on my own world and culture, perhaps by letting me see it through the eyes of a different kind of creature entirely, from a planet light-years away? These qualities are not only among those which make science fiction good, they are what make it unique. Be it never so beautifully written, a story is not a good science fiction story unless it rates high in at least some of these aspects. The content of the story is as valid a criterion as the style.   —Frederik Pohl

SF is what I point at when I say "SF."   —Damon Knight

INTRODUCTION: WELCOME TO THE FUTURE

Lou Anders

The science fiction genre has been home to many landmark anthology series in its illustrious history, often a staple source of groundbreaking work. The saying goes that we see so far because we stand on the shoulders of giants. In this case, the idea behind *Fast Forward*—that of presenting a new, unthemed science fiction–only anthology series of original material—owes its inspiration to the late Damon Knight and his prestigious and influential Orbit series, which ran twenty-one volumes from 1966 to 1980. Orbit itself took inspiration from Star Science Fiction, the first SF anthology series of them all, which ran six volumes from 1953 to 1959 and was edited by the great Frederik Pohl, whose wonderful definition of science fiction—which serves as close to a theme as this anthology has—opens this book. Damon Knight's definition, by contrast, is the better known, more humorous; and while it points out the problems inherent in definitions of any kind, it is of lesser use in this context. If I may offer my own definition, it is this: Science fiction is a tool for making sense of a changing world. It is *the* genre that looks at the implications of technology on society, which in this age of exponential technological growth makes it the most relevant branch of literature going. We've lived through at least one singularity with the birth of the Internet, and the way this technology has transformed everyone's lives in just a few short decades cannot be overlooked or downplayed. But this is only the start—we have a biotech and a nanotech boom still to come—and the close of the twenty-first century will look absolutely nothing like its inception. The future has overtaken the present, and things are speeding up. This hasn't ever been true in history before to the extent that it is true now. As Bob Dylan wrote, "The times they are a-changin'."

Theodore Sturgeon defined science fiction's strength as its ability to "ask the next question" in an ongoing dialogue that takes us from the present into the future. The future, as the saying goes, exists first in imagination, then in will, then in reality; and the types of dreams we dream today will determine the world we and our children live in tomorrow. Our world is dreaming some dark dreams now. We need to dream better, as if our life depended on it. Because it does. To a very real extent, we live today in the science fiction of the past. The nanotechnological research going on today was first envisioned in Philip K. Dick's 1955 story "Autofac," which introduced the concept of micromachines able to construct duplicates of themselves. We walk around with Bluetooth-enabled earclips that look like nothing less than the Borg implants of *Star Trek*, talking on communication devices deliberately modeled on Kirk's communicator, and while our music is increasingly digital, the compact discs that have yet to give up the ghost were actually modeled on the big silver discs that Mr. Atoz and his clones used in the library from the episode "All Our Yesterdays." Asimov gave us the word "robotics" and Gibson the word "cyberspace." Our communication satellites were dreamed up by Sir Arthur C. Clarke in 1945, and our personal computers were first envisioned by author Murray Leinster back in 1946 in his short story "A Logic Named Joe." (Not only did Leinster envision the PC, but he understood that it would be used for television, news, horoscopes, dating, stock trading, weather, and all the "junk" that fills up so much of our inboxes. As has been said before, anyone could have predicted the automobile, but it would take a science fiction writer to predict the traffic jam.)

"Science fiction is critical to progress in science," says geologist Robert Peckyno in an interview posted on the science and science fiction blog *Meme Therapy* (June 15, 2006). "Visionaries who radically change the world are often thought of as crackpots, and fiction has been the inspiration for many great ideas. Tsiolkovsky, Goddard, Oberth, von Braun, and Korolev are collectively the foundation of rocketry today—every one mentioned being inspired by the Jules Verne story 'From the Earth to the Moon.' Go to any NASA facility and you will find desks with models of the *Enterprise* and *Starfury*. Science fiction helps to provide the dreams and puzzles that today's engineers and scientists try to bring to life."

But it is the future of science fiction itself (and that of science fiction publishing) that some have called into question, and lately it seems as if the very idea of the future has been under threat. Certainly, respect for science and the scientific method has come under attack in recent times. In his essay "The Omega Glory," Pulitzer prize–winning author Michael Chabon writes:

> I don't know what happened to the Future. It's as if we lost our ability, or our will, to envision anything beyond the next hundred years or so, as if we lacked the fundamental faith that there will in fact be any future at all beyond that not-too-distant date. Or maybe we stopped talking about the Future around the time that, with its microchips and its twenty-four-hour news cycles, it arrived. Some days when you pick up the newspaper it seems to have been cowritten by J. G. Ballard, Isaac Asimov, and Philip K. Dick. . . . This is the paradox that lies at the heart of our loss of belief or interest in the Future, which has in turn produced a collective cultural failure to imagine that future, any Future, beyond the rim of a couple of centuries.

Chabon is talking about the imagination of the wider world, not the community of science fiction writers who have always labored to create a myriad of tomorrows. But it's no secret that our field is changing, that the most popular books today are works of epic fantasy, or that we're inundated with post–*Buffy the Vampire Slayer* tales of werewolf detectives and sexy women who battle the supernatural. We hear talk about the graying of the field as the readership for the "good stuff" ages and dwindles. We worry about the shrinking of the midlist, as many deserving practitioners who sell in respectable numbers are squeezed out of their publishing houses in the pressure to produce another Stephen King or Laurell K. Hamilton. We wonder if the inundation of high-tech gadgetry in our society makes our potential readership proverbial fish that cannot see the science fiction waters all around them. And always, it is harder to be brilliant than it is to be merely competent.

Recently, I came across another explanation of our genre, again on *Meme Therapy*, from the wonderful Robert Charles Wilson (July 2, 2006):

> The one compelling idea that recurs constantly in science fiction from H. G. Wells onward is human contingency—which boils down to three statements: The world in the past was a very different place than it is now; the world we live in could have been a very different place than it is; and the world will inevitably become a very different place in the future. These assertions may seem obvious, but I believe they're counterintuitive, like the idea that the earth revolves around the sun. Our lives are simply too short to give them real visceral meaning. So we have to use our imagination, we have to literalize the possibilities, we have to engage the truth that dinosaurs really did once wander over the prairies, that the Confederacy really might have bargained with England and won its independence, that human activity really might change the climate or sterilize the seas.
>
> Internalize this deeply enough and you do end up with a slightly distanced worldview. You learn not to trust appearances, which is always a valuable lesson, and you realize that no human institution, good or bad, secular or religious, cultural or technological, is fore-ordained or guaranteed to last.

There you have it. Science fiction *is* skepticism. Science fiction *is* rationalism. Science fiction is the notion that there *are* other perspectives out there, other modes of thinking, other ways of being than those in front of your nose, worlds beyond your current understanding. Science fiction opens the mind to the notion of change. Science fiction is enlightenment packaged in narrative.

And why is this in itself important? What makes this agenda—and it is an agenda—relevant beyond that of other genres or mainstream works? As Gardner Dozois wrote in the introduction to his anthology *Galileo's Children: Tales of Science vs. Superstition* (Pyr, August 2005):

> Even today, the pope interdicts cloning, the president of the United States pushes to make stem cell research illegal, mention of the theory of evolu-

tion is banned from textbooks and explanations of "creation science" are inserted instead, and politicians of both political parties vote against money for space exploration or any other kind of research where the instant up-front financial benefit to the bottom line is not immediately evident.

The battle of science against superstition is still going on, as is the battle to not have to think only what somebody else thinks is okay for you to think. In fact, in a society where more people believe in angels than believe in evolution, that battle may be more critical than ever.

One of the major battlefields is science fiction, one of the few forms of literature where rationality, skepticism, the knowledge of the inevitability of change, and the idea that wide-ranging freedom of thought and unfet-tered imagination and curiosity are *good* things are the default positions, taken for granted by most of its authors.

. . . [S]cience fiction provides one of the few places in modern letters where the battle between science and superstition is openly discussed and debated, and that makes those who write it, as well as those brave charac-ters they write about, embroiled in the age-old struggle to prevent the con-trol of the human mind and the suppression of the human spirit, "Galileo's Children" in a very real way indeed.

I don't think there could be a clearer case as to why our "escapist literature," as it is so often called, is so important, or as to why it is never *just* escapism—not even at its most embarrassing levels. Even absurd cinematic blockbusters like *Star Wars* (for all it has to answer for) have their part to play in turning on the minds of people everywhere to the wonders of the universe and the possibilities of technology.

Despite fears to the contrary, I see a rise in science fiction as a long-term trend, aided by the pace of technological developments in the real world. At the 2006 Winter Olympics, US and Canadian skiers were wearing "smart armor" inside their normal clothing. Known as d3o, a futuristic flexible material that hardens into armor on impact, the skintight outfits look as much like a superhero's pajamas as anything Tobey Maguire or Christian Bale ever donned. And the Net itself is nothing if not science fiction realized. It is with much irony that I note that now, decades after J. G. Ballard proclaimed that the Space Age was over, it is the children of the "inner space" his own

New Wave writings ushered in—the dot-com billionaires who first crafted William Gibson's cyberspace in reality—who are now leading the charge to privatization of the race to the heavens. Space Adventures, who previously sent three space tourists with extremely deep pockets to the International Space Station, has announced plans to build a $265 million spaceport in the United Arab Emirates, with help from Texas venture capital and a Russian aerospace firm. And Richard Branson is building a (slightly cheaper!) $225 million spaceport in New Mexico for his Virgin Galactic. Virgin Galactic? The very name sounds like something out of *Barbarella*. Long-term, the real Space Age is only beginning, and the literature that charts our future there can only benefit.

While back on the ground, our increasingly technological society is making it increasingly hard for the mainstream to deny that we do in fact *live in the future*. Who better to explain this accelerated age than the science fiction writers, those who have tools honed over a century of experiment and experience for examining the ramifications of change?

It is to this end, and in this spirit, that *Fast Forward* is offered. As author and critic John Clute says, "SF accustoms us to looking; it does not, in the end, tell us what we are going to have to see. SF is the window, not the view." Here, then, are twenty-one windows on the future, as seen through the imagination of twenty-three different talents. Their collective visions take us from the far future to the day just after tomorrow. In their hands, science fiction is indeed a tool for making sense of a changing world. It's not the only such tool, but it is an amazingly effective one. Who knew enlightenment could be so much fun?

YFL-500

Robert Charles Wilson

Multiple award winner and nominee Robert Charles Wilson is a fabulously inventive writer who always manages with his tales to pull fresh jaw-dropping concepts from out of the worn fabric of science fiction. In my previous anthology, FutureShocks, *he created the world of the Rationalization, a time in which the majority of human occupations have been rendered obsolete by advances in robotics, leaving humanity with too much time on its hands. Although this story shares no characters in common with "The Cartesian Theater," it is set in the same post-Scarcity world, explores similar concerns as the previous tale, and is every bit as fascinating.*

He knew her name and a few salient details. She was a dole gypsy, no fixed address, lived by the docks, slept with friends or in the lightless nooks of aibot factories or, weather permitting, under a tent on the beach. She earned no money and subsisted on her dole annuities, but—and this was among his first impressions of her—she wore brightly dyed clothing and gaudy flecks of expensive jewelry, and maybe that should have told him something, but it didn't.

Gordo had been coming to Doletown every day for more than a month, searching for her. He didn't pretend to be anything but a modestly wealthy artist slumming among the willfully unemployed. Every morning he rose from a dreamless sleep and left his neat, expensive apartment to ride down the columnar deeps of the city to Doletown. He didn't mention her name there—he dared not be that obvious—but he made friends quickly among the would-be and has-been aesthetes who comprised so large a percentage of the Doletown population, and he kept his ears open. He dropped his own name by way of a calling card. "I'm Gordo Fisk," he would say, extending his hand, and the response might be a raised eyebrow of recognition or envy or scorn. Yes, *that* Gordo Fisk. The transrepresentationalist. Briefly famous, yes. Though that was fading.

Apart from her name, all he really knew about her was that she had visited the Bonnuit Sleep Clinic in the early spring of 2110—three years ago now. Because he couldn't name her directly, he discreetly mentioned the Bonnuit instead. It turned out a lot of Doletown types had visited the Bonnuit in the past, not because they had trouble sleeping but because the clinic was conveniently located and had sponsored a research program that ran until late last year. The clinic would pay volunteers a generous tithe just for sleeping in a monitored bed with devices attached to their craniums. A noninvasive night's work and a nice way to pick up pocket change when the free food, shelter, and consumer chits guaranteed by the Rationalization seemed not quite sufficient.

So her name eventually came up in conversation. Her name was Iris Seawright, and before too long Gordo found himself on a beach where the salt air smelled rank and the concrete bastions of wave/tide power stations rode the blue horizon like floating castles. It was late in the day, and a casual group of dole gypsies had assembled to build a bonfire. They stacked driftwood and flotsam while public-safety aibots flitted overhead with motherly concern. In the light of the setting sun, the flying aibots looked like seabirds made of amethyst or amber.

Iris Seawright came out of a green hempen tent, shielding her eyes, and Gordo, still meters away, knew at once that he had found her. She had been described to him, of course, but he suspected he would have known her anyway. She was everything he had imagined but more specific—somehow, more *incarnate*. She wasn't remarkably tall or short. Her face was elfin and sun-browned. She wore gauzy fabrics that flag-danced in the breeze from the ocean, and her golden hair was tied with a ribbon and dangled carelessly down her back. Her rings sparkled. So did her eyes.

Gordo's heart did double beats as he tried to maintain his calm. This, after all, was what he had been searching for for so long. This, or some sense of his own authenticity.

‖

Three years ago, Gordo had gone to the Bonnuit Clinic to confess a shameful secret and to seek a cure.

The physician he saw that day was one Dr. DuBois, a man his own age. Dr. DuBois welcomed him into one of the interview rooms attached to the clinic's luxurious main atrium. The Bonnuit Clinic catered expensively to the worried well. The Rationalization guaranteed medical care to anyone who needed it, but if you wanted a human physician—not one of those competent but affectless or obsequious aibots who staffed the curbside hospitals—you had to pay money for the privilege. Perversely, the most expensive of these facilities specialized in the most trivial non-life-threatening complaints. See a machine for appendicitis: see a human being for your soul. Or so people said, up on the sunlight levels of the city.

Gordo's complaint was not physical, exactly, but neither was it wholly spiritual. Now that he had screwed up the courage to come here, he found it enormously difficult to confess.

"Your sleep is disturbed," Dr. DuBois said encouragingly.

"Yes . . . well . . . in a way."

"Are you reluctant to confide in me? Believe me, Mr. Fisk, there's nothing to be apologetic about. I see people every day—people who share your problem, I'm sure, if you'll only explain to me what it is. Can't fall asleep? Medication doesn't work for you? Nightmares? Existential discomfort?"

For any of those problems he would have consulted an aibot physician or neurologist. But there were some things you simply didn't want to say to a machine. That delicacy of feeling was no doubt what kept Dr. DuBois in business.

"I don't dream," Gordo said, almost choking on the words.

The doctor betrayed no disapproval or disgust. Why would he? Gordo's shame was specific to himself: to his situation, his history.

"Most likely you *do* dream," DuBois said congenially, "and simply don't remember having done so. Dreams are elusive, Mr. Fisk. Slippery by nature. They're seldom what we expect."

"I don't dream, or I don't remember my dreams—it's all the same—though I truly believe I don't dream at all, Dr. DuBois; that's what it feels like, although I can't prove it."

"That must be disturbing. Even so, I have patients who might envy you. They suffer terribly from nightmares."

Dr. DuBois was being even-handed, injecting a sense of proportion. Gordo shrugged. He would have welcomed a nightmare. He would have thrown a party for it.

"Well," Dr. DuBois said, "we can certainly work with you, Mr. Fisk, identify the problem and address it, but before we begin may I ask why you find this dreamlessness so particularly troubling?"

"I'm an artist."

The doctor's eyebrows rose. "Fisk? I'm thinking of the Fisks who created the Mt. Merapi Series—but surely you're too young—"

"Tomas Fisk was my father." And Arcela Fisk was his mother, he might have added. Both were responsible for the Mt. Merapi installation, not to mention dozens of other less-grandiose works of static art.

Gordo had been apprenticed into the static arts since childhood, had willingly and eagerly accepted the role of heir-apparent that had been thrust upon him by his parents and, when they retired, by their eager public following. But he was thirty years old now, and to this point he had produced only workmanlike and undistinguished public installations, commissioned by businesses and municipalities more interested in his marketable name than in the final product. Like his parents Gordo was a transrepresentationalist, but his work had gathered only tepid applause, and his status within the movement was fragile. He had overheard himself being dismissed at gallery openings and sophisticated parties.

Worse than that, though—or at the root of it—was this inability to dream. He had been raised in a household and in a community that valued all things invisible or mysterious in human nature: things the aibots (presumably) didn't share. Visions, eccentricity, madness of the nonviolent sort, hallucinatory journeys, dream quests—dreams! His parents had discussed their dreams in minute detail at the breakfast table. As a child Gordo had willingly and eagerly joined in these conversations, and his mother and father had praised the vividness and gaudiness of his youthful fantasies. But the dreams dried up when he hit puberty, and Gordo had been reduced to silence or embarrassing fiction. He could not bring himself to say, "I don't dream anymore; my nights are black, seamless oceans of nothingness; I lie unconscious for eight hours and wake knowing I've slept; but I no longer dream." He could hardly admit it to himself, even now. It would have been like confessing that he was hollow inside, an empty vessel from which all visionary content had been drained.

He explained this to Dr. DuBois while blushing and studying the floor.

Dr. DuBois appeared to give the issue somber thought. Then he said, "Thank you for your frankness. I understand now. We'll work up your case, Mr. Fisk, and we'll find out what's gone wrong. And then we'll fix it."

Gordo liked the sound of that.

‖

He observed Iris Seawright surreptitiously as he circled the bonfire, not wanting to spook her, not wanting their meeting to seem anything but natural. Night fell while he watched her, and there was the sound of waves lapping the littoral, the tide offering up bits and pieces of the world as it had been before the population decline and the Rationalization—wasteful plastic things, salt-bleached jugs and bottles like the pallid carcasses of extinct crabs. Public-safety aibots still flitted prissily overhead, keeping watch to make sure the flames didn't spread, dodging sparks that whirled up from the burning driftwood. There was conversation and singing, and Gordo saw couples and threesomes vanishing behind a concrete tidal wall to make love in the sandy darkness. Iris, he was pleased to see, listened to the music, chatted with friends, but essentially kept to herself. There was a certain singleness about her.

She finally settled on a log a comfortable distance from the fire, her face an intoxicating patchwork of firelight and moonshadow, among a group of people with whom Gordo had recently made friends. He drifted that way and nodded at the familiar faces. Before long he was introduced to her. Gordo Fisk, Iris Seawright. Pleased to meet you. The chorus of biographical data: Gordo is an artist. A *successful* artist. Lives up in the sunlight levels, a transrepresentationalist, maybe you've heard of him.

Iris, who had not yet pronounced more than a sentence, cocked her perfect head at him and said, "No. Name's not familiar."

"Iris don't follow the arts," someone else chimed in. "Iris's one of the original originals."

"Pure dole gypsy," a second voice said.

"Does as she wills."

"A free spirit."

"Goes where the wind blows."

Et cetera. Gordo ignored all these incantations, because Iris was smiling at him now. She patted the log beside her, and he sat down, entranced.

He had known she would be beautiful.

Of course there had been no guarantee of that. As Dr. DuBois had once said, "She could be anyone." The code on her file had indicated her gender but nothing else. She could have been a child. She could have been an old woman stooped and angled by the years. She could have been monstrously ugly. There was no telling.

But Gordo had known, in some inexplicably powerful way, that she would be beautiful. He remembered something his father had often said (imperially, as he said most things, pronouncing a great truth): "If there is no such thing as a beautiful dream, Gordo, there can be no such thing as a beautiful mind."

So he had known that her mind, at least, would be beautiful. But he had suspected the rest of her would be, too. He had anticipated the youth and lightness of her, the fearlessness of her gaze, even the wrinkles of curiosity and (perhaps) joy at the corners of her eyes.

He put those things out of his thoughts, however, and simply talked to her—small talk, the only kind of talk available to strangers; the weather, the night, the stars; while he memorized the look of her and while she likewise checked him out, one moment meeting his eyes with her own, the next looking at his shoes or his clothing or away into the night and the sea. Her voice was light and musical, her vocabulary simple, her grammar and syntax uncomplex. Her hands moved when she spoke, illustrating her sentences like twin trained birds.

He had known, he had known.

Cautiously, not wanting to push anything but conscious of the connection he had already made, he asked her to dinner the following night. She said yes, that might be nice. Come around about evening tomorrow, she said.

"Where?" he said.

"Oh, here. I'll be here somewhere. I'll look for you," she said.

Dr. DuBois had performed an intricate test on Gordo to determine the cause of his anoeiric fugue—his dreamlessness. What happened was, Gordo went to the Bonnuit Clinic at an appointed hour, was helmeted with neurological inductors of the latest and subtlest kind, was given a hypnagogic potion to make him sleep, and was installed in a monitoring bed while he waited for the drug to affect him. He asked whether the drug would *make* him dream: he had experimented with other substances reputed to have that effect, but they had done nothing for him.

"No," Dr. DuBois said, "this is only to put you to sleep, and to compress the equivalent of an eight-hour night into half that time—it does nothing to foster or inhibit REM states. How do you feel so far?"

"Well—*sleepy*," Gordo admitted. His limbs had grown heavy, and he found himself listlessly uninterested in his body, the doctor, the room, his senses, anything at all. Dr. DuBois said reassuring things, and soon Gordo slept: the only evidence of which was, he woke again.

"No dreams," he reported.

He had slept the regulation four hours under the influence of the drug. Dr. DuBois had meanwhile interviewed patients, gone for lunch, written the introduction to a journal article, and returned to Gordo's bedside. "We'll see about that," he said.

They adjourned to a consultation room where DuBois was already running a collation of the session's results. Numbers scrolled down the screen of the doctor's analytical engine, followed by something that interested Gordo more: a patchwork of elementary colors, chiefly gray, blue, black, separating and reconjoining like oil on water.

Dr. DuBois studied these results. The sequence seemed to run no more than a minute. Dr. DuBois ran it twice, frowning.

Gordo said, "What is that?"

"Your four hours of sleep. From the inside. The devices you wore on your head monitored your brain activity. They're extremely subtle machines, Mr. Fisk. They can register the discharge or inhibition of a single neuron, the ebb and flow of an entire alphabet of neurotransmitters, the activity or inactivity of individual synapses and ion channels. They know where these events happen in the brain and what they signify in macroscopic and behavioral terms. They can distinguish between rage and pain, laughter and grief, love and hate. All these things and a thousand more are condensed into numbers and represented schematically in compressed time."

"Transrepresented," Gordo said, because this was what the transrepresentational movement in the arts was all about: taking real-world data and making beautiful abstractions of it.

"In a sense," Dr. DuBois agreed, "in a sense."

"And it can tell when I'm dreaming?"

The doctor hesitated a long moment. "Yes."

"And was I?"

Another pause. "No."

Gordo was unsurprised.

"But this is only an isolated test," Dr. DuBois said. "You didn't dream *this time*. Most patients do, but in your case—well—"

Gordo watched the colors evolve and dissolve on the screen. "So what does a dream look like, if this isn't one?"

"Here—I can show you an example, if you like."

He rooted through his desk for a file folder to which a slip of digital memory was attached and fed the slip into a port of the analytical engine. The screen immediately flushed with pearlescent filigree, with subtle paisleys and exfoliating neon fractals.

Gordo watched, wide-eyed. Then he glanced at the file folder. On it was written an identity code: YFL-500.

Gordo arrived at the beach at the appointed hour, but the wind was chilly and carried a periodic, stuttering drizzle—he was afraid she wouldn't show up. He waited under a sheltering abutment as the time came and the time passed. At sea, under veils of rain, aibot cargo ships drifted like gray window-less cities. Gordo had abandoned all but the faintest hope and was about to head back to the intracity lifts when he spotted a swirl of magenta behind the curve of a retaining wall: her cape. He ran to her, grinning and shivering.

"You're wet," she said, and he said, "I'll be all right. Thank you for coming. I was hoping you would. Are you hungry? Where do you want to eat?"

"You pick. Somewhere nice."

Somewhere uptown, she meant. Somewhere she couldn't afford to go without exhausting her dole allowance. Well, that was a reasonable request. He meant to show her a good time. So he folded his rain cape back into its pack and took her up the lifts to a premium mallway in which there was an Ethiopian-style restaurant he had discovered last year. The restaurant was quiet and dark and staffed entirely by human beings. Most menial food chores (like menial chores of every other kind) were customarily performed by aibots, so the waitstaff here were almost certainly paid fabulous wages for lending that last touch of *biologique* to the all-organic ambiance. And that premium was reflected in the prices on the menu, at which Iris's eyes widened prettily. Gordo didn't mind. He was happy to give her this; she deserved it—though he could not let his adulation show, for it might lead her to suspect his motives. His motives were as pure as arctic ice—well, relatively pure—but it wouldn't do to reveal them too soon. Might scare her away.

He asked her about her life.

She had been born into a large family somewhere south of Eugene, Oregon, she said, and they had all been content to subsist on the dole. The automation of the economy, the Entrepreneurial Expert System that guided and governed machine/machine production and exchange, had enabled an idyllic childhood. No one lacked for food, shelter, and an income large enough to allow that individual to function as a consumer (and thus a perceptible unit in the global calculus of economic intercourse). Iris was educated—she could read and write English—but she had never been any kind of scholar, and her spiritual life, she said, consisted of a deep need not to linger too long in any single place. "I like to move around," she said.

"It's true what they said about you at the beach, then. Free spirit."

"Yeah, I guess." She shrugged. "Whatever that means."

Gordo was not in the least disappointed that Iris wasn't an intellectual or an artist. Better that she wasn't, perhaps. Any trace of self-consciousness would have marred her perfect authenticity. After all, it wasn't the content of her mind he had come to love. It was the raw fecundity of it.

"But it's boring talking about myself," she remarked over the wine. "What about you? People say you're famous."

"Not famous. I do static art, Iris. No one who does that gets really famous, not famous the way video stars and lurid novelists are famous. Well-known in certain circles, you could say."

She smiled coquettishly. "Certain circles. Huh. You paint pictures?"

"No. I create objects."

"What kind of objects?"

"I'm a transrepresentationalist. You must know what that means."

"Doletown people talk about it. I never paid much attention. You make things that represent other things."

"I re-represent data as a pleasing abstraction."

That was the dictionary definition, and it was true enough if you allowed a certain latitude to the word "pleasing." What was important was that the original dataset should be drawn from the physical world—from sunspot cycles, say, or the microwave radiation generated by variable stars, or (as in the case of his parents' Mt. Merapi installation) the seismic waveforms of a simmering volcano. The artist's job was to reconfigure the data in a fashion that was striking in a visual or tactile sense, to reconfigure it as art. To find patterns in it, even (or especially) meaningless patterns: accidental deviations from randomness, without scientific value but enormously useful when employed as a line or a contour or a color. To chisel abstract beauty from the sullen rock of science.

It was something aibots didn't do; thus it had the virtues of rarity and unrepeatability, a product as purely human as a pearl is purely oyster.

"And," Iris said, folding a hunk of injira around a dollop of curried goat, "this makes money for you?"

"From time to time, it does."

"I wish I could see one of your, um, things."

"Maybe you can," Gordo said, concealing his excitement. "My best-known piece is on display not far from here."

"What's it like?"

"I can't really describe it. A column two feet wide by eight feet tall. Like glass or ice—but not glass or ice."

"What's it about? I mean, what's the dataset? What'd you base it on?"

"That's a secret," Gordo said, smiling in spite of himself.

"Well, what's it called?"

"YFL-500."

Therapy didn't work. Drugs didn't work. Dr. DuBois grew frustrated with Gordo's intractable dreamlessness. It was a frustration Gordo had lived with every day of his adult life.

"Clearly," the doctor said, "all the physiological functions of sleep are being adequately performed. There are even what you might call *traces* of dreams, the brain doing the sort of nocturnal dusting and cleaning that keeps us all sane. What you lack, Mr. Fisk, is the usual vocabulary of images and slipshod narrative that a layman means by the word 'dream.'"

"Figured as much," Gordo said.

He had been back to the clinic five times. Five times, sleep had been induced and his sleeping brain monitored in substantive detail. Five times, the result had been the same: undifferentiated neurological murk.

And each time, by way of contrast, Gordo had asked to see the kaleidoscopic flash and gnarl of the file marked YFL-500. And Dr. DuBois had indulged him, perhaps sensing that this was all the satisfaction Gordo was going to get from his costly consultation. "Is this *typical*?" Gordo asked.

"More typical than your productions, Mr. Fisk, but actually it's close to the opposite end of the scale—if you can imagine a linear scale for intensity of dreaming."

He had imagined just such a thing. "Who did it come from?"

"A volunteer. It was part of our baseline study."

"What volunteer?"

"I can't say. I'm constrained by confidentiality protocols."

"May I have a copy of it?"

"I can't see how that would be useful to you. What's on the file is really just numbers. To see it this way you'd need to sort the data according to an appropriate algorithm."

"That's not a problem."

Gordo imagined the wheels turning in Dr. DuBois's head. "What are you saying, Mr. Fisk—that you want to make *art* of it?"

"I collect datasets of all kinds," Gordo said humbly.

"Well, but again, the question of confidentiality—"

"You can scrub any notation regarding the individual source. I don't want names or circumstances. Just the anonymous raw material."

"I see. Irregular. But, hm, harmless, I suppose, as long as you don't publish the raw data or use the name of the clinic." Perhaps thinking, as before, that it would be at least a souvenir, something to carry away from an expensive course of treatment that had not yielded a cure or anything close to one.

"I'll be very careful," Gordo said.

He had not yet taken the full measure of Iris Seawright, but he had seen enough to know she was something he couldn't ever be—spontaneous, simple, and on some level visionary. She looked at him admiringly as they rode a crowded masslift to the gallery where several transrepresentationalist works had recently been mounted for display. Not a prestigious venue, because he was no longer an especially prestigious artist, but respectable enough that it cost money to get inside the vast and luxurious hall. Gordo had begun his career as a disappointment and he had peaked with YFL-500, which everyone admitted was a masterpiece. There had been some interest in the pieces that followed, but if you charted his career as a graph it would have displayed but a single spike, and he still wasn't sure whether the inspiration was his or, ultimately, hers.

"Oh my God," Iris whispered when they entered the Corridor of the Static Arts, a glass-ceilinged cathedral enhanced by moonlight and patrolled by child-sized aibots with formal clothing and enormous eyes. "This is so fucking nice!"

There were no class barriers in these days of the Rationalization—snobbery of all sorts, but no lines one literally couldn't cross. Iris could have come here (or to any number of similar galleries or museums) at any time. Many of her Doletown friends did, although as aspiring and unsuccessful artists, the attitude they brought with them was usually disdainful and dismissive. Gordo was pleased that Iris was an exception.

Here were displayed items of transrepresentationalist statuary, sculpture, and painting of varying degrees of sophistication. The enormous room was dominated by Moses Bolden's *Voices of Time*, distilled from a map of variations in the cosmic background radiation. A couple of nocturnal visitors stood at the foot of it, gawking. Much admired, that piece, although to Gordo it looked like nothing more than a series of arcane symbols carved into a luminescent half-dome, more idiosyncratic than beautiful, and trite in its labored sense of mystery. But Iris's lovely eyes widened when the structure radiated semitones of blue and azure. If he did not much care for the art, he enjoyed her enjoyment of it. And was briefly jealous. She asked, "Did you do this?"

"No."

"So which one is yours? Show me yours."

"That's why we're here, Iris."

He escorted her down the arched and curving corridor. Except for the spaces where works of art were appropriately lighted, the entire gallery was dim. The early-evening rainfall had passed, and beyond the glass wall on the right a crescent moon shone over the city's peaks and canyons. Iris was impressed by the politeness of the custodial aibots. "I guess that's the difference between Uptown and Doletown. Up here the aibots keep their distance."

"This is it," Gordo announced, suddenly nervous.

Iris stopped short. He had steered her this way purposely, so that she would be surprised by YFL-500 rather than absorbing it from a distance. It had been placed at a curve in the corridor for that very purpose, a challenge to the glassy ceiling and the stars.

Gordo discovered he could not speak. This was a moment he had long contemplated—long hoped for, long feared. And now that it had arrived he found himself seizing up like a faulty machine.

"Huh!" Iris said at length.

What did he want from her? Praise? No. No praise was due him. What he had hoped was that she might recognize the piece, might feel some unconscious kinship with it.

She moved around YFL-500 slowly, following its internal lace and filigree and the boldness of its structure. She extended her hand as if to touch it, then pulled back. "Wow . . . how'd you make this?"

"It's a question of, of—well, technically, each micron-layer of crystals, and every crystal in each layer, is polarized so that it refracts or absorbs light. The polarization is binary . . . it's code, and the span from top to bottom is a timescale. It's a portrait of an event—"

"What event?"

He hesitated. He hovered on the brink, it seemed to him, of a vast abyss. "I've never told anyone—"

"Well, you don't have to tell, if you want to keep it secret."

"It's a dream," he said, almost gasping at his own audacity.

"A dream? Really? Someone's real dream?"

"A dream as recorded by very sensitive neurological machinery. But what makes it art is that I found the *narrative* in the data. Do you see it, Iris? Caught in the crystal? Like a shadow hidden by a rainbow. It begins at the top, that ghost of clarity, and it pulses, it expands and contracts according to its own logic, and it vanishes, down below, into chaos, into fractured light."

"Like a prism," Iris said.

"Yes, like a prism, in a sense, but—"

"Is it *your* dream? A dream you had?"

"I don't dream," Gordo said aloud for the second time in his life. He felt numb, weightless.

"That's too bad," Iris said, and she gave YFL-500 another thoughtful look. "Anyway," she said. "It's very pretty."

There was no way to tell her how difficult, how exacting the work had been.

He had taken the binary file YFL-500 to his studio with fierce anticipation. What he had seen on the display panel of Dr. DuBois's analytical engine had already been a crude act of transrepresentation—raw and ridiculously literal as it was, it hinted at the riches the file might contain. The data was complex, but (like a dream) not entirely random, and to Gordo it was a mute command: Carve my beauty out of this stone of numbers. Make tangible what lies beyond the power of words.

He hacked at the data for six months before he began to recognize the major and minor chords embedded in it. The stacked, polarized crystals were his own idea. He had commissioned his tools from an aibot prototyper, three times attempted a rendition, and three times failed to achieve the effect he was aiming for.

As he worked he could not help speculating about the source of the data, the dreamer of the dream. Dr. DuBois had said this was a "particularly rich and vivid" dataset, but might not *any* dream yield some similar strange beauty? (Excepting the products of his own gray sleep.) Gordo suspected not. And it was as he envisioned this hypothetical dreamer—a woman, he was almost certain—that the work finally attained the coherence it needed.

In due time the finished piece was debuted. He called it YFL-500 after the numbered Bonnuit file and refused to publicly divulge the source of his data. At first the piece aroused no particular attention, but word quickly spread among the community of critics and opinion makers and, in time, the art-literate public. It was called a remarkable departure for an artist who previously had been considered too pedestrian to create anything of lasting worth. By such faint but real praise his name was once more elevated, and before long Gordo began to think of himself as a genuine artist.

In time he went back to see Dr. DuBois.

"I have no new therapy for the dreamless," the doctor said, "unless something else is bothering you? Insomnia, perhaps?"

"Actually," Gordo said, "what I want is more data."

More dreams. More raw material. The more intricate the better, he explained.

"But this is unethical," Dr. DuBois protested.

"No more unethical than the first time you did it."

"Even so—even with the names and details deleted, these measurements were given to us in trust. They were donated for a specific purpose, for research. Contracts to that effect were signed. If anyone were to discover that they had been manipulated for mass entertainment—"

"Hardly mass," Gordo said. *Hardly entertainment*, he thought.

"The piece you created must have been lucrative, though, yes?"

"It made some money for me. But more important—"

"In this context, shouldn't I decide what's important? What you're looking for, it seems to me, is a kind of silent partner."

"I suppose so."

Dr. DuBois waited. Gordo measured the pause and then said, "You want to be compensated for the risk."

"We can work out the details later," the doctor said.

As they left the gallery, Iris asked him where he lived.

"Couple levels up," Gordo said. "Not far. Come for a drink?"

"Yeah," Iris said, "I'd like that."

He keyed the door and let her in with mounting excitement. Not just sexual excitement, though that was definitely an ingredient. She seemed willing, and the thought of making love to the woman who was the source of

YFL-500 was almost unbearably tantalizing. But he took nearly as much pleasure simply in being near her, in a place as private as his home. Gordo was a private man, by and large. Only his most intimate friends had visited him here. Was Iris an intimate friend? Not yet. But there was a kind of unspoken intimacy between them, the shared space of her unconscious mind, with which he had long since fallen in love—not that she was aware of that, of course.

And in time he might ask other intimacies of her.

"Super nice place," Iris said, tossing her rain cape over the back of a sofa.

"I like it," Gordo said. "Mostly for the view."

She went to the window that constituted one wall of the apartment. In sunlight it would have rendered the exterior world as a shadowy forest of cliff-like habitats, roof gardens, turbines, blunt concrete aibot hives. By night the window was clear as fine crystal. Here was the crescent moon again, pale against the glistening vertical lightscape of the city. Firefly aibots darted between tall buildings; cargo drones cruised above the city with weightless ease.

Iris gave the city a cursory glance and paced the room, stopping to admire this or that of his possessions.

Gordo owned a few antiques, a few valuable contemporary pieces. She paused by a mahogany table on which was displayed the only object he owned that had been crafted by his father. She picked it up—a little cavalierly, Gordo thought—and inspected it.

"A seashell," she said.

"Not exactly. The root dataset was a recording of wave impacts on the shore of a beach somewhere in the Pacific. It was rendered as a Fibonacci series—that's why it looks like a conch shell. A little joke."

"It's a joke?"

"In a way. Hold it up to the light."

She did, and a faint sound emerged from the bell-like opening.

"It stores photonic energy and rereleases it as mechanical vibrations. The sound reflects the original data."

"The sea!" Iris said, grinning.

Gordo nodded. The piece had always struck him as painfully obvious, almost a novelty item. But even as a minor work of Fisk *pere* it would command a large sum at auction—more than any work of his own except YFL-500.

She put the shell back in its place and looked, in turn, at a glass sculpture by Bekaa, a two-hundred-year-old Tiffany lamp, and a framed Eberhardt.

"You must be fucking rich," she said.

He shrugged.

"You're cute, too. Do you have anything to drink?"

Good idea. His mouth was dry. "Glass of wine?"

"Is the wine an antique too?"

"The word is 'vintage.'"

"Good vintage?"

"Not bad."

"I'd like that," she said, settling down on the sofa, loosening a button on her blouse.

There had been other dreams, other works. YMG-004. YFX-037. EMG-200. Pick of the files, Dr. DuBois assured him. Dreams gaudy and vivid, dreams subtle and complex. Gordo had made art of them, and the work was good, it was professional, it was attractive.

But—despite his best efforts—none of these pieces possessed the verve and color of YFL-500.

"Perhaps," Dr. DuBois offered, "it's the dreamer, not the dream."

Gordo had already considered that possibility. "I would love to meet the woman who was the source for YFL-500."

"What makes you think the subject was a woman?"

"Intuition. Wishful thinking."

"A waking dream?"

Gordo smiled wanly. "You could say that."

"Well, you're right. It *was* a woman."

Gordo's pulse sped up. "I thought that information was confidential."

"Anything I tell you," Dr. DuBois said, leaning over his desk and giving Gordo a meaningful look, "I tell you in confidence. Correct?"

Gordo nodded.

"And will stay that way?"

"Of course."

"Frankly, our partnership to date hasn't been as lucrative as I'd hoped."

"I've done everything I can—"

"Oh, I understand, Mr. Fisk." They were still "Mr. Fisk" and "Dr. DuBois" to one another, despite the intimacy of their financial arrangement. "I don't blame you at all. Still, I can't help thinking that if we had access to the original *source* of YFL-500, we might recover some momentum."

"What are you saying? That you want to contact her? Get her back in the clinic?"

"No! I don't want to have any contact with her at all. That would make me legally vulnerable . . . and I'd like to hang on to my medical license. No; I think *you* should contact her."

"And then what?"

"See what happens. Aren't you curious?"

Achingly curious. The only reason he hadn't proposed this to DuBois was that he had imagined the physician would be shocked. He should have known the doctor's ethics were flexible. That fact had been pretty firmly established.

"She's younger than you, she's not of your station in life. She's a dole gypsy, and I don't have a firm address for her. But I can describe her."

Gordo said, "I imagine she's beautiful."

"Not bad-looking."

"Hair short? Hair long?"

"Long, and tied down her back. At least when she came in here three years ago to sell us a dream."

"But even if I find her, that doesn't solve our problem."

"Ideally, you won't just *find* her. You'll befriend her. Grow close to her. Close enough that you can arrange the recording of another dream, or two, or more."

"Convince her to come and see you, you mean?"

"No, no—as I said, I want no direct connection with this. But the gear that records nocturnal brain activity needn't be as bulky as what we use here. In fact, I've prototyped some much stealthier inductive devices. Things you could install in a pillow, say, or a bed frame."

"And record her dreams without her knowledge? Isn't that a criminal act?"

"I've never heard of such a prosecution. Define it any way you want, Mr. Fisk. Do it, or don't do it. All I'm saying is, I can supply you the technology. And her name. Don't you at least want to know her name?"

||

By the second round of drinks Iris had shed her diaphanous blouse and put her feet up on Gordo's mahogany living-room table. The table was an antique. Antiques, like therapy, could not be manufactured by aibots. It was a costly table. Gordo thought her feet looked just fine, resting there. Exquisite, he thought, those feet. Small, pale, flawless. Also not manufactured by aibots.

"This has been nice, Gordo," she said. "I mean really nice. Thank you."

Gordo sipped his drink and thought it might be going to his head, possibly because he was tired. Or he was tired because the drink was going to his head. Or something. He tried to assemble his thoughts. She seemed inclined to stay: should he record her dreams tonight? (If they slept at all.) Or wait for another night, presuming there would *be* another night? Prospects seemed bright. Maybe better to forget about Dr. DuBois's spyware for now. Make love for the sake of making love. For the sake of her perfection.

No, not perfection. Perfection was not what he wanted or expected. If anything, Gordo thought, Iris Seawright seemed a little simple-minded, or at least not well educated. But she ran deep. He knew that: he had seen what was inside her. He had built a monument to her long before he'd ever met her.

She nestled into his shoulder and put her hand on his thigh.

"How are you feeling?" she asked.

"A little woozy," he said.

"Yeah. That's how it starts."

"What starts?"

She ignored the question and stood up. Gordo remained seated. Getting up didn't seem like a good idea, somehow.

"What would you say is the most valuable small thing you own, Gordo?"

"Valuable?"

"On the resale market. *Small* thing. Not, like, real estate. Something you have in the apartment. Something portable."

Gordo wondered what the point of this was but found himself answering, again, honestly: "The Fibonacci seashell," he said. "After that . . . I suppose the psalter on the mantel. It's silver and it's very old. Other things . . . some of the furniture . . ."

"Smaller than furniture," Iris said, and she was putting her blouse back on, looking curiously businesslike, unaffected by the drink (though why a mere two glasses of wine should have taken him so strongly he failed to understand). . . .

He opened his mouth and answered her questions in detail, as if she were an insurance adjuster; then she said, "And do you have a bag, a backpack, anything like that?"

He answered that question too. She was almost unbearably beautiful, Gordo thought, moving around the apartment methodically, gathering up his possessions and tucking them into his old camping pack. He didn't want to close his eyes, because he might not be able to will them open again. He realized he had been drugged.

He said, "What did you give me?"

"Relax," Iris said. "It's the same stuff they give you to make you sleep at the Bonnuit Clinic. Bunch of us from the beach used to go there to sell dreams. And rip off a dose or two when the docs weren't looking."

"You gave me a drug? So you could steal my things?"

"I don't think of it as theft," Iris said.

"What?"

"Royalties," she said.

Gordo was silent for what might have been a minute or an hour. His thoughts were becoming incoherent. Finally he said, "How did you know?"

"Well, you don't have to be a genius to draw a conclusion. YFL-500 was the code they put on my file at the clinic."

"You have . . . a good memory."

"'Nearly eidetic.' A teacher told me that once. Then she told me what 'eidetic' meant. She said if I cared at all about schoolwork I could be a great scholar. But remembering isn't the same as understanding."

"Maybe that's why. Why you dream so vividly."

"Maybe." She shrugged. "So that was really my dream, huh? Made into art. Wow."

Gordo nodded groggily. Wow. He watched as she stuffed the Fibonacci seashell, his father's legacy to him, into the backpack. "No point stealing that," he said. "Everything's microtagged. And that piece is well known. If you put it on auction—"

"Who said anything about stealing? It's a *gift*, right, Gordo?"

"No," he said helplessly.

"Well, then, report it. We'll go to court. But I might have to mention YFL-500, and the clinic, and that doctor you must be paying off. Motive and all that."

Gordo would have slumped deeper into the sofa, had that been possible.

"Don't worry," she said. "You'll sleep soon. Before you do, though, Gordo, I have to ask: why me? Couldn't you steal someone else's dream?"

"Not as good. I tried."

"Or a dream of your own? Oh—right. You don't dream." Gordo considered that statement, and she mistook his expression for misery. "Don't be so fucking hard on yourself. You do okay. Data's just data, right?"

She had seemed beautiful. She *was* beautiful. He could not dispel the illusion. She possessed not just a superficial but a profound beauty. A beauty invisible. He had believed in it. He had believed in it fiercely. It had seemed so real.

He closed his eyes.

"Sleep, baby," Iris said. "Maybe this time you'll dream."

"But I did." Even with his eyes closed he could see her. The vision of her. The vision he had made, though it did not entirely fit her: it was, he realized, a transrepresentation, a very fine one, delicate and beautiful, and he was sorry to lose it, but it was slipping away now, lost in morning light.

"I did," he said, or tried to say. "I dreamed," he said into her absence. "I dreamed of you."

THE GIRL HERO'S MIRROR SAYS HE'S NOT THE ONE

Justina Robson

Widely acknowledged as one of the best of the new British hard SF writers, Justina Robson expertly mixes vanguard speculations with achingly personal concerns, melding hard science with warm emotion better than anyone else working today. Science and sexuality, nanotech and neurosis, action and anxiety—she takes us from the depths of her humanity to the heights of the stars. The New York Times *recently praised Robson for "the exquisite precision and thoughtfulness of her writing," a characteristic that is always in evidence, even (especially) when she is at her most playful. Here, fun and heartache mix in equal measures in a tale set in the aftermath of her novel* Mappa Mundi, *when the software of the human mind is too easily updated.*

The eternal youth and optimism, the always-forwards energy of the Girl Hero makes her feel lethargic whenever she stops for coffee at her favorite bookstore. She is living in a Base Reality not unlike Prime, the original reality old Earthers used to share before Mappa Mundi, except it has fifty more shades of pink and no word for "hate." Her reality is called Rose Tint, and it was the one relatively mild hacker virus she was glad to catch. Of course, she would think that about it now. . . .

The Girl Hero feels there is something missing about herself, but she cannot name it. She has always felt this way, since she was tiny at her father's knee. He showed her a fly that had landed on the back of his hand. She looked closely, marveling at how small it was, how neat, how industrious as it cleaned its pretty glass wings. She remembers how he smashed it flat with his other hand. He was so fast. He had the reflexes of ten men, and he was a Hero, too.

Oh, one other thing that is missing about her is her name . . . a bout of flu stole it from her when she was in her teens, not so long ago. She keeps it written on the inside of her wrist in indelible ink that she rewrites every three days. She doesn't look at it much. Only when someone asks. The coffee barista has his name written on a badge: Marvin.

"Thank you, Marvin," she says as she takes her drink. The establishment is guaranteed clean. Little tablet boxes of Mappacode are sold at the counter, but they don't come under the Infection Bill: too minor, too common, and not particularly useful—they offer mnemonic upgrades for popular music charts, fashion, current affairs, and the stock markets so you can always have something to say and know what to buy. The information is stored somehow in proteins that only unfurl when they reach the right places in the brain— the places where Mappaware has created ports for them. They are inert otherwise, and when they have delivered the goods they break up into amino acids and provide spare nutrition. The Girl Hero takes a Mode one and pops it with the first steaming sip of espresso.

The Girl Hero picks at the cardboard band around her coffee cup and goes to take a seat in the window. She is dismayed to learn from the Modey that tweed pencil skirts are in. They are the worst kind of skirt for kicking. She sips and looks around her and wonders for the millionth time if she should save her money and risk a remodel. But she doesn't know what to do if she isn't a Hero. A Hero wouldn't. The preference is disturbing—would she really like it if she hadn't agreed to this job at the careers' meeting? Too late to wonder. It was a road not taken. She will never know who . . . (she looks at the inside of her wrist) . . . Rebecca might have been if she had chosen some different option. She hopes that Rebecca would have wanted to be a Hero anyway.

In the eternal present moment of the Hero's world Rebecca waits, waits, waits for her assignment without anxiety or hope. On other faces she sees various expressions of emotions that fit a task: executives focused and intent on work, an artist dreaming as he stares into nowhere through the wall opposite him, girls bent to their schoolwork rising and falling in the perfectly timed bursts of concentration and relaxation that allow them maximum efficiency in their learning and their fun. They are like seals at play, bobbing in and out of the water. Their chat and laughter rises like bubbles, thinks the Girl Hero, and she feels a twinge of envy, though she had her time and doesn't want it back.

A man in a dark suit as unmemorable as yesterday's news glides past and casually leaves his magazine on her table. She knows him for an Attaché, a man from the ministry who delivers duties to her kind, and that the magazine is a job offer in the eternal post-Mappa economy of the fight against the Cartomancers. She needs a job. She wants to move out of her mother's house.

On page fifty-nine her secret message awaits her. It is typed on tissue paper and all the "o"s are offset, which means it is a mission of the most extreme danger and highest importance. How typical, she thinks, that these things should come together. She rubs some hand cream into her knuckles to hide the thick, dry calluses from years of smashing her fists into concrete walls.

The message instructs her to take a journey to Pointe-Noire, in Congo. It is a place riddled with Cartoxins and the illegal breeding pens of the black market traders who design animals of exquisite savagery and intelligence for the use of the criminal underworld. Most of them will be remapped for various tasks, and they will not know mercy, fear, or any debilitating survival instinct. Once there she will go to a jungle compound and find a certain man and kill him. He is a bad man. She does not know his crimes, but they are probably something to do with writing or disseminating rogue viruses and/or Maps, because these are now the only crimes there are in the absence of what used to be known as Free Will. It is sure that if he were not so bad he would not be hiding out in such a place in the hopes that nobody would dare to follow. The vestiges of her sympathy for desperate men with missions for mankind are not stirred.

She folds the tissue paper and puts it in her handbag. She goes to the bathroom and has to queue. The bathroom is located in the Self-Help section of the bookstore. The Girl Hero has no need for this. She is slightly mystified by the titles, and by the need of books in a world where everything can be eaten. She does not like to look at them. They seem to ask questions of her, and when her back is turned they whisper like schoolchildren.

As she is washing her hands the Girl Hero feels an unpleasant feeling. It is like something scattering inside. She imagines she is made from swarms of rats that have just noticed a terrible thing and are running, running, running for their lives. She often feels this. It is doubt. It comes along after a certain time period when she has had nothing heroic to do. She puts the lid on the toilet down and sits there, taking up someone else's pee time as she gets out a vanity mirror from her handbag and opens it up. One half of the clamshell is an ordinary mirror. The other half has its own face, a kind of pixie that looks exactly like the Girl Hero. It came with the job. She suspects it is a transmitter device that talks directly to her Mappaware to sort out glitches. If she were more dedicated to keeping her appearance groomed than she is, possibly it would deal with her doubts for her.

"Mirror, mirror," says the Girl Hero, and need say no more.

"You want to go," says the mirror. "And you will." It always says this. The Girl Hero finds it very reassuring. She always asks. Her real question has not yet been answered and she doesn't bother to say it, but the mirror replies all the same, "He is not the one."

She closes the mirror and puts it away, satisfied that its prophecies are correct. Despite her bad feeling, this encounter will not be the last. She will not die today. A Girl Hero always trusts her mirror.

The Girl Hero goes shopping for a tweed pencil skirt and knee-high boots with heels. On her way to the airport she stops to text her mother that she will be home late, do not save any dinner, she will get some at the takeaway. Her mother is a Perky Waitress and will be satisfied with this latchkey message, not curious, not alarmed; she might bring home plastic boxes filled with peach pie and put them on the countertop for . . . Rebecca . . . to find when she comes in. Peach pie tastes of sweet, fulfilling safety and sleep. Two bites would be enough.

At the check-in desk she sees another Girl Hero, but one with a robot dog companion. She feels a sudden pang of envy and wants to introduce herself, to ask something that brims to her lips with urgent importance, though it can't make itself into words without a listener . . . but the other Hero is in a hurry. She runs off towards a departure gate with a flip of curly brown hair over the top of her practical backpack and grabs up her ammunition clips from the security guard without breaking stride. Her robot dog races beside her.

The Girl Hero . . . Rebecca . . . has no weapons to check. She deals only in kung fu. Her handbag is very small, just big enough for makeup, the mirror, and her phone. She looks up the price of robot dogs while she waits to board her flight. They are expensive. She thinks a real one would be better, but of course there is a problem with quarantine and the endless inoculations. She couldn't possibly afford one. Robots cannot catch diseases, so they are immune to all but the most specific and local of memetic assaults. A robot is much better, but the Girl Hero imagines a warm body, soft fur, regular breathing in a real rib cage moving under her hands, and brown eyes looking at her with unconditional love.

On the flight a man is seated beside her. He makes small talk about her job with the unconscious impulses of all businesspeople. She tells him she is a secretary, which is true, when she is not being a Hero. He sells virtual real estate. He shows her one of the communities he administers: a condo by the sea, to let, all mod cons, barely the cost of a sandwich per month and unlimited online access. He is persuasive, but Heroes are not easily sold. She declines. Her feet swell uncomfortably in the boots. She takes a limousine from the airport to her hotel, where she has a room already booked for her by the ministry.

Pointe-Noire is a township with only a small centre adequately defended and habitable. Beyond the line of automatic fire lie teeming swarms of wildlife so bestial and savage, so tightly packed, that every moment of their existence is a matter of do or die. They are the testbed of Hellmemes and other horrors cooked up in the mobile Cartomancy sweatshops that creak and grind through the jungle; metal behemoths covered in solar panels and electrical deterrents.

Beyond the hotel perimeter fence it is still night but will soon be day. In that blue hour there is a slight lull in the slaughter and terror as sleepy creatures of dark trade places with waking creatures of light.

The Girl Hero hires a personal jetcar and lands a few miles from town, close to the house where He lives, this criminal, or whatever he is. Her little capsule glides down within his ranch home's Sphere of Influence—a forcefield of protection maintained by a mini reactor. There are no monsters inside, but two muddy fields of marsh grass and the foot-high remains of stripped trees lie between her and the buildings. She regrets the boots now.

Outside the house there are fences and inside the fences are real dogs, mastiffs with serial killers' eyes. The Girl Hero walks to the gate, pulling her boot heels free of the mud with every step, thinking the leather will be ruined. She does not feel like strangling a dog. Her inner world has become the gray blank place she associates with Heroism. It is familiar and strangely disappointing. She doesn't know what she was expecting from a life devoted to exacting justice and defending the world from evil, but this was not it. Beyond the forcefield at her back the dawn chorus of howls, screams, roars, and whimpers greets the veteran sun.

There's a fence and a gate too. In the gatehouse there is a person. Where there is a person, there is an easy way in.

The Girl Hero says she is selling virtual real estate. She shows the guard her mirror and, as he peers at this strange kind of identification, she knocks him unconscious. He crumples without a sound.

Close by two monsters in the forest clash foreheads in a dominance fight, and the air is split by a crack like thunder. If the animals assaulted the shield they could get through it easily, but the shock of sudden pain has always prevented them from making this discovery. As they stumble about, stunned but undaunted by mortal combat, they avoid its gossamer shimmer at all costs. The Girl Hero shakes her head at them.

As she frisks pockets for codes, keys, cards, or whatever the Girl Hero is overcome by a sense of déjà vu. It is one of those nasty moments where, certain this is not a memory, because she has never been here before, she understands it is an omen. She hesitates and feels the man's still-beating heart under her hand. Her hand forms the shape of a crane's bill and delivers a rapid, extreme strike. It does not break the bone, but it doesn't have to. The shock is sufficient.

She could not have let him live, of course. He would have woken up sooner or later, and she does not know how long she has to be here. She feels mildly surprised at her action, and faintly sad that this is all she feels. Her finger stings her. She looks down and finds she has broken a nail. She spends a moment fixing it with her little kit of glue and tape, packed neatly into a thimble. She has the shakes, however, and her mend does not hold. She tapes the thimble onto the end of her finger instead. It is made of gold and once was the barque of a fairy queen, or so she likes to imagine. The Girl Hero wonders if it will defeat the power of her strike, but she doesn't take it off.

The Girl Hero locates the keys to the inner house and gets into the armored golf cart, which takes her through the fence territory of the dogs. It has sealed sides. The dogs run and bark alongside the cart. The whine of the electric motor is inappropriately cheerful. Insects whirl and scream around in the light, involuntary and designed carriers of diseases to change the mind—they are indistinguishable from the real things. The sun crests over the forest's edge, and a flight of red-winged insectivores takes to the air, flocking in the rising heat in a way that makes the air look syrupy. The Girl Hero takes out her mirror and adjusts her lip gloss. She thinks about what to order from the takeaway and decides she will have a Chinese.

At the end of the golf cart's route she is let into the house by machines who do not care that she is here to kill the master. Like so many of his kind he has run short of henchpersons whose instincts might favor him and now relies on mechanicals. Not popular, thinks the Girl Hero, and frowns a tiny frown to go with her tiny pang of sorrow. On the polished wood of the hallway her boots make hollow sounds.

There is a cook, a person doing some menial tasks, and a man who throws carcasses to the dogs. None of them are interested in stopping her when they see her coming, so the Girl Hero wearily locks them into the storeroom. She makes a note to herself on her mobile, so she does not forget to call help for them once she has left the scene. Lying on the kitchen counter is a plate of cream cakes, freshly defrosted, their chocolate iced tops coated in condensation sweat. She would like to eat them all. With the ease of a lifetime of denial, she barely registers the desire.

The bad man is in the living room, enjoying a glass of juice. His heavy frame is silhouetted against the rapacious sky as he looks out over a balcony towards the thin blue veil of the Sphere and beyond. Whatever he has loaded, it would naturally include a lot of processors to bypass any fear he might feel at her arrival. She feels that this is possibly a meeting of equals, her legally enhanced mind against his self-made one. There is a kind of honor code to be observed.

The Girl Hero puts her handbag on the table. He turns around at the small sound. His eyes begin to measure the distance to the door, but they falter halfway. He has recognized her and that an attempt to escape will be futile. She watches him relax as resignation takes the place of fear in his look. Perhaps it is genuine, but no reaction could be taken at face value in the circumstances. They are already too far along the road of combat.

"Would you like a drink?" he asks. He is wearing some kind of Japanese robe and looks like he has led a full life, she thinks. His short legs are planted firmly. He has no intention of running. Perhaps he will not put up a fight. Her stomach rumbles and she feels a slight pain there. She shakes her head—no. She can't do anything distracting to her, even if she thinks it would be safe—and for some reason she does feel safe now.

He is a long way across the room. She starts to walk.

"Do you know why you are here?"

She assumes he means does she know what he has done. She's not really interested. She shakes her head.

"Do you know why you are?"

The Girl Hero hesitates. He has deployed the Defense of Existential Crisis and she should ignore it boldly, defeat it with a witty and humorous line, but recently she hasn't thought of any of these. She only thinks of them later, long after the person who should have been rebuked is dead. It is her biggest weakness. She has read books of aphorisms, but *A lot of knowledge fits an empty head* seems inappropriate and is the only thing that comes to mind.

"I am a poet," he says.

It seems unlikely, she thinks. Why would anyone want to kill a poet? But, then again, why not? "Was your verse offensive?" she asks. Why did she engage? The only sensible thing to do is to break his neck and leave. What is she talking for? She adds quickly, "It isn't important. You are on the list."

"Do you know your masters and their ideas, Girl?" he asks, backing away rapidly as she advances with a firm, librarian's tread. His voice gets a bit higher, but it remains steady. "Do you know why you don't want to know?"

"It's not my place," she says, and unaccountably finds she has stopped walking. She does know why. She has *chosen* not to know.

There are two sides to this war of memes: the side of the Directive, which advocates managed and secure social design for the safety and well-being of all, and the side of the Cartomancers, which wants anarchy at any cost, a free market without limits. Both of them have to contend with the Wild in which Mappaware and Mappacode have become attached to the genetic strands not only of their original carriers, the viruses, but also of bacteria. There is no doubt it will soon spread (if it hasn't already) into the DNA of larger species. The Girl Hero never had gotten her head quite around the science or the politics of it. It's not a Hero's business to do all the thinking about the rights and wrongs. Her remit is much smaller. Justice for the wrongdoer and safety for the calm world of Perky Waitresses, Secretaries, and peach pie. And whiskery skittery rats.

The Bad Man takes a nervous sip of juice. The scream and murder of the jungle increases as the full circle of the sun appears clear of the trees. What a dreadful place, thinks the Girl Hero. She realizes she has reached a kind of stalemate but doesn't understand why she can't break it. She watches the Bad Man drink and set down his glass carefully on a coaster on a nice, smooth table.

"What's your name?"

She didn't expect this question even though an effort to become more intimate with an attacker who is more powerful is an obvious tactic. She opens her mouth, determined to answer, but nothing comes out. She looks to the inside of her wrist. She shouldn't tell him, so she keeps her mouth shut. "Rebecca" rings no bells for her. It could be a barcode for all it means. Her stomach starts to gnaw at her.

"I'm Khalid," he says, and nods with a faint, social smile. He glances at her wrist, and a moment of pity firms his lips.

A vicious streak of envy cuts across her mouth like the taste of lemon. Suddenly she wants the reassurance of the mirror, that tonight is not the night, but she left her bag on the table. It gets in the way and drags her arm when she has to punch.

"Wouldn't you like to understand what happened to you?"

"What is this, exam night?" She is determined not to be distracted by flimsy philosophizing. She doesn't care about the answers to his tiresome inquiries, but for some reason she thinks about the books, snickering behind her back. She wants to go home, get duck in plum sauce, get a shower, give her mother a cup of tea, and go to bed. In the morning she has work again because it is still three days until the weekend. Besides, the answer to his question is surely obvious. She says it without knowing she's going to until she starts, "I caught a bad purge. That's all. No big. Look." She flashes her wrist at him.

"Everything in the world and the Wild is written, Rebecca, just like your name," he says. He keeps a close watch on her, and she on him, in case he runs away, in case she doesn't.

Damn, she sees he has reached the wall. His free hand darts with the speed of desperation towards a control hidden there. He fumbles. She darts across the gap, jumps and kicks. Her skirt rips. Her boots are too tight. She knocks him aside but lands on her ass. Some kind of alarm is sounding like a bleating goat. Angry with herself she glares at him.

"The Sphere control," he says with satisfaction. "In a minute it will vanish and the Wild will come in." His face is pasty under its smooth olive plumpness, but triumphant.

She sees clearly that a lot now stands between her and the evening she had planned. She looks out, to where her car is hidden, beyond the cleared land. One minute? "But my mirror says you're not the one," she tells him firmly. Suddenly her belief in the mirror is wavering.

She looks into the eyes of the bad man. He looks back at her, without attempting to move. She says, "If you reset the device I will let you live." She tells herself she does not mean it. She hasn't made a mistake. She wouldn't betray the contract. A Hero would do what it takes to save the world.

"I think you will not," says the bad man, becoming amused.

"Don't just lie there," she says, lying there.

"Why not?" he asks. "I can see up your skirt from here. Nice underwear."

"I mean it," she says, meaning it to her own surprise. "I will let you live."

"Ah, thanks, " he says, "but if it wasn't you, it would just be some other Girl Hero coming along in a day or two, and I've done my time. There's nothing left I want to do I haven't done, and I'm not much for repeats. The Directive has no real defense against the Cartomancy, and neither have a chance against the Wild, not in the end. The life of ideas is already a literal thing. We used to transmit them inadequately with words, and soon they will transmit themselves through nature, through biology, in ways that bypass what small shred of choice may ever have existed. So, I think I'll just stay here, if it's all the same to you. It's a bit more satisfying if you die along with me than if you get to escape, and I wish I was a bit different but I was free of the Map all my life and I have to bow to my taste for justice in my own way. I hope you can understand that."

"But I want to live!" the Girl Hero says.

"I don't think so," Khalid observes. His voice is mild. "I knew when you walked in and hesitated that you were the one."

The bleat alarm goes off. Without it the mindless fury beyond the Sphere seems twice as loud. The Girl Hero leaps to her feet and tries the device by the window. She cannot make it work. The blue tissue of force begins to fade. The blazing ruddy glare of beyond starts to color it a deep purple. The Girl Hero thinks about the cakes on the counter, the innocent dogs, the people in the storeroom, her mother.

She glares down at him. "Why didn't they stop the Wild a long time ago?"

He shrugs. She sees that he does not know. "The day it was discovered there was a faster way to change people's minds than simply by talk or the gun, then it was already decided. If you were hoping for a final insight into human nature . . ." He trails off and looks distracted as the color of the room changes from a soft shadowy umber to bright yellow. The Sphere has gone.

The Girl Hero makes a dive and slides the length of the table. She picks up her handbag and takes out her mirror. She no longer has the gray, flat feeling of Heroism, and she wants to see if that has changed her face.

It has. The incipient wrinkles at the edges of her eyes and between her brows have gone. She is as smooth and pretty as she was the first day she took up office. On the other side of the mirror the pixie looks out towards the clear edge of the forest where it seems that a starving, boiling mass of vegetable and animal is slowly billowing towards them.

"Oh my," says the mirror. "Look out! He's getting away."

The Girl Hero feels a surge of desperation and anger quite unusual for her. She spins around just in time to catch sight of Khalid slithering through the narrow black gap of a secret doorway he has opened in the paneling. She is after him like a shot, but her muddy feet slip a little and she can't grab hold of him as she intended. She makes it through the gap anyway and runs through the narrow, wooden corridor after him, her skirt seam ripping a bit more up the thigh with every furious stride. How could she fall for a distraction? How could she have entertained the idea that he was telling the truth about never having acquired the Map? Just look at this ridiculous compound with its guards and gates and dogs and cook. Listen to him give his Villainous Speech. She and he are both products of Stock Narrative 101, however many upgrades and individual variations they may have acquired . . . and now her rage is like hell itself.

The corridor winds and slopes down. Khalid skids and loses a shoe. The escape chute opens to a broad decking with an escape car tethered to it, its air-bladder fully primed with helium. The engine ticks over, its rotors whir softly in the thick and humid air. Khalid is forced to pause, hand fighting his pocket for the key. The Girl Hero cocks her arm and throws the mirror in a dead flat spin. It strikes him on the back of the head and he falls to his knees. Around him the broken bright pieces scatter, fragments of sky.

"I want to see what's real!" she screams. "Why did you have to be a liar?" She is crying. This is impossible. She needs the mirror, and rushes up to him. She tries to pick up the pieces, but behind the glass all the circuitry is broken. There should be some word for what she feels when she looks at him, a word not like "fuchsia" or "madder" or "carmine" or "rose" or "sugar" or "candy." It should be a word for rats turning and scuttling back with red eyes, teeth bared, tails like little ramrods. Maybe the word is "Rebecca."

Khalid blinks at her with panic beginning to make him sweat. "What did you expect?" He had located the key.

The car door opens as a wave of warm air, full of thunder, ripples slowly across them. Rain starts to fall and there comes the screeching and shrilling of agony, the sputter of electrical things and burning fur as creatures test the weakening perimeter fence. Khalid snatches a mask from his pocket and wraps it across his face with his free hand as he scrabbles to his feet. He makes a lunge for the door. The Girl Hero watches him with the Rebecca feeling and jumps after. She makes the sill and he attempts to push her out backwards, but he's weak, a big soft geek type who's all brain and no brawn. She kicks him in the chest and slams the door after them.

"Take me with you," she says. "They'll send other Heroes. You need me."

He looks up from the floor and croaks, "I did okay so far . . ."

"You were dead when I walked in the door. And if you say no, you still are," the Girl Hero assures him, picking him up by the shirtfront and hauling him to the passenger seat of the little craft. "Shit," she says, safe, for now. "What about your people? Can't leave them . . ."

"Have to leave them," he gasps, still winded. "No time."

No Hero would ever leave them.

Khalid slams a hand to the controls, and the car begins to lift off. "Anyway, why should you care? Killed enough for a lifetime. . . ."

She opens her mouth to protest, but the breath she took doesn't go anywhere, just leaves her inflated. As she delays the aircar rises smoothly into the sky above the treetops. From the windshield she can see the dogs running back and forth in their prison, barking.

"You should let them out," she said, sitting down slowly in the pilot's seat. "It's cruel to keep dogs that way." They fly for a time in silence, avoiding the Directive Patrols but with no other plan.

"Can you ever get rid of it?" Rebecca asks in a quiet voice. "Mappaware? Ever?"

"You can tell it not to work," Khalid says. "That's all." He hands over a small black box shaped like a cigarette pack with a single button on it. "We use them a lot. When you get too much infestation, you go unstable. This clears it. Then you start again."

Rebecca remembers him fumbling in his pockets. Zap. Not the door. Her. "You got me."

Khalid nodded. "And me. Works in a range."

Rebecca presses the button, over and over. Nothing happens. "Now what? Why aren't I different then?"

"That takes time," he says, sighing wearily. "Lots of time. Have to grow, think, do things . . . take more code or not . . . left alone you'll change on your own."

"Like in the old days." She puts the box into her own pocket, which is almost too small. She wishes she had not forgotten her bag. For a moment she thinks about Chinese food and her home, all the stuffed animals in a row, her mother's scent. . . . "Where to?"

Khalid shrugs. "I wait until I pick up a beacon. Most likely spot is still over the Congo area somewhere. Just follow the river."

"And then?"

"Set down, make new friends in the Cartomancy, carry on. . . . Write something, test it, purge it. Try to figure out how to create antimemes against the worst plagues . . . not much."

Rebecca nods. It's not much, but it is enough.

SMALL OFFERINGS

Paolo Bacigalupi

One of the most exciting authors currently making a splash in the short story scene, Paolo Bacigalupi recently took the Theodore Sturgeon Memorial Award for his novelette "The Calorie Man." I'm indebted to Gordon Van Gelder for introducing me to Paolo, who proved to be as wonderful a person as he is a wordsmith, and to Paolo himself for agreeing to constrict his talent into this short tale so that he could fit into an already bloated book. Not always for the squeamish, Paolo often shows us near futures that are as convincing as they are unsettling. The following tale is no exception.

Readouts glow blue on driplines where they burrow into Maya Ong's spine. She lies on the birthing table, her dark eyes focused on her husband while I sit on a stool between her legs and wait for her baby. There are two halves of Maya. Above the blue natal sheet, she holds her husband's hand and sips water and smiles tiredly at his encouragement. Below it, hidden from view and hidden from sensation by steady surges of Sifusoft, her body lies nude, her legs strapped into birthing stirrups. Purnate hits her belly in rhythmic bursts, pressing the fetus down her birth canal, and toward my waiting hands.

I wonder if God forgives me for my part in her prenatal care. Forgives me for encouraging the full course of treatment.

I touch my belt remote and thumb up another 50 ml of Purnate. The readouts flicker and display the new dose as it hisses into Maya's spine and works its way around to her womb. Maya inhales sharply, then lies back and relaxes, breathing deeply as I muffle her pain response in swaddling layers of Sifusoft. Ghostly data flickers and scrolls at the perimeter of my vision: heart rate, blood pressure, oxygenation, fetal heart rate, all piped directly to my optic nerve by my MedAssist implant.

Maya cranes her neck around to see me. "Dr. Mendoza? Lily?" Her words slur under the drugs, come out slow and dreamy.

"Yes?"

"I can feel it kicking."

My neck prickles. I force a smile "They're natal phantasms. Illusions generated by the gestation process."

"No." Maya shakes her head, emphatic. "I feel it. It's kicking." She touches her belly. "I feel it now."

I come around the natal sheet and touch her hand. "It's all right, Maya. Let's just relax. I'll see what we can do to keep you comfortable."

Ben leans down and kisses his wife's cheek. "You're doing great, honey. Just a little longer."

I give her hand a reassuring pat. "You're doing a wonderful thing for your baby. Let's just relax now and let nature take its course."

Maya smiles dreamily in agreement and her head rolls back. I let out a breath I hadn't known I was holding and start to turn away. Maya lurches upright. She stares at me, suddenly alert, as if all the birthing drugs have been lifted off her like a blanket, leaving her cold and awake and aggressive.

Her dark eyes narrow with madness. "You're going to kill it."

Uh-oh. I thumb my belt unit for the orderlies.

She grabs Ben by the shoulder. "Don't let her take it. It's alive, honey. Alive!"

"Honey—"

She yanks him close. "Don't let her take our baby!" She turns and snarls at me. "Get out. Get out!" She lunges for a water glass on her bedside table. "Get out!" She flings it at me. I duck and it shatters against the wall. Glass shards pepper my neck. I get ready to dodge another attack but instead Maya grabs the natal sheet and yanks it down, exposing her nude lower half splayed for birth. She claws at her birth stirrups like a wolf in a trap. I spin the dials on my belt remote, jam up her Purnate and shut off her Sifusoft as she throws herself against the stirrups again. The birthing table tilts alarmingly. I lunge to catch it. She flails at me and her nails gouge my face. I jerk away, clutching my cheek. I wave to her husband, who is standing dumbly on the opposite side of the birth table, staring. "Help me hold her!"

He snaps out of paralysis; together we wrestle her back onto the table and then a new contraction hits and she sobs and curls in on herself. Without Sifusoft, there is nothing to hide the birth's intensity. She rocks against the pain, shaking her head and moaning, small and beaten. I feel like a bully. But I don't restart the painkillers.

She moans, "Oh God. Oh, God. Oh. God."

Benjamin puts his head down beside her, strokes her face. "It's okay, honey. It's going to be fine." He looks up at me, hoping for confirmation. I make myself nod.

Another Purnate-induced contraction hits. They're coming fast now, her body completely in the grip of the overdose I've flushed into her. She pulls her husband close and whispers. "I don't want this, honey. Please, it's a sin." Another contraction hits. Less than twenty seconds apart.

Two thick-armed female orderlies draped in friendly pink blouses finally come thumping through the door and move to restrain her. The cavalry always arrives too late. Maya brushes at them weakly until another contraction hits. Her naked body arches as the baby begins its final passage into our world.

"The pretty queen of the hypocritic oath arrives."

Dmitri sits amongst his brood, my sin and my redemption bound in one gaunt and sickly man. His shoulders rise and fall with labored asthmatic breathing. His cynical blue eyes bore into me. "You're bloodied."

I touch my face, come away with wet fingers. "A patient went natal."

All around us, Dmitri's test subjects scamper, shrieking and warring, an entire tribe of miscalibrated humanity, all gathered together under Dmitri's care. If I key in patient numbers on my belt unit, I get MedAssist laundry lists of pituitary misfires, adrenal tumors, sexual malformations, attention and learning disorders, thyroid malfunctions, IQ fall-offs, hyperactivity, and aggression. An entire ward full of poster children for chemical legislation that never finds its way out of government committee.

"*Your* patient went natal." Dmitri's chuckle comes as a low wheeze. Even in this triple-filtered air of the hospital's chemical intervention ward, he barely takes enough oxygen to stay alive. "What a surprise. Emotion trumps science, once again." His fingers drum compulsively on the bed of an inert child beside him: a five-year-old girl with the breasts of a grown woman. His eyes flick to the body and back to me. "No one seems to want prenatal care these days, do they?"

Against my will, I blush; Dmitri's mocking laughter rises briefly before dissolving into coughing spasms that leave him keeled over and gasping. He wipes his mouth on his lab coat's sleeve and studies the resulting bloody smear. "You should have sent her to me. I could have convinced her."

Beside us, the girl lies like a wax dummy, staring at the ceiling. Some bizarre cocktail of endocrine disruptors has rendered her completely catatonic. The sight of her gives me courage. "Do you have any more squeegees?"

Dmitri laughs, sly and insinuating. His eyes flick to my damaged cheek. "And what would your sharp-nailed patient say, if she found out?"

"Please, Dmitri. Don't. I hate myself enough already."

"I'm sure. Caught between your religion and your profession. I'm surprised your husband even tolerates your work."

I look away. "He prays for me."

"God solves everything, I understand."

"Don't."

Dmitri smiles. "It's probably what I've missed in my research. We should all just beg God to keep babies from absorbing their mother's chemical sludge. With a little Sunday prayer, Lily, you can go back to pushing folate and vitamins. Problem solved." He stands abruptly, coming to his full six and a half feet like a spider unfolding. "Come, let us consummate your hypocrisy before you change your mind. I couldn't bear it if you decided to rely on your faith."

Inside Dmitri's lab, fluorescent lights glare down on stainless-steel counter-tops and test equipment.

Dmitri rustles through drawers one after another, searching. On the countertop before him, a gobbet of flesh lies marooned, wet and incongruous on the sterile gleaming surface. He catches me staring at it.

"You will not recognize it. You must imagine it smaller."

One portion is larger than an eyeball. The rest is slender, a dangling sub-section off the main mass. Meat and veiny fatty gunk. Dmitri rustles through another drawer. Without looking up, he answers his own riddle. "A pituitary gland. From an eight-year-old female. She had terrible headaches."

I suck in my breath. Even for Chem-Int, it's a freak of nature.

Dmitri smiles at my reaction. "Ten times oversized. Not from a vulner-able population, either: excellent prenatal care, good filter mask practices, low-pesticide food sources." He shrugs. "We are losing our battle, I think." He opens another drawer. "Ah. Here." He pulls out a foil-wrapped square the size of a condom, stamped in black and yellow, and offers it to me. "My trials have already recorded the dose as dispensed. It shouldn't affect the statistics." He nods at the flesh gobbet. "And certainly, she will not miss it."

The foil is stamped, NOT FOR SALE, along with a tracking number and the intertwined DNA and microscope icon of the FDA Human Trials Division. I reach for it, but Dmitri pulls it away. "Put it on before you leave. It has a new backing: cellular foil. Trackable. You can only wear it in the hospital." He tosses me the packet, shrugs apologetically. "Our sponsors think too many doses are walking away."

"How long do I need to wear it before I can leave?"

"Three hours will give you most of the dose."

"Enough?"

"Who knows? Who cares? Already you avoid the best treatment. You will reap what you sow."

I don't have a retort. Dmitri knows me too well to feed him the stories I tell myself, the ones that comfort me at 3 AM when Justin's asleep and I'm staring at the ceiling listening to his steady honest breathing: *It's for our marriage. . . . It's for our future. . . . It's for our baby.*

I strip off the backing, untuck my blouse and unbutton my slacks. I slip the derm down under the waistband of my panties. As it attaches to my skin, I imagine cleansing medicine flowing into me. For all his taunts, Dmitri has given me salvation, and suddenly, I'm overwhelmed with gratitude. "We owe you, Dmitri. Really. We couldn't have waited until the trials finished."

Dmitri grunts acknowledgment. He is busy prodding the dead girl's bloated pituitary. "You could never have afforded it, anyway. It is too good for everyone to have."

||

The squeegee hits me on the El.

One minute, I'm sitting and smiling at the kids across the aisle, with their Hello Kitty and their Burn Girl filter masks, and the next minute, I'm doubled over, ripping off my own mask, and gagging. The girls stare at me like I'm a junkie. Another wave of nausea hits and I stop caring what they think. I sit doubled over on my seat, trying to keep my hair out of my face and vomiting on the floor between my shoes.

By the time I reach my stop, I can barely stand. I vomit again on the platform, going down on hands and knees. I have to force myself not to crawl down from the El. Even in the winter cold, I'm sweating. The crowds part around me, boots and coats and scarves and filter masks. Glittering news chips in men's sideburns and women with braided microfilament glo strands stepping around me, laughing with silver lipsticks. Kaleidoscope streets: lights and traffic and dust and coal diesel exhaust. Muddy and wet. My face is wet and I can't remember if I've fallen in the murk of a curb or if this is my vomit.

I find my apartment by luck, manage to stand until the elevator comes. My wrist implant radios open the apartment's locks.

Justin jumps up as I shove open the door. "Lily?"

I retch again, but I've left my stomach on the street. I wave him away and stumble for the shower, stripping off my coat and blouse as I go. I curl into a ball on the cold white tiles while the shower warms. I fumble with the straps on my bra, but I can't work the catch. I gag again, shuddering as the squeegee rips through me.

Justin's socks are standing beside me: the black pair with the hole in the toe. He kneels; his hand touches my bare back. "What's wrong?"

I turn away, afraid to let him see my filthy face. "What do you think?" Sweat covers me. I'm shivering. Steam has started pouring up from the tiles. I push aside the cotton shower curtain and crawl in, letting the water soak my remaining clothes. Hot water pours over me. I finally drag off my bra, let it drop on the puddled tiles.

"This can't be right." He reaches in to touch me, but pulls away when I start gagging again.

The retching passes. I can breathe. "It's normal." My words whisper out. My throat is raw with vomit. I don't know if he hears me or not. I pry off my soggy slacks and underwear. Sit on the tiles, let the water pour over me, let my face press against one tiled wall. "Dmitri says it's normal. Half the subjects experience nausea. Doesn't affect efficacy."

I start retching again but it's not as bad, now. The wall feels wonderfully cool.

"You don't have to do this, Lily."

I roll my head around, try to see him. "You want a baby, don't you?"

"Yeah, but . . ."

"Yeah." I let my face press against the tile again. "If we're not doing prenatal, I don't have a choice."

The squeegee's next wave is hitting me. I'm sweating. I'm suddenly so hot I can't breathe. Every time is worse than the last. I should tell Dmitri, for his trial data.

Justin tries again. "Not all natural babies turn out bad. We don't even know what these drugs are doing to you."

I force myself to stand, lean against the wall and turn up the cold water. I fumble for the soap . . . drop it. Leave it lying by the drain. "Clinicals in Bangladesh . . . were good. Better than before. FDA could approve now . . . if they wanted." I'm panting with the heat. I open my mouth and drink unfiltered water from the shower head. It doesn't matter. I can almost feel PCBs and dioxins and phthalates gushing out of my pores and running off my body. Good-bye hormone mimics. Hello healthy baby.

"You're insane." Justin lets the shower curtain fall into place.

I shove my face back into the cool spray. He won't admit it, but he wants me to keep doing this; he loves that I'm doing this for him. For our kids. Our kids will be able to spell and to draw a stick figure, and I'm the only one who gets dirty. I can live with that. I swallow more water. I'm burning up.

Fueled by the overdose of Purnate, the baby arrives in minutes. The mucky hair of a newborn shows and recedes. I touch the head as it crowns. "You're almost there, Maya."

Again, a contraction. The head emerges into my hands: a pinched old man's face, protruding from Maya's body like a golem from the earth. Another two pushes and it spills from her. I clutch the slick body to me as an orderly snips the umbilical cord.

The MedAssist data on its heart rate flickers red at the corner of my vision, flatlines.

Maya is staring at me. The natal screen is down; she can see everything we wish prenatal patients would never see. Her skin is flushed. Her black hair clings sweaty to her face. "Is it a boy or a girl?" she slurs.

I am frozen, crucified by her gaze. I duck my head. "It's neither."

I turn and let the bloody wet mass slip out of my hands and into the trash. Perfume hides the iron scent that has blossomed in the air. Down in the canister, the baby is curled in on itself, impossibly small.

"Is it a boy or a girl?"

Ben's eyes are so wide, he looks like he'll never blink again. "It's okay, honey. It wasn't either. That's for the next one. You know that."

Maya looks stricken. "But I felt it kick."

The blue placental sack spills out of her. I dump it in the canister with the baby and shut down Maya's Purnate. Pitocin has already cut off what little bleeding she has. The orderlies cover Maya with a fresh sheet. "I felt it," she says. "It wasn't dead at all. It was alive. A boy. I felt him."

I thumb up a round of Delonol. She falls silent. One of the orderlies wheels her out as the other begins straightening the room. She resets the natal screen in the sockets over the bed. Ready for the next patient. I sit beside the biohazard bin with my head between my legs and breathe. Just breathe. My face burns with the slashes of Maya's nails.

Eventually I make myself stand and carry the bio-bin over to the waste chute, and crack it open. The body lies curled inside. They always seem so large when they pour from their mothers, but now, in its biohazard can, it's tiny.

It's nothing, I tell myself. Even with its miniature hands and squinched face and little penis, it's nothing. Just a vessel for contaminants. I killed it within weeks of conception with a steady low dose of neurotoxins to burn out its brain and paralyze its movements while it developed in the womb. *It's nothing.* Just something to scour the fat cells of a woman who sits at the top of a poisoned food chain, and who wants to have a baby. *It's nothing.*

I lift the canister and pour the body into suction. It disappears, carrying the chemical load of its mother down to incineration. An offering. A floppy sacrifice of blood and cells and humanity so that the next child will have a future.

THEY CAME FROM THE FUTURE

Robyn Hitchcock

Self-styled "retrodelic" musician Robyn Hitchcock expertly blends Bob Dylan–esque minstrel rock with Lewis Carroll sensibilities that dazzle and delight even as they chart the edges of death and decay. His music is aglow with wonderful tensions, a predilection for examining the unpleasantness of raw nature in all its savage glory stretched over catchy pop melodies. As he says of himself, "As a thinking person I'm completely in despair, but as a kind of creature I'm quite happy." His original band, The Soft Boys, took the inspiration for their name from science fiction surrealist William S. Burroughs's novel The Soft Machine, *so it is only fitting that this very literary lyricist contributes an SFnal poem to this volume of future fiction. Reminiscent of ideas expressed in Michael Chabon's essay "The Omega Glory," the poem explores the lost promise of tomorrow as reflected in the shortcomings of today.*

They came from the future
Once upon a time
In silver suits and confident helmets
Reflecting our sun and historic stars.

They came to shake our hands
And laze by fountains in their silver torsos
Pushing back their helmets to receive
Dandelions from Earth girls and
Blow them away.

"Easy when you know how," said the wise ones.

Their clean-cut hair and fresh teeth
Caressed our breeze.
They handed out postcards of their world,
Electric toothbrushes, sunlight so strong it
Flowed from them in chrome.
The local boys aped them,
Dressed like them when they could get the gear.

Then they changed:
They came now from a rough sad world that
Imitated ours. Stolen mirrors, bacteria, wild teeth framed in stubble
Tired breath.
No one wanted to kiss them.

They carried DO NOT TOUCH placards and tried to thrust leaflets into
   shopper's hands.
Which nobody could read.
But the photos showed a frightened monkey in a noose.
The girls walked round them
And the boys, our silver boys, ganged up on them in dark stairwells.

The wise ones sat in cafes, eating leaves and shoots.

Our world has lost its shine,
Though there's still money to polish it.
Radiance comes in jars.

The wise ones shake their heads
But they've had a lot of practice
And pack away their stalls.

Boys are angry, girls are scared
Bloated like carcasses, dwindled to bones:
The future isn't what it was
And somebody must pay.

The boys, our boys in silver blade patrols, caught one last refugee.
I saw them take him one grim green dawn
Pushing him backwards through the mall, pushing him down against the
　　wall
They finished him with stones:
He had nothing to offer them.
Our sunlight framed his dying shadow.

After that, no one came from the future:
We've reached it, after all.
Too real to dream, the clouds protect me from the rising sun.
Stars keep their distance
Tattooed on a ceiling we no longer dream of reaching.
Not this way, not as us
Not the silver boys, no way.

Yet, this is no time to be sour—the hour is now, and it's our turn
To visit them.

Ready, boys?

PLOTTERS AND SHOOTERS

Kage Baker

Best known for her novels and short stories featuring the mysterious Company, a twenty-fourth-century corporation in control of time travel technology that employs agents throughout history, Kage Baker's tales are always full of wit and whimsy. But who doesn't yet know what a wonder Kage Baker is? Or what fun it is to dive into another of her so-original speculations. What can I say? Only that she has done it again.

I was flackeying for Lord Deathlok and Dr. Smash when the shuttle brought the new guy.

I hate Lord Deathlok. I hate Dr. Smash too, but I'd like to see Lord Deathlok get a missile fired up his ass, from his own cannon. Not that it's really a cannon. And I couldn't shoot him, anyhow, because I'm only a Plotter. But it's the thought that counts, you know?

Anyway, I looked up when the beeps and the flashing lights started, and Lord Deathlok took hold of my little French maid's apron and yanked it so hard I had to bend over fast, so I almost dropped the tray with his drink.

"Pay attention, maggot-boy," said Lord Deathlok. "It's only a shuttle docking. No reason you should be distracted from your duties."

"I know what's wrong," said Dr. Smash, lounging back against the bar. "He hears the mating call of his kind. They must have sent up another Plotter."

"Oh, yeah." Lord Deathlok grinned at me. "Your fat-ass girlfriend went crying home to his mum and dad, didn't he?"

Oh, man, how I hated him. He was talking about Kev, who'd only gone Down Home again because he'd almost died in an asthma attack. Kev had been a good Plotter, one of the best. I just glared at Deathlok, which was a mistake, because he smiled and put his boot on my foot and stood up.

"I don't think I heard your answer, Fifi," he said, and I was in all this unbelievable psychological pain, see, because even with the lower gravity he could still manage to get the leverage just right if he wanted to bear down. They tell us we don't have to worry about getting brittle bones up here because they make us do weight-training, but how would we know if they were lying? I could almost hear my metatarsals snapping like dry twigs.

"Yes, my Lord Deathlok," I said.

"What?" He leaned forward.

"My lord yes my Lord Deathlok!"

"That's better." He sat down.

So okay, you're probably thinking I'm a coward. I'm not. It isn't that Lord Deathlok is even a big guy. He isn't, actually; he's sort of skinny, and he has these big yellow buck teeth that make him look like a demon jackrabbit. And Dr. Smash has breasts and a body odor that makes sharing an airlock with him a fatal mistake. But they're *Shooters*, you know? And they all dress like they're space warriors or something, with the jackets and the boots and the scary hairstyles. Shracking fascists.

So I put down his Dis Pepsy and backed away from him, and that was when the announcement came over the speakers:

"Eugene Clifford, please report to Mr. Kurtz's office."

Talk about saved by the bell. As the message repeated, Lord Deathlok smirked.

"Sounds like Dean Kurtz is lonesome for one of his little buttboys. You have our permission to go, Fifi."

"My lord thank you my Lord Deathlok," I muttered, and tore off the apron and ran for the companionway.

Mr. Kurtz isn't a dean; I don't know why the Shooters call him that. He's the Station Manager. He runs the place for Areco and does our performance reviews and signs our bonus vouchers, and you'd think the Shooters would treat him with a little more respect, but they don't because they're *Shooters*, and that says it all. Mostly he sits in his office and looks disappointed. I don't blame him.

He looked up from his novel as I put my head around the door.

"You wanted to see me, Mr. Kurtz?"

He nodded. "New arrival on the shuttle. Kevin Nederlander's replacement. Would you bring him up, please?"

"Yes, sir!" I said, and hurried off to the shuttle lounge.

The new guy was sitting there in the lounge, with his duffel in the chair beside his. He was short and square, and his haircut made his head look like it came to a point. Maybe it's genetic; Plotters can't seem to get good haircuts, ever.

"Welcome to the Gun Platform, newbie," I said. "I'm your Orientation Officer." Which I sort of am.

"Oh, good," he said, getting to his feet, but he couldn't seem to take his eyes off the viewscreen. I waited for him to ask if that was really Mars down there, or gush about how he couldn't believe he was actually on an alien world or at least in orbit above one. That's usually what they do, see. But he didn't. He just shouldered his duffel and tore his gaze away at last.

"Charles Tead. Glad to be here," he said.

Heh! That'll change, I thought. "You've got some righteous shoes to fill, newbie. Think you're up to it?"

He just said that he was, not like he was bragging or anything, and I thought, *This one's going to get his corners broken off really soon.*

So I took him to the Forecastle and showed him Kev's old bunk, looking all empty and sad with the drillholes where Kev's holoposters used to be mounted. He put his duffel into Kev's old locker and looked around, and then he asked who did our laundry. I coughed a little and explained about it being sent down to the planet to be dry-cleaned. I didn't tell him, not then, about our having to collect the Shooters' dirty socks and stuff for them.

And I took him to the Bridge where B Shift was on duty and introduced him to the boys. Roscoe and Norman were wearing their Jedi robes, which I wish they wouldn't because it makes us look hopeless. Vinder was in a snit because Bradley had knocked one of his action figures behind the console, and apparently it was one of the really valuable ones, and Myron's the only person skinny enough to get his arm back there to fish it out, but he's on C Shift and wouldn't come on duty until seventeen hundred hours.

I guess that was where it started: B Shift making such a bad first impression.

But I tried to bring back some sense of importance by showing him the charting display, with the spread of the asteroid belt all in blue and gold, like a stained-glass window in an old-time church must have been, only everything moving.

"This is your own personal slice of the sky," I said, waving at Q34-54. "Big Kev knew every one of these babies. Tracked every little wobble, every deviation over three years. Plotted trajectories for thirty-seven successful shots. It was like he had a sixth sense! He even called three Intruders before they came in range. He was the Bonus Master, old Kev. You'll have to work pretty damn hard to be half as good as he was."

"But it ought to be easy," said Charles. "Doesn't the mapping software do most of it?"

"Well, like, I mean, sure, but you'll have to *coordinate* everything, you know? In your head? Machines can't do it all," I protested. And Vinder chose that second to yell from behind us, "Don't take the Flying Dynamo's cape off, you'll break him!" Which totally blew the mood I was trying to get. So I ignored him and continued:

"We've been called up from Earth for a job only we can do. It's a high and lonely destiny, up here among the cold stars! Mundane people couldn't stick it out. That's why Areco went looking for guys like us. We're free of entanglements, right? We came from our parents' basements and garages to a place where our powers were *needed*. Software can map those rocks out there, okay; it can track them, maybe. But only a human can—can—smell them coming in before they're there, okay?"

"You mean like precognition?" Charles stared at me.

"Not exactly," I said, even though Myron claims he's got psychic abilities, but he never seems to be able to predict when the Shooters are going to go on a rampage on our turf. "I'm talking about gut feelings. Hunches. Instinct! That's the word I was looking for. Human instinct. We outguess the software seventy percent of the time on projected incoming. Not bad, huh?"

"I guess so," he said.

I spent the rest of the shift showing him his console and setting up his passwords and customizations and stuff. He didn't ask many questions, just put on the goggles and focused, and you could almost see him wandering around among the asteroids in Q34-54 and getting to know them. I was starting to get a good feeling about him, because that was just the way Kev used to plot, and then he said:

"How do we target them?"

Vinder was so shocked he dropped the Blue Judge. Roscoe turned, took off his goggles to stare at me, and said:

"*We* don't target. Cripes, haven't you told him?"

"Told me what?" Charles turned his goggled face toward the sound of Roscoe's voice.

So then I had to tell him about the Shooters, and how he couldn't go into the bar when Shooters were in there except when he was flackeying for one of them, and what they'd do to him if he did, and how he had to stay out of the Pit of Hell where they bunked except when he was flackeying for them, and he was never under any circumstances to go into the War Room at all.

I was explaining about the flackeying rotation when he said:

"This is stupid!"

"It's sheer evil," said Roscoe. "But there's nothing we can do about it. They're Shooters. You can't fight them. You don't want to know what happens if you try."

"This wasn't in my contract," said Charles.

"You can go complain to Kurtz, if you want," said Bradley. "It's no damn use. *He* can't control them. They're Shooters. Nobody else can do what they do."

"I'll bet I could," said Charles, and everybody just sniffed at him, because, you know, who's got reflexes like a Shooter? They're the best at what they do.

"You got assigned to us because you tested out as a Plotter," I told Charles. "That's just the way things are. You're the best at your job; the pay's good; in five years you'll be out of here. You just have to learn to live with the crap. We all did."

He looked like a smart guy, and I thought he wouldn't need to be told twice. I was wrong.

We heard the march of booted feet coming along the corridor. Vinder leaped up and grabbed all his action figures, shoving them into a storage pod. Norman began to hyperventilate; Bradley ran for the toilet. I just stayed where I was and lowered my eyes. It's never a good idea to look them in the face.

Boom! The portal jerked open and in they came, Lord Deathlok and the Shark and Iron Beast. They were carrying Piki-tiki. I blanched.

Piki-tiki was this sort of dummy they'd made out of a blanket and a mask. And a few other things. Lord Deathlok grinned around and spotted Charles.

"Piki-tiki returns to his harem," he shouted. "What's this? Piki-tiki sees a new and beautiful bride! Piki-tiki must welcome her to his realm!"

Giggling, they advanced on Charles and launched the dummy. It fell over him, and before he could throw it off they'd jumped him and hoisted him between them. He was fighting hard, but they just laughed; that is, until he got one arm free and punched the Shark in the face. The Shark grabbed his nose and began to swear, but Lord Deathlok and Iron Beast gloated.

"Whoa! The blushing bride needs to learn her manners. Piki-tiki's going to take her off to his honeymoon suite and see that she learns them well!"

Ouch. They dragged him away. At least it wasn't the worst they might have done to him; they were only going to cram him in one of the lockers, probably one that had had some sweaty socks left in the bottom, and stuff Piki-tiki in there on top of him. Then they'd lock him in and leave him there. How did I know? They'd done it to me, on my first day.

If you're sensible, like me, you just shrug it off and concentrate on your job. Charles wouldn't let it go, though. He kept asking questions.

Like, how come the Shooters were paid better than we were, even though they spent most of their time playing simulations and Plotters did all the actual work of tracking asteroids and calculating when they'd strike? How come Mr. Kurtz had given up on disciplinary action for them, even after they'd rigged his holoset to come on unexpectedly and project a CGI of him having sex with an alligator, or all the other little ways in which they made his life a living hell? How come none of us ever stood up to them?

And it was no good explaining how they didn't respond to reason, and they didn't respond to being called immature and crude and disgusting, because they just loved being told how awful they were.

The other thing he asked about was why there weren't any women up here, and that was too humiliating to go into, so I just said tests had shown that men were better suited for life on a Gun Platform.

He should have been happy that he was a *good* Plotter, because he really was. He mastered Q34-54 in a week. One shift we were there on the Bridge and Myron and I were talking about the worst-ever episode of *Schrödinger's Rock*, which was the one that had Lallal's evil twin showing up after being killed off in the second season, and Anil was unwrapping the underwear his mother had sent him for his thirty-first birthday, when suddenly Charles said: "Eugene, you should probably check Q6-17; I'm calculating an Intruder showing up in about Q-14."

"How'd you know?" I said in surprise, slipping my goggles on. But he was right; there was an Intruder, tumbling end over end in a halo of fire and snow, way above the plane of the ecliptic but square in Q-14.

"Don't you extend your projections beyond the planet's ecliptic?" said Charles.

Myron and I looked at each other. We never projected out that far; what was the point? There was always time to spot an Intruder before it came in range.

"You don't have to work *that* hard, dude," I said. "Fifty degrees above and below is all we have to bother with. The scanning programs catch the rest." But I sent out the alert and we could hear the Shooters cheering, even though the War Room was clear at the other end of the Platform. As far out as the Intruder was, the Shark was able to send out a missile. We didn't see the hit— there wouldn't be one for two weeks at least, and I'd have to keep monitoring the Intruder and now the missile too, just to be sure the trajectories remained matched up—but the Shooters began to stamp and roar the Bonus Song.

Myron sniffed.

"Typical," he said. "We do all the work, they push one bloody button, and *they're* the heroes."

"You know, it doesn't have to be this way," said Charles.

"It's not like we can go on strike," said Anil sullenly. "We're independent contractors. There's a penalty for quitting."

"You don't have to quit," said Charles. "You can show Areco you can do even more. We can be Plotters *and* Shooters."

Anil and Myron looked horrified. You'd have thought he'd suggested we all turn homo or something. I was shocked myself. I had to explain about tests proving that things functioned most smoothly when every man kept to his assigned task.

"Don't Areco think we can multitask?" he asked me. "They're a corporation like any other, aren't they? They must want to save money. All we have to do is show them we can do both jobs. The Shooters get a nice redundancy package; we get the Gun Platform all to ourselves. Life is good."

"Only one problem with your little plan, Mr. Genius," said Myron. "I can't shoot. I don't have the reflexes a Shooter does. That's why I'm a Plotter."

"But you could learn to shoot," said Charles.

"I'll repeat this slowly so you get it," said Myron, exasperated. "*I don't have the reflexes*. And neither do you. How many times have we been tested, our whole lives? Aptitude tests, allergy tests, brain scans, DNA mapping? Areco knows exactly what we are and what we can and can't do. I'm a Plotter. You're just fooling yourself if you think you aren't."

Charles didn't say anything in reply. He just looked at each of us in turn, pretty disgusted, I guess, and then he turned back to his console and focused on his work.

That wasn't the end of it, though. When he was off his shift, instead of hanging out in the Cockpit, did he join in the discussions of graphic novels or what was hot on holo that week? Not Charles. He'd retire to a corner in the Forecastle with a buke and he'd game. And not just any game: targeting simulations. You never saw a guy with such icy focus. Sometimes he'd tinker with a couple of projects he'd ordered. I assumed they were models.

It was like the rest of us weren't even there. We had to respect him as a Plotter; for one thing, he turned out to have an uncanny knack for spotting Intruders, days before any of the rest of us detected them, and he was brilliant at predicting their trajectories too. But there was something distant about the guy that kept him from fitting in. Myron and Anil had dismissed him as a crank anyway, and a couple of the guys on B Shift actively disliked him, after he spouted off to them the way he did to us. They were sure he was going to do something, sooner or later, that would only end up making it worse for all of us.

They were right, too.

When Weldon's turn in the rota ended, he brought Charles the French maid's apron and tossed it on his bunk.

"Your turn to wear the damn thing," he said. "They'll expect you in the bar at fourteen hundred hours. Good luck."

Charles just grunted, never even looking up from the screen of his buke.

Fourteen hundred hours came and he was still sitting there, coolly gaming.

"Hey!" said Anil. "You're supposed to go flackey!"

"I'm not going," said Charles.

"Don't be stupid!" I said. "If the rest of us have to do it, you do too."

"Why? Terrible repercussions if I don't?" Charles set aside his buke and looked at us.

"Yes!" said Myron. Preston from A Shift came running in right then, looking pale.

"Who's supposed to be flackeying? There's nobody out there, and Lord Deathlok wants to know why!"

"See?" said Myron.

"You'll get all of us in trouble, you fool! Give me the apron, I'll go!" said Anil. But Charles took the apron and tore it in half.

There was this horrified silence, which filled up with the sound of Shooters thundering along the corridor. We heard Lord Deathlok and Painmaster yelling as they came.

"Flackey! Oh, flackey! Where are you?"

And then they were in the room and it was too late to run, too late to hide. Painmaster's roach crest almost touched the ceiling panels. Lord Deathlok's yellow grin was so wide he didn't look human.

"Hi there, buttholes," said Painmaster. "If you girls aren't too busy making out, one of you is supposed to be flackeying for us."

"It was my turn," said Charles. He wadded up the apron and threw it at them. "How about you wait on yourself from now on?"

"This wasn't our idea!" said Myron.

"We tried to make him report for duty!" said Anil.

"We'll remember that, when we're assigning penalties," said Lord Deathlok. "Maybe we'll let you keep your pants when we handcuff you upside down in the toilet. Little Newbie, though . . ." He turned to Charles. "What about a nice game of Walk the Dog? Painmaster, got a leash anywhere on you?"

"The Painmaster always has a leash for a bad dog," said Painmaster, pulling one out. He started toward Charles, and that's when it got crazy.

Charles jumped out of his bunk and I thought, *No, you idiot, don't try to run!* But he didn't. He grabbed Painmaster's extended hand and pulled him close, and brought his arm up like he was going to hug him, only instead he made a kind of punching motion at Painmaster's neck. Painmaster screamed, wet himself, and fell down. Charles kicked him in the crotch.

Another dead silence, which broke as soon as Painmaster got enough breath in him for another scream. Everybody else in the room was staring at Charles, or I should say at his left wrist, because it was now obvious there was something strapped to it under his sleeve.

Lord Deathlok had actually taken a step backward. He looked from Painmaster to Charles, and then at whatever it was on Charles's wrist. He licked his lips.

"So, that's, what, some kind of taser?" he said. "Those are illegal, buddy."

Charles smiled. I realized then I'd never seen him smile before.

"It's illegal to buy one. I bought some components and made my own. What are you going to do? Report me to Kurtz?" he said.

"No; I'm just going to take it away from you, dumbass," said Lord Deathlok. He lunged at Charles, but all that happened was that Charles tased him too. He jerked backward and fell over a chair, clutching his tased hand.

"You're dead," he gasped. "You're really dead."

Charles walked over and kicked him in the crotch too.

"I challenge you to a duel," he said.

"What?" said Lord Deathlok, when he had enough breath after his scream.

"A duel. With simulations," said Charles. "I'll outshoot you. Right there in the War Room, with everybody there to witness. Thirteen hundred hours tomorrow."

"Fuck off," said Lord Deathlok. Charles leaned down and displayed the two little steel points of the taser.

"So you're scared to take me on? Chicken, is that it?" he said, and Myron and Anil obligingly started making cluck-cluck-cluck noises. "Eugene, why don't you go over to the Pit of Hell and tell the Shooters they need to come scrape up these guys?"

I wouldn't have done that for a chance to see the lost episodes of *Doctor Who*, but fortunately Lord Deathlok sat up, gasping.

"Okay," he said. "Duel. You lose, I get that taser and shove it up your ass."

"Sure," said Charles. "Whatever you want; but I won't lose. And none of us will ever flackey for you again. Got it?"

Lord Deathlok called him a lot of names, but the end of it was that he agreed to the terms, and we made Painmaster (who was crying and complaining that his heartbeat was irregular) witness. When they could walk they went stumbling back to the Pit of Hell, leaning on each other.

"You are out of your mind," I said, when they had gone. "You'll go to the War Room tomorrow and they'll be waiting for you with six bottles of club soda and a can of poster paint."

"Maybe," said Charles. "But they'll back off. Haven't you clowns figured it out yet? They're used to shooting at rocks. They have no clue what to do about something that fights back."

"They'll still win. You won't be able to tase them all, and once they get it off you, you're doomed."

"They won't get it off me," said Charles, rolling up his sleeve and unstrapping the taser mounting from his arm. "I won't be wearing it. You will."

"Me?" I backed away.

"And there's another one in my locker. Which one of you wants it?"

"You've got *two*?"

"Me!" Anil jumped forward. "So we'll be, like, your bodyguards? Yes! Can you make more of these things?"

"I won't need to," said Charles. "Tomorrow's going to change everything."

‖

I don't mind telling you, my knees were knocking as we marched across to the War Room the next day. Everybody on B and C Shifts came along; strength in numbers, right? If we got creamed by the Shooters, at least some of us ought to make it out of there. And if Charles was insanely lucky, we all wanted to see.

It was embarrassing. Norman and Roscoe wore full Jedi kit, including their damn light sabers that were only holobeams anyway. Bradley was wearing a Happy Bat San playjacket. Anil was wearing his lucky hat from *Mystic Antagonists: The Extravaganza.* We're all creative and unique, no question, but . . . maybe it isn't the best idea to dress that way when you're going to a duel with intimidating mindless jerks.

We got there, and they were waiting for us.

Our Bridge always reminded me of a temple or a shrine or something, with its beautiful display shining in the darkness; but the War Room was like the Cave of the Cyclops. There wasn't any wall display like we had. There were just the red lights of the targeting consoles, and way in the far end of the room somebody had stuck up a black light, which made the lurid holo-posters of skulls and demons and vampires seem to writhe in the gloom.

The place stank of body odor, which the Shooters can't get rid of because they wear all that black bioprene gear, which doesn't breathe like the natural fabrics we wear. There was also a urinal reek; when a Shooter is gaming, he doesn't let a little thing like needing to pee drive him from his console.

All this was bad enough; imagine how I felt to see that the Shooters had made war clubs out of chlorilar water bottles stuck into handles of printer paper rolled tight. They stood there, glowering at us. I saw Lord Deathlok and the Shark and Professor Badass. Mephisto, the Conquistador, Iron Beast, Killer Ape, Uncle Hannibal . . . every hateful face I knew from months of humiliating flackey-work, except . . .

"Where's the Painmaster?" said Charles, looking around in an unconcerned kind of way.

"He had better things to do than watch you rectums lose," said Lord Deathlok.

"He had to be shipped down to the infirmary, because he was complaining of chest pains," said Mephisto. The others looked at him accusingly. Charles beamed.

"Too bad! Let's do this thing, gentlemen."

"We fixed up a special console, homo, just for you," said Lord Deathlok with an evil leer, waving at one. Charles looked at it and laughed.

"You have got to be kidding. I'll take *this* one over *here*, and you'll take the one next to it. We'll play side by side, so everybody can see. That's only fair, right?"

Their faces fell. But Anil and I crossed our arms, so the taser prongs showed, and the Shooters grumbled but backed down. They cleared away empty bottles and snack wrappers from the consoles. It felt good, watching them humbled for a change.

Charles settled himself at the console he'd chosen, and with a few quick commands on the buttonball pulled up the simulation menu.

"Is this all you've got?" he said. "Okay; I propose nine rounds. Three sets each of *Holodeath 2*, *Meteor Nightmare*, and *Incoming Annihilation*. Highest cumulative score wins."

"You got it, shithead," said Lord Deathlok. He took his seat.

So they called up *Holodeath 2*, and we all crowded around to watch, even though the awesome stench of the Shooters was enough to make your eyes water. The holo display lit up with a sinister green fog, and the enemy ships started coming at us. Charles got off three shots before Lord Deathlok managed one, and though one of his shots went wild, two inflicted enough damage on a Megacruiser to set it on fire. Lord Deathlok's shot nailed a patrol vessel in the forefront, and though it was a low-score target, he took it out with just that one shot. The score counters on both consoles gave them twelve hundred points.

Charles finished the burning cruiser with two more quick shots—it looked fantastic, glaring red through its ports until it just sort of imploded in this cylinder of glowing ash. But Lord Deathlok was picking off the little transport cutters methodically, because they only take about a shot each if you're accurate, which he was. Charles pulled ahead by hammering away at the big targets, and he never missed another shot, and so what happened was that the score counters showed them flashing along neck and neck for the longest time and then, *boom*, the last Star Destroyer blew and Charles was suddenly way ahead with twice Deathlok's score.

We were all yelling by this time, the Shooters with their chimpanzee hooting and us with—well, we sort of sounded like apes too. The next set went up and here came the ships again, but this time they were firing back. Charles took three hits in succession before he seemed to figure out how to raise his shields, and the Shooters started gloating and smacking their clubs together.

But he went on the offensive real fast, and did something I'd never thought of before, which was aiming for the ships' gunports and disabling them with one shot before hitting them with a barrage that finished them. I never even had time to look at what Deathlok was doing, but his guys stopped cheering suddenly—and when the set ended, he didn't even have a third of the points Charles did.

The third set went amazingly fast, even with the difference that the gun positions weren't stationary and they had to maneuver around in the middle of the armada. Charles did stuff I would never have dared to do, recklessly swooping around and under the Megacruisers, *between* their gunports for cripes' sake, getting off round after round of shots so close it seemed impossible for him to pull clear before the ships blew, but somehow he did.

Lord Deathlok didn't seem to move much. He just sat in one position and pounded away at anything that came within range, and though he did manage to bag a Star Destroyer, he finished the set way behind Charles on points.

I would have just given up if I'd been Deathlok, but the Shooters were getting ugly, shouting all kinds of personal abuse at him, and I don't think he dared.

I had to run for the lavatory as *Incoming Annihilation* was starting, and of course I had to run all the way back to our end of the Gun Platform to our toilet because I sure wasn't going to use the Shooters', not with the way the War Room smelled. It was only when I was unfastening that I realized I was still wearing the taser, and that I'd done an incredibly stupid thing by leaving when I was one of Charles's bodyguards. So I finished fast and ran all the way back, and there was Mr. Kurtz strolling along the corridor.

"Hello there, Eugene," he said. "Something going on?"

"Just some gaming," I said. "I need to get back—"

"But you're on Shooter turf, aren't you?" Mr. Kurtz looked around. "Shouldn't you be going in the other direction?"

"Well—we're having this competition, you see, Mr. Kurtz," I said. "The new guy's gaming against Lord—I mean, against Peavey Crandall."

"Is he?" Mr. Kurtz began to smile. "I wondered how long Charles would put up with the Shooters. Well, well."

He said it in a funny kind of way, but I didn't have the time to wonder about it. I just excused myself and ran on, and was really relieved to see that the Shooters didn't seem to have noticed my absence. They were all packed tight around the consoles, and nobody was making a sound; all you could hear was the *peew-peew-peew* of the shots going off continuously, and the *whump* as bombs exploded. Then there was a flare of red light and our guys yelled in triumph. Bradley was leaping up and down, and Roscoe did a Victory Dance until one of the Shooters asked him if he wanted his light saber rammed up his butt.

I managed to shove my way between Anil and Myron just as Charles was announcing, "I believe you're screwed, Mr. Crandall. Care to call it a day?"

I looked at their scores and couldn't believe how badly Lord Deathlok had lost to him. But Lord Deathlok just snarled.

"I don't think so, Ben Dover. Shut up and play!"

It was *Meteor Nightmare* now, as though they were both out there in the Van Oort belt, facing the rocks without any comforting distance of consoles or calculations. I couldn't stop myself from flinching as they hurtled forward; and I noticed one of the Shooters put up his arms involuntarily, as though he wanted to bat away the incoming with his bare hands.

It was a brutal game; *nightmare*, all right, because they couldn't avoid taking massive damage. All they could do was take out as many targets as they could before their inevitable destruction. When one or the other of them took a hit, there was a momentary flare of light that blinded everybody in the room. I couldn't imagine how Charles and Lord Deathlok, right there with their faces in the action, could keep shooting with any kind of accuracy.

Sure enough, early in the second round it began to tell. They were both getting flash-blind. Charles was still hitting about one in three targets, but Lord Deathlok was shooting crazily, randomly, not even bothering to aim so far as I could tell. What a look of despair on his ugly face, with his lips drawn back from his yellow teeth!

Only a miracle would save him, now. His overall score was so far behind Charles's he'd never catch up. The Shooters knew it too. I saw Dr. Smash turn his head and murmur to Uncle Hannibal. He took a firm grip on his war club. Panicking, I grabbed Anil's arm, trying to get his attention.

That was when the Incoming klaxons sounded. All the Shooters stood to attention. Lord Deathlok looked around, blinking, but Charles worked the buttonball like a pro and suddenly the game vanished, and there was nothing before us but the console displays. There was a crackle from the speakers—the first time they'd ever been used, I found out later—and we could hear Preston screaming, "You guys! Intruder coming in fast! You have to stop! It's in—"

"Q41!" said Uncle Hannibal, leaning forward to peer at the console readout. "Get out of my chair, dickwad!"

Charles didn't answer. He did something with the buttonball and there was the Intruder, like something out of *Meteor Nightmare*, shracking enormous. It was in his own sector! How could he have missed it? *Charles*, who was brilliant at spotting them before anybody else?

A red frame rose around it, with the readout in numbers spinning over so fast I couldn't tell what they said, except it was obvious the thing was coming in at high speed. All the Shooters were frantic, bellowing for Charles to get his ass out of the chair. Before their astounded eyes, and ours, he targeted the Intruder and fired.

All sound stopped. Movement stopped. Time itself stopped, except for on the display, where a new set of numbers in green and another in yellow popped up. They spun like fruit on a slot machine, the one counting up, the other counting down, both getting slower and slower until suddenly the numbers matched. Then, in perfect unison, they clicked upward together on a leisurely march.

"It's a hit," announced Preston from the speakers. "In twelve days thirteen hours forty-two minutes. Telemetry confirmed."

Dead silence answered him. And that was when I understood: Charles hadn't missed the Intruder. Charles had spotted it days ago. Charles had set this whole thing up, requesting the specific time of the duel, knowing the Intruder would interrupt it and there'd have to be a last-minute act of heroism. Which he'd co-opt.

But the thing is, see, there are *people* down there on the planet under us, who could die if a meteor gets through. I mean, that's why we're all up here in the first place, right?

Finally Anil said, in a funny voice, "So . . . who gets the bonus, then?"

"He *can't* have just done that," said Mephisto, hoarse with disbelief. "He's a *Plotter*."

"Get up, faggot," said Uncle Hannibal, grabbing Charles's shoulder.

"Hit him," said Charles.

I hadn't unfrozen yet, but Anil had been waiting for this moment all day. He jumped forward and tased Uncle Hannibal. Uncle Hannibal dropped, with a hoarse screech, and the other Shooters backed away fast. Anil stared down at Uncle Hannibal with unholy wonder in his eyes, and the beginning of a terrible joy. Suddenly there was a lot of room in front of the consoles, enough to see Lord Deathlok sitting there staring at the readout, with tears streaming down his face.

Charles got out of the chair.

"You lost," he informed Lord Deathlok.

"Your reign of terror is over!" cried Anil, brandishing his taser at the Shooters. One or two of them cowered, but the rest just looked stunned. Charles turned to me.

"You left your post," he said. "You're a useless idiot. Myron, take the taser off him."

"Sir yes sir!" said Myron, grabbing my arm and rolling up my sleeve. As he was unfastening the straps, we heard a chuckle from the doorway. All heads turned. There was Mr. Kurtz, leaning there with his arms crossed. I realized he must have followed me, and seen the drama as it played out. Anil thrust his taser arm behind his back, looking scared, but Mr. Kurtz only smiled.

"As you were," he said. He stood straight and left. We could hear him whistling as he walked away.

It wasn't until later that we learned the whole story, or as much of it as we ever knew: how Charles had been recruited, not from his parents' garage or basement, but from Hospital, and how Mr. Kurtz had known it, had in fact *requested it*.

We all expected a glorious new day had come for Plotters, now that Charles had proven the Shooters were unnecessary. We thought Areco would terminate their contracts. It didn't exactly happen that way.

What happened was that Dr. Smash and Uncle Hannibal came to Charles and had a private (except for Myron and Anil) talk with him. They were very polite. Since Painmaster wasn't coming back to the Gun Platform, but had defaulted on his contract and gone down home to Earth, they proposed that Charles become a Shooter. They did more; they offered him High Dark Lordship.

He accepted their offer. We were appalled. It seemed like the worst treachery imaginable.

And yet, we were surprised again.

Charles Tead didn't take one of the stupid Shooter names like Warlord or Iron Fist or Doomsman. He said we were all to call him *Stede* from now on. He ordered up not a bioprene wardrobe with spikes and rivets and fringe, but . . . but . . . a three-piece suit, with a *tie*. And a bowler hat. He took his tasers back from Anil and Myron, who were crestfallen, and wore them himself, under his perfectly pressed cuffs.

Then he ordered up new clothes for all the other Shooters. It must have been a shock, when he handed out those powder blue shirts and drab coveralls, but they didn't rebel; by that time they'd learned what he'd been sent to Hospital for in the first place, which was killing three people. So there wasn't so much as a mutter behind his back, even when he ordered all the holoposters shut off and thrown into the fusion hopper, and the War Room repainted in dove gray.

We wouldn't have known the Shooters. He made them wash; he made them cut their hair; he made them shracking salute when he gave an order. They were scared to fart, especially after he hung up deodorizers above each of their consoles. The War Room became a clean, well-lit place, silent except for the consoles and the occasional quiet order from Charles. He seldom had to raise his voice.

Mr. Kurtz still sat in his office all day, reading, but now he smiled as he read. Nobody called him *Dean Kurtz* anymore, either.

It was sort of horrible, what had happened, but with Charles—I mean, Stede—running the place, things were a lot more efficient. The bonuses became more frequent, as everyone worked harder. And, in time, the Shooters came to worship him.

He didn't bother with us. We were grateful.

ARISTOTLE OS

Tony Ballantyne

Tony Ballantyne blew my socks off with the story "The Waters of Meribah," which appeared originally in Interzone 189. *I didn't know anything about Tony, beyond my original impression that he was a genius, and then I met him on a pirate ship in Glasgow and found out he was also a very nice guy. There was nothing for it but to have him in* Fast Forward.

Turning on a computer has a whole different feel nowadays, but I had to write this somehow.

I'm running CP/M now. If that doesn't mean anything to you, then it soon will. It's an old operating system from the seventies: A *Platonic* OS. Lots of people are installing it.

It's only a few months since I heard the term *Platonic Operating System*.

I wish I hadn't. I wish I'd never listened to my brother.

"Can you fix it?" I asked. Ken was gazing at the screen with that half smile on his face he always has when he's doing me a favour.

"It's not broken," he snorted. "You just had the security settings turned up high. The computer must have detected unsuitable words in your files."

"What are you implying ?"

Ken gave a laugh. "Don't be so sensitive. They're there to stop children accessing inappropriate stuff on the Internet. Of course, most children would have no problems turning them off. Don't worry. I'll soon have things sorted."

"Oh, good."

He tapped away, the clacking of the keys the only sound in my half-empty flat. So much space to fill with half the furniture gone . . .

There seemed to be empty spaces in the conversations between Ken and me too, lately. Just like this one.

"Do you want some more coffee?" I asked, breaking the silence.

"Yes, please." He held out a flowered mug, one that Jenny must have overlooked when she disengaged her possessions from mine. "And how about a spot of brandy in it?" he added. "It's cold out there."

He leaned back in the elderly chair and gave a dramatic sigh. "Of course," he declared, "the *big* problem here is that you are still using a *Platonic* operating system."

Ken has this way of dropping conversational hooks, then sitting back and looking smug whilst he waits for you to bite on them. Normally I'd just ignore him, even say something sarcastic, but—just like when you speak to the tax office—you're always polite to the person who is fixing your computer.

"Platonic operating system?" I asked. "I thought it was just Windows, like everyone uses."

He laughed at that.

"Windows, Linux, Mac OS. They're all the same. They model the real world inside your computer. Whether you're running a spreadsheet to do your household accounts, or playing a car racing game, you're just running an imperfect model of the real world."

He looked at me again, another one of those little pregnant pauses. I was the one who went to university, he was saying. I was the one who studied philosophy; he had left school to become an electrician.

"Okay," I said. "Plato said that humans experienced the world like a group of people sitting inside a cave, watching the shadows of reality that dance on the walls before them. Are you saying that my computer just does the same? Models shadows on a wall?"

"You got it," said Ken sliding a plastic case from his pocket and holding it up for me to see. "This is something new. It dispenses with the paradigm that the computer only *models* the real world. This operating system makes the assumption that everything input is real."

I took the case from him and turned it over in my hands. There was a shiny CD-ROM inside, half hidden by a torn piece of paper on which were scrawled the words "Aristotle OS."

"What's the point of that?" I asked.

"You'll see." He pressed a button, and the DVD tray on my computer slid smoothly open.

"Ken," I began, "I'm perfectly happy with my computer the way it is. All I want to be able to do is write articles and lesson plans. Maybe try to keep track of my spending—"

It was too late. He had already dropped the disc into the tray and was beginning to type at the keyboard.

"Now," he said. "Where's my coffee?"

Ken eventually left two hours later with a promise to meet at our mother's house for dinner the following Sunday. I didn't hold out much hope. Something would come up; an old acquaintance would buttonhole him in a pub somewhere. Either that or he would lose track of time, busy downloading more illegal stuff from the Net. It had been a long time since he had made a family meal. I looked across at my guitar, gathering dust in a lonely corner. It was longer still since Ken had come around on a Wednesday night so we could rehearse together. I couldn't remember the last time we had played a gig. . . .

I busied myself with tidying up the kitchen. I had an article to write, but, truth be told, I was putting off starting it. I didn't want to see what Ken had done to my poor computer. His modifications tended to complicate my life, not simplify it. They were all done in good faith, of course, but sometimes I longed for the days of my old AMSTRAD word processor with its green screen and simple commands. I groaned as I saw my PC, its screen, once a familiar pale blue, now shining at me in bright orange.

Maybe I should mark a set of essays ready for tomorrow's lessons.

Still the orange screen seemed to be staring at me.

"Okay," I said, seating myself before it. "Let's see what Ken has done this time."

The screen looked pretty much the same as before, apart from the bright orange background. I clicked START and launched my accounts spreadsheet.

It was exactly as I had left it. Neat columns showing my monthly income and expenditure. Ken had been hassling me to use a copy of the Money Management software he had installed, but I preferred this. I could understand it. I had control. I could spot mistakes. Just like that one there.

I was saving up for a car. Each month I transferred what I could into my savings account. That month I had mistyped an entry. £10 instead of £100. That was easily rectified. I clicked in the cell and made the change. An error message flashed up on the screen.

Reality dysfunction. £10 is not £100

"I know that," I muttered. "I made a mistake." I tried the correction again and received the same error message.

"Bloody Ken."

I picked up the plastic disc case, still lying by the keyboard, and read the scrawled insert. *Aristotle OS.* That was a clue, of course.

"Come on now, Jon," I said to myself. "You can figure this out. Ken said that this was not a Platonic OS. This does not model reality. . . ."

It made a certain sort of sense, when you thought about it. Aristotle believed that Plato had got it wrong. Reality wasn't something that existed "behind" us and could only be seen as shadows; it wasn't something that could only be modeled with our reason. Aristotle believed reality was that which we perceived through our senses.

What senses did a computer have? Inputs. Keyboard presses and mouse clicks. Digital samples of sounds and images played into their memories a byte at a time. If the keyboard had said there was £10 in the savings account this month, then £10 there was. If the keyboard later on said there was £100, then the computer would want to know which was right. It would be like me opening my wallet and finding £100 in crisp notes there, when minutes before there had only been £10. I'd want to explain the change.

I gazed at the screen. What was the point of my computer acting like this? Well, it was easily fixed. I entered another £90 in the cell below the £10. There. Now I had £100 in my savings account.

If only mistakes in life could be remedied so easily.

‖

I grew to like the Aristotle OS. It came into its own when I was typing up long articles. I came to rely on the little messages that flashed up as a piece of work took shape.

J Davies cannot have published *An Introduction to Existentialism* in 1982 *and* 1984

or

Grumman cannot have been born both French and German

It had other uses too. Ways of making you think; of confronting you with your own assumptions.

Why do you begin so many sentences with the word "Hopefully"?

or

Why give £40 to *Feed the Homeless* when this month you threw out food to the value of £45?

Why indeed? I resolved to be more careful with my shopping. I would eat everything that I bought. There was half a lettuce going brown in the bottom of the fridge. I boiled a couple of eggs and made a salad with it.

My first inkling that something was not quite right came when Ken phoned late one night, maybe three weeks after he had installed Aristotle.

"Hey, Jon . . ." His speaking was slurred. I could hear the clink of glasses in the background, the muffled sound of laughter made by men drinking in a pub after hours.

"Ken," I said. "It's two o'clock in the bloody morning. Can't it wait?"

"Jon, have you been using your computer?"

"Of course I've been using my computer. Why have you rung me in the middle of the night to ask me that?"

"No. No. I don't want another pint. No. Whiskey." His voice was muffled. I could picture him standing there, that way he did, phone cradled at his neck, shaking his hand in a "drink" gesture at the barman. "No. No Jon. That should be okay. Of course you should use your computer. Just don't connect it to the Internet."

"What? Why not? How am I supposed to read my mail? Look Ken, what's the matter with you?"

The line went dead.

I went back to bed and stared at the ceiling. I couldn't go back to sleep. My mind drifted inexorably to Jenny. What was she doing now? I wondered. After half an hour of torturing myself I got up and went into the lounge and picked up my guitar, blew the dust off it. I tried to play something, but the strings were old and I couldn't tune them.

The picture on my computer screen was of Ken and me, standing on the summit of Ben Nevis. It was a cold scene, gray cloud swirled over the lifeless vista: rocks and rubble and the remains of a building. A man in a yellow waterproof coat and thick woolen hat could be seen squatting there, stirring a pan on a portable stove. Steam from hot soup rose into the air.

Ken was dressed in a thin jumper and coat; on his feet was a pair of old training shoes. He looked as if he had wandered out of a pub in Fort William with a couple of his mates and decided to climb the mountain for a laugh.

That's exactly what he had done.

He was holding up a can of Tennants Super Lager for the camera to see. I stood by him, in my old Craghoppers jacket, looking seriously concerned for my brother's well-being.

A picture paints a thousand words. . . . This one captured the moment perfectly. It told the viewer everything they needed to know about my relationship with my brother.

Just one thing. I've never been to Ben Nevis.

How had the computer managed to superimpose me onto that picture?

Ken almost looked embarrassed when he came around.

"Look," I said. "Look!"

I clicked the mouse, flicking through picture after picture on the screen. Me in front of the Taj Mahal; a strange city of silver towers, the Houses of Parliament clearly visible nestling amongst them; an airplane the like of which I'd never seen, flying over a blasted plain.

"Where have they come from?" I asked. "I certainly didn't put them there."

"No," said Ken. "It's Aristotle. It's trying to make sense of contradictory data. Let me explain." He looked around for inspiration. "I know; it's better if you close your eyes. . . ."

I stared at him. He looked a mess.

"You stink of beer," I said. "When are you going to sort yourself out?"

He looked angry.

"I've got nothing to sort out. Look, close your eyes. I'm trying to explain it to you. Do you want me to fix your computer or not?"

That threat was always there. I closed my eyes. "Now what?"

"Now imagine an orange. Are you doing that? Imagine the feel of its skin, that slightly waxy, warm sensation. Imagine pressing your thumbs into it, forcing a hole, juice squirting over your hands, that sharp citrus smell in your nose—"

"Is there a point to this?" I said, my eyes tightly closed.

"Yes. Open your eyes. Look at me. Now, tell me. How do you know what you just experienced was imagination and not the real thing?"

"Is this some sort of philosophical question. 'Am I a butterfly dreaming I am an Emperor?'"

"No. I'm dealing with facts, not some philosophical bollocks. Listen, I'll tell you how you know the difference: the signals in the neurons in your brain that fired when you imagined the orange were not as strong as they would have been if you had *really* handled one. The same neurons fired, but there was a difference in the magnitude of the signal."

"If you say so. . . ."

"I do say so. Well, your computer can't do that. For a computer, a memory location is either on or off. It holds something in memory, it accepts an input, it has no way of knowing if what it has stored is real or imaginary. You connected your computer to the Internet. It has encountered all sorts of data out there. Games, models, jokes—some things that are just plain wrong. But it has no way of knowing what is real and what is made up. It tries to resolve what it sees as contradictory realities. Your pictures are an example of your computer doing just that."

"Oh. So what are you going to do about it?"

He held out another disc. This one read *Kant 2.0*. "This'll sort it out."

"Why don't I just go back to Windows?"

"You can't. Aristotle won't let go. It refuses to accept a Platonic OS as valid. It will upgrade to Kant, though. Don't ask me why."

I gave a grim smile. "I know why." It wasn't often I managed to put one over on my brother where computers were concerned. "Kant built on Aristotle's materialism. He distinguished between the thing in itself, and the way it appears to an observer. He said that we only experience the world through the forms of time and causality. I'm guessing that the upgrade on that disk will give my computer just enough of a context to make sense of the world."

Ken swayed as he looked from me to the computer. His clothes smelled of stale cigarette smoke.

"Whoever thought that philosophy could be useful?" he said sarcastically.

"Whoever designed the program on that disk, I imagine," I replied sweetly.

Kant 2.0 seemed to do the trick. The composite picture of me and Ken at the top of Ben Nevis was efficiently separated into its component parts and placed in a query folder, along with other files with ambiguous dates. I went through the folder at my leisure, assigning the files to their correct context.

Picture files "Jon Paris.jpg" and "Ken Eiffel Tower.jpg" have the same date. Merge Yes No ?

They had the same date because both files would have been newly created when I copied them across from my old computer. Piece by piece I separated my life back out, disentangling it from the imaginary web in which it had become entangled.

I found it quite therapeutic. Like playing my guitar.

All seemed to return to normal. Until I came home late one evening from college and found a message on the screen.

hi jon gone to mallons with charlotte and najam back late don't wait up jen xxx

It was from Jenny. There was no doubt about it. She regarded ignoring punctuation or the shift key as a way of demonstrating her refusal to take my work seriously. It was "only writing," after all.

But what was she playing at, e-mailing me now?

Her number was still on my mobile. I dialed her. She answered on the third ring.

"Jon. What do you want?"

The sound of her voice still hurt, especially when it was twisted into something so suspicious and hostile.

"Me?" I replied. "What do *you* want? What do you mean, you've gone to Mallon's?"

"Why shouldn't I go to Mallon's?" she said. "It's Charlotte's birthday." I could hear the sound of a jukebox playing in the background: wine bar jazz, bland saxophones over a Latin clave. The sort of MOR crap I hate. "Anyway," she snapped, "what's it got to do with you? Are you spying on me?"

"What?" I looked at the computer screen again, just to confirm that I wasn't seeing things. "Spying on *you*? No. I got your message."

"What message? Jon, stop pissing me around."

And at that the line went dead.

I stared at the screen for a while; then I went to close the message down. A prompt appeared on the screen.

Save changes to file? Yes No

After a long moment, I clicked on the Yes button.

‖

I don't think I could name the exact moment I realized I was not living my real life. It was a slow process of comprehension, a picture that gradually took form as the different pieces slotted into place. It was like watching an image downloading from the Internet on a slow connection.

Here there was an e-mail from Jenny telling me that she would meet me at the Tate at seven that night.

Here was confirmation of two tickets to see Chris Smither at the Half Moon in Putney. Two tickets, one for me, one for Ken.

Here was a picture of Jenny and me riding on a boat down the dark stripe of the Thames, late on a warm July evening. London rose up on either bank outlined in red and yellow and white lights. What a delightful scene for a wedding reception. I could see Charlotte in the background, looking beautiful as the bride.

Here was confirmation of a flight to Geneva, and later on there was picture of Ken and me sitting on the terrace of a refuge high in the Italian Alps. Ken was holding up a glass of water to the camera to say "cheers!" His nose was burned red by the sun; he looked happy and healthy and utterly relaxed, and I felt suddenly stifled by the half-empty room in which I sat. South Street was so dull and lifeless compared to the world on my screen. I stared again at Ken, looking so peaceful. When was the last time I had seen him so happy with nothing but a glass of water in his hand?

That was my computer. That was Kant 2.0. It viewed the world through keyboards and scanners and microphones, and built up a pattern of life through causality and time that was as optimized and validated and free from illogicality as was anything else on my computer. My new OS didn't understand about repression and self-destruction and pride and all those other human traits in which Ken and I had steeped our lives. On the screen I could see my PC living out my life for me as it should have been lived, if only I had the courage and the sense to have seized my opportunities as they came along.

And it made me feel sick to my soul to see it, because there, dancing in the pixel light of my dim room, there was no room for excuses or dreams or might-have-beens. That was a picture of my failure in negative, a successful life painted for all to see in twenty-four-bit glory.

▌▌

Ken rolled up at my house two nights later. It was half past ten; there was still forty minutes' worth of drinking time left in the pubs, but I guess his money had run out. I offered him a coffee; he accepted it with a decent measure of brandy poured in for luck.

"Ken," I said. "Why didn't we go and see Chris Smither?"

He sat back on my old sofa, knocking yesterday's newspaper onto the floor, and took a big drink.

"Chris Smither?" His eyes lit up for a moment. "Yeah—he did that cool arrangement of Statesboro Blues. How did that go again?"

He put his mug down on the carpet and began to play air guitar. "Doo dn doo dn dah dah . . . Wake up Mama, turn your lamp down low . . . doo dnn . . ." He shook his head. "I don't know. We just didn't have the time, I suppose."

He mimed some more, singing to himself. Ken used to play the guitar a lot: he was very good. Way better than me. I pulled my computer chair up so that I was sitting closer to him.

"Why not?" I asked. "Why didn't we have time? It's not like we ever do anything. I spend my evenings sitting here at a computer typing out lesson notes and articles that are never published. What about you?"

"I don't know. I guess I was busy. You know how it is. . . ."

"Busy doing what? Ken, we used to go to a concert at least once a week. You used to love listening to live music."

"I still do."

"No you don't. Ken, we'd have been at the concert if you hadn't been 'too busy.'"

I tapped at the keyboard and brought up the picture of Ken sitting outside the refuge in the Alps, glass of water in his hand.

"Looks good, doesn't it?" I said. He didn't seem surprised to see it. I pressed home my point.

"We'd have taken that holiday if you hadn't decided to stay in the pub and have another drink. That"—I pointed to the PC—"knows the logical thing would have been to put down your beer and come with me to the travel agents."

"What does it know?" said Ken dismissively.

"That you're an alcoholic."

The words were out before I could stop them. Ken held my gaze for a lengthening time, and then both our eyes slid back to the computer screen.

"Have you been on the Internet lately?" he asked, changing the subject.

"Just for e-mail. Research, that sort of thing."

"Have you looked at the news sites?" There was an edge of danger in his voice.

"I prefer to read the papers." I looked at the tangled mess of yesterdays *Guardian* being ground into the floor by his restless feet. He stood up suddenly.

"Come here," he said, walking to my computer.

He opened the web browser and typed in an address at the top: news.bbc.co.uk.

My Internet connection is slow. The words and pictures dropped into place piece by piece, slowly revealing the picture of the world as understood by Kant 2.0.

There were pictures of cities full of gleaming towers.

A classroom full of beaming black children.

A field of tanks, painted in rainbow colors, flowers growing amongst their tracks.

A spaceship sitting on the red rocky surface of Mars.

I turned to Ken.

"That's not true, is it?" I said. "None of it is real."

"No," said Ken. "But it could be. If we really wanted it."

There was another of those deepening silences that seemed to have infected our lives. Eventually, he held out his mug.

"More coffee?" I said.

"Yes. Don't forget the brandy."

THE SOMETHING-DREAMING GAME

Elizabeth Bear

Elizabeth Bear's Jenny Casey trilogy (Hammered, Scardown, Worldwired) *has been kicking up quite a storm, enough to put her on my radar even if she hadn't been the 2005 winner of the John W. Campbell Award for Best New Writer. Fortunately, due to a fortuitous meeting at Book Expo America, I was able to invite her into* Fast Forward *and experience her genius firsthand.*

It's autoerotic asphyxiation, but nobody's admitting *that*.

The children get jump ropes or neckties or shoelaces, or they just do it to each other, thumbs under chins buried in baby fat. With childish honesty, they call it the pass-out game, the fainting game, the tingle game. The something-dreaming game, too.

When it's mentioned in the papers, journalists coyly obscure the truth. With Victorian prudishness, they report that the children strangle each other to get "high." Because society thinks that children that young—nine, ten—aren't *supposed* to experience erotic sensation. The reality that kids don't always do what they're supposed to—am I the only one who remembers my own confused preadolescent sexuality?—gets disregarded with fantastic regularity.

But the truth is that they do it for the tingle through their veins, the arousal, the light-headedness, and the warmth that floods their immature bodies. Like everything else we do—as individuals, as a species—it's all about sex. And death. Yin and yang. Maybe if we admitted what was going on, we'd have a chance of stopping it before more die.

It's the things we don't talk about that become the monsters under the bed.

The game is autoerotic asphyxiation. You would hope the smart ones wouldn't do it alone, wouldn't do it at all.

But my Tara was as smart as they come.

Tara must have learned the game at the hospital, when she had her implant finalized. It was the cutting edge of therapy, a promising experimental treatment. An FDA trial; she was lucky to be selected.

The implant is a supercomputer the size of the last joint of my thumb, wired into my daughter's brain. Tara has RSD, reflex sympathetic dystrophy syndrome, a disease resulting in intense, uncontrollable neuralgia. Which is to say, her nerves hurt. *Transcendently.* All the time.

The implant interrupts the electrical signals that cause the brain to register the sensations. The computing power is quantum, supplied by a Bose-Einstein condensate, and no, I don't know what that means or how it works, any more than I know how a silicon chip works, or a vacuum tube.

What matters is, it worked.

Two weeks after Tara returned to school, I got a phone call from Silkie Mendez's mother. I was still at work; Tara was in after-school enrichment, and her dad was supposed to pick her up. I'd get her after dinner.

It's the real mark of domesticity. You become somebody's mother, somebody's father. A parent, not a person at all.

But at work, I still answered my phone, "Doctor Sanderson."

"Jillian. It's Valentina. We have to talk."

You get to know the tone, so-carefully-not-panicking. A mother scared stiff, and fighting with every ounce of rationality to override the brain chemicals and deal with a threat to her child with smarts rather than claws and teeth. "What's wrong?"

Her breath hissed over the pickup on her phone. Cell phone, I thought, and there was noise in the background. Human bustle, an intercom, stark

echoes off polished tile. I've been in private practice since my psychiatric res-
idency, but you never forget what a hospital sounds like. "Val, is Silkie okay?"

"She will be," Val said. The sob caught in her throat and she choked it
back. "The doctor says she—Jillian, uh, she'll be fine—"

One thing I'm good at is getting people to talk to me. "Val, just say it.
You don't have to soft-pedal, okay?"

I heard her gulp. She sniffled and took a breath, the phone crackling as she
pressed it against her hair. "Silkie says Tara taught her how to hang herself."

||

First, there's the pressure.

A special kind of pressure, high under Tara's chin, that makes her feel
heavy and light all at once. She kneels by the chair and leans across the edge,
because if she faints, the chair will roll away and she won't choke.

She's always careful.

After the pressure she gets dizzy, and her vision gets kind of . . . narrow,
dark around the edges. It's hard to breathe, and it feels like there's something
stuck in her throat. Prickles run up and down her back, down her arms where
the pain used to be, and a warm fluid kind of feeling sloshes around inside
her. She slides down, as things get dark, and then she starts to dream.

But not like nighttime dreams. These are special.

When Tara dreams the special way, she hears voices. Well, no, not voices. Not
voices exactly. But things. Or sees things. Feels them. It's all jumbled together.

But there's a sky, and she walks out under it. It's not any kind of sky she's
seen. It's big and pale, and seems . . . flat, and very high up. There aren't any
clouds, and it looks dusty under the big red sun.

It might be a desert. She's read someplace that deserts have skies like that.
And it's not just a picture. Tara can taste it, feel the pebbles under the soles of
her shoes, the heat baking off the cracked tarmac. Except the tarmac isn't really
tarmac: like it, but chocolate-brown, or maybe that's the dull red dust.

And Tara doesn't think they have people like Albert in the kinds of
deserts she'd get to on a plane.

As for Albert, he's a long, segmented being like a giant centipede, though he can't be a centipede because of the inverse square law. Which says that if you breathe through a spiracle, you can't breathe if you get that big. Of course . . .

. . . he isn't necessarily an *Earth* arthropod. And when she watches him, she sees all his segments swelling and relaxing, independent of each other. They each seem to have a top and bottom plate that slide rather than one hard shell like an arthropod would have. So it's more like armor than an exoskeleton. And Albert isn't his real name, of course, but Tara doesn't know his real name, because she can't talk to him.

He has a lot of legs, though, and lots of little fine claws and then two big bulky claws too, like a lobster instead of a crab. He chitters at her, which freaked her out the first few times, and grabs her hand with one knobby manipulator. It's all right. She's already reaching out, too.

‖

I didn't call Tara's father, just arrived to pick her up at the usual time. I'd talk to Tara first, I decided, and then see what I was going to say to Jerry. He's a good guy, works hard, loves his kid.

He panics. You know. Some people do. Tara doesn't, not usually, and so I wanted to talk to her first.

She sat in the back, big enough to be out of a booster seat but not big enough to be safe with the airbags yet. She was hitting a growth spurt, though; it wouldn't be long.

RSD has all sorts of side effects. There are people who think it's psychosomatic, who dismiss it, more or less, as malingering. I got some resistance from my mom and my sister when we decided to go ahead with the surgery, of the she's-just-doing-it-for-attention and she'll-outgrow-it sort.

My Tara was a brave girl, very tough. She broke her arm on the playground a few days after her eighth birthday. I didn't figure out there were other issues until the cast was off and she was still complaining that it hurt. And then, complaining that it hurt more, and the hurt was spreading up her shoulder and down her side. And her right hand was curling into a claw while it took us nine months to get a diagnosis, and another ten months after that to get her into the trial, while she suffered through painkillers and physical therapy.

I watched in the mirror as she wriggled uncomfortably under her shoulder belt and slouched against the door, inspecting bitten fingernails. "How was school?"

"Fine," she said, turning to look out the window at the night rushing past. It was raining slightly, and she had rolled her window down to catch the damp air, trailing her fingers over the edge of the crack.

"Hands in the car, please," I said as we stopped under a streetlight. I couldn't see in the darkness if her eyes were bloodshot, or if those shadows under her chin were bruises.

Tara pulled her fingers back, sighing. "How was work, Mom?"

"Actually, I got a call from Mrs. Mendez today."

Her eyes widened as I pulled away from the stop sign. I forced my attention back to the road. "Am I in trouble?"

"You know it's very dangerous, what you taught Silkie to do, don't you?"

"Mom?" A plaintive question, leading, to see how much I knew.

"The fainting game. It's not safe. People die doing that, even grown-ups." Another stop sign, as she glared at her hands. "Silkie went to the emergency room."

Tara closed her eyes. "Is she okay?"

"She will be."

"I'm always careful, Mom—"

"Tara." I shifted from second to third as we rolled up the dark street and around the corner to our own house, the porch light gleaming expectantly by the stairs, light dappled through the rain-heavy leaves of the maple in the front yard. "I need you to promise me you'll never do that again."

Her chin set.

Wonderful. Her father's stubborn mouth, thin line of her lips. Her hair was still growing back, so short it curled in flapper ringlets around her ears and on her brow.

"Lots of kids do it. Nobody ever gets hurt."

"Tara?"

"I can't promise."

"*Tara.*" There are kids you can argue with. Tara wasn't one of them. But she could be reasoned with. "Why not?"

"You wouldn't believe me." And she didn't say it with the petulant defiance you might expect, but simply, reasonably, as an accepted annoyance.

"Try me."

"I can't promise," she said, "because the aliens need me."

Albert chitters again. It's hot. Really hot, and Tara wants water. But there never seems to be any water here. Albert tugs her hand. He wants her to follow. She goes with him and he takes her the same way he always does. Toward the big steel doors, and then down into cool darkness, the hum of big fans, and then he'll bring her underground and there will be a thing like a microphone, only at her height, not a grown-up one. And she'll talk and sing into it, because that seems to be what Albert wants her to do, while luminescent colors roll across his armor plates in thin, transparent bands.

She's never seen anything alive here. Except Albert.

She talks into the microphone, though, sings it silly songs and talks about things. Her mother and father, and the divorce. The time in the hospital, and the friends she made there. Insects and arthropods, bicycles and card games. Her friends and teachers, and how happy she is to be back in a real school.

Colors rippling across his carapace impatiently, Albert waits. They've done this before.

I blamed the implant. Nobody likes to think her kid is experiencing symptoms of undifferentiated schizophrenia, after all. I rescheduled for the next day and took the morning off and we made an emergency appointment with Dr. al-Mansoor.

Tara waited outside while I went in to talk to the doctor. She looked bleary-eyed under the scarf tucked over her hair, the flesh slack over her cheekbones and shadowed around the eyes. I like Dr. al-Mansoor. And it was pretty obvious she hadn't planned on being in the clinic at 7 AM to see us, but she'd managed to get there.

I put a cup of coffee on her desk before I sat down. She took it gratefully, cupping lean fingers around the warm paper, her wedding ring flashing as she lowered her head over the steam. "You have a concern, Jill?" she asked.

Her given name is Hadiyah, but I always have to remind myself to use it, even though we'd gotten to be good friends over the last four months or so. I think she respected the questions I asked. None of the other parents were in the medical profession.

I looked down at my own coffee cup and cleared my throat. Best to just say it. "I think there's a problem with Tara's implant."

They'll catch her if she tries it here. So Tara sits and folds her hands and tries not to rock impatiently, first in the waiting room and then in the office while Mom and Dr. al-Mansoor talk, mostly over her head. There's a dollhouse on the ledge, though, along with some other toys that Tara is mostly too old for, and Tara busies herself with the dolls and the furniture until she gets bored, and starts running the red fire truck back and forth along the ledge. She stages a four-alarm fire and a rescue, complete with hook-and-ladder work on the dollhouse, though the sizes are off and the dolls have to make a death-defying leap from the second floor to be caught at the top of the ladder by a half-scale fireman.

She's totally lost track of the grown-up conversation, and they're not talking about her now anyway but about some other girl in the trial, though Dr. al-Mansoor is very careful not to say her name. "She hasn't had any similar ideations, though. . . ."

The conversation stops, and Tara looks up to find Mom and Dr. al-Man-soor staring at her. "Did I do something wrong?"

"Tara," Dr. al-Monsoor says, smoothing her scarf over her hair, "where did you learn to play the fainting game?"

Tara bites her lip. Her hair falls across her eyes and she pushes it back. She never *promised* not to tell. "At the hospital," she says, dragging it out. She turns back to the dollhouse and saves another Ken doll from the flames.

"Who taught you?"

This Ken doll didn't jump hard enough. He falls short of the ladder, and the miniature fireman lunges frantically to catch him. He gets one of Ken's outreached hands, and clutches it. Firemen have gloves, big rubber ones, so it must be the gloves that are slipping in the sweat, not Ken's hand. Ken sways perilously as the fireman hooks his feet in the rungs of the ladder and hauls on his hand, Tara mimicking both Ken's cries for help and the fireman's reassurances.

The grown-ups are silent, watching. Until Tara's mother clears her throat and says, carefully, "Tara? Did you hear the question?"

"One of the other girls," Tara says, letting Ken rock back and forth a little, hands slipping. She watches him carefully. Maybe if the fireman slides a little higher, ladder rungs gouging his tummy, he can keep his grip. Oh, no, gasps Ken. Don't worry, I've got you! cries the fireman.

"Which girl?"

Tara shrugs. She won't remember. That's not a lie, and they can't make her remember, either. The fireman hauls Ken up once his predicament stops being interesting.

Tara prefers a happy ending.

"Tara," Mom says, quietly, "she could be in a lot of danger. You have to tell us."

It takes a long time. But eventually, she does.

I barely knew Jodi Carter. She was older than Tara, twelve or thirteen, and they hadn't been roommates. But they'd spent time together, in the common room or the girls' bathroom.

I wondered how many other girls Jodi had taught the fainting game. At least, from what Dr. al-Mansoor said, it didn't seem like she was having the hallucinations. I was guiltily glad it wasn't my job to answer either of those questions.

Dr. al-Mansoor and I had a hasty conference while Tara banged around a little more with Barbie dolls and fire trucks. My worry that Tara was the only child to report some sort of hallucination after receiving the implant was enough to make my hands cold.

We got Tara checked in—back in her old room, in fact—and Dr. al-Mansoor put her under observation. No restraints, but she'd be under fifteen-minute checks, though the room had a one-way window so she'd at least have the illusion of privacy.

I argued for the right to sleep in the waiting room. Dr. al-Mansoor countered with an offer of her office couch. Tara and I went home to fetch her pajamas and get her some lunch while Dr. al-Mansoor and Mrs. Carter had a long talk with Jodi, who was already checked in for observation of her apparent hallucinations.

Afterwards, Dr. al-Mansoor and I sat and drank more coffee—worse coffee, this, from the staff room pot, lightened with artificial creamer and too sweet because that was the only way it was drinkable—out of chipped mugs, and waited while one of the clinic staff got Tara settled in. She was furious that I'd told her she had to stay, and after she had exhausted herself on a temper tantrum and two sulks, I decided it was just as well if I gave her a little time alone to get the leftover wrath out of her system. At least Tara wasn't a kid who held grudges.

"I didn't know about this fainting game thing," Dr. al-Mansoor said, blowing over her coffee.

"It's not new." Pediatric psychiatry isn't my specialty, but you hear things, pick up around the edges in the journals. "Like inhalant abuse. Every generation figures it out, or anyway some of them do. The question is—"

She nodded. "And then there's the whole issue of whether the implant is causing hallucinations."

"Only when she's on the verge of unconsciousness."

"And a hypnagogic state doesn't do it. Sleep's no good. It's got to be hypoxia."

My turn to stare into my coffee. "Apparently. What do you think of the character of the hallucinations?"

"Some alien entity trying to communicate with her? It's a common marker for schizophrenia."

"But that's the only symptom she's got. No mood swings, she's obviously rational—"

Dr. al-Mansoor smiled. "Odd, isn't it?" And then she cocked her head to one side as if *she* were listening, and held up one finger to silence me. "Oh," she said. "You know, I may have something here."

The plastic chair creaked under me when I resettled my weight. It wasn't late, just after lunch, but it felt like six or seven o'clock at night. I was a little shocked every time I glanced at my watch. Busy day. "Well, don't keep me in suspense."

"The implants use a quantum computer chip."

"Tell me something I didn't know."

"Well, the chips were all manufactured at the same time, right? And the same place. Probably all from one condensate. So what if there's quantum interference? I mean"—she waved her long, elegant hand beside her face, her diamond flashing—"what if the chips can transmit electrical patterns back and forth between the girls? Feebly. And when their synapses are already mis-firing from the hypoxia, those patterns get overlaid, and Tara's subconscious mind translates those signals into symbols, as they would in a dream—"

"The symbol being some kind of alien trying to communicate. Is that possible? The transferal, I mean." What I knew about quantum mechanics could be written on an index card, but it sounded . . .

Hell, it sounded like an excuse not to pull the chip that was Tara's promise of a normal life out of her head. It might be a straw, but it wasn't a bad-looking straw.

She made a face, pulling her jaw back and flattening her lower lip, and then wrinkled her nose. "I guess so?"

"Why is it only Tara?"

"There's something wrong with her chip? Or something right with it. If that is what's going on, it's functional telepathy."

"That would mean there wasn't any problem, really."

"Other than half the clinic strangling themselves for the fun of it, you mean."

"Right." I thumped back in my chair. I'd lurched forward at some point, without realizing it. "That. Tara won't promise. She thinks her alien friend needs help."

"If she promises, can you trust her?"

"Tara? Yes. What about Jodi?"

"I'll ask Mrs. Carter what she thinks. We'll have to address it with all the kids. One of the staff is making calls. Tara seems a special case, though. For her, we could edge the voltage down a little and maybe get rid of the hallucinations, if my guess is right. Which it probably isn't. But that might affect pain management."

"Right," I said. I put my half-empty cup down on the edge of Dr. al-Mansoor's desk. "I'll go talk to her. If asking nicely doesn't work, there's always extortion."

Mom comes back before dinner, and takes Tara down to the cafeteria to eat. Tara likes the cafeteria. There's always something she doesn't get at home very often. Today it's meatloaf and apple pie, with brown gravy. The meatloaf, not the pie.

Mom's watching her worriedly, and pushing kidney beans and cottage cheese—and other stuff Tara can't figure out why anybody would eat—around on her salad bar plate. "Dr. al-Mansoor thinks the things you're seeing are feedback from the implant," she says, when Tara is halfway done with her meatloaf.

"I think it's from the implant," Tara agrees. She'd picked out a mockneck shirt to hide the bruise across her throat. Mom frowns at it. "But maybe not feedback. I've been thinking about Albert."

"Albert?"

"The alien." Tara slashes her fork sideways. "I don't think it's just him. I think it's a whole species."

Mom leans forward, arms folded behind her fussed-at plate. "He told you his name?"

"No." Tara drops her fork and jerks her hands back and forth beside her head. "He talks in colors or something. He's Albert because of Albert Einstein." She drinks some milk and picks up the fork again. "But he keeps wanting me to talk in a microphone into a computer. I think he's trying to learn how *I* talk. Anyway, I think he's in trouble. He needs help."

"What kind of help?" Mom starts chasing the kidney beans around her plate again, pretending like she's only being polite.

"I don't *know*," Tara says. She stops herself abruptly, chews and swallows the mouthful of mashed potatoes before mom can yell at her. She reaches out and picks a hard, round red grape off her mother's plate, waiting for the nod of permission. It crunches sweetly between her teeth. She takes another one. "I just . . . it seems really important."

"How do you know?"

"I just know."

Mom picks up one solitary kidney bean on the end of her fork and stares at it. She slips it into her mouth and chews slowly. "Tara," she says. "It's more important that you don't risk your life playing the fainting game anymore. If Albert's real, and he's a grown-up scientist, even if he's an alien, he'd agree with me. Don't you think?"

"I'm always careful. That's the problem. I think if I had just a little more time with him, we could *talk*."

"It doesn't matter how careful you are. It's dangerous."

"Mom—"

"*Tara*." Mom puts her fork down, and uses *that voice*. "Promise me."

Tara finishes her meal in silence, while Mom stares at her and doesn't eat another thing. They're going to make her sleep in the hospital bed tonight, with the lights that don't go off and the shadows behind the one-way mirror all the time.

It's okay. She can sleep anywhere. And she has a plan.

I was supposed to sleep on the couch. Predictably, I spent the entire night in the observation room. Tara seemed to be sleeping, under the pale blue light, her hair fanned out on the pillow and her knees drawn up against her chest as always. I sat and watched her with the observation room lights off, so every time Dr. al-Mansoor or the staffer came in for the check, a wedge of light fell across the floor and dazzled me for a minute.

Each time, they paused in the doorway, glanced through the window for a moment, smiled at me, and withdrew. I think Dr. al-Mansoor was hoping I'd fall asleep on the bench. Not quite.

At two in the morning, Tara began to thrash.

She kicked the covers off and rolled out of bed, rolled *under* the bed in the space of time it took me to hit the call button and dive for the connecting door, shouting her name. I crawled after her, scrabbling on hands and knees. The metal railing caught my shoulders, knocking me off my knees and onto my belly, and I squirmed after her. She jammed herself into the space by the head of the bed and curled on her side, knees drawn up, hands pressing me back, pressing me away. Battling, until her arms went soft and her feet kicked, or I should say shivered.

I couldn't hear her breathing.

I got my hand around the slender flexible bones of her ankle and pulled. She went limp as I dragged her out, and first I thought she was making herself dead weight, but when I got her into the light I saw how limp she was. I thought it was the light turning her blue, but then the door thumped open and the light came on and I could see it was her skin, as well.

You're supposed to check the airway. Her mouth fell open, slack, and I ran my fingers into it. Her tongue hadn't fallen back, but I thought my fingers brushed something smooth and resilient, hard, at the back of her throat.

"Jillian," Dr. al-Mansoor said, her hand on my shoulder.

"She's choking," I said, and let her pull me out of the way. "I think she palmed a grape at dinner. I didn't think—" Stupid. *Stupid.* No, I didn't *think* at all.

Dr. al-Mansoor yanked off her rings. They rattled on the floor, disregarded, gold and diamonds knocked aside as she straddled my daughter's hips, straightened her neck. She placed the heel of her interlocked hands under Tara's breastbone, and I loved her with all my heart.

I remembered Tara crowding away from me under the bed, her eyes wide and wild, her desperation. Tara was the smartest kid I've ever known. She'd had swimming courses, first aid courses. She was ten. Not a baby, just ask her. She knows more about entomology and dinosaurs and stellar astronomy than I ever will.

She'd known I'd come after her. She'd known I could save her. She'd jumped out of the bed so I would see that she was in distress. And she'd crawled away from me, buying time.

They talk about possession. After a crisis, you hear people say they have no idea what they were doing.

I knew exactly what I was doing. I reached down and grabbed Dr. al-Mansoor's wrists and held on tight. "Jillian, let go," she said. "It's just the Heimlich maneuver."

Her face was inches from mine, her eyes red with sleeplessness rather than asphyxiation. Her scarf had fallen back, and her hair was all tangled over her shoulders. It didn't matter. We were all women here.

"Thirty seconds," I said.

She stared at me. She leaned against my hands, but I held on to her wrists. Tight.

"*Brain damage*," she said.

Dreams can happen *fast*. The length of the REM cycle affects it, of course, but sometimes even when they seem to take hours, days, they're over in seconds. Just the forebrain trying to make symbolic sense of electrical noise kicked up by the random signals firing up the brainstem. "Hadiyah. Thirty seconds. Twenty seconds. Let her talk to Albert."

She licked her lips. And then she jerked her chin sharply, and I saw her mouth move, counting. Fifteen, fourteen, thirteen—

‖

Albert is waiting. He's in a hurry, too. This time, he grabs Tara's hand in his manipulator without preamble and almost drags her into the tunnel, his many legs rippling indigo-azure-gold as they race underground. But this time it's different, dream-different, the microphone gone and a kind of control panel in its place, not made for Tara's hands. She stops, confused, just inside the arched doorway and waits for Albert to show her what to do. And isn't it funny, now that she thinks about it, that the doorway is tall enough for her, when Albert's only two feet high?

He takes the controls in his manipulators. They move over the keypad with arachnid grace. "Tara," the air says.

"Albert?" At her voice, colors ripple across the panels before him. He turns, regarding them with every evidence of thought in the tilt of his expressionless face on the ball-jointed neck. She shouldn't try to guess what he feels. She knows that.

She does it anyway. "You figured out how to talk to me."

"I did," he says. "Come here. Put your hands on the plate. We don't have much time."

"Before my mother stops us?"

He chitters at her, his antennae bristling. "Before the program ends. This is a simulation. I am the last remaining, and we used the last of the power to reach you. We looked and looked, and you were the first we found."

"You're *dying*?"

"Our sun is dying," he says, and her face crumples painfully. She sniffs back stinging. "Soon, the computers will fail. We've lived in them for a very long time. The rest have gone ahead, to conserve power. I chose to stay and search."

"But you can't—I just got to *talk* to you—"

"Will you let me give you our history?"

"Of course," she says, reaching out. He stops her, though, as sharply as he urged before, his manipulator indenting the flesh of her hand.

"Wait," he says. "I will put it in your brain. You have to give permission. It could change you."

She stops. His manipulator is cool and hard, the surface sandpapery. "Change?"

"Make you more like us."

She looks at him. His antennae feather down, lying against his dorsal surface like the ears of an anxious dog. He's still. Maybe waiting, she doesn't know. "And if I don't you die."

"We die," he says. "Either way."

She stares at him. The stinging in her eyes grows worse, a pressure in her sinuses and through her skull. She pulls her hand from his manipulator, reaches out resolutely, and places both palms on warm yellow metal as the first tear burns her cheek.

"Don't mourn." The voice is uninflected, but his palp reaches out softly and strokes her leg. "You will remember us."

We made it to nine. I yanked my hands back, Hadiyah pressed hers down. The first push didn't do it. She realigned, lips moving on what must have been a prayer now, and thrust forward sharply, the weight of her shoulders behind it.

Something glistening shot from Tara's lips and sailed over Hadiyah's shoulder, and Tara took a deep harsh breath and started to cough, her eyes squinched shut, tears running down her cheeks.

"He's gone," she said, when she got her breath.

She rolled over and grabbed my hands, and wailed against my shoulder like a much younger child, and would not be consoled.

There's enough room in Tara's implant for three or four Libraries of Congress. And it seems to be full. It also seems like she's the only one who can make sense of the information, and not all of it, and not all the time.

She's different now. Quieter. Not withdrawn, but . . . sad. And she looks at me sometimes with these calm, strange eyes, and I almost feel as if *she's* the mother.

I should have stopped her sooner. I didn't think.

At least she hasn't tried to strangle herself again.

Hadiyah suggested we not *tell* anybody what had happened just yet, and I agreed. I won't let my daughter wind up in some government facility, being pumped for clues to alien technology and science.

I won't.

She's ten years old. She's got school to get through. We'll figure the rest of it out in our own time. And maybe she'll be more like herself again as time goes by.

But the first thing she did when she recovered was paint a watercolor. She said it was a poem.

She said it was her name.

NO MORE STORIES

Stephen Baxter

One of the acknowledged kings of Big-Concept Hard SF, and a worthy successor to his sometimes writing partner Sir Arthur C. Clarke, Stephen Baxter's imagination spans from the prehistoric to the far future. He has crafted tales of woolly mammoths, penned the only authorized sequel to H. G. Wells's The Time Machine, *and shown us alternatives to our current space program. Stephen was in my first original anthology,* Live without a Net, *and it's a pleasure to have him in again.*

"It's strange to find myself in this position. Dying, I mean. I've always found it hard to believe that things will just go on afterwards. After *me.* That the sun will come up, the milkman will call. Will it all just fold up and go away, when I've gone?"

These were the first words his mother said to Simon, when he got out of the car.

She stood in her doorway, old-lady stocky, solid, arms folded, over eighty years old. Her wrinkles were runnels in papery flesh that ran down to a small, frowning mouth. She peered around the close, as if suspicious.

Simon collected his small suitcase from the back of the car. It had a luggage tag from a New York flight, a reminder that he was fifty years old, and that he did have a life beyond his mother's, working for a biotech company in London, selling gen-enged goldfish as children's pets. Now that he was here, back in this Sheffield suburb where he'd grown up, his London life seemed remote, a dream.

He locked the car and walked up to his mother. She presented her cheek for him to kiss. It was cold, rough-textured.

"I had a good journey," he said, for he knew she wouldn't ask.

"I am dying, you know," she said, as if to make sure he understood.

"Oh, Mother." He put an arm around her shoulders. She was hard, like a lump of gristle and bone, and didn't soften into the hug.

She had cancer. They had never actually used that word between them. She stepped back to let him into the house.

The hall was spotless, obsessively cleaned and ordered, yet it smelled stale. A palm frond folded into a cross hung on the wall, a reminder that Easter was coming, a relic of intricate Catholic rituals he'd abandoned when he left home.

He put his suitcase down.

"Don't put it there," his mother said.

A familiar claustrophobia closed in around him. "All right." He grabbed the case and climbed the stairs, fourteen of them as he used to count in his childhood. But now there was an old-lady safety banister fixed to the wall.

She had made up one of the twin beds in the room he had once shared with his brother. There wasn't a trace of his childhood left in here, none of his toys or books or school photos.

He came downstairs. "Mother, I'm gasping. Can I make a cup of tea?"

"The pot's still fresh. I'll fetch a cup and saucer." She bustled off to the kitchen.

He walked into the lounge.

The only change he could see since his last visit was a fancy new standard lamp with a downturned cowl, to shed light on the lap of an old lady sitting in the best armchair, facing the telly, peering at her sewing with fading eyes. The old carriage clock still sat in its place on the concrete 1970s fireplace, a legacy from a long-dead great-uncle. It was flanked by a clutter of photos, as usual. Most of them were fading color prints of grandchildren. Simon had no grandchildren to offer, and so was unrepresented here.

But the photos had been pushed back to make room for a new image in a gold frame. Brownish, blurred and faded, it was a portrait of a smiling young man in a straw boater. He had a long, strong face. Simon recognized the photo, taken from a musty old album and evidently blown up. It was his grandfather, Mother's dad, who had died when Simon was five or six.

Just for a moment the light seemed odd to him. Cold, yellow-purple. And there was something strange beyond the window. Pillowlike shapes, gleaming in a watery sun. He saw all this from the corner of his eye. But when he turned to look directly, the light from the picture window turned spring green, shining from the small back garden, with its lawn and roses and the last of the azalea blossom. Maybe his eyes were tired from the drive, playing tricks.

"It's just for comfort. The photo."

The male voice made Simon turn clumsily, almost tripping.

A man sat on the sofa, almost hidden behind the door, with a cup of tea on an occasional table. "Sorry. You didn't see me. Didn't mean to make you jump." He stood and shook Simon's hand. "I'm Gabriel Nolan." His voice had a soft Irish burr. Maybe sixty, he was small, round, bald as an egg. He wore a pale jacket, black shirt, and dog collar. He had biscuit crumbs down his front.

Simon guessed, "Is it Father Nolan?"

"From Saint Michael's. The latest incumbent."

The last parish priest Simon remembered had been the very old, very frail man who had confirmed him at age thirteen.

Mother came in, walking stiffly, cradling a cup and saucer. "Sit down, Simon, you're blocking the light."

Simon sat in the room's other armchair, with his back to the window. Mother poured out some tea with milk, and added sugar, though he hadn't taken sugar for three decades.

"Simon was just admiring the portrait of your father, Eileen."

"Well, I don't have many pictures of my dad. You didn't take many in those days. That's the best one, I think."

"I was saying. We find comfort in familiar things, in the past."

"I always felt safe when my dad was there," Mother said. "In the war, you know."

But, Simon thought, granddad was long dead. She'd led a whole life since then, the life that included Simon's own childhood.

Mother always was self-centered. Any crisis in her children's lives, like Mary's recurrent illness as a child, or the illegitimate kid Peter had fathered as a student, somehow always turned into a drama about *her*. Now somehow she was back in the past with her own father in her own childhood, and there was no room for Simon.

Mother said, "There might not be anybody left who remembers Dad, but me. Do you think we get deader, when there's nobody left who remembers us?"

The priest said, "We live on in the eyes of Christ."

Simon said, "Father Nolan, don't you think Mother should talk to the doctor again? She won't listen to me."

"Oh, don't be ridiculous, Simon," Mother said.

"Best to accept," said Father Nolan. "If your mother has. Best not to question."

They both stared back at him, seamless, united. Fifty years old he felt awkward, a child who didn't know what to say to the grown-ups.

He stood up, putting down his teacup. "I've some shirts that could do with hanging."

Mother sniffed. "There might be a bit of space. Later there's my papers to do."

Another horror story. Simon fled upstairs. A little later, he heard the priest leave.

The "papers" were her financial transactions, Premium Bonds and tax vouchers and battered old bankbooks.

And the dreaded rusty biscuit box she kept under her bed, which held her will and her life insurance policies, stored up in the event of a death she'd been talking about for thirty years. It even held her identity card from the war, signed in a childish hand.

Simon always found it painful to sit and plod through all this stuff. The tin box was worst, of course.

Later she surprised him by asking to go for a walk.

It was late afternoon. Mother put on a coat, a musty gabardine that smelled of winter, though the bright April day was warm.

Simon had grown up in this close. It was a short, stubby street of semi-detached houses leading up to a main road and a dark sandstone wall, beyond which lay a park. But his childhood was decades gone, and the houses had been made over out of all recognition, and the space where he'd played football was now jammed full of cars. Walking here, he felt as if he were trying to cram himself into clothes he'd outgrown.

They crossed the busy main road, and then walked along the line of the old wall to the gateway to the park. Or what was left of it. In the last few years the park had been sliced through by a spur of the main road, along which cars now hissed, remote as clouds. Simon's old home seemed stranded.

Simon and his mother stuck to a gravel path. Underfoot was dogshit and, in the mud under the benches, beer cans, fag ends, and condoms. Mother clung to his arm. Walking erratically she pulled at him, heavy, like an unfixed load.

Mother talked steadily, about Peter and Mary, and the achievements and petty woes of their respective children. Mary, older than Simon, was forever struggling on, in Mother's eyes, burdened by difficult kids and a lazy husband. "She's got a lot to put up with, always did." Peter, the youngest, got a tougher time, perceived as selfish and shiftless and lacking judgment. Simon's siblings' lives were more complicated than that. But to Mother they were ciphers, dominated by the characteristics she had perceived in them when they were kids.

She asked nothing about his own life.

Later, she prepared the evening meal.

As she was cooking, Simon dug his laptop out of his suitcase, and brought it down to the cold, formal dining room, where there was a telephone point. He booted up and went through his e-mails.

He worked for a biotech start-up that specialized in breeding genetically modified goldfish, giving them patterns in bright *Finding Nemo* colours targeted at children. It was a good business, and expanding. The strategy was to domesticate biotech. In maybe five or ten years they would even sell genome-sequencing kits to kids, or anyhow their parents, so they could "paint" their own fish designs.

It was a bit far off in terms of fifty-year-old Simon's career, and things were moving so fast in this field that his own skills, in software, were constantly being challenged. But the work was demanding and fun, and as he watched the little fish swim around with "Happy Birthday, Julie" written on their flanks, he thought he glimpsed the future.

His mother knew precisely nothing about all this. The glowing e-mails were somehow comforting, a window to another world where he had an identity.

Anyhow, no fires to put out today. He shut down the connection.

Then he phoned his brother and sister with his mother's news.

"She's fine in herself. She's cooking supper right now. . . . Yes, she's keeping the house okay. I suppose when she gets frailer we'll have to think about that. . . . I'll stay one night definitely, perhaps two. Might take her shopping tomorrow. Bulky stuff, you know, bog rolls and washing powder. . . .

"Things are a bit tricky for you, I suppose." Exams, school trips, holidays. Mary's ferocious commitment to her bridge club—"They can't have a match if I don't turn up, you know!" Peter's endless courses in bookkeeping and beekeeping, arboriculture and aromatherapy, an aging dreamer's continuing quest to be elevated above the other rats in the race. All of them reasons not to visit their mother.

Simon didn't particularly blame them. Neither of them seemed to feel they *had* to come, the way he did, which left him with no choice but to be here. And of course with their kids they were busier than he was, in a sense.

Mother had her own views. Peter was selfish. Mary was always terribly busy, poor lamb.

She'd once been a good cook, if a thrifty one, her cuisine shaped by the experience of wartime rationing. But over the years her cooking had simplified to a few ready-made dishes. Tonight it was boil-in-the-bag fish. You got used to it.

After they ate, they spent the evening playing games. Not Scrabble, which had been a favourite of Simon's childhood. She insisted on cribbage, which she had played with her father, in her own childhood. She had a worn board that must have been decades old. She had to explain the arcane rules to him.

The evening was very, very long, in the silence of the room with a blank telly screen, the time stretched out by the pocks of Uncle Billy's carriage clock.

In the morning he came out of his bedroom, dressed in his pajama bottoms, heading for the bathroom.

Father Gabriel Nolan was coming up the stairs with a cup of tea on a saucer. He gave Simon a sort of thin-lipped smile. In the bright morning light Simon saw that dried mucus clung to the hairs protruding from his fleshy nose.

"She's taken a turn for the worse in the night," said the priest. "A stroke, perhaps. It's all very sudden." And he bustled into Mother's bedroom.

Simon just stood there.

He quickly used the bathroom. He went back to his bedroom and put on his pants and yesterday's shirt.

Then, in his socks, he went into Mother's bedroom. The curtains were still closed, the only light a ghostly blue glow soaking through the curtains. It was like walking into an aquarium.

She was lying on the right-hand side of the double bed she had shared with Dad for so long. She was flat on her back, staring up. Her arms were outside the sheets, which were neatly tucked in. The cup of tea sat on her bedside cabinet. Father Nolan sat at her bedside, holding her hand.

Her eyes flickered towards Simon.

Simon, frightened, distressed for his mother, was angry at this smut-nosed, biscuit-crumby priest in his mother's bedroom. "Have you called the doctor?"

Mother murmured something, at the back of her throat.

"No doctor," said Father Nolan.

"Is that a decision for you to make?"

"It's a decision for her," said the priest, gravely, not unkindly, firmly. "She wants to go downstairs. The lounge."

"She's better off in bed."

"Let her see the garden."

Father Nolan's calm, unctuous tone was grating. Simon snapped, "How are we going to get her down the stairs?"

"We'll manage."

They lifted Mother up from the bed, and wrapped her in blankets. Simon saw there was a bedpan, sticking out from under the bed. It was actually a plastic potty, a horrible dirty old pink thing he remembered from his own childhood. It was full of thick yellow pee. Father Nolan must have helped her.

They carried her down the stairs together, Simon holding her under the arms, the priest taking her legs.

When they got to the bottom of the stairs, it went dark on the landing above. Simon looked up. The stairs seemed very tall and high, the landing quite black.

"Maybe a bulb blew," he said. But the lights hadn't been on, the landing illuminated by daylight.

Father Nolan said, "She doesn't need to go upstairs again."

Simon didn't know what he meant. Under his distress about his mother, he found he felt obscurely frightened.

They shuffled into the lounge. They sat Mother in her armchair, facing the garden's green.

What now?

"What about breakfast?"

"Toast for me," said Father Nolan.

Simon went to the kitchen and ran slices of white bread, faintly stale, through the toaster.

The priest followed him in. He had taken his jacket off. His black shirt had short sleeves, and he had powerful stubby arms, like a wrestler. They sat at the small kitchen table, and ate buttered toast.

Simon asked, "Why are you here? This morning, I mean. Did Mother call you? I didn't hear the phone."

Father Nolan shrugged. "I just dropped in. I have a key. She's got used to having me around, during this, well, crisis. I don't mind. I share my duties at the parish." He complacently chewed his toast.

"When I was a kid, you smug priests used to make me feel like tripping you up."

Father Nolan laughed. "You're a good boy. You'd never do that."

"'A good boy.' Father, I'm fifty years old."

"But you're always a little boy to your mother." He nodded at the fridge, where photographs were stuck to the metal door by magnets. "Your brother and sister. You're the middle one, yes?"

"Sister older, brother younger."

"Mary and Peter. Good Catholic names. But it's unusual to find a Simon *and* a Peter in the same Catholic family."

"I know." Since Simon had learned about Simon Peter the apostle, he had sometimes wondered if Mother had chosen Peter's name on purpose—as if she was disappointed with the first Simon and hoped for a better version. "They've both got kids. I'm sure she'd rather one of them was here, frankly. Grandkids jumping all over her."

"You're the one who's here. That's what's important."

Simon studied him. "I don't believe, you know. Not sure if I ever did, once I was able to think for myself. You can be as calm and certain as you like. I think it's all a bluff."

Father Nolan laughed. "That's okay. What you choose to believe or not is irrelevant to the destiny of my immortal soul. And indeed yours."

It had been a very long time indeed since Simon had even considered the possibility that he might have a soul, some quality that might endure beyond his own death.

He shivered, and stood up. "I think I need some air. Maybe I'll buy a paper."

"We'll be fine here."

"Help yourself to tea. It's in the—"

"Winston Churchill caddy. I know." Father Nolan smiled, and chewed his toast.

He walked up the close, towards the park.

This stub of a road had seemed endless when he was a child. Full of detail, every drain or stopcock cover or broken paving stone a feature in some game or other. Now he felt a stab of pity for a child who perhaps could have done with a bit more stimulation.

But the close seemed long today, stretching off ahead of him, like the hours governed by Uncle Billy's clock.

And though the sky was clear blue, the light was odd. Weakening. Once he'd sat through a partial eclipse over London, a darkening that was not the setting of the sun but an eerie dimming. That was what this was like. But there was no eclipse due today; he'd have known.

It took an effort to reach the top of the close. And more of an effort to wait for a gap in the stream of dark, anonymous cars, and to cross to the footpath by the park wall.

He walked along the wall, letting his fingers trail along the grubby, wind-eroded sandstone. It had happened so quickly. Would mother really never make this little journey again? Was that awful bagged fish really the last meal the woman who had fed him as a baby would ever make for him? Grief swirled around in him, unfocused. He thought vaguely about the calls he would have to make.

At the gate, he stopped.

There was no park. No sooty oak trees, no grass, no dogshit.

He saw a plain, a marsh. The sunlight gleamed from a sheet of flat, green, sticky-looking water. Pillowlike shapes pushed out of the water, their surfaces slimy crusts, green and purple.

Nothing moved. There was no sound.

Of the park, the parade of shops beyond, there was no sign.

It was like the scene he thought he had glimpsed through his mother's lounge window yesterday. But that had been from the corner of his eye, and had vanished when he looked directly. This was different.

He turned away. The main road was still there, the cars streaming along.

Carefully, he walked back down the road, and into the close. Every step he took towards home made him feel more secure, and the daylight grew stronger.

He didn't dare look back.

||

At home, Father Nolan was still sitting with mother. It wasn't yet lunchtime.

Simon got himself a glass of water and went to the dining room. He booted up his laptop. He dialed into work, to check his e-mails. He was trying not to think about what he'd seen.

He got error messages. The work site didn't exist.

He heard Father Nolan climbing the stairs, a splashing sound, the toilet flushing. Emptying a bed pan, maybe.

He tried Google. That still existed.

There was a word that had come into his head when he thought about what had become of the park. *Stromatolite.* He Googled it.

Communities of algae. A photo showed mounds just like the ones on the park. Heaped-up mats of bacteria, one on top of another, with mud and sand trapped in between. They had their own complexities, of a sort, each mound a tiny biosphere in its own right.

And they were very ancient, a relic of the days before animals, before insects, before multicelled creatures of any kind.

He followed links, digging at random, drawn by his own professional interest in genetics. The first stromatolites had actually been the height of complexity compared to what had gone before. Once there had been nothing but communities of crude cells in which even "species" could not be said to exist, and genetic information was massively transferred sideways between lineages, as well as from parent cell to offspring. The world was muddy, a vast cellular orgy. But if you looked closely it had been fast-evolving, inventive, resilient.

Google failed, the browser returning a site-not-found error message.

And then the laptop's modem reported it couldn't find a dial tone.

It seemed to be growing darker. But it wasn't yet noon. He didn't want to look out of the window.

Father Nolan walked in. "She's asking for you."

Simon hesitated. "I'd better call Mary and Peter. They ought to know."

The priest just waited.

At his first try, he got a number-unobtainable tone. Then the dial tone disappeared. He tried his mobile. There was no service.

It was very dark.

Father Nolan held out his hand. "Come."

In the lounge the curtains were drawn. The excluded daylight was odd, dim, greenish. The only strong light came from mother's fancy new reading stand.

The telly was like an empty eye socket. Simon wondered what he would find if he turned it on.

Mother sat in her armchair, swathed in blankets. Of her body only her face showed, and two hands that looked as if all the bones had been drawn out of them. There was a stink of piss and shit, a tang of blood.

Father Nolan sat beside mother on a footstool, the bedpan at his feet.

"I probably ought to thank you for doing this," Simon said.

"It comes with the job. I gave her the Last Rites, Simon. I should tell you that."

Mother, her eyes closed, murmured something. Father Nolan leaned close so he could hear, and smiled. "Let tomorrow worry about itself, Eileen."

Simon asked, "What's happening tomorrow?"

"She asked if there will *be* a tomorrow."

Simon stared at him. "When I was a kid," he said slowly, "I used to wonder what would happen when I die. It seemed outrageous that the universe should go on, after I, the center of everything, was taken away. Just as my mother said to me yesterday.

"Then I grew up a bit more. I started to think maybe everybody feels that way. Every finite mortal creature. The two things don't go together, do they, my smallness and the bigness of the sky?"

Father Nolan just listened.

Simon stepped towards the window. "What will I see if I pull back the curtain?"

"Don't," said Father Nolan.

"Do *you* know what's going on?"

"I'm here for her. Not you."

"If I ask you, will you tell me?"

The priest hesitated. "You're a good boy. I suppose you deserve that."

Simon touched Uncle Billy's clock, pressed his palm against the wall behind it. "Is any of this real?"

"As real as it needs to be."

"Is this really the year 2010?"

"No."

"Then when?"

"The future. Not as far as you might think."

"People are different."

"There are no people."

"I don't understand."

"No. But you're capable of understanding," Father Nolan said. "It's no accident you work in biotechnology, you know. It was set up that way, so if you ever asked these questions, you'd have the background to grasp the answer."

"What has my job got to do with it?"

"Nothing in itself. It's where things are leading. Those Day-Glo fish you sell. How do you *do* that?"

Simon shrugged. "I don't know the details. I do software. Gene splicing, basically."

"You splice genes from where?"

"A modified soya, I think. Other sources."

"Yes. You swap genes around, horizontally, from microbes to plants to animals, even into people. It's a new kind of gene transfer—or rather a very old one."

"Before the stromatolites."

"Yes. You're planning to put this gene-transfer technology on the open market, aren't you?"

It was like the drive to put a PC in every home, a few decades back. The domestication would start with biotech in the mines and factories and stores. Home use would follow. Eventually advanced home biotech kits, capable of dicing and splicing genomes and nurturing the results, would become as pervasive as PCs and mobile phones. Everybody would have one, and would use it to make new varieties of dogs and budgies, exotic orchids and apples. To create a new life-form and release it into the world would be as easy as blogging.

Simon said, "It's the logical next step, in marketing terms. Like putting massive computing power in the hands of the public. That would have seemed inconceivable, in 1950. And the secondary results will be as unimaginable as the Internet once was. Do you think it's immoral? Unnatural?"

Father Nolan grinned. "If I were what I look like, perhaps I'd think that."

"What are you, then?"

"I'm the end-product of your company's business plans. Yours and a thousand others."

It was a question of accelerating trends. The world's genetic inheritance would become open source. And then, a generation later, the technology would merge with the biology.

"It was only a few decades after your birthday-card goldfish that things took off," Father Nolan said. "Remarkable. Only a few decades, to topple a regime of life that lasted two billion years."

"And things were different after that."

"Oh, yes. Darwinian evolution was *slo-ow*. For all the fancy critters that were thrown up, there was hardly a change in the basic biochemical machinery across two billion years.

"Now there are *no* non-interbreeding species. Indeed, no individuals. The Darwinian interlude is over, and we are back to gene sharing, the way it used to be.

"And everything has changed. Global climate change became trivial, for instance. With the fetters off, the biosphere adapted to the new conditions, optimizing its metabolic and reproductive efficiency as it went.

"And then," he said, "off into space."

These words, simply spoken, implied a marvelous future.

"Who is my mother?"

"We are in a lacuna," Father Nolan said.

"A what?"

"A gap. A hole. In the totality of a living world. Sorry if that sounds a bit pompous. Your mother is a part of the totality, but cut away, you see. Living out a life as a human once lived it."

"Why? Is she being punished?"

"No." He laughed. "It's the contrary. She wanted to do this. It's hard to express. We are a multipolar consciousness. She is part of the rest of us—do you see? She was an expression of a global desire."

"To do what?"

"Not to forget." He stood up. Grave, patient, he had the manner of a priest, despite his hairy nose, his stained shirt. "I think you're ready." He led Simon to the window, and pulled back the curtain.

Green stars.

❚❚

The garden was gone.

The rest of the house was gone. The close, the park, Sheffield—*Earth* was gone, irrelevant. Mother had been right. It had all been placed there as a stage set for her own life. But now her life had dwindled to the four walls of this room, and the rest of it could be discarded, for she would never need it again.

Just green stars. Simon pressed his ear to the window. He heard a reverberation, like an immense bell.

"Earth life turning the galaxy green. Our thoughts span light-years. But we don't want to forget how it was to be human." Father Nolan smiled. "It's a paradox. Without *loss*, we have in fact lost so much. As you said—the strange tragedy of being mortal in an unending universe. There's no more poetry. No more epitaphs. No more *stories.* Just a solemn calm."

"Mother wanted to experience it. Human life."

"On behalf of the rest of us, yes."

"And what are *you*, Father?"

Father Nolan shrugged. "Everything else." He let the curtain drop, hiding the green stars.

The electric light was dimming.

Father Nolan sat down beside Mother and held her hand. "Only a few more minutes. Then it will be done."

Michael sat on the other side of his mother. "What about me?"

"You're only here for her."

"But I'm conscious!"

"Well, of course you are. She chose you, you know. You always thought she didn't love you, didn't you? But she chose you to be beside her, at the end, when all the others—Peter, Mary, even her own father—have all gone. Isn't that enough?"

"Do I have a soul, Father?"

"I'm not qualified to say."

Mother turned her head towards him, he thought. But her eyes were closed.

"Help me," Simon whispered.

Father Nolan looked at him. Then he closed his eyes and bowed his head. "In the name of the Father, and of the Son, and of the Holy Ghost. Amen."

Simon said, "Bless me, Father, for I have sinned."

The glow of the single bulb faded slowly, to black.

TIME OF THE SNAKE

A. M. Dellamonica

A. M. Dellamonica compares being a writer to being Spider-Man. "It may not always be easy—at times, it can be terribly hard. Sometimes you even want to quit. But story-telling is a form of superpower; once it gets hold of someone, it will express itself one way or another." Someone who understands the web slinger so well can't help but take her responsibilities as a writer seriously. After all, with great storytelling power . . .

My offworlder allies don't trust me.

Squid, we call them, though their home planet is named Kabuva. They're twelve feet in length from top to tip, see, with bullet-shaped caps that pull tight over a spaghetti of tentacles. When they bell out these caps, they look less like calamari and more like giant umbrellas. The Brits used to call them "brollies," as a matter of fact, back before England was annihilated.

All the players in this game have nicknames. The other human army wrangling for control of Earth calls itself the Friends of Liberation. Pompous, right? We've shortened it to Fiends.

As for us, the squid-sponsored Democratic Army, we're the Dems. "It's either Dems or us," the Fiends say. Bad pun; they end up taking over the world, they'll probably outlaw laughing.

It's just after dawn on a sunny July morning and I'm humping through East Los Angeles with a squad of ten heavily armed and overtired squid fry.

Squid-squad, get it? Hence the song. *How many Fiends can a squid-squad squash?*

It doesn't help that squid armor is silly looking—essentially an upside-down mussel shell that hooks to their bullet-shaped caps. When the going gets hot, they yank in their tentacles and seal the carapace tight, firing weapons from inside the all-but-impregnable canister. Once sealed in, though, they can barely move.

The newest fry teedle along on the tips of their tentacles, shell all but shut. Vets tend to leave it half open, on the grounds that the carapace sensors don't work for shit.

We're here today because Intelligence has designated this neighborhood so thoroughly infiltrated by Fiends that there's no way to tell the bad guys from noncombatants. An evac order's gone out, and now we're one of the squads going block to block ensuring each house, shop, and low-rise is empty. Behind us floats a demolition ship, hanging just over the rooftops like a big blimpy starfish. Every time we give the all-clear on a building, the ship glides in and starts dusting the structure to nothingness.

Once this whole area is flattened, the squid will compile a few dozen sky-scrapers for the humans who lived here. These buildings will be wired, so that any Fiendish conversations go straight to Kabuva Intelligence. The general idea is neighborhood Fiends will have to move elsewhere . . . those that do will be tagged as probable hostiles and rounded up for interrogation.

Bluto, on point, goes rigid and the squad snaps to alertness. He rips an apartment door off its hinges.

"Cantil?" The unit commander, Loot, caresses the back of my neck; this is his idea of a nudge.

"Anyone in there?" I call, first in American and then in Spanish. The amplifier built into my face mask makes my voice come out officious and strident, anything but reassuring. "It's okay. Come out and you won't be harmed."

The response is a pepper of bullets from antique machine guns, and the squad barges in happily. I wait in the hall. Loot's a good guy, as squid go; he doesn't expect me to pitch in when they're beating on probable civilians.

Screams, thumps, punches. The firing stops. I inhale a dense reek of gun-powder. Ah, the good old days.

Soon enough they're hauling out the troublemakers: a mother and son maybe, both netted like trout. The boy is unconscious; livid sucker marks show he's been throttled. The woman is shrieking.

Loot asks: "What is she saying?"

I tilt up my mask, taking the opportunity to poke a stick of gum into my mouth, and kneel beside her. "Ma'am? Nobody's going to hurt you. We need to evacuate—"

"We ain't leaving!" she yells.

I turn to Loot. "She doesn't want to leave her home. I doubt she's a Fiend."

"We'll see." A bloom of mildew-pink within his cap betrays irritation. "We are falling behind the other teams."

The others are probably doing cursory checks. Plenty of squid are fed up with being unable to tell Fiends from allies. If a few stubborn humans get dusted with their houses, they probably figure it's a bonus. Loot's more conscientious . . . and his family connections mean he can get away with it.

Now the woman bellows in sudden rage, glaring past my legs at a squid I've dubbed Gollum. He's lingering over the trussed-up son, poking a tentacle into the boy's mouth, getting a taste of him.

I vault over her, shoving the offworlder's carapace. "Cut it out."

Loot kills the fight before it can begin, bringing Gollum to heel. Then he orders Squiggly to haul the prisoners back to the evacuation team, effectively reducing our strength by ten percent. More, really—Squiggly's worth three of Gollum.

"Your son'll be okay," I tell the woman. "I can see he's breathing."

Her reply doesn't require translation; every squid in California knows "Fuck you, traitor," when they hear it. I let the words glide over my skin, light as the rush of sweat raining down my face.

"Building is empty," Loot reports. We pull out, and the floater drifts in to demolish the low-rise.

"The strip mall next?" I ask.

"Yes," he says, and we move out. "Tell me something, Cantil?"

"Sure."

"This city lies on a major fault line, does it not? Wouldn't it make sense to take the population inland?"

"You saying your fancy nano-built condos can't handle the occasional earthquake, Lieutenant?"

Gollum smacks me, accidentally-on-purpose, for dissing Kabuva architecture. Loot flicks him back into line.

"Of course they can. But if the land's unstable—"

"You can't just uproot all of L.A."

"You could build somewhere tectonically stable—house everyone in a tenth of the land area," throws in Bluto.

It's a fight not to sigh. You wouldn't believe how offworlders can go on and fucking on about urban sprawl. "People like to live near the beach."

That gets a ripple of amusement from the platoon. As far as these guys are concerned, humans can't swim. Take a squid to a dive shop, he'd probably laugh himself into a stroke.

Mmmm, interesting thought. I file it away, cracking out a fresh stick of gum before I close up my mask.

At the strip mall we check a liquor store and a magazine shop. Both are empty, eminently dustable. Troops poke into a third, bored. All routine until there's a flash and a series of whumps—modified car airbags, from the sound. Three squid race out of the shop. A black cloud follows: toner from photocopiers, almost certainly. The stuff gets everywhere, burns their skin, infiltrates their delicate gills.

"Why didn't you say there was a print shop?" Loot, furious, hitches two tentacles into my armpits and takes a full taste of me.

"I didn't know!" My pulse goes haywire as he hoists me to my tiptoes. "It says Office Furnishings."

He runs a tentacle around my forearm, checking blood pressure, suspicious. I wait, chewing my gum furiously and trying to get my breath under control. When they're calm they're decent lie detectors, but you never know when a squid might decide you're stringing him along, not because you are but just because he's upset.

Calm. Focus on concrete things. I watch the remainder of the squad heading back into the shop. They come out a minute later carrying what's left of Harpo, webbing up the dead fry in grim silence. My runaway heart slows as the wounded lift him gently and start limping to the rear.

"Down to half strength now," Kramer grumbles.

"Pull back." Loot still hasn't let go. "We'll dust the retail block."

Bluto asks: "We're moving on to the single-family dwellings?"

"Perhaps." He shakes me. "Are there signs, Cantil? What do they say?"

"People don't put signs on their houses. Numbers, names, sometimes, but—" I glance ahead. The other squads' demolition ships are fifteen to twenty blocks ahead of us.

"What about that?" He unfurls an anger-white tentacle, pointing. Definitely worked up now, not so keen to believe the copy shop thing's not my fault.

I swallow. "It's an old 'For Sale' sign—the owners tried to sell the house."

"And that?"

"Beware of dog," I translate. "Look, pick any house. Any street. I'll go in first."

"And lead us into a trap?"

"You've seen my file, Loot." I press my face mask against his armor, glaring into his cap. Sweat flows off me, soaking the sticky tentacles holding me up. "You know I hate everything Fiendish."

Gollum scoffs. "Easy to say."

"You want me to take point? I'll take point. Fuck, you can take my vest off. Pick the house, Loot, send me in."

No response. I let fury take over, popping catches on my protective vest. "I'll go naked, how's that?"

"Wait." Finally releasing me, Loot knots a couple tentacles in a ritual gesture of apology and presses them against my shoulder.

"Cantil in front works for me," Gollum snarls.

Ignoring him, Loot says: "Let's move on."

Five houses into the next block, we find a family chained to the pipes in their basement.

There are four of them: mama, papa, grandma, and a daughter who's maybe twelve. They're white, old Euro from the looks of them. This probably isn't the first time they've been displaced.

The old woman shrieks in a foreign tongue.

"What is she saying?"

"Not sure—I think they might be Greek."

"You don't speak Greek?" Bluto asks accusingly. As if, you know, I'm a moron.

"American, Spanish, Mandarin, French, and Kabuva."

This gets me the usual response. "But Greek's just another Euro dialect, isn't it?"

Sighing, I try the girl. "Come on, honey, you must've been born here. Speak American? *¿Habla Español?*"

She does a burrow into Mama's leg.

"We'll cut them free," decides Loot. "Apply taser patches." Gollum gleefully presses the patches against the back of each human's neck.

"One wrong move, we zap you into a coma," he warns. I make gestures, trying to get the idea across via charades. Granny waves her evil-eye pendant oh-so theatrically. The squid, forced to crowd together in the low-ceilinged basement, are nevertheless relaxing their guard. It's cooler out here than in the sun.

Only Loot remains sharp.

Toady shoves Papa away from the end of the pipe, brandishing a mini-saw. Meanwhile, Bluto unrolls the first body restraint, his tentacles roiling fluidly as he flaps the net out like a rug.

The mini-saw bites into the pipe, sending up a stream of sparks. The whole family starts wailing and shrieking; you'd think they were being murdered.

Loot turns to me in exasperation.

"Sorry," I say. "It's all Greek to me."

Just then Toady's saw breaks through the pipes. Gas belches out. Loot reacts quickly, jerking Bluto and Gollum away from the billow of white fog.

The gas is high-end stuff, no improvised booby trap this time. Toady and Kramer collapse like punctured balloons. Granny and the girl fall atop them as Loot hits the tasers.

Mama and Papa Fiend must have ditched the taser patches somehow. They're loose, armed and firing.

Quarters are close. Bodies, human and offworlder, are surging everywhere. I'm drawing a bead on Papa when four Fiends in sensor-clouding capes drop out of the T-bar ceiling. Gollum clamps his shell shut, a hair too late. The caped human drives a firespike into the carapace before it locks. A whoosh of heat—the smell of grilled seafood fills the air.

Nerve gas and flame spikes, I think. This little operation is well funded.

I'm aiming at a caped Fiend when I feel a flamespike against the nape of my neck.

"Guns down." It's Mama Fiend, speaking American.

"She's telling us to surrender," I say.

Loot and Bluto grope at each other, tentacles twining in the squid equivalent of nonverbal communication.

"Now," Mama says. "Or I burn your head off."

"Come on, they're going to waste me." I stare across the room at Loot. He's a good-enough guy, in his way, but we're not the same species. He'll clamp his armor and take his chances. It's what they do, every time.

But no. Flesh darkening with frustration and fear, they surrender.

"What now?" I ask, feeling oddly giddy. She thumps me upside the head, just a warning, no real damage. Loot, bless his weird offworlder heart, fluffs his cap protectively.

"It'll be all right," he tells me. "Tell her she has three minutes before our backup takes the roof off this dwelling."

Before I can translate, we hear the whump of surface-to-air packets. A high-pitched shriek and a thunderclap follow; a few seconds later, the ground shakes. Upstairs, windows shatter.

"That'd be your air support biting dirt," explains Mama Fiend unnecessarily.

Loot's strange, moist skin mottles in an unreadable roil of emotions. "Tell her we'll send missiles."

"He says they'll bomb you from orbit."

"They aren't going to dust their own people," Mama Fiend says. Her pals are gleefully using the squad's own restraints to bind the surviving squid onto wheeled palettes. One of them is setting up a webcam, pointing it at Loot's face as they wrench off his mussel shell and the hydrator that keeps his skin moist.

"It seems Intel was right for a change," he says calmly.

"Sir?"

"A new-hatched fry could see this neighborhood really is Fiendish. What do you suppose their plan is?"

I shrug. "We're alive, so Command can't bomb."

"We're bait," he agrees. "They'll draw the other squads back to rescue us."

"Into a trap." I nod. This street lies at the bottom of a gently rising wave of cookie-cutter houses. If Fiends are dug in all along the hill, the slaughter will be unthinkable. "It'll be kill at will."

Flashes of blue-white fury bloom across his translucent, helpless body, but what can he do? It's all been very neatly planned.

"It won't work," he says finally. "We'll lose a few squads here, but you'll all die."

You. A bit of a chill.

"Tell them," he says, and I realize he just wants me to pass the word along.

"What's he saying?" asks Mama Fiend.

I let out a long breath. "Basically? They rock, we suck, we're all gonna die."

Mama laughs. "Let him know we don't need a traitor on-hand to translate his bullshit."

Loot fluffs again—probably caught the word "traitor." "Tell them you're a prisoner, Cantil. Say we forced you to help us."

Poor guy. Impulsively, I knot my bony fingers into a sign of friendship, then press both hands into the flesh of his webbed-up tentacle, giving him a last taste of my damp palms and dirty fingers. "Thanks for everything, Loot."

"Come on." Mama Fiend drags me toward the door, leaving her minions to watch the hostages.

He bellows in fractured American as we disappear down the hall. "Don't hurt! Not hurt! Cantil!"

But Cantil is flaking away, all but gone. He was never more than a false skin, and it is good to finally shed him.

Mama Fiend, whose name is Debra Notting, hits a remote on an antique iPod. The basement fills with the sound of me shrieking in agony. We pass through an old bedroom, where a redheaded girl is pouring two pints of blood—mine, donated a couple months back—onto a stained mattress.

Deb points at my shoes. I slip them off, along with my sweat-stained socks, and kick them into a corner. There won't be a body, but there's a lot of my DNA in here now. Given the way Dust can obliterate a person from existence, you can never know for sure if someone's alive or dead.

"Spit your gum onto the floor?" the girl suggests.

"Can't—it's laced with drugs," I reply, undertone.

Beyond the bedroom is a squalid john whose tub is full of broken tile. A crude tunnel has been hacked into its wall; we head down and then east for two hundred feet, coming up in another basement. The battle wranglers are here, crouched in a sensor-proof tent, peering into portable datascreens and murmuring orders into headsets. The others are tracking the incoming squid squads that are heading back to rescue Loot and his fry.

"Demolition ships are clearing off," reports one old man.

"Told you, Deb," I say. "They're too pricey to risk when we've got surface-to-air."

"What happened with the ship we hit?" she asks.

"Four survivors, pinned down in the Hamiltons' backyard," a wrangler answers.

"The squid receiving video of their captured platoon?"

"Affirmative." He tilts a screen and we see Loot and the others, bound tightly onto the pallets, taser-patched and already drying out. I make myself smile. It's always important at this point to look solid, loyal.

The mental shift of gears is harder this time.

"One squad's almost back to Sycamore Drive," a wrangler reports. "Permission to fire?"

"No," Deb says. "Wait until they're closer. We're wasting five hundred troops here. To make it worth the blood, we need to draw in and kill as many as we can. I want lots of bait, well-placed bait."

"They'll deploy," I say. It took me months of careful maneuvering to get onto Loot's squad. Months of minty chewing gum that made me sweat like a pig and smell ever so faintly sweet. Months of shooting Fiends and telling dumb Dem jokes and worrying that Kabuva Intel would figure out I'd been behind the bloodbath last year in Altanta. "The lieutenant's mother will throw half the West Coast Command in here if she thinks it'll get Loot back."

"You sez," Debra replies, but she's smiling.

"Been right so far, haven't I?"

"No," she says.

"No? I brought him right here, on time."

"Yeah." She taps the screen. "You also said he'd sell you out."

It's true. Loot came through, unlike all the other squid I've so carefully betrayed. My voice, when I answer, is steady: "Kid's an idealist, the real deal. Had to happen eventually, I guess."

"Almost a shame we're gonna kill him, huh?"

She's watching me carefully.

"Almost," I agree. If I do feel a pang, if the game is suddenly less fun than it used to be, how's she going to know? I'm a serpent. I lie.

"Okay." She smiles. "Time you scrambled. I'm sure you've got a hot date with a new identity."

"I'm going after the spaceport in Tulsa," I say. There's no harm in telling. Everyone in the room took slow poison as soon as my squad passed the copy shop. The squid will overrun this position eventually—there's no avoiding that. But they won't be interrogating anyone but grunts.

She draws back the cover on another tunnel. "This one leads to the sewers. There's a truck waiting."

"Thanks." Still barefoot, I ease onto the ladder.

To my surprise, Deb gives me a hug before I can go. "Thanks for setting the stage."

"Make a good show of it," I reply, squeezing back. For a second, the hard tissue of her muscles feel strange. Almost alien.

Letting me go, she salutes.

Then she turns back to her work and I start down the ladder, leaving my friends and enemies together, locked in the endless dance of mutual annihilation.

THE TERROR BARD

Larry Niven and Brenda Cooper

"Kath and Quicksilver" was one of my favorite stories of 2005. It originally appeared in the November issue of Asimov's, *and I was so taken with its intriguing far-future setting that I invited Larry and Brenda to collaborate again for this volume. I was delighted when they said yes, but even more delighted when their contribution arrived and I realized that they had penned a sequel to that fantastic tale.*

Venus, near death, nipped at Earth's old orbit. Earth, barren and abandoned, spun in a new place, halfway to Mars's orbit, eased outward by the sun's diminishing mass. The swollen sun engulfed Mercury's orbital path. Yet it had not, so far, eaten Mercury, for Mercury now spun in a new path, between Venus and Earth. Mercury was lighter now; its heavy iron core partially spent as reaction mass to move it away from its hungry mother sun. It had all happened hundreds of thousands of years ago.

They had salvaged Mercury, Kath and Quicksilver. Over tens of thousands of years, Mercury's salvage had paid Kath's and Quicksilver's rescue debt, and then, finally, unexpectedly, yielded profit. Kath had donated most of the credit to the Clade. Quicksilver would have owned half. She had tried to save funds in his name, but the Bear Clade was growing, and greedy, and needed much to sustain itself and educate itself.

Kathlerian sat in her living room in Valles Marinaris, bent forward, arms resting on her knees. Sweat poured down her face, tickling her nose as she stared intently at the vid-wall in front of her. She was watching an escape pod leave Mars, flying through a dilating window in the Roof of the Red World, heading for Pluto.

Kath had the resources to leave. But half of her own human control group—the Bear Clade—did not. The AIs and others didn't value them enough to save them.

The sun was growing, was expected to grow for another two hundred thousand years or so. An eye-blink, to a star. From time to time it spat out a shell of high-velocity gas, and everybody scrambled for shelter.

Sol poured heat through the atmospheric barriers its citizens had erected. Most who could leave Mars had gone, or queued for ships that would leave in the next few years. Some waited to see Venus die; Mars would be a good vantage point. Soon, only the unwanted and the uncaring would be left.

She had nearly forgotten the presence of a tall dark man with ice blue eyes. She reached for Charter's hand and squeezed it.

The escape pod shrank to a bright pinprick of light. Kath switched the video screen to show the alien starship *Thousand Flowers*, still against a field of still stars, its size impossible to guess with no points of reference.

"Don't blink," she whispered, watching Charter's pursed lips. The ship suddenly slipped away to a pinprick of reflected light, moving so fast it seemed to belong in an immersion sim or a movie. She whispered, "What a machine."

"You're nuts," he said, pulling his hand away, standing, stretching. The shadow of his tall thin frame touched her face.

She loved Charter with all her heart, but the Bear Clade tied up her soul. Jerian Wale 9000, the Clade's founder, had chosen half the Clade. They were on their way to Charon already. Kath *would* save the rest before the sun baked Mars into something like Mercury used to be.

She needed Quicksilver.

He had been a teacher once. The teacher's mind had been recorded and imposed on the magnetic flux tube that ran between Mercury and an expanding sun. He had survived in that state for a billion years and more. Pulling Mercury out from the sun had ruptured the flux tube, of course. Now an uninitiated, fallow copy of Quicksilver lay in Jerian Wale's data banks on Mars, not exactly alive, not exactly dead.

Charter turned toward her, his thin face mostly in shadow. Faint light from the silent wall-screen painted a halo above his dark hair. "We don't know anything about the HighJin. Their intent is as opaque as their technology."

Kath stood and faced Charter, speaking forcefully. "They came from the stars to watch the sun's transformation. They want to use Mercury as a base. Set up equipment and watch Venus die. They're scientists; we're subjects. Kind of like us studying ants. But they want *my* anthill, and I plan to give them permission in exchange for certain rights."

"If you're an ant, will they protect your hill?"

She looked past him. "They won't protect Mercury. Neither will I."

He frowned. "We've never even seen a HighJin. Not once. Hell, I don't know if the AIs have seen one. You're the first human we know of they've even talked to."

She nodded. No need to respond; it was his way of thinking through a challenge. When the HighJin first arrived, two hundred years ago, everyone thought they'd come to rescue humanity from their dying sun. Humans had never broken the speed of light, but the HighJin had, barely. Surely aliens who could do that were wizards come to save humanity. Or at least give them a lifeboat.

But they'd never offered. They'd watched and recorded.

At first they'd acted as if no one else existed in Sol system. Their inaction had turned Charter's curiosity, and almost everyone else's, to anger.

Ten years ago they'd started talking. First to the AIs, and then, through them, to Kathlerian 771.

Charter said, "You own salvage rights to Mercury. That's not the same as owning the planet. No one owns a planet."

That had been decided by the World Courts long ago. Kath said, "Mercury's no better than salvage now. No one can get close, except the HighJin. They say they can take the heat. What difference does it make who owns it? I'm giving a good death to two worlds."

Charter shook his head, looked away, and then back. "I fell in love with your courage. That doesn't help my nerves."

She stared up into his eyes. "It will be okay. Really." She struggled to look as calm as her words.

His voice sounded strangled. "I can't go to Charon without you."

She knew. They'd been together a thousand years. "You'll go with me? To Mercury?"

He nodded.

"We can take a copy of Quicksilver?"

A jerky shake of his head. "The technology is too old. We can't talk to it. We can take the record along and read it into the flux tube."

"The new flux tube's formed? Is it strong enough?"

This time, Charter nodded.

"Did Jerian take a copy of Quicksilver with him?"

Charter spread his arms wide: he didn't know who had what copies of whom where. A little fear fluttered along her spine. She'd be risking the only copy of the man—once man—who'd saved her life so long ago.

Her eyes and mouth tightened in frustration; her nostrils closed like tiny fists; her ears curled tight against her head. Two deep breaths. Three. Her ears unfurled. The Clade mattered more than Quicksilver. Hundreds of thousands of living humans weighed against one who was currently dead.

Charter sighed. "Jerian left the culls. The Bear Clade families he took to Charon were the half he wanted. Perfect health, no sociopaths, no gene twists—"

"No imagination. He left you, love."

"His choice."

"I'm going to save them. You. All of you."

He opened his arms toward her.

If you're going to love, she reminded herself, *love completely. Trust.* She stepped into Charter's embrace, let him fold her in his arms, let her muscles relax against his. She reached her face up and offered and received a long, deep kiss that warmed her to the core. She whispered to her house. "Lights up. Chairs conversational. Cinnamon, low."

The room changed around them as Kath and Charter savored another kiss. A hint of cinnamon brushed Kath's nostrils.

Kathlerian's silver butler intruded with a bottle of syrah from Kath's cellar, and then Kath sent the message <*Contract terms agreed to. Two humans.*> to the HighJin ship, using an encrypted band of Solnet Three. She and Charter shared the wine and held hands, comfortable. She'd loved him longer than she'd loved anyone else.

She glanced up through the window, where a huge red sun shone through the Roof of the Red World. Behind Charter's head she made an obscene gesture, a death sign. She settled deeper into Charter's arms and drifted to sleep, her cheek on his shoulder.

The next morning Kath walked out onto her observation deck. She had already said her good-byes. Not directly, but they'd be recognized as such once she was gone. There was no one left she needed to talk to.

Her gaze swept Mars's rugged horizon, one low rim of the Valles Marinaris showing between rooftops. Severely filtered light, all the Roof of the Red World allowed in, threw a blanket of bright points across streets and parks and tall buildings. Below her, figures walked and ran in the park, flashing in the dappled light. Over half appeared to be Clade members, but the day's heat would soon drive her kind inside, leaving the park to those with metal or gene-altered or hybrid bodies better able to dump heat and stay cool.

And down there, living side by side with the Clade, a thousand thousand variations. Quasi-humans shaped to hundreds of varied ideals. Human-machine hybrids, machines with the minds of men, machines with the minds of machines in robotic bodies, and machines with no bodies—Artificial Intelligences, patterns that lived in Mars's vast information architecture.

Cooling systems couldn't keep up anymore. Sweat beaded her arms. She idly whispered, "Fan," and a soft warm breeze came from above her, making the deck slightly more comfortable. Her ears curled up, shutting the noise out, letting her stay quiet inside her thoughts.

Old Jerian had once tried to stop the Bear Clade from reproducing until after the sun settled. He had lost *that* battle. Kath had been on Mars a quarter million years; fifteen children, two or three at a time, years apart, salves to loneliness. After ten grandchildren, she'd lost track. Almost? There was one grandson: Lysle 8951. Lysle was thirty now. An artistic prodigy, like Charter was a math prodigy. Jerian didn't like prodigies. He'd left Lysle behind.

Kathlerian recalled lovers, men and women and one hybrid. Only a few, really, considering all the years. Two or three she still missed. She didn't even know if they were on Mars now. And out there, scattered in tens of locations on Mars, the rest of the Bear Clade. As early a version of humanity as anyone could find. Medical procedures let them stay young as long as they chose, but there had been no other modifications since Jerian founded the Clade. The last of a race.

Much of Bear Clade was related to her by now.

Quicksilver would help her. Sure he would. He would.

It felt hard to leave. She might never return. And it would all be different, anyway. If she succeeded, the Clade would scatter, and most would live. If she didn't . . .

She held her picframe in her hands for a moment, watching it cycle. Lysle 8951, complete with freckles and a short, almost square nose under bright yellow-gray eyes. Then Lysle in front of an air-mural, Lysle's own work, that still toured Newton's streets. Next, a picture of the Kathlerians. Three times, there had been a fad to name kids after her. She had a single picture of a hundred Kathlerians. Jerian had taken less than half the Kaths to Charon. Two wedding pictures and a picture of her third Joplee, her third mechanical bodyguard/teacher/friend; this one had died in one of the occasional attempts on her life. She set the picframe down and sighed.

Working through Solnet Three, Kath sent a note to Sol System's second-biggest entertainment network, Hyunet. <*Ready? I'll give you what I promised. Keep your word: no leaks.*>

She ordered her house closed and booked transportation.

She'd been packed for a week. There was no need to wait for a reply—the second-biggest network wanted to become the biggest, and it would pay her enough if she succeeded. If not, well, the sun would finish what it had started a quarter of a million years ago.

They flew to Mars's Outpoint Station, which in a closer orbit had been the moon Deimos. In the station bar they ate a scratch meal and watched the sun reflect brightly at them from the nano-engineered shield that swathed most of Mars. The out-facing side's silvery finish stung their eyes with light.

A silver biped stopped opposite them and chimed.

Kath eyed it. Long arms, long legs now retracting, solar panels already folded, a short, thin torso and a small head; it looked almost like a metal butterfly. One of the many standard bodies often inhabited by AIs without the funds to design their own.

"I am Joy Ten." It nodded its tiny silver head, the size of Kath's closed fist. "You are Kathlerian 771 and Charter 1802 of the Bear Clade."

"Yes."

"I will be your guide and interpreter. I am a fully sapient AI, level four, representing the HighJin. Our transport is in dock twelve. Follow me?"

||

Joy Ten led them to a black mushroom with patches of rounded window around the cap.

The ships of Sol System came in near-infinite variety. This ship didn't look so alien, but Kathlerian paused to look it over. Though humans had long since harnessed nanotech to make flawless materials, Kathlerian had never seen a shipskin so perfect, so unblemished. Surely it wasn't new? There should be debris marks, or scratches from maintenance bots, or something.

Joy Ten showed a squat cargo bot an opening for Kath's pallet of carefully packed cameras and electronics, and for Charter's smaller but oh-so-precious cargo: Quicksilver, housed now in Bose-Einstein condensate memory-ware, in a box the size of a small desk. As soon as the cargo bot started, Joy Ten took the two travel cases and held them balanced, arms extended front and back, one case on the end of each arm. It walked slowly up a narrow stairway and stopped before a smooth curved wall, just below the cap. Joy Ten's head bobbed, and an oval door opened in front of it. Beyond the door: blackness.

Kath grabbed Charter's hand, suddenly awkward. She hadn't been off Mars in thousands of years.

His grip on her hand was dry. He smiled. "New territory. After you."

She swallowed and ducked through the door.

The silver of Joy Ten's overlong appendages and the dull black of their travel cases were mirrored on shiny bluish surfaces inside the alien ship. Subdued light rose from a glowing strip inset under their feet as they walked through an otherwise featureless corridor. Kath and Charter followed the AI forward into what must be a control room near the front of the mushroom cap. Their footsteps made almost no sound.

The tip was a window. Kath looked out on a circle bright with stars, edged with the thin strutwork of the docking web. A thrill ran through her. The last time she had chosen so audaciously she had nearly lost her life, but the gamble had given her Mercury, had shaped her from that moment. She had been a child then, too stupid to understand what she risked. This time, the stakes lived in her bones like an electrical current, sharpening her senses.

Two acceleration couches opened like blossoms, obviously meant for humans. Unidentifiable symbols decorated the smooth walls. Joy Ten helped them strap down their belongings, then themselves. The couch's softness surprised Kath. The restraints felt like gossamer. The HighJin were considerate.

Joy Ten folded into a corner, locking itself against the wall, legs retracted, long arms over its knees, and became still.

The docking cage disappeared. Thrust pushed Kath back against the couch, flattening her, turning the pillowy couch into a wooden plank. Her lungs burned.

As the thrust fell away, Kath's mood lightened, as if her worries evaporated with her weight. After five years of speaking through interpreters and sending and receiving terse notes, of detective work to ferret out any possible scam, of transferring money and signing agreements, she was really in the alien ship—or on her way. She was sure now: this little mushroom shuttle was a component, a lifeboat, of *Thousand Flowers*.

Joy Ten emerged from the corner to offer food and drink. Kath was famished. She and Charter held the trays between their toes.

Hours later the robot served them again. Charter protested. "Joy Ten, that's just what we had for lunch."

"Yes."

"You bought these at Outpoint, right? What else did you get for us?"

A wall rolled back over storage space. Kath looked. "Charter? I'm sorry."

He was already chuckling. "Joy Ten, you've bought eighty boxes of Miracle Meal, curry flavor."

"Yes, and fruit juice. I do not see a problem. Bear Clade are omnivores. You can eat anything."

Kath sighed. It was always the little things.

Joy Ten emerged from the corner five times a day to feed them. Otherwise the AI ignored them. They played memory chess and told each other stories to pass the time. Two days passed . . . and she woke to see the HighJin ship.

Charter was asleep. She reached across the space between the acceleration couches and shook his shoulder, then pointed directly ahead of them. From a distance, *Thousand Flowers* was a featureless cylinder, a long thin pipe that blocked ever more stars as they neared it. As they began deceleration, the outside of the cylinder devolved into a multifaceted garden of strange shapes.

Kath whispered softly to Charter. "I swear I can see things growing and changing on that ship."

He squinted. "It must be an optical illusion."

"These are aliens."

"I'll watch."

An hour later, he gave in. "I see what you see, but I don't believe it."

When Joy Ten unfolded from its corner, Charter asked it, "Would you describe the *Thousand Flowers* to me? The outside."

Joy Ten refilled their water bulbs and handed them Miracle Meal (curry) and bulbs of astherid juice. Kath thought it hadn't heard, but finally it said, "'*Thousand Tools*' would be a more apt name. The HighJin took a chemical route to creation. *Thousand Flowers*, and this transport for that matter, are assembled by organic processes. What humans do inorganically, with computer programs and nanotechnology, the HighJin do with organic programming."

"So the ship is alive?" Kath asked, glancing over at Charter. Charter watched the ship rather than the AI. He loved figuring out how things worked.

She turned her attention back to the AI, who said, "Chemistry is not necessarily life." With that, Joy Ten folded back into the corner.

Kath shook her head. "Why won't it give us more information? Maybe they haven't told it very much."

"I hope the information you *do* have is good," Charter replied dryly.

The mushroom-ship inverted, turning stem-inward to the cylinder. They drifted backwards. Mars glowed like a tiny sun from this distance; a trick of the shielding. She watched the little red spark, taking deep belly breaths, settling herself into a psychologically ready state to meet the aliens.

The ship surged hard. They became weightless.

Kath and Charter unstrapped from their couches and followed Joy Ten down the corridor in the stem, toward *Thousand Flowers*. The corridor had changed. They'd had gravity when they boarded back at the station, and they'd walked through a featureless tube. Now, smooth handholds protruding from the same corridor (surely the same one!) allowed them to pull themselves forward. As before, Joy Ten carried their luggage, one piece held by each foot. The handholds shone, greasy in the faint light, soft and slightly warm under Kath's palms. As before, a single strip of light provided orientation.

By now they must be *inside* the larger ship. They'd certainly traveled at least twice as far as when they had boarded the transport. Kath didn't recall seeing an entry point; the corridor had been seamless. "Charter, did you see a doorway between the transport and this corridor?"

"No."

Joy Ten stopped in front of them and turned towards one side of the cylinder. A door dilated.

They entered a large room, nearly as featureless as the corridor. In a corner, a wall glowed. After the door closed behind them, Joy Ten said, "Orient this way," and turned itself so its feet were on the side wall. Kath and Charter followed its lead, and Kath's stomach flipped as gravity surged, pulling her feet to the wall, until suddenly her perspective clicked and her feet hugged the floor. She stood. How did they *do* that?

"This will be your quarters. You will be protected from the effects of acceleration and radiation here." Joy Ten pointed toward the panel. "You may use this panel to request anything the HighJin can provide. Klio?"

The panel glowed brighter. "I am Klio, a full sentient AI, level fifty."

Smarter than Joy Ten, then. Anything over thirty was virtually unrestricted. Fifties didn't bother with humans. Kath fought back a wave of awe. "Hello, Klio," she said. "I'm pleased to meet you. When might I see our hosts?"

"I will be your interpreter." No accent. Its silken neuter voice might have uttered human speech every day. "This screen, this entire room, has been designed for you."

Kath glanced around the empty room. "May we have a tour of the ship?"

"No."

Kath scowled. She could hardly command the HighJin to show themselves, but she *had* expected to finally see her enigmatic hosts. She looked at the bare floors. "What should we sleep on?"

Two beds rose out of the floor, dark rectangles with no covers. Kath's cheeks warmed. "We'd prefer one bed."

One bed sank again. What else did they *need*? "Sink, bathing and elimination facilities. Running water."

A door dilated, and behind it, a full fresher fitted for humans . . . but there weren't any angles. It all looked melted. Then the door became wall again, and Kath said, "Show me how to open the wall, or leave the door open."

The door opened. Kath frowned. "Will you show me how to do that?"

"You do not have the necessary circuitry."

"Fine. Leave it open." She wasn't about to have to ask an AI for permission every time she needed to use the fresher.

Charter spoke. "A table and chairs."

Kath smiled at him and squeezed his hand. "Kitchen."

A square table and rounded chairs appeared, all black like the beds, greasy looking and smooth like the corridor and the handholds. Klio said, "Your food will be brought to you."

"Klio," Charter asked, "Are you modified to interface with this ship?"

"I've accepted patch sequences of programming from the HighJin. The result is different from AIs merging here. Separation remains; there is an interface between me and the programming that is HighJin. After all, I am light and they are matter."

Kath frowned. "When can I talk to the HighJin?"

Klio said, "When you talk to me, you are talking to them. Let me order you a meal. We have attempted to improve on Joy Ten's efforts. Joy Ten will stay with you."

Charter spoke. "We would rather be alone. Can we call for Joy Ten when we want?"

"Yes, but let it serve you. That is its chosen task."

"We can't leave this room, right?" Kath asked.

"You do not have the right circuitry to control the ship surfaces. We require a day to bring you to Mercury."

"I would like to see the flight."

A starfield brightened the screen. "That is Mercury."

A point of light glowed above a wall of red-hot fog. Kath swallowed hard, suddenly wishing she hadn't asked. Mercury had been home, and she'd saved it once. Now, she was about to kill it. "Thank you."

Joy Ten brought them a tree branch laden with fruit. Kath gaped; Charter laughed. The little red spheres were half-familiar; they might have been purchased from some lunar or asteroidal colony. "Omnivore," Charter said, grinning.

They gorged on the fruit.

The bed conformed perfectly to Kath's hips and shoulders and head. Kath and Charter slept, and stretched, and cuddled, and read.

In the viewscreen, Mercury didn't move.

The next morning, the sky hadn't moved. Deep red fringe of sun, black sky, dust of stars and one bright point. Charter asked, "Wasn't this ship supposed to be *fast*?"

"I have never seen *Thousand Flowers* in flight," Joy Ten said, and returned to its corner.

Hours later Joy Ten brought them a root vegetable, baked, the size of Charter's forearm. While they were eating it, Mercury exploded in their faces.

There had been no sense of motion. Suddenly the sky was all glare-pink baked rock. Charter spasmed like a dying man, ears and nose and mouth clenched tight.

Kath slapped Charter's ridged stomach to get him to breathe again. "They spent all that time gearing up," she said.

"We're still in a hurry," Charter said.

Mercury was brighter than she remembered, lit by the expanding sun. Dark specks on the surface resolved to leftover habitats and old mining machinery. The hulk of a dead space-barge. Klio's voice interrupted her. "Locking into low Mercury orbit. Three hours to disembarkation."

Kath and Charter gathered their things, piling them in a spot Joy Ten pointed out. The room returned to its original blankness. Charter took Kath's hand. "It looks like an empty slate now."

She giggled. "Maybe I'll redecorate when we get back."

They boarded the mushroom ship, accompanied by Joy Ten. The ship dropped fast, plunged toward the surface of Mercury in a hot red glare. It landed in relative darkness at the edge of the sunward side.

Mercury had been scoured clean of dust. Rounded rocks and crater walls looked melted. A wistful sadness settled over Kath. Charter had never seen Mercury pristine, Mercury normal, Mercury before the sun scoured it, but she had: sharp jagged rocks and steep crater walls. Edges.

Klio ordered the transport to transform from ship to habitat. As far as Kath could tell, it didn't grow, or at least it didn't add mass. It changed, became a single thick-walled space, morphing around them until their cargo pallet rested in the center of a large empty room.

Kath and Charter enlisted Joy Ten's help to unpack the pallet Kath had carefully designed back on Mars. Charter watched Joy Ten fold open the bulky radiation suits Kath had commissioned two days after her original contact with the HighJin. Charter examined them, looking pleased.

She pulled out a single old-fashioned chess set with real wood pieces. "Yeah, I know. Sentimental. I made room for it." The feel of something so *human* in her hand brought tears to her eyes. It had been a gift from Lysle 8951. His yellow-gray eyes sparkled momentarily in her memory.

Klio spoke up, its voice pouring through Joy Ten. "We've established a tenuous connection with Solnet Three. Your absence is being discussed. What is a 'terror bard'?"

Kath bristled. "Not me! Nobody's going to die."

Charter said, "Search the net, Klio. You can find records of terror bards. There was a whole religion, the Companions, part of a sect called, um—"

"Data on the Companions has mostly been erased or classified. I have mention of Jestlyn Ward 006, who directed a meteorite at a city named Los Legiones and rode it down," Klio said. "I have the Ayatolah Warner, who smuggled a thermonuclear device into Ceres."

"Well, you know more than I do. There hasn't been a terror bard in a long time."

"But why has there ever been?"

AIs didn't kill each other. Charter glanced at Kath; he shrugged. "People can live practically forever, with luck. Every so often, one or another decides he's had enough. Most of them don't take anyone else with them, but some do. A terror bard is making a statement. Warner thought the Ceres bureaucracy had robbed him. Jestlyn Ward classed the Los Legiones sensories as demonic. The Companions committed genocide against . . . well, a forgotten people. Klio, I'm only a hundred and ten thousand years old. I don't empathize with wanting to kill so much that I'm willing to die for it."

Klio said, "Good," in the same silky voice.

"All right, Klio. When will the rover be ready?"

"Now."

"Thank you."

She stood next to Quicksilver's rectangular case. She spoke to the case. "Ready?"

Klio: "Do you like the rover?"

She'd given specs for use, not design specs. She nodded, pleased with the machine's simplicity; a heavily shielded small platform with six wheels, and a closed box at the front for two Bear Clade humans.

Together, they manhandled Quicksilver's radiation-shielded box into the rover and strapped it down. They added shielded cameras and mounting rods, filling almost all the spaces in the rover. They lurched slowly forward as first Kath, then Charter, learned the controls.

Crossing into the light felt like driving into the sun itself.

Sol took up a frightening amount of sky, a ball of brightness arching across more than half the heavens. Their helmets blocked the glare; they could look directly at the sun for a few moments at a time. Every kilometer or so, they stopped; one of them crawled out of the cab, worked a camera and mounting stick free from the pile surrounding Quicksilver's box, and with the help of a mechanical arm, planted the stick and decorated it with a tiny camera.

If Charter was Hansel and Kath Gretel, planting camera crumbs to lead them home, then the sun was the witch and the waiting oven and every other evil thing from every fairy tale that had survived the billions of years. It took six exhausting hours to crawl and stop and crawl their way to Midnight Dome, the only place on Mercury with the right vintage systems in place. During the whole journey, she felt as if the Clade stood in a silent spectral line along the rover's tracks, watching her, nodding when she planted a camera, their ghostly gray eyes filled with hope.

The Dome sat tilted: land beneath it had wrinkled. Antennas and other external objects had melted into odd-shaped lumps and run down the dome's exterior.

It recognized Kath as she and Charter drove up. A door rolled open. They drove inside. Darkness surrounded them, except for the elongated rectangle of bright light that spilled into the doorway from the rover.

"Light," Kath requested.

No response. Well, they'd expected problems. "Dome! This is Kathlerian 771. Lights, please!"

A single tiny light bloomed down a long corridor, then winked out.

Charter touched her hand, the gesture awkward in his thick suit. "You rest. I'll work on this."

She identified Charter to the dome and gave him as many rights as she had. With those, Charter could take more. As soon as he clambered out, she lay across the rover's narrow seat and slept. Once, light bloomed throughout the dome, waking her. She smiled and curled back into sleep. In her dreams, she played chess with Quicksilver, losing again and again.

When he woke her, Charter's unprotected blue eyes looked dark with exhaustion. "You took your helmet off!" she exclaimed, reaching for the latches of her own.

He nodded. "Habitat's good. Warning bells will tell us if it goes bad again."

She gave him a puzzled look. She was careful; he was more careful.

He grinned at her and pointed toward the top of the dome. "We're already standing just under death."

She tucked her helmet under her arm and shook her head. The air smelled stale and warm, and her forehead broke instantly into a sweat. She reached toward the neck of her suit, then thought better of it. Charter was still suited, and carried his helmet with him.

Working environmental systems implied working computers. "What do you know about the core computing?" she asked.

"If you run diagnostics while I sleep, we can load Quicksilver right after."

While the diagnostics ran, Kath wandered the silent halls of her old home, half expecting her childhood self to round a corner and greet her.

She shook Charter awake four hours later. "We're ready."

Two more hours passed before Charter grinned at her. "Say hello."

Her voice shook. "Quicksilver?"

Silence.

Charter whispered. "He'll be disoriented. He won't know how long he's been out."

"I know," Kath hissed back softly. Then, louder. "Quicksilver. It's me, Kathlerian."

Charter's voice again. "Mercury is different now, but he'll feel like he left it yesterday. The flux tube is different. Trust me. He'll be all right."

Kath grinned. "I trust you." She took advantage of the free face time and kissed Charter, hard.

He whispered, "Quicksilver won't remember you as an adult."

She kissed him again. "You do."

They toured the vast empty dome. Kath stepped over a maintenance robot that whirred up next to her and stopped dead at her feet. "Not exactly mint condition, but not too bad for a place that's older than me."

Hours passed before Quicksilver's cheery, childish voice filled her right ear. "Kathlerian 771?"

"Quicksilver? You okay?"

"Diagnostic still running. I remember giving Jerian permission to copy me. I was . . . afraid to die." Silence. "But we both lived."

She finally spoke words there hadn't been time for a quarter million years ago. "Thank you for saving me."

"This is Mercury. I'm in the Mercury flux tube. Surely you didn't move us back to the sun?"

"No, the sun swelled to us."

Silence.

"Tell me what you plan."

She sat up, wrinkling her nose. She needed a shower. She said, "Every mind in Sol System wants to watch the sun swallow Venus. An audience of trillions. But there's no way to get close, and too long to wait. We won't wait. We're going to send Mercury smashing into Venus and knock them both into the sun, years early. It'll be spectacular beyond anything the Solnets are expecting, except for Hyunet, because they're working with me. Microcams can't get close enough to the sun, not get in and stay in. Too hot. But a planet has enough mass to dump heat into. I've been scattering cameras over Mercury. Hyunet will have the only close-up view of the whole thing. It will make enough money to save the rest of the Bear Clade."

Five heartbeats passed before Quicksilver said, "I hear pain in your voice. Tell me what happened while I lay dormant. It's been thousands of years."

She grimaced. "Hundreds of thousands." She wriggled to find a comfortable place to sit, glanced at Charter, who sat still, listening, and then she started near Quicksilver's last memories. "When we got away from the sun, and you had . . . been moved into Jerian Wales's data bank and I couldn't talk to you—you didn't finish our last chess game!—I swore I wouldn't abandon family again, that I wouldn't disobey the Clade and wander off. That . . . that after this whole world was moved to save me . . . I'd matter." Her voice held firm, her words coming from her core self. "I'm grateful every day for my life. Grateful to you, grateful for Mercury. You must feel how much mass the planet has lost."

"Unevenly mined."

"People wanted the metal and minerals as the exodus to Pluto moved in waves from Mercury to Mars." She shifted again, off-balance in the suit, wishing she trusted the aged dome more. "They're abandoning Mars soon. They wrapped the planet in an envelope to reflect heat and radiation away, and it's almost past working."

She told him about the Clade, about Jerian taking half, and leaving some of the best, leaving Lysle. She described Lysle 8951's yellow-gray eyes and the chess set he'd given her. "How can I leave Mars if I have to leave so many behind to die?"

"And you need me to throw Mercury into Venus? What happens to me then?" Quicksilver sounded like a five-year-old. He always had; that was *his* voice. It hadn't been as heart-wrenching when she was a child herself. "I died before. The me after the copy."

"You don't remember it."

"I remember being afraid of it. You want me to commit suicide for you a second time."

"For the whole Clade. You did it for just me, once."

"I don't know the Clade."

She swallowed, her throat suddenly dry.

Quicksilver was silent for a long time before it asked, "Kathlerian 771, could you hurl yourself into a fire even if you knew you had a copy kept safe somewhere?"

Her fingernails dug furrows in her palm. The only copy of Quicksilver she was sure of was in her hands, as endangered as herself. "If it would save Lysle 8951."

"If it would save someone you didn't know?"

Nothing mattered as much as saving the Clade. "Yes," she lied.

Quicksilver said, "I don't know if I would save who you have become. When you were younger, you cared whether or not I would die."

She hung her head. "We'll keep you . . . we'll keep this copy safe."

"If it's *your* decision for *me* to die, *then you murder me*. Go away and let me think."

Tears stung the corners of Kath's eyes.

They took the rover back, driving from the dark of the dome into the impossible bright of the sunward side, and across the ragged landscape until the sun had nearly set.

The habitat was not there.

Charter drove them to where it had been, pointed at the deep lines where the weight of it had landed and, eventually, left, as a mushroom ship. Their belongings were neatly stacked on a rock, tied down. Kathlerian eyed Quick-silver's storage box, strapped to the rover. If the HighJin abandoned them, she had killed—*murdered*—them all.

Even through the darkened faceplate of his helmet, Charter's blue eyes narrowed with anger as his voice pinged across the radio in her ear. "I told you they wouldn't care about your plans."

"If Quicksilver sends us into Venus, the money will go to the Clade anyway. I didn't set this up so we had to live to succeed. You knew that."

"I don't want to die."

Quicksilver had said the same thing. "I don't want you to die either. I don't want to die. None of us does." She scanned the sky. Had the HighJin really left? "Klio?" she asked.

There was a pause of over a second. Then, "We overheard you," Klio said. "We are like Quicksilver. There is only one of us, and we could die if you do what you plan and there is . . . a failure. We will watch what Quicksilver does, and then we will make our own choices."

It didn't seem to matter what she did.

Charter slid away from her, as far from her as he could get on the wide bench. Thinking.

Kath frowned at him, an expression he couldn't see. She wanted to go back to the dome, but it was sunward, and offered more dangers.

She'd best let Quicksilver decide for himself. He'd do this. He would.

Charter's abandonment cut the closest. She slid over near him. He ignored her. She spoke softly, "Love. Charter, my lover."

After a while he reached one heavy suited arm out and set it over her shoulder. *Clank.* She felt its weight through the padding in her suit. The faceplate of his helmet was still turned away from her.

Finally he whispered, "Are we just waiting to die?"

"I'm waiting for Quicksilver to start us off."

"It doesn't matter what Quicksilver does. It matters what the HighJin do."

She didn't tell him he was wrong. She'd handed the ability to save the Clade to Quicksilver.

"Shall we explore?" he asked.

That was how she got stranded on Mercury the first time, exploring when she should have been readying to leave. When she should have been listening to her elders. She looked at Quicksilver's box again. "No. I need to stay by our copy of my friend."

He turned toward her, and his eyes were rimmed with red.

They slept. Kath woke to Charter's voice in her head, via the radio. "We're moving."

She felt a slight change in weight, in balance. A tremor. The old crater must be jetting ionized iron. "Which way?"

"Toward Venus, toward the sun."

Bless Quicksilver. The Clade would be safe. She'd built enough smarts into the media contract to assure that.

"Klio?" she queried.

Her heart beat slowly into the silence.

"Klio?" Her voice was louder, a little strident.

"We will copy Quicksilver, and he will decide whether or not we take you."

Kathlerian's eyes widened, but the HighJin would not see that. "You made a deal with me."

"But you did not make a deal with Quicksilver. He is teaching us more about humans than the AIs have, more than you did."

What would the old teacher tell the HighJin? *Now* she realized how little of her life she had known Quicksilver. He had been an icon. She sat close enough to Charter to feel him draw toward her. Humans were used to feeling outnumbered. She made a private channel between them and said, "Love."

"Love," he repeated, but the tones she heard were of fear.

She would have preferred defiance to fear, but Charter was who he was. "We are going to the dome," she told Klio.

There was no response. Kath looked at the pile of their belongings, then at Charter. "We'd better take anything we want."

"Do you want anything?"

"I have what I wanted most. When Hyunet pays off, the Clade will have enough money to save tens of thousands of them. Now I want to save you."

"And Quicksilver?"

The question ripped through her. "Of course."

If the HighJin didn't return, they'd burn. Death was death, for any of the

Clade. Quicksilver was not Clade, but she had killed him. Played one life against thousands. Perhaps she *should* die with Quicksilver. But choosing death wasn't in her. She climbed down from the rover and retrieved the chess set, setting it on the seat beside them. They rode back to the dome. As soon as she stripped off her helmet, Kath called out, "Quicksilver!"

"Yes?"

"I'm sorry." She shouted it. "I'm sorry, I was wrong!"

Three heartbeats, four.

His high, childish voice said, "You weren't wrong. I am still human enough to save the Clade."

She licked her lips. "I will save your copy if I can." Was she pleading for his life or for hers? For Charter's? For all of them? "Quicksilver, what kind of human were you? Like Bear Clade?"

"Not very. Largely cyborg and not so long-lived. Kath, the HighJin transport ship comes. They will copy me out of the flux tube."

"We brought the copy we restored you from."

"That copy does not know what you did. Leave it here."

"You will live."

"*I* will not. There will be a copy of me left behind. It is not the same. I will remain here, and keep Mercury on course. Small corrections may be needed to the end."

Kath raised an eyebrow at Charter.

He shook his head. "A solid trajectory will guarantee a course for Venus. You don't need to stay and burn."

Quicksilver said, "I should commit suicide first? No, *I* will live every moment left to me."

Kath drew in a sharp breath. Quicksilver had been Vance Hordon, a teacher. He was teaching her now. The words tore from her, ripping away a scar built by too many years of life. "I will never leave any being with no choice again."

Two hours later, the HighJin mushroom ship landed outside the Dome. The light of its engines balled and gathered below it, like a flaming pillow, and the ship settled peacefully onto the surface. The light around it winked out. The lock appeared as if a mouth yawned in the side of the vehicle.

They suited up and left the dome.

A squat black robot emerged from the HighJin ship, trundled past them on six wheeled feet. They followed it inside the dome, and sat by the door, breathing overheated air, waiting for Quicksilver or Klio or the black robot to say if they were needed. No one asked for them. When the robot went back out the dome door, they went out with it.

The rover followed the robot, climbing into a tunnel in the side of the ship. Kath and Charter followed the rover into the tunnel, immediately relieved to be free of the fire above them.

Nothing greeted them. They found the soft acceleration couches and the gossamer restraints and strapped themselves in. The HighJin did not provide them a view of anything, although they had enough light to see each other. The pity in Charter's eyes made her glad of the distance between them.

A viewscreen lit. A tiny dark ball with flames licking its edges, the only resolved hard thing against a background of sunfire. The view zoomed in. "That's from one of the cameras we set up," Charter whispered.

She nodded. Venus expanded. The second-largest network was undoubtedly busy becoming the largest. No terror bard had ever done anything so *big*. "Klio," Kath whispered, "can you show me the Solnet feeds so I can watch them too?"

Venus filled half the screen, wreathed in fire, fire behind it. Dancing fire, a nest of shock waves, as if the edge of the sun reached toward it. The goddess of love prepared to burn in her mother's embrace.

She watched Mercury, blinking. "Can I talk to Quicksilver from here?"

"He asked to die alone."

Charter reached for her hand.

A new viewscreen popped up, a talking sim. "Reports claim a clandestine force has moved Mercury into a collision path with Venus. Mercury, of course, moved once before. Powerful Bear Clade member Kathlerian 771 is rumored to be on the alien ship near Mercury. Charges have been filed against Kathlerian as a terror bard."

She frowned. "Terror bards kill people. I killed a rock, and I saved thousands of people." She'd killed Quicksilver, and saved the Clade. "And one person." She nearly choked on the words.

The sim continued. "The world court is even now declaring the destruction of Venus a capital crime."

Kath's ears curled. She pulled them relaxed with her hands. The sun was destroying Venus. Would destroy Mercury, soon. And Quicksilver. The flux tube would be wild with harmonics and shock waves. Did such a being feel pain? She remembered the days just before they'd left Mercury's original orbit, when Quicksilver had been there and gone and there and gone and she'd thought she'd lost him.

Hours passed. Venus filled the whole screen. Flame licked in front of the camera. Details of Venus's surface resolved. Bumps that used to be volcanoes, low valleys that used to be deep rift valleys. Like Mercury, Venus was a partly melted planet. The thick atmosphere was long since boiled away.

Surely Quicksilver was dead, now. The part of him she had killed. The rest slept—a copy that would recall her betrayal. She shivered, guilty and sorry.

Screens darkened one by one as cameras winked out, failing in the heat. Mercury was gone. Quicksilver.

She glanced up at the single camera view remaining, the perspective from *Thousand Flowers*. Mercury tiny and Venus huge, two bright cores whose edges mingled, then joined. Matter shattered and twisted, blazing balls and strings, a kitten's fire toy, two central cores tumbling, tied together, bright arcs of flame linking the two. Brilliant shards of planet transforming into flame and falling, falling, flaming, through the vaguely defined rim of the flaming sun. Everything fire. A bright spot marked the merged planet's passage for a long time, slowly dissipating into the currents of the red, swollen sun.

Afterimages burned in her retinas.

When the impact began to replay on the communication nets, she closed her eyes and breathed out slowly. Even if she didn't make it back to Mars, she had staff competent enough to get her people off Mars.

Hell with the Solnets. What would the HighJin do with her now?

Another view bloomed. The ship, *Thousand Flowers*, and Mercury while it still lived. The near recorded past. The mushroom ship detached from *Thousand Flowers*, and landed sunward on Mercury. Kath saw herself standing by Charter watching the black robot disembark. The cameras did not follow the robot, but stayed on the mushroom ship. Its smooth skin quivered and bunched and turned from dark to darker. Kath had barely noticed. Now she said, "It's burning, isn't it?"

Charter's voice was awed. "More than that, Kath. It's healing itself as it burns." He took her hand in his before he asked Klio, "Is the ship all right?"

"It will never rebond with *Thousand Flowers*. It had to separate itself or cause *Thousand Flowers* to live through its pain. Separate, it cannot rebond. This is how we re-create ourselves. It chose its path, chose to save Quicksilver."

Kath swallowed. "After I gave Quicksilver no choice." How much choice had the mushroom ship really had?

Charter's face shown with discovery. "We thought we had never seen you, but we have. We are in you." His voice quickened, his curiosity overwhelming him. "You are . . . you must be . . . a multiple being of some kind? A hive?"

"We are one. We are parts. Parts are less than the one if they are alone."

On the screen, the mushroom ship, with them inside it, floated free to *Thousand Flowers*, like a baby whale next to its parent.

"What will happen to it?" Charter asked. "To us?"

"It wants to take you with it."

"Where?" Kath asked, barely breathing. The alien wanted them?

"Where do you want to go?"

Kath didn't think she could go to Mars. Too many beings would condemn her choices. She had destroyed Mercury. The sun would have done that, but still . . . emotions might run high, fueled by the media. She had used the media, and they had not hesitated to use her in return. She'd bargained for the life of her Clade, not for her reputation.

The voice of Hyunet said, "No details of Venus and Mercury remain, but the mass still orbits within the sun's outer envelope. In its way, it is beautiful." It was: a scarlet comet. "The sign of the terror bard will orbit within the red-hot vacuum that is currently the sun's photosphere for decades or centuries."

Only in the heat of the moment were they calling her a terror bard. In a few hundred years, the Venus fireball would be etched away, the scandal would leak away, and she could win back her citizenship in court.

"Give us a few moments?" she asked.

"Of course."

Kath turned to Charter. "I can only talk to Quicksilver if he's in a flux tube."

Charter kissed her, catching on quickly. "You're being audacious again."

"And you like that?"

He smiled. "Yes."

Kath leaned into him, reached her face up, and kissed him. "You won't mind not getting to Charon?"

"After *that*?"

"Klio?" Kath requested the AI's attention. "Klio—we want to go to Jupiter. There is a flux tube between Io and Jupiter. Quicksilver might be able to live in it. I need to talk to him."

Silence.

"Can your ship live well there? At Jupiter?"

Klio again. "Yes, we can. We thought you'd never ask."

Kath settled into Charter's arms. "I'm sorry."

Klio and Charter answered at once. "I know."

P DOLCE

Louise Marley

Music often plays a role in Louise Marley's fiction, which is no surprise given that she has a Master of Music degree and has spent over two decades working as a professional singer, appearing with the Seattle Opera and touring internationally. The two taboo topics one should never mention at a dinner party—religion and politics—often figure strongly in her work as well. But it is that soft, sweet touch she employs when crafting her characters that makes all her fiction so compelling.

Frederica Daniels lay on the elaborately appointed hospital bed as if frozen. Her skin was the dull white of the olive blossoms brushing the window above her head. Her eyes did not so much as flicker beneath their shadowed lids. Her brown hair hung in limp strands beneath the cap of sensors, almost indistinguishable from the wires that fell over her shoulders and looped off to the emitter array. Kristian looked down at her, surprised by a feeling of sharp disappointment.

She had been romanticized by the media discussions and net reports. Kristian had expected her to look like the formal, touched-up sort of photos the reporters used, mostly showing her at the piano, her plump figure draped in evening attire. Gazing at her now, Kristian couldn't help thinking how distressingly plain she was. She had a high, rather lumpy forehead, almost nonexistent eyebrows, a thick nose, thin lips. She had been twenty-four at the time of Insertion. She was twenty-five now. Young, brilliant, much-mourned scholar. The lost girl.

The technician stepped behind the emitter array and did something with the dials. Kristian bent closer to the bed, searching for some sign of life. Even her chest barely seemed to move, only an infinitesimal rise and fall as she breathed. *Where are you, Frederica?*

The technician, a physician's assistant from the Insertion Clinic in Chicago, grimaced at him across the jumble of machinery. "She won't know you're there, I'm afraid. There's been nothing since the beginning. We lost her the very first day."

"How did you know?"

The PA nodded to the bank of machinery filling one entire wall. The Mediterranean sun glinted on its dials and silver flatscreens. "You know how the Insertion process works?"

"Brain-wave mapping, as I understand it. Codify the consciousness."

"Right. And copy it into the temporal coordinates you want. Those screens are blank because hers disappeared."

"What disappeared?"

"Her consciousness. The chart of her brain waves. The doctors have tried everything, but they can't find it. Can't get it back."

Kristian stared down at the unprepossessing form of Frederica Daniels. Other than the shallow rise and fall of her bosom, she lay utterly, absolutely still upon the hospital bed. Tubes ran from her nose, from her mouth, from the veins in her hands.

The PA went on talking, outlining the prep process, but Kristian tuned him out. He had reviewed it exhaustively on the plane to Pisa.

It could have been himself lying there on the bed. The approval of Frederica Daniels's application to be Inserted meant the denial of Kristian's. Too expensive, the Insertion Clinic said, to fund two musicologists. Kristian's credentials were solid, but Frederica's were blazingly impressive, even without her family connections. She had earned her bachelor's at eighteen, her master's at twenty. Her DMA was pending the very research that had placed her on this bed.

Frederica Daniels had been destined for high scholarship from childhood. She was the only child in a family that boasted more than one well-known musician and academic. Her elite schools had groomed her in every way to become the most impressive Brahms scholar of several generations.

Kristian Nordberg's background could hardly have been more different from Frederica's. Born to working-class parents who would never understand his obsession with a composer dead more than two hundred years, Kristian had worked and struggled his way through school. Frederica and Kristian had both set their sights on the answer to one small question of performance practice, but in the end, it was to have been Frederica who would solve the puzzle. Her dissertation was to have preceded his own, making his work redundant. He had been struggling with acceptance of that when word came that things had gone awry with her Insertion.

It wasn't that the Insertion Clinic cared about what Brahms meant by *p dolce*, of course. What they cared about was adding another scholar's research to their already impressive list. Having an obscure musicological puzzle solved increased their credibility with their donors, many of whom were art patrons as well as supporters of scientific innovation. But Kristian and Frederica, and performers and musicologists over the centuries, cared passionately about this small, obscure marking in Brahms's work. And Kristian understood why Frederica had won, and he had lost. He had read her master's thesis, but more importantly, he knew her background. He understood her connections.

But now, shockingly, everything had changed. Frederica lay like a corpse on the bed, and the Insertion clinicians had run out of ways to try to recover her. They had no option left but to call in Kristian, the runner-up, the second choice. This failure of Insertion had made headlines around the world in academic and in scientific circles. This failure had stopped their work dead. Kristian was their last hope of finding out what had gone wrong, and he had jumped at the chance.

Kristian kept his eyes closed for a long moment, fighting the vertiginous feeling that came with Insertion. He reminded himself, as he struggled against nausea, that it wasn't physical. Still, he felt rocked by it, as if he were upside down.

He gathered his resolve, swallowed, and opened his eyes.

He found himself standing in a dirt lane, just outside a rock-walled garden. A scrolled cast-iron gate stood slightly open. Climbing roses spilled over the crooked wall and twined through the gate's pattern. Everything seemed to glow with abnormally yellow sunshine, as if some sort of filter had been removed. The air looked so clean he could imagine it tingling in his lungs.

It's all real, he reminded himself. *It's completely real. I'm the only thing that's not.*

He was, of course, only an observer. He had been told it would be like watching television, seeing and hearing, but unable to touch, taste, or smell. In the actual event, Kristian found the analogy a poor one. The sensation of being present in 1861 Castagno, in the hills of Tuscany, was so vivid that he thought if he were to pinch himself, it would hurt. Ahead he saw the old stone houses, a dozen of them, named for the months of the year, crowding together over narrow cobbled streets. To his left, the lane fell away steeply down the hill to the valley. Three days before, in his own time, he had driven through that valley, past factories and gardens and shops. Now he saw nothing but open ground, scattered olive trees, the twisted balletic forms of grapevines.

The gate before him shone in the sun. He passed into the garden of the little villa, wishing he could feel the cushion of moss beneath his feet, the shade of the drooping Italian pine on his head. No television screen could so perfectly convey what this must be like, the air sweet with the scent of roses, their petals stirred by a light breeze coming down from the hills.

And then he heard it. It was the dark-light sound of a fortepiano—a real fortepiano, not a twenty-first-century imitation—coming from the villa. He took a deep breath—did his body, in its own time, take a deep breath?—and moved to the front door.

It seemed obtrusive, outrageous, to simply pass through the door and into the house, but of course he could not knock. Nor could he wait for the door to be opened. He must simply pass through, a ghost, a shade, an uninvited and unseen guest.

He stepped forward, or felt as if he did. Kristian Nordberg, or at least the essence of him, codified and measured and Inserted into another time, moved over the doorstep of Casa Agosto and went inside.

She saw him slip through the door, diffidently, a little guiltily, very much as she herself had done six months before. She saw him, and she trembled in her hiding place.

Frederica knew who Kristian Nordberg was. Her father had monitored the application process at the Insertion Clinic, had made calls to the president of the board and the director of the program. She knew all the five names on the short list, and she knew how close Kristian Nordberg had come to winning the grant. She had looked him up. His credentials impressed her, especially because he had been a scholarship student. He had earned a master's degree in piano performance from Julliard, and was already teaching at Oberlin.

It was his press photo that had made her heart sink. Kristian was a handsome man: blond, lean, and tall. Just the kind of man who would never give Frederica Daniels a second look.

She had known since early adolescence how plain she was, even ugly. After a brief bout with bulimia, which she found disgusting, she had given up on her figure, deciding that being slender would not help to make her pretty. She poured herself, instead, into her studies, delighting her parents and her teachers. The Insertion was to be the crowning achievement of an already stellar academic career. She would become the preeminent Brahms scholar in the world, would be invited to speak at conferences, offered chairs at universities, have her dissertation picked up by a national publisher. She, and she alone, would truly understand what the Master had meant by marking his scores *p dolce*.

Frederica had never planned to lose herself in the nineteenth century, nor had she intended to hurt anyone. She had intended merely to observe, as all the other Inserted subjects had done. She had intended to listen, and learn how the simple marking of *p dolce* was interpreted by the Master. Her offense was, she believed, one of impulse, of temptation too great to resist. And whether one judged it kindly or cruelly, she could not—she *would* not—retreat now. Frederica Daniels had never, in all her life, felt so happy.

She had no doubt Kristian had come looking for her. In truth, she had half expected this development, and had only wondered if she would recognize whomever they sent. No one had seen her own entrance, of course. She had spent her first hours flitting past the inhabitants of the villa like a curious spirit. She had known Johannes immediately, but it had taken a bit longer to puzzle out the cook's identity, and the gardener's, because her Italian was not so good as her German. Even her German was modern, and some days had passed before she felt confident of her nineteenth-century pronunciation. Still, disregarding the language difficulties, she had slipped into her hiding place by the end of that first afternoon.

Now she watched Kristian mimicking her own movements of that first day, passing through the sun-washed *salotto*, the high-ceilinged *cucina*, wandering upstairs to inspect the *camera da letto* with its shutters thrown wide to let in the summer breeze. She followed him there, watching as he peered from the window, glanced into the dressing room, ran a hand over the wide, plushly comforted bed.

Ah, the bed.

Even thinking of this morning gave her a shiver of ecstasy. It had been very early, before the cook had arrived, before even the sun had crept past the eastern hills. The memory made her long for the day to pass so that she could return there, could feel again the rush of his passion, the opening of herself, could give herself over to his unfettered desire.

Kristian turned abruptly from the bed, and stared at her in the doorway. He would think, of course, that she could not perceive him. She went to the bureau and took out a handkerchief, as if that was what she had come for. She heard a questioning chord on the fortepiano, heard his deep voice calling her name. She turned her back on Kristian and hurried downstairs, her silken skirts whispering over the dark wood. Johannes was waiting for her.

Kristian gazed at her in wonder. She had borne eight children, he knew, and was the veteran of hundreds of concert performances, a wonderful composer in her own right. How many times he had gazed at the old pictures, trying to imagine what she truly looked like, how she played, what charm she had that had drawn two of the nineteenth century's greatest composers to her side. And here she was.

She was as appealing as Frederica Daniels was plain. She had white skin, abundant dark hair caught up in some complicated arrangement, and dark eyes. The grief of her husband's recent death shadowed those eyes, but she was lovely nonetheless. Kristian followed her to the door of the bedroom and watched her graceful descent to the first floor. He had not expected her to be here. It was not in the histories, the diaries, the letters. How hard the two must have worked to keep this visit secret!

A voice called, "Clara! *Komm' mal her!*"

Kristian slipped down the stairs after her.

The scene in the sunny little salon was like something from a painting. The Master himself sat upon the bench of the fortepiano, and Clara settled herself beside him, her long-fingered hand caressing his sleeve, her cheek just touching his shoulder. He chuckled—a rich, contented sound—and moved a sheaf of paper closer to her. She bent forward to look at it, her hands automatically reaching for the keyboard. She began to pick out a chord progression, and then a fragment of melody. He shifted to his left, and she smiled up at him as she moved closer to the keyboard. A moment later the flowing sounds of a lied rolled from the instrument. Clara hummed the vocal line as she played, and the Master nodded, following her reading, smiling.

Kristian stared at them in awe, forgetting all about his mission for the moment. This was a historian's dream. He hardly breathed, striving to hear every detail, every nuance. There, did Clara stress that agogic accent? And there, did she slur the bass line more than later pianists thought was right? Of course, this little piece had no *p dolce* marking, he knew that, but still! The variations of dynamic, the stretching of the largo, the languid legato . . .

He brought himself up short. It was important to concentrate. For all he knew, Frederica had been lost through just such indulgence, forgetting who and what she was in the thrill of discovery. He must look for her, must look everywhere. The Clinic had promised him that if he was successful in bringing her back, he would have his own Insertion. The prize would be his, after all, if only he could find her.

He forced his eyes away from Johannes Brahms and Clara Schumann, and turned toward the little courtyard behind the villa.

The translational effects of the codification were supposed to make him able to perceive her. His mind would "see" her mind, would recognize her presence. The director had given him four hours. "No longer," he had said emphatically. "If we lose another one, the university will kill the program, and that would be a terrible waste."

Kristian had promised. Four hours.

With the music following him, he searched. She had to be within a one-hundred-yard radius of the Insertion locus. The codification began to fail if the traveler moved beyond that distance. Kristian was to examine the house, the garden, the courtyard, and the street adjacent to Casa Agosto. He could go no farther.

He looked in the courtyard, peering behind rose vines and under a splintered wooden table. He looked over the back gate, where the narrow street wound between the other eleven houses of Castagno. He sidled between the house and the stone fence, coming out again into the front garden. A gardener stooped over a bed of flowers, but Kristian saw no one else. He went back in the house, and found Clara and Johannes being served luncheon at the kitchen table. Except for the cook and the gardener, it seemed they had the villa to themselves.

He stood in the doorway and watched the two of them. An idyll, he thought. That's what this was. A tryst, which no one was ever to know about.

But Frederica had discovered it.

Where are you, Frederica? Where are you hiding?

The *vitello* was like butter upon her tongue, the *pomodori* and the mozzarella bursting with essences of sunshine and clean earth and fresh water. She closed her eyes, letting the flavors flood her mouth. Nothing in Chicago had ever tasted like this. Never in her life had she felt the way she did here: sensuous, satisfied, utterly alive. She couldn't be expected to return to the pallid sensations of a cold, worn-out world, not when there was this cornucopia of feeling and sound and taste!

No. Absolutely not. This Kristian would simply have to go back empty-handed and frustrated. And though Hannes was beginning to talk about returning to Vienna, Clara must not leave. She had letters from her children asking for her return, and it was unfortunate for them, perhaps. But they were not so young anymore, after all. And the concert dates . . . well, the agents could find other pianists. Clara could not leave Castagno. Frederica would not allow it.

Kristian followed Clara and Johannes back to the fortepiano, and lingered in a corner as they resumed playing. The Master had put aside the sheaf of lieder, and had brought out a thick manuscript. Kristian followed the German well enough to understand that it was the Quartet in A Major they were working on, though the niceties of discussion eluded him. There was, however, as he knew very well, that special marking at the end of one movement. *P dolce*, the Master had written. Kristian waited, hoping, willing them to reach it.

Literally, of course, *p dolce* meant "soft, sweet." But musicologists had argued for nearly two centuries about what Brahms meant in terms of true nineteenth-century performance practice. What made the passage "sweet"? Some asserted it was a question of tempo, of dragging just a bit. Others thought it had more to do with the way the keys were struck, or the way the *motif* was expressed. It was a small, much-debated detail, and the only way the true answer could come was through Insertion. Frederica had won, and then lost, the right to find it.

It was Kristian's turn. The alternate, the second-place winner. Here he was, and here was Brahms, with his collaborator. And it was coming, the passage he knew so well. He recognized the cadences leading to it, and he could picture the printed score in his mind, that enigmatic notation . . . they were almost there. . . .

❚❚

She felt his attention on them, and it washed over her, all at once, why he remained in the *salotto* when he should have been searching Casa Agosto high and low for her.

P dolce. He thought he would find out what it meant, and he would go back, even having failed to retrieve her, with the prize. *P dolce.*

No. She would not allow that, either. Why should he, who had everything else, have this? He had looks, and popularity, and friends. This was hers, and hers alone!

She seized Johannes's arm, lifting his hand from the keyboard just before he reached the passage. He turned to her in surprise, and she threw her arms around his neck and kissed him, deeply, tightly. Let Kristian watch this! Let him see for himself! The mysteries of Johannes—mind, body, soul, and music—were hers. She would give up none of them!

Hannes's breath quickened against hers, and his body stirred. She melded herself against him, feeling his heat, breathing in the scents of tobacco and wool and sweat. He chuckled against her hair, and whispered, *"Liebchen,"* before he swept her up in his arms and started for the staircase.

Though her head was already swimming with desire, she glanced over his shoulder, and saw Kristian in the very center of the room, staring after them, openmouthed. She buried her face in Hannes's lapel to hide the cat's smile that crept across her face.

❚❚

Kristian resumed his search. He looked in every corner, every closet, every nook and cranny of the villa. Suppose the translational effect didn't work? After all, it had never been tried before. Suppose she was here, but he couldn't perceive her—could she perceive him?

Frederica, Frederica. They want you back. Where are you?

He found nothing. He went outside again, moving carefully and cautiously past the garden, back into the street. He turned toward the other houses of Castagno and moved just a little farther. Almost immediately he felt the *shifting*, the slight dizziness, that meant he had reached the perimeter of the locus.

He stopped where he was, gazing back at Casa Agosto. His time was almost up. His heart pounded with frustration as he watched the house, as the sun sank behind the hills, the sky darkened into evening. And then, as shadows stretched around him, the curtains in the upstairs bedroom twitched.

Someone was at the window, looking down on the street. On him.

The next moment, Kristian was opening his eyes in the twenty-first century. His body lay surrounded by clinical equipment, and the physician's assistant bent over him, brow furrowed.

When Kristian stirred, the technician breathed a sigh, and straightened. Kristian struggled upright, and saw that the director was also present, a look of relief brightening his tired face.

"I'm glad you're here," Kristian said. "I want to try again."

They made him wait three days. He had to describe what he had seen and experienced over and over again, first to the director, and then to two clinicians, who compared his notes with those of the other six Insertion subjects. They nodded over his account of reaching the outer edge of the locus, and they frowned over his being unable to perceive the missing Frederica.

"Are you sure," he asked them, "that the translational effect works?"

"It has to," one of the clinicians told him. He was a thin, intense man in his sixties, whose entire life had been devoted to developing the Insertion process. "We were very careful to align your brain mapping with the previous subject's. Your codification includes key recognition triggers which should enable you to perceive her presence in the Insertion. We've checked and double-checked, run the simulation thirty times. You should perceive her easily."

"What if she's not there?"

The other clinician shook his head. "She couldn't leave. She would snap back here the moment she moved outside the perimeter of the locus."

"But where could she hide?"

The first clinician gave an expressive shrug.

Frederica was furious to see him return. He appeared in the *salotto* just as she and Hannes had begun work.

She had played the A Major Quartet before, of course, but Hannes didn't know that, and she took pleasure in his admiration of what he believed to be her sight-reading of the score. She was halfway through the opening movement of the A Major Quartet when Kristian showed up. He watched her from the doorway, a curious expression on his face. She missed a fingering, and had to stop. Anger made her cheeks burn, and she kept her eyes down so Hannes wouldn't see it.

"What's wrong, *Liebchen*?" he asked.

She shook her head. "Nothing, Hannes, nothing at all. It's brilliant." There was nothing she could do but ignore Kristian's presence. He had not detected her the last time, and she had no reason to think he would now. Still, she had hoped never to see him here again.

She turned back a page, and massaged her fingers for a moment. "I'll start again." She found a place to begin, and resumed playing, with Hannes frowning, nodding over something that pleased him, sometimes muttering to himself about the harmonies.

She pressed on, enjoying the feel of the real ivory beneath her fingertips, the easy flow of the notes. After a few minutes, she even began to enjoy having an audience, albeit an uninvited one. She kept her eyes fixed on the score, though she knew it by heart, had played it from memory many times. Once she had made the mistake of playing a later version of one of Hannes's pieces, startling him with the improvements she added on what he thought to be a first reading. Since then, she had been careful to play what was on the page before her.

It was when she reached the scherzo that she realized Kristian was behind her, looking over her shoulder at the score, at her hands upon the keyboard, at the Master listening to his creation being played for the first time. At the end of the finale would come that enigmatic marking. *P dolce.*

She knew now what Hannes meant by it. She had heard it under his own competent although undistinguished hands, and then under Clara's brilliant ones. She understood it now, though she would never write that dissertation.

Still, she would not—*could* not—let this interloper steal it away from her! Even thinking about Kristian Nordberg completing his dissertation on the dynamic markings of Brahms before she could finish hers—whether she meant to finish it or not—renewed her fury, made her pulse thrum in her throat, her cheeks flame.

She had felt just such fury when Clara Schumann had tried to banish her from her mind.

It was the music that had made it possible for her to slip inside Clara's consciousness. Clara—poor, pretty Clara—knew nothing of brain mapping or codification, or of Insertion. Even the Insertion people had never realized how thoroughly she, Frederica, understood the process. She had quite deliberately hidden that from them, some instinct driving her.

Clara had been playing *"Wiegenlied,"* singing softly, with the Master standing beside the open window, listening to his fragile, perfect lullaby. Frederica had been floating through the rooms, imagining what it must be like to feel the linen of the curtains, to taste the fresh ravioli being rolled out in the kitchen. Clara had been lost in the music, and Frederica, without forethought, without really meaning to, simply . . . *inserted* herself. It had been an instinctive, almost childlike action. She wanted to be there, wanted to be in Clara's mind, in Clara's lovely body, to feel what she felt, to know what it was like. . . .

At first Clara had not known she was there. She had gone on playing, and then risen to go to her lunch with Hannes. Frederica, through Clara's senses, savored the richness of the ravioli, delighted in the brush of silk and fine lawn against Clara's skin, reveled in the maleness of Hannes's scent, the tinge of cigar smoke and bay rum. The two of them had strolled in the garden, and then had decided to walk down through the little town's steep streets. They moved out through the gate, and into the lane, but as they turned toward the other eleven houses of Castagno, Frederica felt that sudden vertigo, the wrenching sensation of being upside down or sideways or—

She couldn't let it happen. If Clara moved beyond the locus, she would be cast out, and if she did not withdraw, she would be snapped back to the clinic, that cold white bed strung with wires and dials.

Energized by fury, she had gripped Clara's mind with her own, her greater intellect as sharp as cat's claws over the other woman's unsuspecting consciousness. She had been aware, dimly, of the spasm of anguish that had shot through Clara Schumann. More immediately, she knew that Clara had stopped dead in her tracks, clutching her temples, crying out as if something had struck her.

Hannes, solicitous as always, had scooped her up in his strong arms and carried her back inside Casa Agosto and up the stairs to the bedroom. He laid her upon the bed, and lay down beside her to comfort her in what he took to be a sudden migraine. Frederica, drunken with power, with opportunity, clung to him, first as if in pain, and then with increasing passion. They made love in the hot Italian afternoon, as the birds sang in the olive trees, and Frederica, even at the moment of ecstasy, her first glorious understanding of physical passion, never loosened her hold on Clara's mind.

It had become habit now, something as automatic as playing two-handed scales. At first Clara had cried out for release, for freedom, but over the intervening months, her struggles had grown weaker and weaker, until at last they faded away altogether. In all that time, she had never once left the garden of Casa Agosto. Occasionally, Hannes was compelled to go back to Vienna for some engagement or other, but Clara cancelled every commitment she had, and stayed in Castagno. When Hannes quizzed her, she pled the need to rest, the need for solitude. She wrote to her children, assuring them she was recuperating from a mild but persistent illness, and that she would return in due course. She wrote to her agents and assured them she could not possibly concertize until she was well again. She spent her days in reading, playing, strolling in the little garden. She spent her nights in passion. Frederica came, almost, to believe that she *was* Clara Schumann. Even her playing had improved, amplified by Clara's gifts, and by the sensual atmosphere of Casa Agosto.

And then Kristian Nordberg appeared.

She stumbled a little in the *allegretto*, recovered herself. She turned the page, and saw that it was there, above the final staff, that marking that meant "soft, sweet," but also meant something else. Something Kristian wanted to understand.

Abruptly, she lifted her hands from the keys.

Had Kristian had the use of his voice at the moment Clara Schumann stopped playing, he would have cried out. She had been at the very point of showing him, of solving the problem of his research! It was as if she knew just what he wanted to hear, as if she deliberately stopped short of the *p dolce* marking so he would not learn what the Master meant by it! As if—

Kristian's mind rocked with the implication. He moved back, away from the pair at the piano, and stared at their backs. Surely she could not be— surely it was not possible—

But she turned at that moment, her great dark eyes wide, her full lips curving. And he knew. He couldn't understand how, not yet, but he knew. Frederica Daniels was *in* Clara Schumann. She had, bizarrely, possessed her.

The immorality of it, the unfairness, the complete and utter selfishness of such a thing rendered him, for the moment, incapable of thought. He stared at her, and she stared back, and he understood that she perceived him perfectly. She knew he was there, and she had no intention of giving him what he wanted.

Brahms turned to her, murmuring a query. Clara—Frederica— responded with a slight shake of her head, a gentle touch of her hand to her brow. Moments later, the Master was solicitously helping the traitoress up the stairs to rest. Kristian hovered where he was, powerless to intervene.

At first the director wouldn't believe him. He explained, again and again, that she had stopped short of playing the *p dolce* section twice, that there was no doubt in his mind it was deliberate, that she had looked directly at him, out of Clara's eyes. "She saw me," he said. "She knew I was there."

"But she couldn't—there is no way for one person to—"

Kristian made an irritated noise. "Of course she could!" he snapped, frustration making him impatient. "She *inserted* herself, don't you see?"

The director shook his head. It was the technician who said, softly, "The codification makes it possible. We made it easy for her."

Kristian nodded to him. "Of course. The question is, what do we do about it?"

"If we pull the plug, she'll die."

"Her body will die," Kristian said. "Who knows what will happen to her consciousness? She's perfectly comfortable in someone else's body."

"Perhaps we have to leave her there, then," the director said glumly. "If she dies, her father will dismantle the whole program. He has the connections to do it."

"We can't leave her!" Kristian protested. "She's taken over someone else's life!" Someone beautiful and fragile, he thought, though he didn't say so. Someone who had suffered enough already.

"This isn't supposed to be possible," the director said. "Changing the past . . ."

"We don't know if she's changed anything," Kristian said. "There's no record of Clara Schumann joining Brahms in Castagno that summer of 1861, but that doesn't mean it didn't happen."

"I just don't know what to do."

"Well, I do," Kristian said, standing, moving back to the hospital bed to look down on Frederica Daniels's still form. "I'm going back again."

She saw him the moment he returned. It was an odd sensation, a *seeing* not with the eyes, but with her consciousness. She knew that was true, and yet the impression of perceiving Kristian through the usual conduit of retina, ganglia, and optic nerves was unshakeable. He simply was there, all at once, and his physical image—projected, she imagined, by his own consciousness—was clear and consistent.

He knew. She could see that he knew.

She smiled at him, and lifted her head in the way she knew set off her creamy neck, the roundness of her chin. She touched her abundant hair, and let her fingers trail down her cheek.

Kristian's eyes hardened at her teasing. He gazed at her, his mouth set, his shoulders stiff with anger. She didn't care. There was nothing he could do. She was in complete control, and had even begun to suspect Clara was gone, vanished, vanquished.

She had been about to take up the sonata once again, but now she set it aside. Hannes had gone out for a walk, and would be back soon. She rose, turning her back on the presence of Kristian Nordberg, and went out to the kitchen to order a pot of tea. As the cook set the kettle to boil, she gazed dreamily out the window. The olive blossoms had begun to drift to the ground, and the fruit was beginning to set. The pastel houses, tumbling across the little hillside in their charming fashion, glowed gently in the afternoon sunshine. Frederica savored every sensual detail. Surely, there was no more beautiful place in the world than this, not even in Vienna.

She smiled to herself at the stir in her loins, and leaned forward to watch Hannes climb back up the steep street.

It was surprisingly, disturbingly easy, Kristian found. All the study of processes, all the diagrams and formulas and programming language came to his aid. Brahms stepped in through the arched doorway, and Kristian— smoothly, without hesitating—*inserted* his own consciousness into the Master's. It was like beginning a new piece of music, but one so similar to others that the fingerings came naturally, that he could anticipate the harmonic structure, the tempo and dynamic changes. It was, oddly, like putting his hand into a glove, like slipping his feet into comfortable boots. He was inside the other's mind and body, so thoroughly integrated that he trembled with the Master's shock at his presence.

But compunction was a feeling he couldn't afford, not at this moment.

He tried to transmit a sense of calm, of reassurance. It was difficult. He had to concentrate on the sensation of walking, of turning, of speaking. He said Clara's name, and she turned to him, embraced him, pressed her lips to his. He tried to respond naturally. If she guessed . . . if she knew what he had done . . . it would never work.

He didn't dare speak to her in his modern-day German. After the briefest hesitation, he decided to chance Italian. "*Si fa una piccola passeggiata, carissima?*" he whispered into her cloud of hair.

She giggled, and pulled away to admonish him with one white finger. In her perfect nineteenth-century German, she said, "I will walk with you a moment in the garden, Hannes. But the tea is almost ready."

He circled her waist with his arm, and turned toward the door, keeping his eyes averted. Surely, he thought, if she were to look into his eyes, she would perceive him there. Her body was pliant beside him as they stepped out into the shade of the olive trees. The grass was soft beneath their feet, the sun warm on their uncovered heads. Clara's skirts brushed Brahms's leg, a feeling almost more intimate than the touch of her lips. Kristian took a deep breath, and was surprised to find that he could smell the fresh air, the trees, the trailing roses that climbed the stone wall. His hand tingled with the warmth of Clara's body, and he realized he was hearing things with physical ears, the clink of the gardener's spade against a stone, the humming of the cook as she moved about the kitchen—Rossini, that was, *L'Italiana*. He would have to think about this later, about the sharp difference between physical perception and that which was purely mental. But now—now he must concentrate on Frederica.

They completed a circuit of the house, stepping around a little pile of bruised and faded olive blossoms the gardener had raked up. They reached the gate, and Frederica turned back, to go inside.

Kristian seized her arm with his hand—with Brahms's hand—and caught her back.

She turned, eyes suddenly wide. "Hannes?" she breathed.

He opened the gate with his other hand, and pulled her toward it.

"Hannes!" she cried.

He tightened his grip, knowing the fragile white skin would be bruised, unable to prevent it. He kept his eyes on the street, on the gate, anywhere but on her face.

"What are you doing? *Nein, Liebchen, nein!*"

She struggled, and Kristian had to take hold of her with both hands, and drag her, stumbling, resisting, out through the gate.

With a tremendous effort, she pulled back. The delicate hand-stitching of her lawn dress tore at the shoulders. She whirled, and tried to go back inside the garden.

Kristian grunted "Goddammit" under his breath. He seized her by the waist, and yanked her roughly backward. He had never, in all his life, behaved so violently.

And now she understood. She turned to him, her pupils wide with shock and fear. "Oh, no," she moaned.

"Yes!" he said firmly. "Let her go, Frederica. Let Clara go."

"No," she pleaded, "please, no. You don't understand! I—"

He picked her right off her feet, and took two steps out into the lane. The moment he reached the perimeter of the locus he began to feel the blurring of his consciousness. He took another step, wishing there were another way, wishing he could take the time to explore Brahms's mind. Learn about *p dolce* . . .

P dolce—the meaning was there, in the Master's mind. If only he could hold on to it. . . .

Another step, and Kristian's head began to spin. The woman in his arms kicked and screamed, but with every step he took, her cries grew fainter, her struggles weaker.

Kristian grew weaker, too. His hands slipped on her body, his grip loosening as the Insertion failed. He stumbled forward, one more shaky step. He had to drag her far enough outside the locus, but his hands were nerveless, and his feet could no longer feel the ground.

His vision faded, and the world turned upside down.

Kristian opened his eyes to the white walls and gleaming steel and chrome of the clinic. He drew a ragged breath and turned his head to look at the other bed, where Frederica lay. The director and the technicians were gathered around her, staring at the monitors. The physician's assistant had his fingers on her wrist, and a technician was hurriedly injecting something into the Y-port of her IV. The monitors were alive with movement, lines and waves dancing across the screens.

"She's back?" Kristian croaked.

The director turned to him. He nodded, but his face was drawn. "She's back. But she's not waking up."

One of the technicians came to help Kristian untangle himself from the wires and cords, remove the sensor cap, slip off the pressure cuff, and detach the heart monitor. Kristian coughed, and reached for a glass of water. He cleared his throat, and started to stand, but the dizziness of transition overwhelmed him. He sank back again, and the technician put a hand on his shoulder. "Wait," he told Kristian. "Give it a minute."

Kristian sat and stared across the room at Frederica Daniels. She was back, and yet she wasn't. She lay still except for the slight rise and fall of her chest. Not even her eyelids moved.

"Will she be all right?" he asked quietly.

"We don't know." The technician shook his head. "There's no reason she shouldn't. Her codification is intact. Her screens came alive at the same moment you woke up."

Kristian watched Frederica for a long time, and wondered.

Discover magazine's reporter came to interview Kristian the day after he defended his dissertation. It took Kristian some time to tell his story. He tried to explain what Insertion felt like, though he warned the reporter that it was hard to put into words. He described what Brahms looked like, what Casa Agosto looked like, what Castagno of 1861 looked like. He spoke guardedly, having promised the director, of finding the "lost" girl and bringing her back. He left out Frederica's possession of Clara Schumann, and his own of Johannes Brahms.

"But if you brought her back—then why won't she wake up?"

"I don't know. None of us understands it."

"Then how do you know you *did* bring her back? Perhaps her consciousness is still in the nineteenth century."

Kristian only shrugged. He did know, because in 1862, Clara Schumann had resumed concertizing after a six-month hiatus. But he couldn't explain that without revealing what had really happened.

"Tell me why you did this, Dr. Nordberg. Why risk Insertion, especially after what happened to Miss Daniels?"

"I wanted an answer to an old question of performance practice. Brahms sometimes wrote *p dolce* on his scores, but he never explained exactly what it meant. It was essential to my dissertation."

He didn't say that Frederica had wanted the same thing, but that now it appeared she would never write her dissertation. Only he and the director knew that Frederica had done her damnedest to keep Kristian from writing his.

The reporter smiled. "Ah. You must have learned what you needed to know."

Kristian leaned back in his chair, in his comfortable office in the music department, where he had just been offered the Llewellyn Chair for Musicology. "I did," he said. "Indeed I did. I learned it from the Master himself."

JESUS CHRIST, REANIMATOR

Ken MacLeod

Ken MacLeod has been a force in British hard SF and space opera since he burst on the scene in 1995 with The Star Fraction. *A recipient of several awards, and a nominee for many more, his work is always smart in tone, broad in scope, deep in theme. I have wanted to work with Ken for some time, but the timing hasn't been right before now. I love the tale that follows and the truth that resonates in its subtle message.*

The Second Coming was something of a washout, if you remember. It lit up early-warning radar like a Christmas tree, of course, and the Israeli Air Force gave the heavenly host a respectable F-16 fighter escort to the ground, but that was when they were still treating it as a UFO incident. As soon as their sandals touched the dust, Jesus and the handful of bewildered Copts who'd been caught up to meet him in the air looked about for the armies of the Beast and the kings of the earth. The only soldiers they could see were a few terrified guards on a nearby archaeological dig. The armies of the Lord hurled themselves at the IDF and were promptly slaughtered. Their miraculous healings and resurrections created something of a sensation, but after that it was detention and Shin Bet interrogation for the lot of them. The skirmish was caught on video by activists from the International Solidarity Movement, who happened to be driving past the ancient battlefield on their way to Jenin when the trouble started. Jesus was released a couple of months after the Megiddo debacle, but most of the Rapture contingent had Egyptian ID, and the diplomacy was as slow as you'd expect.

Jesus returned to his old stomping ground in the vicinity of Galilee. He hung around a lot with Israeli Arabs, and sometimes crossed to the West Bank. Reports trickled out of a healing here, a near-riot there, an open-air speech somewhere else. At first the IDF and the PA cops gave him a rough time, but there wasn't much they could pin on him. It's been said he avoided politics, but a closer reading of his talks suggests a subtle strategy of working on his listeners' minds, chipping away at assumptions, and leaving them to work out the political implications for themselves. The theological aspects of his teaching were hard to square with those previously attributed to him. Critics were quick to point out the discrepancies, and to ridicule his failure to fulfill the more apocalyptic aspects of the prophecies.

When I caught up with him, under the grubby off-season awnings of a Tiberias lakefront cafe, Jesus was philosophical about it.

"There's only so much information you can pack into a first-century Palestinian brain," he explained, one thumb in a volume of Dennett. "Or a twenty-first-century one, come to that."

I sipped thick sweet coffee and checked the little camera for sound and image. "Aren't you, ah, omniscient?"

He glowered a little. "What part of 'truly man' don't you people understand?" (He'd been using the cafe's Internet facilities a lot, I'd gathered. His blog comments section had to be seen to be believed.) "It's not rocket science . . . to mention just one discipline I didn't have a clue about. I could add relativity, quantum mechanics, geology, zoology. Geography, even." He spread his big hands, with their carpenter's calluses and their old scars. "Look, I really expected to return very soon, and that everyone on Earth would see me when I did. I didn't even know the world was a sphere—sure, I could have picked that up from the Greeks, if I'd asked around in Decapolis, but I had other fish to fry."

"But *you're*"—I fought the rising pitch—"the Creator, begotten, not made, wholly God as well as—"

"Yes, yes," he said. He mugged an aside to the camera. "This stuff would try the patience of a saint, you know." Then he looked me in the eye. "I am the embodiment of the Logos, the very logic of creation, or as it was said in English, 'the Word made flesh.' Just because I *am* in that sense the entirety of the laws of nature doesn't mean I *know* all of them, or can override any of them. Quite the reverse, in fact."

"But the miracles—the healings and resurrections—"

"You have to allow for some . . . pardonable exaggeration in the reports."

"I've seen the ISM video from Megiddo," I said.

"Good for you," he said. "I'd love to see it myself, but the IDF confiscated it in minutes. But then, you probably bribed someone, and that's . . . not something I can do. Yes, I can resurrect the recent dead, patch bodies back together and so on. Heal injuries and cure illnesses, some of them not purely psychosomatic. Don't ask me to explain how." He waved a hand. "I suspect some kind of quantum hand-wave at the bottom of it."

"But the Rapture! The Second Coming!"

"I can levitate." He shrugged. "So? I was considerably more impressed to discover that you people can *fly*. In metal machines!"

"Isn't levitation miraculous?"

"It doesn't break any laws of nature, I'll tell you that for nothing. If I can do it, it must be a human capability."

"You mean any human being could levitate?"

"There are recorded instances. Some of them quite well attested, I understand. Even the Catholic Church admits them."

"You could teach people to do it?"

"I suppose I could. But what would be the point? As I said, you can fly already, for all the good that does you." As if by coincidence, a couple of jet fighters broke the sound barrier over the Golan Heights, making the cups rattle. "Same thing with healing, resurrections of the recent dead, and so on. I can do better in individual cases, but in general your health services are doing better than I could. I have better things to do with my time."

"Before we get to that," I said, "there's just one thing I'd like you to clear up. For the viewers, you understand. Are you telling us that after a certain length of time has passed, the dead can't be resurrected?"

"Not at all." He signaled for another pot of coffee. "With God, all things are possible. To put it in your terms, information is conserved. To put it in my terms, we're all remembered in the mind of God. No doubt all human minds and bodies will be reconstituted at some point. As for when—God knows. I don't. I told you this the first time."

"And heaven and hell, the afterlife?"

"Heaven—like I said, the mind of God. It's up in the sky, in a very literal sense." He fumbled in a book-bag under the table and retrieved a dog-eared Tipler. "If this book is anything to go by . . . I'm not saying you should take *The Physics of Immortality* as gospel, you understand, but it certainly helped *me* get my head around some of the concepts. As for hell . . ." He leaned forward, looking stern. "Look, suppose I tell you: if you keep doing bad things, if you keep refusing to adjust your thoughts and actions to reality, you'll *end up in a very bad place*. You'll *find yourself in deep shit*. Who could argue? Not one moral teacher or philosopher, that's for sure. If you won't listen to me, listen to them." He chuckled darkly. "Of course, it's far more interesting to write volumes of Italian poetry speculating on the exact depth and temperature of the shit, but that's just you."

"What about your distinctive ethical teaching?"

He rolled his eyes heavenward. "*What* distinctive ethical teaching? You'll find almost all of it in the rabbis, the prophets, and the good pagans. I didn't come to teach new morals, but to make people take seriously the morals they had. For some of the quirky bits—no divorce, and eunuchs for the Kingdom and so forth—I refer to my cultural limitations or some information loss in transmission or translation."

I'd already seen the interrogation transcript, and the blog, but I had to ask.

"Could you explain, briefly, the reason for the delay in your return?"

"Where I've been all this time?"

I nodded, a little uneasy. This was the big one, the one where even those who believed him could trip up.

"I was on another planet," he said, flat out. "Where else could I have been? I ascended into heaven, sure. I went up into the sky. Like I said, levitation isn't that big a deal. Gravity's a weak force, not well understood, and can be manipulated mentally if you know how. Surviving in the upper atmosphere, not to mention a raw vacuum, wearing nothing but a jelebah—now *that's* difficult. As soon as I got behind that cloud I was picked up by an alien space ship that happened to be passing—you can call it coincidence, I still call it providence—and transported to its home planet. I'm not at liberty to say which, but—assume you can't go faster than light, think in terms of a two-way trip and a bit of turnaround time, and, well—you do the math."

"Some people," I said, trying to be tactful, "find that hard to believe."

"Tell me about it," he said. "They'll accept levitation and resurrection, but I mention an extrasolar civilization and I'm suddenly a fraud and a New Age guru and a flying saucer nut. Talk about straining at gnats and swallowing camels." He shrugged again, this time wincing slightly, as if there was a painful stiffness in one shoulder. "It's a cross I have to bear, I guess."

What I was thinking, completely irreverently and inappropriately, was the line *you jammy bastard!* from the scene in *Life of Brian*. I'd stumbled at this point, like so many others. It was all too Douglas Adams, too von Däniken, too much a shaggy god story. Just about the only people who'd swallowed it so far were a few Mormons, and even they were uncomfortable with his insistence that he really hadn't stopped off in America.

We talked some more; I thanked him and shook hands and headed back to Lod airport with the interview in the can. When I glanced back from the corner, Jesus was well into a bottle of wine and deep conversation with a couple of off-duty border cops and an Arab-Israeli tart.

I couldn't pitch the interview as it stood—there was nothing new in it, and I needed an angle. I settled on follow-up research, with scientists as well as theologians, and managed to pull together an interdisciplinary meeting in Imperial College, London, held under Chatham House rules—quotes on the record, but no direct attributions. The consensus was startling. Not one of the clergy, and only one of the physicists, thought it at all probable that we were looking at a return of the original Jesus. They all went for the shaggy god story.

"He's a Moravec bush robot," an Anglican bishop told me, confidently and in confidence.

"A what?" I said.

He sketched what looked like a tree, walking. "The manipulative extremities keep subdividing, right down to the molecular level," he said. "That thing can handle individual atoms. It can look like anything it wants, walk through walls, turn water into wine. Healing and resurrection—provided decay hasn't degraded the memory structures too far—is a doddle."

"And can it make Egyptian Christians float into the sky?" I asked.

He pressed the tips of his fingers together. "How do we know that *really* happened? His little band of brothers could be—more bush robots!"

"That's a stretch," said the Cambridge cosmologist. "I'm more inclined to suspect gravity manipulation from a stealth orbiter."

"You mean the ship's still up there?" That was the Jesuit, skeptical as usual.

"Of course," said the cosmologist. "We're looking at an attempt to open a conversation, an alien contact, without causing mass panic. Culturally speaking, it's either very clever, or catastrophically inept."

"I'd go for the latter," said the Oxford biologist. "Frankly, I'm disappointed. Regardless of good intentions, this approach can only reinforce religious memes." He glanced around, looking beleaguered ("like a hunted animal," one of the more vindictive of the clergymen chuckled afterwards, in the pub). "No offense intended, gentlemen, ladies, but I see that as counterproductive. In that part of the world, too! As if it *needed* more fanaticism."

"Excuse me," said the bishop stiffly, "but we're not talking about fanaticism. Nor is he. He is certainly not *preaching* fanaticism. Personally, I'd almost prefer to believe he *was* the original Jesus come back. It would be quite a vindication, in a way. It would certainly make the African brethren sit up and take notice."

"You mean, shut up about gay clergy," said the Jesuit, rather unkindly.

"You see?" said the Oxford man, looking at me. "It doesn't matter how liberal he sounds, or how any of them sound. It's all about authoritative revelation. And as soon as they start arguing on that basis, they're at each other's throats." He sighed, pushing biscuit crumbs about on the baize with a fingertip. "My own fear is that the aliens, whoever they are, are right. We're too primitive a species, too *mired* in all this, too infected by the mind virus of religion, to be approached in any other way. But I'm still afraid it'll backfire on them."

"Oh, there are worse fears than that," said the computer scientist from Imperial, cheerfully. "They could be hostile. They could be intentionally aiming to cause religious strife."

That statement didn't cause religious strife, exactly, but it came damn close. I waited until the dust and feathers had settled, then tried to get the experts to focus on what they all actually agreed on. As I said, the consensus surprised me. It added up to this:

The supposed Second Coming had no religious significance. The man calling himself Jesus was almost certainly not who he claimed to be. He was very likely an AI entity of some type from a post-Singularity alien civilization. Further interventions could be expected. Watch the skies.

I wrapped all this around the interview, ran a few talking-head sound bites from the meeting through voice-and-face-distorting software filters, and flogged it to the Discovery Channel. This took a couple of weeks. Then I caught the next El Al flight from Heathrow.

I was sitting in a room with a dozen men, one of them Jesus, all sipping tea and talking. All of them were smoking, except Jesus and myself. I'd caught up with him again in Ramallah. The conversation was in Arabic, and my translator, Sameh, was so engrossed in it he'd forgotten about me. I must admit I was bored.

I was, of course, excited at the idea that this man, if he was a man, represented an alien intervention. I was just as excited by my doubts about it. There was, as the bishop had implied, something quite tempting about the notion that he was who he said he was. The original Jesus had explained himself in terms of the religion of his place and time, and had in turn been explained in terms of contemporary philosophy. It begins in the arcane metaphysics of Paul's letters, and in the Stoic term "Logos" in John, and it continues all the way to the baroque Platonic and Aristotelian edifices of theology. So it was perhaps not entirely strange that *this* Jesus should explain himself in modern philosophical terms from the very beginning.

Right now, though, he was trying to explain himself to Muslims. The going wasn't easy. I couldn't follow the conversation, but I could hear the strain in the voices. The names of Allah and the Prophet came up frequently. For Muslims, Jesus is a prophet too, and there were plenty of the faithful who didn't take kindly to this man's claims. The gathering here, fraught though it was, was the most sympathetic a hearing as he was likely to get.

In terms of publicity Jesus wasn't doing too well. He'd had his fifteen minutes of fame. Religious leaders had refused to meet him—not that he'd asked—and even the scientists who were prepared to speculate publicly that he was an alien were reluctant to do anything about it. I mean, what could they do about it—cut him up? The defense establishment may have taken seriously these scientists' claims about alien intervention, but there's only so many times you can draw a blank looking for a stealth orbiter before you conclude that there's *no* stealth orbiter. The general feeling was that something odd had happened, but nobody could be sure what, and for all anyone knew it could have been a bizarre hoax. There were photographs, videos, eyewitness accounts, radar traces—but that kind of evidence can be found any month in *Fortean Times* and debunked every quarter in *Skeptical Inquirer*.

The only people—apart from his own small following, most of it online—who paid close attention to his activities were fundamentalist Christians. Not because they believed him. Oh, no. They believed *me*. That's to say, they believed the religious and scientific experts I'd cited in the documentary. They were quite happy with the notion that he was an alien entity of some kind. To them, an alien meant a demon. Worse, a demon walking around in human shape and claiming to be Jesus could only mean one thing: the Antichrist.

I only found that out later.

Handshakes all round. Smiles. Frowns. Jesus and two of the men—followers, I'd gathered—went out. I and Sameh accompanied them into the muddy street. Breezeblock buildings, corrugated zinc roofs, mud. Ruins here and there. It was nearly dusk. Lights in windows, braziers at stalls, the smell of frying chicken. A big Honda people-carrier drove slowly down the crowded, potholed street, conspicuous among old Renaults and VW Polos and Yugos.

We stood about—a moment of uncertainty about where to go next. Some problem with the traffic. Sameh was talking to the followers, Jesus was gazing around, and I was fiddling with the camera.

I saw a flash. That is to say, for a second I saw nothing else. Then I saw nothing but sky. Everything had become silent. I saw two bright lights moving fast, high above. My legs felt wet and warm. I pressed the palms of my hands on damp gravel and pushed myself up to a sitting position. I could see people running around, mouths open, mouths working; cars accelerating away or coming to a halt; everything covered with gray dust; but I could hear nothing. A little way down the street, smoke rose from a flowerlike abstract sculpture of bent and twisted metal: the Honda, its wheels incongruously intact.

I saw Jesus run towards it. Sameh and the two followers were facedown on the street, hands over the backs of their heads. They didn't see what I saw. I don't know how many people saw it. He leaned into the wrecked Honda and started hauling out the casualties. He dragged out one corpse, whole but charred. He laid it down and pulled out something that might have been a torso. Then he clambered in and started heaving out bits of bodies: an arm, half a leg, a bearded head. More. It was like the back of a butcher's shop.

He vaulted out again and knelt on the road. I saw his hands move, with effort in the arms, as if he was putting the bits together. He stood up. Three men stood up beside him. They looked down at the rags that clothed them, and then at the wreck of their vehicle. They raised their arms and cried out praise to Allah. Jesus had already turned his back on them and was hurrying towards me. He wore jeans and scuffed trainers, a shirt and sweater under a new leather jacket. He was looking straight at me and frowning.

Sound and pain came in a rush. My ears dinned with yells, car horns, screams. My thighs felt—

I looked down. My thighs felt exactly as you would expect with a chunk of metal like a thrown knife in each of them, stuck right into my femurs. I could see my blood pumping out, soaking into the torn cloth. Everything went monochrome for a moment. I saw his hands grab the bits of metal and tug. I heard the grate of the bones. I felt it, too. I heard a double clatter as the metal shards fell on the road. Then Jesus laid his hands on my legs, and leaned back.

"Up," he said.

He held out a hand. I caught it and stood up. As I got to my feet I saw the pale unbroken skin of my thighs through the ripped fabric. My camera lay crushed on the ground. Sameh and the two followers picked themselves up and brushed themselves off.

"What happened?" I asked Jesus, but it was Sameh who answered.

"Another targeted killing," he said. "That Honda. I knew it had to be a Hamas big shot inside." He stared across at the wreck. "How many?"

I pointed at the men, now the center of a small crowd.

"None."

"None?"

"They had a miraculous escape," I said.

Jesus just grinned.

"Let's go," he said.

We departed.

Jesus had a knack for making his movements unpredictable. I and Sameh stayed with him and his followers, jammed in the back of a taxi, to Jerusalem. Through the wall, through the checkpoints. Jesus nodded off. The followers talked to Sameh. I sat bolt upright and replayed everything in my mind. I kept rubbing my thighs, as if I had sweaty hands. When we got out of the taxi at the hotel Jesus seemed to wake up. He leaned forward and said, "Would you like to meet me tomorrow, privately?"

"Yes," I said. "Where?"

"You know where the tours of the Via Dolorosa start?"

I nodded.

"There," he said. "Alone."

I was still struggling for a remark when the taxi door slammed.

❚❚

I pushed past guides and through coach parties, looking for him. He found
me. He had a camera hung from around his neck and a big hat on his head,
a white T-shirt under his jacket. We fell in at the back of a dozen or so people
following a guide who shouted in English. I think they were Brits. Jesus rub-
bernecked with the rest of them.

"I saw the Gibson film on DVD," he said.

"What did you think of it?" I asked, feeling a little smug.

"I liked it better than yours," he said.

"I just report," I said.

"You could have done better," he said. "'Moravec bush robot!' I ask you."

"I'm sorry," I said. "Do you deny it?"

He looked at me sharply. "Of course I deny it. What use would a robot
be to you?"

"And the whole alien intervention hypothesis?"

The crowd stopped. The guide declaimed. Cameras clicked. We shuffled
off again, jostling down an alley.

"Yes, I deny that also."

"And any other natural explanation?"

His lips compressed. He shook his head. "If you mean a hoax, I deny that
too. I am who I say I am. I *am* the natural explanation."

The man in front of us turned. He wore a baseball cap with a Star of
David, and his shirt was open at the neck to display a small gold cross on a
chain. He reached inside his heavy checked jacket.

"Blasphemer," he said.

He pulled out a handgun and shot Jesus three times in the chest.

I grabbed Jesus. Two men barged out of the crowd and grabbed the
assassin. He'd already dropped the gun and had his hands up. The two men
wrestled him to the ground at gunpoint, then dragged him to his feet.
Screams resounded in the narrow space.

"Police!" the men shouted. One of them waved a police ID card, like it wasn't obvious. I learned later that they'd been shadowing Jesus from the beginning.

The assassin held his hands out for the plastic ties. He kept staring at Jesus.

"Save yourself now!" he jeered. One of the undercover cops gave him the elbow in the solar plexus. He doubled, gasping.

Jesus was bleeding all over me. "Lay off him," he wheezed. "He doesn't know what he's done."

The man strained upright, glaring.

"Playacting to the end, demon! I don't want forgiveness from you!"

Jesus waved a hand, two fingers raised, in a shaky blessing, and sagged in my arms. I staggered backwards. His heels dragged along the ground. One of his shoes came off.

It took a long while for the ambulance to nose through the narrow streets. Jesus lost consciousness long before it arrived. I stayed with him to the hospital. The paramedics did their best—they're good with gunshot wounds in the Holy Land—but he was dead on arrival.

Jesus, DOA.

I couldn't believe it.

I watched every second of the emergency surgery, and I know he was a man.

The autopsy should have taken place within twenty-four hours, but some procedural dispute delayed it for three days. I managed to attend. It didn't even take much effort on my part—I was a witness, I had identified the body when it was pronounced dead. On the slab he looked like the dead Che Guevara. The pathologists opened him up, recovered the bullets, removed organs, and took tissue samples. Results came back from the labs. He was human right down to the DNA. So much for the bush robot theory. There was a burial, and no resurrection. No levitation and no infinitely improbable rescue. Some people still visit the grave. One thing I'm sure of: this time, he's not coming back.

There was a trial, of course. The assassin, an American Christian Zionist, disdained the prompting of his lawyer to plead insanity. He proudly pleaded guilty and claimed to be acting to thwart the attempts of the Antichrist to derail the divine plan for the End Times. I was a witness for the prosecution, but I suspect my testimony had as much effect as the rantings of the accused in the eventual ruling: not guilty by reason of temporary insanity. The assassin did six months in a mental hospital. After his release he made a splash on the US fundamentalist lecture circuit as the hero who had shot one of the Devil's minions: the false messiah, the fake Christ. The man he killed wasn't the real Antichrist, it's been decided. The Antichrist is still to come. Millions still await the real Rapture and the return of the real Jesus.

Perhaps it was some obscure guilt about my own inadvertent part in Jesus' assassination that drove me to research his writings and the live recordings of his sayings and miracles. They're all online, and the authentic ones are carefully kept that way by his followers: online, and authentic. There's enough apocryphal stuff in circulation already, and far more interest in him than when he was alive.

The odd thing is, though, that if you trawl, as I've done, through his blog posts, his devastating put-downs in the comment sections, and the shaky cell phone and home-video recordings of his discourses, it has an effect on how you think. It isn't a question of belief, exactly. It's more a question of examining beliefs, and examining your own actions, even your thoughts, as if under his skeptical eye, and in the echo of his sardonic voice. It works on you. It's like a whole new life.

SOLOMON'S CHOICE

Mike Resnick and Nancy Kress

Mike Resnick and Nancy Kress, Hugo- and Nebula-winning authors both, need no introduction from me. Mike is a staple of my anthologies, a consummate old pro whom I can always count on to deliver a great and gripping yarn. It's been my privilege to know him for some years now, and I'm always glad to have him on board. Mike always chooses a coauthor for these projects, and I had my fingers crossed he'd pick Nancy. (I may have hinted loudly, too.) Her fiction has impressed me mightily in recent days, but this is my first occasion to work with her. Here's hoping it won't be the last.

Last dark, Eyoli dreamed, again. She woke screaming, again. I huddled with her against the hut wall, where my mother once held me and my grandmother held her, although not like this. I could feel my grandmother's arms around my mother, but for once it brought no comfort. Stroking Eyoli's fur, I pressed her against me until once more she slept in the light of the Three Moons, her small face smoothed free of terror.

Free of memory.

I cannot do this any longer. Tomorrow I will go to the Terrans. Maybe the rumors are true. Maybe they do not have these dreams, as my grandmother remembered hearing. Maybe they can stop Eyoli from having them. It seems incredible, but I am desperate. Let the Council be damned; I must do this for my daughter.

I cannot do less.

"Sir, there's a native outside."

My head snapped up so fast I felt my neck twist. It hurt. "A native?"

"Yes, sir. She seems to want to come in." My adjutant's face showed no shock, because my adjutant made it a point of pride to show nothing to a young spacer, especially to a staff officer, and maybe especially to me. But I was in shock. No native had approached the base in twenty-five years, and I would have bet my medical license that none ever would. And, of course, we stay away from them, too.

It's the least we can do, after what happened so many years ago.

So there was no protocol for this. I rose slowly, blanking the screen of my handheld. A *native*. Perhaps a chance to learn the truth about these strange people, to put scientific fact underneath the suppositions and rumors and, yes, myths. And, of course, a shot at the kind of journal article that established major reputations.

My fingers shook, very slightly, as I laid my handheld on the desk and made sure all room recorders were functional. "Show her in, Corporal. And then leave us."

❚❚

The Terran led me through a door into a small room. My mother had never been on this spot, but my grandmother had, before the Terrans came. It had been a meadow then, and I remembered her playing here with two friends. How young we were then! We ran and hid, giggling, behind a carwollu bush, and then Issimu caught us. The feel of Issimu's hair in the warm sunshine . . . I smiled.

The Terran studied me. I stood straighter and wiped away the smile. I was not, after all, a green girl to be mastered by memory. I have the pride of my line, and it is an old one, and strong. When the Terran motioned to a bright large cushion and sat herself upon another, I, too, sat. And held one hand firmly in the other to still its trembling.

"Hello," something said, and I jumped but did not fall. Then I saw that even though the Terran's lips moved, making strange sounds, the real words came from a small box in her hand. "Don't be afraid, please. I am speaking to you through a translator. That is a machine that changes my language into yours, and yours into mine, so we can understand each other."

My mother had never seen this. My grandmother had never imagined it. My mother watched the first Terran ship come down and said, "Is it real?" My grand-mother, standing beside her, said nothing, but fear ran through her.

The Terran said, "Do you understand?"

"Yes," I said, and the box made a short, unintelligible sound.

"I am called Dr. Rubin. What is your name?" the Terran said. On her bright cushion she did not look quite so tall. Fur on her head only, drab green clothing on her body—the clothing did not look very warm, but then the room was too hot. I began to sweat. "I am Hutaral." I did not give my whole matrilineal, since she had not offered hers.

"Hutaral, you are welcome in our hut."

That was courteous. "How does the box know the language of the Ones?"

She hesitated. I studied her, and all at once what I saw was so shocking that I didn't hear her answer. I rose in panic. "You are a male!"

"Hutaral, I will not hurt you!" Dr. Rubin said, but by that time I had control of myself. Trembling, but in control.

Their males were so big, so strong, so unnatural. Once more I made myself sit on the cushion, and Dr. Rubin and I looked at each other. I kept my eyes from the unmistakable bulge in his tight pants. Finally she—no, he—said through the box, "Your males don't speak, do they? They never leave their huts."

"Of course not," I said. My line was an old and honorable one; we protected our males. They stayed safe at home where they belonged, poor solitary creatures. How would they survive otherwise, with no memories to help them?

"It is different with us Terrans," Dr. Rubin said, and I took heart. "Different" was what I needed, for Eyoli. "Different" and "unnatural." If this Terran could help, I wouldn't care if she—he—were a six-limbed fanged creeper.

"I have come here," I said carefully, "to stop my daughter from dying."

She was incredibly brave.

That was the thought that kept recurring to me, and it was dumb. I should have been concentrating on the visible genetic differences, relating phenotype to the genotype on record, or on her people's culture. But I kept coming back to the bravery. She had come to a Terran base, ululated outside the walls until someone led her inside, asked for the help of people who had inadvertently killed her mother. For I'd viewed all the records from that day twenty-five years ago, and I was sure this was the daughter of one of those natives, the native that had begun it all. The same slight upper body—not all of them are so thin, and we've surreptitiously recorded them for twenty-five years. The same uptilted nose, honey-colored fur, long six-fingered hands. That terrible day we had carefully laid the bodies outside the base perimeter and court-martialed those responsible. It was all that the Navy, new to 539-Beta, could do. That, and respect the natives' refusal to have anything to do with us ever since. They couldn't know exactly what had happened inside, but we had returned to them seven dead and mutilated bodies.

And yet here she sat.

"Hutaral, where do your people come from?"

She blinked rapidly and hung her head, as if in shame. "My great-great-great-grandmother . . . I cannot see her memory clearly."

Quaint phraseology. Or—was their version of their origins perhaps a religious secret, not to be shared with outsiders? But then she said, "My great-great-grandmother was told the story of an Iron Bird from beyond the stars. The Goddess sent it to bring bright seeds that grew into the Ones."

Close enough. The original ship's embryos had included several genetic possibilities, with environmental conditions determining which phenotype expressed. That was the limit of biotechnology in those days. The natives' genome was twice as large as mine—and, by the time humanity arrived here the second time, twice as puzzling. I said, "Did the Goddess care for the seeds after they sprouted?"

"Her iron angels cared for them."

Those would be the first ship's robots, long since rusted away. A more accurate history had survived than anyone could have foretold, back in those dim lost days before the jump drive. But I was a biologist, not a historian. And science had waited twenty-five years for this.

"Hutaral, may I . . . would you permit me to let a machine touch you? It will not hurt you. It will only measure your temperature and your heartbeat."

She blinked rapidly again—evidently a sign of heightened emotion. Then that bravery again, that amazing toughness. Had we selected for it genetically in the original package? Genes were such unpredictable things. They crossbred and jumped and mutated and influenced each other, and so often what you thought you were selecting for ended up far from what you actually got.

"Your machine may touch me," Hutaral finally said, "only if you will help our memories."

I caught my breath. Not just a journal article, but an entire study. Maybe the Assein Prize in Genetics. Why not? This native was the find of the century in xenobiology. Even if she wasn't exactly an alien. "What can't you remember, Hutaral?"

"I can remember all. It is my daughter. She must not Awaken, not ever."

I went still. Not awaken? Were we talking infanticide here? Or prolonging of some sort of coma? Why would—

"She must not go insane," Hutaral said, "or kill herself. Like all the other grandchildren of the seven."

It didn't make any sense. The reference to "the seven"—that could only mean one thing. But I didn't see how it fit. I decided to take the practical route.

"If I am to help your daughter, I must see her," I said. "Can you bring her here, Hutaral?"

"Yes. She must not die like the others," Hutaral repeated. "Not even once."

And what could anybody make of that?

The Terrans are more ignorant than I'd hoped. Almost I didn't go back to them. But then I went home and Eyoli was not there.

My heart froze in my breast. Then I was running through the village, crying to Oddu and Evvico and Imorli. "Where is she? Where is Eyoli? She's gone!"

Horror in their eyes before they, too, left their washing and cooking and ran to woods and river and pond, looking for Eyoli.

I jumped over a hole in the path; it was not there. My mother remembered it from another summer. It is so hard to keep memory sorted when fear fills the huts of the mind! I dodged around a rock, which was there, and ran right into a nest of red creepers. They had not been there in my grandmother's day, and I had not thought to look for them. Sobbing, I tried to free myself from the stinging vines, but I couldn't get loose until Evvico helped me. "We'll find her, Hutaral, we will! And she's a strong child!"

No child is that strong.

But we did find her. Walking into the river at the place of swiftest current, her face ugly with fear and panic and death. Evvico and Oddu and I made a chain of women and pulled her back just before she would have been swept away. Eyoli fought us, and when we had her safely on shore, I screamed at her. "You will not die! You will not go insane! I forbid it!"

Sanity took me then. One of those others had been Evvico's daughter. Evvico looked at me with such grief and pity in her dark eyes that my anger returned, even greater than it had been before. Anger at what? *At all of it, but it came out for Eyoli.*

"Don't you dare die!" I screamed, and hit her with my fist hard enough to knock her out, and so stop all memory.

"Hutaral," Oddu said softly. "Dear heart."

But no "dear heart" was going to help us. No softness. "Tie her up," I said, panting and wet and pressed on by memory—my mother bathing on this riverbank, my grandmother planting breadnuts, my great-grandmother harvesting her small patch of ground. "Tie her tight. I'm taking her to the Terrans now."

In the middle of the night, after I'd failed at sleep for three hours, I sat in the cluttered office of the medical quarters and watched the old records once again.

Repetition dulls everything, even indignation. Without much emotion I watched the holo statements, made after the fact, from the four-soldier scouting party that had found the native who resembled Hutaral, far from her village, and in labor. Premature labor, they'd judged from the fact that no one was with her. They'd put her in the rover and brought her to the doctor at what would become the permanent base, though at the time there was just a jumble of half-unpacked crates and temporary inflatable dwellings. We had landed on 539-Beta only weeks before. The doctor had done what she could, but the native and her infant had both died, the infant instantly, the mother later—which was the problem.

Thus far, nobody had been to blame for anything.

But the doctor had not immediately returned the body to a village—any village—as protocol demanded. Instead, she'd taken tissue samples—not so bad—and performed an unauthorized autopsy—very bad. And she knew it, for she'd performed her xenobiology research in a small inflatable at the very edge of camp, without telling the CO. In the middle of the autopsy, six native women had stormed the inflatable.

The doctor, alone, had grabbed a gun and easily burned down all six. Guards had come running, the doctor had been arrested, and the furious CO had been court-martialed along with her. It had, after all, happened on his watch. The directive came down from the top on Belle Riveau: No further contact to be initiated with natives of 539-Beta.

On my screen, the seven bodies were placed on a cart by weeping fur-covered women and pulled away. The next day, I knew, the entire village had been abandoned. All the preliminary meetings with the natives, who had no idea they were human, all the first calm and fruitful contacts, all the first exchanges of information—all wasted. I turned off the screen and stared at the small brass sculpture on the wall shelf. A caduceus, rod and coiled serpents, exquisitely worked in diamond-fiber. It had cost my father six months' pay. He'd given it to me a year before his death, on the day I graduated from medical school, when he'd practically levitated from pride. His Saul, an officer and a gentleman and a doctor. Of course, all that had occurred before the "regrettable incident" on the *Midian*.

What would my father have said about what happened here on 539-Beta? Avner Rubin, pious as his son is not, would undoubtedly have thrown up his hands in horror and quoted Scripture. "And you shalt not oppress a stranger, or you yourself know the heart of a stranger, seeing you were strangers in the land of Egypt." Or maybe—

"Sir, I'm sorry to interrupt you," my adjutant said on a corner of my screen, "but that native woman is back—with another one, who appears to be unconscious. What should I do with them now?"

I stood abruptly, knocking over my glass of wine, a sleep aid that had failed.

"Bring them to the infirmary," I ordered him, and hurried over to greet them.

Hutaral looked even worse than before: strained, wild-eyed, bedraggled. Her brown fur was matted and dirty. The girl, who looked about twelve, was tied tightly to a two-wheeled handcart, struggling and screaming wordlessly. Her jaw had been broken. Trying not to hurt her more than necessary, I examined the break. "Who hit her?"

"I did," Hutaral said.

"You?" I said, surprised. "This is a bad fracture. I'm going to have to anesthetize her to set it."

Every weary muscle in Hutaral's body tensed, and I wondered what the translator had given her for "anesthetize." But she said nothing. I slapped a patch on the girl and watched her stop thrashing, watched the horror in her eyes dim, watched her slide into unconsciousness.

"Aaaahhhhh," breathed Hutaral, and sat abruptly on the ground.

I had no time for her, nor for much asepsis. I set and wired the jaw, all the time wondering if these people had penalties for child abuse. Originally I had thought Hutaral a caring, if primitive, mother. So much for first impressions. She'd done some serious damage to her daughter. As I was working, I heard a strange sound.

On the ground, Hutaral had begun to weep.

‖

The Terrans can do nothing. All that this Dr. Rubin did was make Eyoli go into true sleep. Sleep is what brings the dreams! Our memories won't come by day until her blood flows begin—Dr. Rubin, a healer, must know that! Is he torturing my child, as his ancestors tortured my mother?

What have I done in bringing Eyoli to this cursed place?

‖

"I don't understand," the CO said. "What does she want?"

"It's not completely clear as yet, sir," I said carefully. Colonel Karenski had a reputation for being fair but hard. Did he know about me, about the *Midian*? Of course he did. I had tried, pathetically, to offset my service record with extreme military polish: shined boots, spotless uniform, salute so sharp it could have cut wood. Karenski slouched in his chair in fatigues, a glass of whiskey in his hand. He looked five times the soldier I would ever be, and he didn't look happy. All I had to impress him was my specialized knowledge.

"Sir, as you undoubtedly know, initial reports on the natives' genome revealed mutated genes on the X chromosome, including not only unique alleles but also long strings of unknown codons that—"

"No jargon, Doctor," Karenski snapped. "Save it for someone who understands it." He stared coldly at me. "You're sure the native approached you, with no previous contact on your side?"

"She sought me out, sir, and asked for my help with her daughter."

"So her daughter would 'not awaken.' And you have no idea what that means?"

"No, sir, I don't. Yet."

"And then she approached you a second time, bringing a child with a broken jaw?"

I didn't think "approached" was the right word for Hutaral's desperate intrusion into the base: ululating, muddy, shivering, weeping, pushing a homemade cart holding a maimed girl. But all I said was, "Yes, sir. I set the jaw. The child is sedated; the native is sitting with her; a guard has been posted. I sent a full report at 0400 hours."

"What are you going to do now?" he asked impatiently.

I wasn't prepared for that question. I was here because I wanted him to tell me what to do, in everything except the scientific procedures. I didn't want to risk the same court-martial charges as my predecessor. My position in the Space Navy was already too precarious.

"Well, sir, I was wondering—"

"Don't wonder, Doctor! What do you propose to *do*?"

I felt myself flush, the mottling of a schoolboy who doesn't know the right answer. Again I fell back on specialization. "First I'll sequence both subjects' genomes and compare them with—"

"Stop." The colonel put down his whiskey. "Of course you'll do whatever medical scans and tests are required or useful or enlightening, if you can do so without objections from the native. I meant, are you going to try to figure out what she wants and give it to her?"

I blurted, "Should I, sir?"

"Yes, damn it! This is our first chance in twenty-five years to establish positive contact with a lost branch of humanity, and you're the one they've approached. Adding anybody else at this point is likely to scare them off. In fact, make sure that the guards keep all weapons out of sight. Keep surveillance unobtrusive and under no circumstances detain them if they wish to leave. Make damned sure you violate neither the letter nor the spirit of Headquarters' directive. Send me reports every two hours unless circumstances make it expedient to delay. And Dr. Rubin?"

"Yes, sir?"

"Do not fuck up this situation. Dismissed."

"Yes, sir." I heard clearly the unspoken word at the end of his sentence: *Do not fuck up this situation, too.* He knew about the *Midian.* "Thank you, sir."

Karenski only scowled.

I ran all the way back to the infirmary. The child—Eyoli, her mother called her—would just be coming out of the anesthetic, and the AI had doubtless finished sequencing both their genomes. My next step was a brain scan. I only hoped that Hutaral had not changed her mind about permitting that.

But she had. They were gone.

$$\text{\textbf{II}}$$

Sleep. He made her sleep. I never imagined such cruelty. Eyoli's only hope was to stay awake without Awakening . . . and the Terran made her sleep.

I pulled her by the hand and we stumbled outside. No one tried to stop us. I pushed Eyoli into the cart. Almost immediately her eyes closed again, but without dreams, thank the Goddess; she didn't thrash around or wake screaming. The stiff cloth around her jaw made her look like someone else, not my child. Of course, she was becoming someone else, many someone elses: my great-great-grandmother Anna, my great-grand-

mother Utetha, my grandmother Ensara, my mother Abalu. I had been so proud on my Awakening Day, to become these women of my line, and prouder still when occasionally I glimpsed the memories of my great-great-great-grandmother, Elena. How many could do that?

As I pushed the cart, heavier every kilometer with Eyoli's weight, it began to rain. I remembered my mother in the rain, younger than Eyoli was now. She had loved it. My grandmother was afraid of thunder. We hid in a cave just beyond that dell, cowering as the great peals crashed overhead and the lightning split the sky. The rain came down harder. I made for the cave.

It opened into solid rock, a shallow depression covered with moonthorn brush, but deep enough to shelter us from the storm. Both Eyoli and I were scratched and bleeding by the time I got her inside. I lit a candle from my pouch. In its wavering light I saw her eyes, the same dark gray as the raining skies, open and staring at me.

"Mother mine," she murmured through the stiff cloth, "make me die. Make me die!"

"No!"

"You don't know," my daughter said, barely intelligible. "You don't know. You don't remember."

I would gladly have taken the burden of memory from Eyoli, but I could not. I, like all daughters, had inherited my mother's memories only up until the day of my birth. But Eyoli had the rest.

She spoke now as if tranced, in despairing quiet, her round child's face twisted in adult horror. "The knives . . . I wasn't dead when the Terran began using the knives. My dead child, your brother . . . he lies there on the table and she raises the knife over him and I can still see." Trance vanished, and Eyoli screamed.

I wrapped my arms around her as tightly as I could. If I had to, I could tie her again . . . but I could not tie her forever. Evvico's daughter, another granddaughter of the Seven, had hung herself from a shipberry tree three days after her Awakening. Both of Amabila's daughters had drowned themselves. Urdu's daughter's mind had snapped and she had set fire to three huts, killing four men, trying to burn out the memories of her grandmother.

Memory, always in need of taming even when sweet, can only bear so much.

I held my daughter as she experienced her grandmother's death—her own death, to the ignorant young—for the tenth time, the twentieth time, forever . . .

▌▌

They were easy enough to follow with the infrared tracker, even through the storm. All the while I raced along, rain lashing me, I kept hearing the colonel's voice in my head: "Don't fuck up this situation." But he had also said to not lose this chance. What if—

I saw the sad little handcart overturned in the rain. Hutaral crouched in a shallow depression in the rock, holding Eyoli to her as if all the forces of Nature had conspired to pull them apart.

"What is the matter?" I asked. "Why did you take her away?"

Hutaral stared at me and said nothing.

At first I thought my translating mechanism wasn't working. I tapped it a couple of times. The tiny light still glowed. "Hutaral, if I have offended you . . ."

"You made her remember," she said at last.

"Remember *what*?" I asked, confused.

"What happened so long ago."

I knew what she was referring to, but it made no sense. "But that was long before Eyoli was born."

She stared at me again without answering.

"Are you saying that she can remember things that happened before she was born?"

Now it was Hutaral's turn to look puzzled, peering at me through her rain-soaked fur. "Cannot the females of your race do so?"

"No, they cannot. Are you telling me you can *all* do this, not just Eyoli?"

"Yes."

"And she is remembering what happened to—"

"To my mother," said Hutaral. "She is more than remembering it. She is"—the translator paused for an instant, trying to come up with an equivalent word—*experiencing* it." Experiencing it. She meant that Eyoli was living that horror over and over, each time as if it were the first. Lying half dead on that table, watching a Terran knife descend into the flesh of your infant who, you believed, was also still alive. Over and over. Dear God, what we had done to these people? I said to Hutaral, a sodden blur in the rain, "I will fix this. I promise you, Hutaral. Now that I understand it, I promise you that I will fix this!" She only stared at me.

He seemed sincere, and if his race were like all males and really could not remember What Has Gone Before, then he could be forgiven for making my Eyoli sleep. I did not know if he could help, but I knew that none of the Ones could.

"Will you trust me?" he asked. "I need to use a few more machines on Eyoli— nothing that will hurt her. I know what to look for now. Please, Hutaral. Just a few more machines."

Did I have a choice? I looked at Eyoli and knew that I did not.

"I will trust you," I said.

It didn't take long: brain scan, skin scrapings, blood test, half a dozen other things for the computer to analyze.

Except that my lab computer couldn't analyze it. Oh, it could do white cell and red cell counts, and it could study the encephelogram and conclude that Eyoli was sane, and it instantly pronounced her to be in perfect health but under great tension. But all it could tell me was that she was different from any person of human stock it had ever analyzed, and that was the whole of it.

Hutaral let me draw blood and take some scrapings from her, and the computer came up with the same conclusion: human stock, healthy, like us in most ways, and it was simply not programmed to understand and analyze the differences. I needed an AI.

That meant I was going to have to awaken Karenski. I didn't dare delay even until morning; I didn't know how long Hutaral would allow Eyoli to stay on the post.

Karenski met me in his office at Headquarters. I'd wanted a screen conference, but apparently the CO did not meet with his officers this way, not
even with one like me. "I just put in an eighteen-hour day," he said angrily,
rubbing his eyes and running his hand through his unkempt hair. "This had
better be good."

"You told me to keep you informed, sir," I noted, shifting my weight
uneasily.

"I didn't tell you to wake me out of a sound sleep."

"It can't wait, sir."

Suddenly he was alert. "All right, let's have it."

"I know what the child's problem is, sir," I said, "and if I don't cure it
quickly she will either kill herself or go mad."

"Well, then, cure it. You don't need my permission."

"It's not that simple, sir."

"Somehow it never is," said Karenski. "Suppose you lay it out for me and
stop giving me sentence fragments, Dr. Rubin."

"All right," I said. "It seems that the females of this human offshoot have
a . . . well, a racial memory is an inadequate term. Once they reach child-
bearing age, which is to say, once they begin menstruating, they can
remember every incident of their progenitors' lives. Not everything of their
mothers'—the mother's memories and experiences are cut off at the moment
of birth, which argues a biological encoding of the inherited memory. But
each female experiences the memories of her maternal grandmother, maternal
great-grandmother, and so on."

"Let me guess," interrupted Karenski, who wasn't stupid. "This kid's
grandmother is either the one our half-baked doctor chopped up on the
assumption it was already dead, or she's one of the half dozen who got to
watch it at close range."

"And now she can't differentiate the memory from the reality. Right now
it only seems to appear to her when she sleeps, or at least it's at its most
potent then, but Hutaral—that's the mother—assures me that soon it will be
with her every second, awake or asleep."

"Poor kid," said Karenski, surprising me. "How do you cure it?"

"I don't know yet," I said. "First I have to find out what caused it."

"I thought you just told me: when she hits a certain age or level of physical maturity."

"I'm not making myself clear," I said. "It's a mutation. No other human stock possesses it. Most mutations serve a purpose. I have to find out what purpose this serves before I decide if it's even a good idea to change it—and then I have to find out *how* to change it."

"And that's your report?"

I shook my head. "No, sir," I said. "I need access to a much more powerful medical computer than the one we have on 539-Beta. My computer recognizes that there are inconsistencies between Eyoli and what we would call normal human women, but it's not complex enough to tell me anything more than that. I'd like to tie into the main computer at the military hospital on 214-Alpha, but I don't have the authority to do so."

"And this should solve the problem?"

"If it doesn't, then it's probably insoluble."

"All right, Dr. Rubin. Give me ten minutes, and then unless you hear otherwise from me, you can access the 214-Alpha computer."

"Thank you for your generosity, sir."

"It's not generosity, damn it! That's not how the military works. But then, you've always had trouble with that, haven't you?"

We stared at each other. Karenski might be a fair man, but he was also a Space Navy commander and it was clear he didn't like having me on his watch. What I had done on the *Midian* would not be forgivable to him, not even if a dozen courts-martial had acquitted me, instead of merely one. Striking a superior officer who was maiming an enlisted man and then briefly disappearing afterward—that should have gotten me a dishonorable discharge, if not the brig. That it didn't, because the superior officer was cruel and oppressive, would never sit well with someone like Karenski. He was too Navy, too establishment, too much a man who, in my father's terms, had never ever been "a stranger in the land of Egypt."

"Dismissed," he said, and I went back to medical quarters. Hutaral had her arms wrapped around Eyoli, who slept uneasily. Hutaral's eyes followed me as I walked past her and sat down at my desk, staring at my timepiece to avoid staring at my father's caduceus. When ten minutes had passed I activated my computer, accessed the computer at the military hospital, and had my computer feed it all the data I'd accumulated. I figured the data would be ten minutes each way in transit, and the hospital computer itself might take a full minute to analyze it and come to some conclusions. That gave me per-haps twenty minutes.

I heated up some coffee. I was aware that Hutaral was watching me. I didn't want to wake Eyoli, so I gestured that she could have some coffee, but she made a face and shook her head.

"Why are you here?" I asked. "My people sleep at night."

"I hope to have a cure very soon," answered the doctor.

"But you are doing nothing," I said.

"My machine is doing it for me," he said, as if that made sense, but of course it didn't.

Eyoli began whimpering in her sleep, and I tried to comfort her.

The doctor watched us bleakly, as if he had bad memories of his own.

Finally the answer came back. The problem was, I didn't know if it made things better or worse. I read it through twice, to make sure I fully under-stood it, and then decided that I was going to have to wake Karenski for the second time in one night.

"Jesus!" said Karenski as his eyes fell on me. "You look worse than the kid."

"You've seen her?" I asked, surprised.

"I'm in charge of this outpost. It's my job to see and know everything that goes on here. But I have a feeling I'm not going to like the next few minutes."

"Sir?"

"You're afraid of me, Doctor. I don't like that in my officers. Just tell me what you found."

"I got the report back from 214-Alpha, sir."

"And?"

"Remember I said that there is always a reason for mutation, that races don't just change for no reason at all?"

"Get on with it," said Karenski. "I'm not a schoolboy."

"It's pretty complex, sir," I said. "The computer suggested environmental reasons for all the mutations—the down that covers them, the sixth finger on each hand, everything."

"And the one causing all this trouble? Is there a way to get rid of it?"

"There's always a way to alter genetic makeup," I said. "But it's not that simple. Millennia ago when Gregor Mendel started crossing peas and studying the results, he decided all traits were controlled by simple dominants or recessives. But—"

"Get to the point," said Karenski impatiently.

"The point is that most genetics aren't that simple. There are partial dominants, incomplete dominants, linked recessives, more things than the layman can imagine."

"I assume what you're leading up to is that this racial memory or whatever we're calling it is linked to something else."

"Yes, sir."

"Does this mean you can't eliminate it?"

"I can eliminate it, sir," I said. "I can eliminate it from Eyoli and Hutaral in less than a day."

"But?"

"I don't know *why* they developed the memory, sir," I said. "Maybe there were poisonous fruits, maybe there were areas of great danger, I don't know— but Nature decided that, in this case, it was the best way to pass along vital survival information. They've been here so long that information is probably no longer vital, but until now it hasn't proven to be a detriment. The thing is, sir, it's sex-linked. Only females have it, and it only arrives with sexual maturity." I took a deep breath and let it out slowly. "According to the computer at the military hospital, the particular genes that are responsible for this are linked to the reproductive system. If I remove the memories, it will so alter the genes that they will run a better than fifty-fifty chance of producing deformed babies."

"How deformed?" asked Karenski.

"I can't be sure, but my best estimate is no eyes. I don't mean blind; I mean no eyes at all. And totally deformed arms and legs. The hands and feet would grow right out of the trunks of the bodies."

I thought I saw Karenski shudder. He said, "So if you get rid of the memories, they'll have sightless deformed babies, and if not, this girl and— what?—maybe half a dozen more will go crazy or kill themselves?"

"More than that, sir," I said.

"I thought I heard reference to 'the Seven.'"

"Yes, sir—but those seven are not the mothers. They're the grandmothers. This is a relatively primitive society, on a relatively uninhabited world. They've had no need to practice birth control; the more farmers and hunter-gatherers they have, the better. I haven't questioned Hutaral specifically, but let's say each of those six surviving females had six offspring. That's thirty-six in Hutaral's generation. Let's say half of them are females, and they each have six offspring. Do you see what I'm getting at, sir? A few have already killed themselves or gone mad, but there could be forty or fifty or more girls who are approaching sexual maturity in the next half-dozen years."

"So a generation goes crazy and probably kills itself, or everyone starts producing deformities."

"In essence, sir."

Karenski paused for a long moment. "Hobson had it easy," he said at last.

"Sir?"

"Hobson's Choice."

"I'm not aware of the reference, sir," I said.

"You will be."

He comes back and lays a hand on my shoulder. Strangely, I do not find it distasteful or intimidating.

"Can you help my Eyoli?" I ask.

He seems troubled. "It depends," he says.

"On what?"

"On many things. I have to think about it tonight. Maybe tomorrow I will know what to do."

"Why can you not cure her now?"

"It is too complicated to explain," he says, and although it sounds like a lie, somehow I know he is not lying.

‖

"I can't do it, sir," I said.

"Exactly what can't you do?" asked Karenski. He watched me closely.

"I can't condemn them to an existence of nightmares, and I can't condemn them to a future of deformed babies—yet if I act I will condemn them to the one, and if I fail to act I'll condemn them to the other." The words came out slowly, painful as vomiting hot lead. I hated being here in front of him again, but I couldn't think what else to do. Couldn't think, couldn't sleep, couldn't eat. I knew I looked a mess—no forced spit-and-polish this time—but it no longer mattered.

Karenski still studied me with that unnerving intensity. "You're a doctor, but you're also an officer. I expect my officers to use their initiative."

"How does initiative enter into it?" I asked. "I'm facing two unacceptable alternatives."

"Well, it's your problem," said Karenski. "But if it were mine, I'd find a third alternative."

I stared at him uncomprehendingly. "A third alternative?"

"Didn't Sherlock Holmes once say that when you eliminated the impossible, whatever was left had to be the truth? Well, when you eliminate the unacceptable, whatever's left must be a viable course of action."

"I have no idea what you're getting at, sir," I said. "If you would just tell me—"

"Then you'd be using *my* initiative, wouldn't you?" he said, scowling. He raised his hand slightly and flipped it sideways, a gesture of both dismissal and disdain. The gesture was what snapped me. I snarled, "It wasn't Hobson, sir. Your history is faulty."

"What?"

"Thomas Hobson, early seventeenth-century Englishman. You said I'd be facing Hobson's Choice, but that term refers to having just one course of action, and it came from a stupid story about taking the horse nearest the livery stable door or no horse at all. But I have two choices, both bad. A better reference for you to use would have been King Solomon with the baby he ordered cut in half. Also a reference suited to my background, isn't it? Sir?"

He leaned forward, "Are you accusing me of anti-Semitism, Dr. Rubin?"

"No, sir."

"I certainly hope not. There is no such thing in the Space Navy—in which, incidentally, you don't seem very happy."

"Irrelevant, sir."

"Maybe not." All at once both his anger and his intensity seemed to vanish. He leaned back in his chair and regarded me from under half-closed eyelids. "The subject is closed, Doctor. I'm going to be off reporting to Sector Headquarters for three days. I expect you to have your problem solved long before I get back."

"I'll try my best, sir," I said stiffly. What had just happened here?

"Good. And once it's solved, Dr. Rubin, I don't expect to be bothered by you in this office ever again. Do you understand?"

"Yes, sir."

"I genuinely hope so."

He saluted, and I had no choice but to salute back and then leave. I had the confused impression that Karenski, despite his dislike, had been trying to tell me something he couldn't say outright. *What? Why?* And what was I supposed to do now? Karenski didn't want me in his command, but he *did* want me to solve the problem of Hutaral and Eyoli. Then, halfway across the base to medical quarters, I saw it. And stopped dead in my tracks, flooded with hope and fear. My fingers shook as once more, this time without authorization, I keyed in the security codes to access the AI on 214-Alpha.

"How much do you love Eyoli?" he asked me.

"She is flesh of my flesh," I answered. "I would die for her.

"Would you live *for her?"*

"I do not understand, Dr. Rubin," I said.

"It is difficult to explain," he said. "I cannot cure her here. But I can cure her, and all the other young girls who descend from the Seven, elsewhere."

"Elsewhere?" I repeated. "Do you mean the mountains, or the flat plains a day's march to the north?"

"No," he said. "I mean another world."

At first I thought he was jesting, but then I saw from his face that he wasn't.

"Another world?" I said. "Why?"

He ran his hand through his head fur, making it all stand up. His strange Terran eyes were red and bright.

"It is very complicated, but if I cure the young women here, they will produce . . . very strange babies, many of which will die at birth."

"And that will not happen on another world?"

"My computer—that is the machine I speak to—tells me that there are two worlds where that will not happen."

I cried, "I do not understand why two worlds will be good for us and all the others will be bad."

"It is not necessary that you understand now," he said. "What I must know is if the descendants of the Seven would be willing to travel to another world, if that meant that the young women would no longer suffer with their memories."

Another world. No longer home. And against that, Eyoli's life. Slowly I said, "If we go, you will make the bad memories vanish?"

"No," he said. "All their *memories will vanish, and will never return."*

I could hardly look at him. No memories. My mother laughing bare-headed in the wind, my grandmother's loving arms around my mother, my great-grandmother waking at dawn just to see the Three Moons rise together. No memories.

"Hutaral, there are no easy answers here," said Dr. Rubin. "If you would rather stay, I will not force you to leave."

"I must confer with all the Ones. How could I alone say? It may be many days before we can reach an agreement."

He shook his head. "I am sorry, Hutaral, but I must have an answer within two days, or it will be too late."

"Are you saying that Eyoli will die in three days?" Terror filled me once again.

"No," he replied. "I am saying that you will not be able to leave after two days."

"But—why?"

The answer was simple enough. If I didn't steal a cargo ship in two days' time, Karenski would be back—and if I hadn't stolen it by then, he'd be sure I was never going to.

I spent the rest of the night studying the star charts, mapping the wormholes, having the computer plot a course to Henderson's World that would keep us light-years from any system where our military was stationed.

That had been my final question to the computer. Even if I took Eyoli and the others away, even if I gave them the drugs that would eradicate their racial memories, there was no way to alter the changes to their genes. They would still be programmed to produce defective babies—and by the same token, there was no sense taking a cross section of males with us, since they were guaranteed to produce such babies.

So I set the AI on 214-Alpha to a truly monumental final task. There were offshoots of humanity on thousands of worlds. Most hadn't changed at all—but some had mutated even more than Hutaral's people had mutated. Was there any human offshoot anywhere in the galaxy with a genome that could negate the harm I would do to Eyoli's and the others' ability to produce normal children?

The AI had to tie into a batch of even more powerful computers—though in this case I think better-informed computers would be more accurate—before it could come up with my answer: the altered grandchildren of the Seven, when mated to the males on Henderson's World or 702-Delta, would produce normal children. The gene for the memories would not recur.

But 702-Delta possessed a military base, and I couldn't land a stolen military cargo ship there. Not even one that Karenski had wanted me to steal, which was what I believed. He wanted to help the natives; he wanted me out of his command; he wanted to avoid any further political incidents with natives. But he wouldn't want to identify a stolen ship as his own, or his already-suspect staff officer as its thief. So 702-Delta was out of the question.

Henderson's World, however, had started out as a farming colony. For all anyone knew, that's what it still was. With one exception it had had no contact with the rest of humanity for fourteen hundred years—but that one exception was a female sailor who had stowed away on a small ship that had put down to make repairs just over a century ago, and before she was returned to her planet she'd been thoroughly examined, and the findings were logged, coded, and forgotten. Those findings included the entire genome in the semen found in her from what had apparently been a very exciting shore leave.

Many more human traits are carried on the X-chromosome than on the Y-chromosome. But not on Henderson's World.

Logging off the terminal, I tried to still the tremor in my fingers. Three days ago I'd been looking forward to publishing a series of papers, possibly winning the Assein Prize, certainly bolstering the career my father had so badly wanted for me. Now my fondest hope was that I had talked a primitive alien female into letting me become an outlaw with a reward on my head.

"We will trust you," I said to Dr. Rubin.

"I hope you will not regret it."

"If you can save our children, we will not regret it."

"Your husbands . . . your partners . . . will be cared for, as will the young males," he said. "I have left instructions."

That I did not understand. "Why would the other Terrans obey someone who steals from them? What if they will not care for the males here?"

"It is me they will be mad at, not the Ones," he replied. "I know one of us did a terrible thing once, but most Terrans are very decent people who will help others whenever they can."

I did not believe it, so I made no answer. Then I thought further and realized that

Dr. Rubin was sacrificing whatever he valued to help us. Maybe Terrans were not what we remembered.

I hope so, or my arguments, which I voiced so passionately, will have condemned sixty-three of the Ones to a terrible existence on another world.

We loaded the ship and took off without incident. That must have been more of Karenski's doing. Had anyone else tried to steal a cargo vessel from the outpost, they'd have been shot down before they hit the stratosphere. Hell, they'd have been stopped and taken into custody before they reached the ship.

According to the navigational computer, it would take four days, traveling at light speeds and traversing seven carefully selected wormholes, to reach Henderson's World. I decided not to contact them until we were within their star system; I didn't want anyone else tracing my signal.

I began treatment on Eyoli and the other girls while we were in transit. The drugs were painless, although most of the girls cried when I pierced their skins with a needle. I had to have Hutaral explain to the others that I was not a direct emotional descendant of the doctor whose actions had precipitated this, and that I was trying to cure the girls, not hurt them.

And after what seemed an eternity, in which I was sure we would be shot out of the ether, we braked to sublight speeds. I could see Henderson's World, green and pastoral, flanked by a pair of moons, on the main viewscreen.

"Is that it?" asked Hutaral, pointing to the image. "The place where our daughters and their daughters will live without the memories and the nightmares?"

"That's it," I said. "Henderson's World, where we will all spend the rest of our lives."

I gazed down at the planet, pristine and lush. If the deebees were right, it would indeed be a promised land, overflowing with milk and honey. Where we would all, every one of us, be strangers.

My father would have understood.

Hutaral said, "You have given everything up to help us."

"Nobody forced me to," I got out over the tightening in my throat. "It was my own decision."

"But you are no longer a doctor," she persisted.

"No," I agreed. "Once the supplies in my bag run out, I am no longer a doctor."

"What shall we call you then, if we cannot call you Doctor?"

I looked again at the pastoral world below, not sure if I wanted to laugh, or cry, or tremble. *Here I am, Lord.*

She repeated, "What should we call you?"

"Moses," I said.

SANJEEV AND ROBOTWALLAH

Ian McDonald

In a review of Ian McDonald's monumental novel River of Gods, *the* Washington
Post *called him "a writer who is becoming one of the best SF novelists of our time." Certainly, he has tapped into the zeitgeist with his recent work, which charts the move from Western-centric science fiction to tales of emerging superpowers. The world of* River of Gods *has proven fodder for several subsequent stories, including the Hugo-nominated novella "The Little Goddess." In the story that follows, McDonald takes us once again into his fascinating and utterly convincing world of mid-twenty-first-century India.*

Every boy in the class ran at the cry. *Robotwar robotwar!* The teacher called after them, *Come here, come here bad wicked things.* But she was only a Business-English artificial intelligence and by the time old Mrs. Mawji hobbled in from the juniors only the girls remained, sitting primly on the floor, eyes wide in disdain and hands up to tell tales and name names.

Sanjeev was not a fast runner; the other boys pulled ahead from him as he stopped among the dal bushes for puffs from his inhalers. He had to fight for position on the ridge that was the village's highpoint, popular with chaperoned couples for its views over the river and the water plant at Murad. This day it was the inland view over the *dal* fields that held the attention. The men from the fields had been first up to the ridge; they stood, tools in hands, commanding all the best places. Sanjeev pushed between Mahesh and Ayanjit to the front.

"Where are they what's happening what's happening?"

"Soldiers over there by the trees."

Sanjeev squinted where Ayanjit was pointing. He could see nothing but yellow dust and heat shiver.

"Are they coming to Ahraura?"

"Delhi wouldn't bother with a piss-hole like Ahraura," said another man whose face Sanjeev knew—as he knew every face in Ahraura—if not his name. "It's Murad they're after. If they take that out, Varanasi will have to make a deal."

"Where are the robots, I want to see the robots."

Then he cursed himself for his stupidity, for anyone with eyes could see where the robots were. A great cloud of dust was moving down the north road, and over it a flock of birds milled in eerie silence. Through the dust Sanjeev caught sunlight flashes of armor, clawed booted feet lifting, antennae bouncing, insect heads bobbing, weapon pods glinting. Then he and everyone else up on the high place felt the ridge begin to tremble to the march of the robots.

A cry from down the line. Four, six, ten, twelve flashes of light from the copse; streaks of white smoke. The flock of birds whirled up into an arrow-head and aimed itself at trees. *Airdrones*, Sanjeev realized and, in the same thought: *missiles!* As the missiles reached their targets the cloud of dust exploded in a hammer of gunfire and firecracker flashes. It was all over before the sound reached the watchers. The robots burst unscathed from their cocoon of dust in a thundering run. *Cavalry charge!* Sanjeev shouted, his voice joining with the cheering of the men of Ahraura. Now hill and village quaked to the running iron feet. The wood broke into a fury of gunfire, the airdrones rose up and circled the copse like a storm. Missiles smoked away from the charging robots; Sanjeev watched weapon housings open and gun-pods swing into position.

The cheering died as the edge of the wood exploded in a wall of flame. Then the robots opened up with their guns and the hush became awed silence. The burning woodland was swept away in the storm of gunfire; leaves, branches, trunks shredded into splinters. The robots stalked around the perimeter of the small copse for ten minutes, firing constantly as the drones circled over their heads. Nothing came out.

A voice down the line started shouting *Jai Bharat! Jai Bharat!* but no one took it up and the man soon stopped. But there was another voice, hectoring and badgering, the voice of schoolmistress Mawji laboring up the path with a *lathi* cane.

"Get down from there you stupid, stupid men! Get to your families, you'll kill yourselves."

Everyone looked for the story on the evening news, but bigger flashier things were happening in Allahabad and Mirzapur; a handful of contras eliminated in an unplace like Ahraura did not rate a line. But that night Sanjeev became Number One Robot Fan. He cut out pictures from the papers and those pro-Bharat propaganda mags that survived Ahraura's omnivorous cows. He avidly watched J- and C-*anime* where andro-sexy kids crewed titanic battle droids until sister Priya rolled her eyes and his mother whispered to the priest that she was worried about her son's sexuality. He pulled gigabytes of pictures from the world web and memorized manufacturers and models and serial numbers, weapon loads and options mounts, rates of fire and maximum speeds. To buy a Japanese trump game, he saved up the pin-money he made from helping old men with the computers the self-proclaimed Bharati government put into every village. No one would play him at it because he had learned every last detail. When he tired of flat pictures, he cut up old cans with tin-snips and brazed them together into model fighting machines: MIRACLE GHEE fast pursuit drones, TITAN DRENCH perimeter defense bots, RED COLA riot-control robot.

Those same old men, when he came round to set up their accounts and assign their passwords, would ask him, "Hey! You know a bit about these things; what's going on with all this Bharat and Awadh stuff? What was wrong with plain old India anyway? And when are we going to get cricket back on the satellite?"

For all his robot-wisdom, Sanjeev did not know. The news breathlessly raced on with the movements of politicians and breakaway leaders, but everyone had long ago lost all clear memory of how the conflict had begun. Naxalites in Bihar, an overmighty Delhi, those bloody Muslims demanding their own laws again? The old men did not expect him to answer; they just liked to complain and took a withered pleasure in showing the smart boy that he did not know everything.

"Well, as long as that's the last we see of them," they would say when Sanjeev replied with the spec of a Raytheon 380 *Rudra* I-war airdrone, or an *Akhu* scout mecha and how much much better they were than any human fighter. Their general opinion was that the Battle of Vora's Wood—already growing back—was all the War of Separation Ahraura would see.

It was not. The men did return. They came by night, walking slowly through the fields, their weapons easily sloped in their hands. Those who met them said they had offered them no hostility, merely raised their assault rifles and shooed them away. They walked through the entire village, through every field and garden, up every *gali* and yard, past every byre and corral. In the morning their bootprints covered every centimeter of Ahraura. Nothing taken, nothing touched. *What was that about?* the people asked. *What did they want?*

They learned two days later when the crops began to blacken and wither in the fields and the animals, down to the last pi-dog, sickened and died.

Sanjeev would start running when their car turned into Umbrella Street. It was an easy car to spot, a big military Hummer that they had pimped Kali-black and red with after-FX flames that seemed to flicker as it drove past you. But it was an easier car to hear: everyone knew the *thud thud thud* of Desi-metal that grew guitars and screaming vocals when they wound down the window to order food, food to go. And Sanjeev would be there: *What can I get you sirs?* He had become a good runner since coming to Varanasi. Everything had changed since Ahraura died.

The last thing Ahraura ever did was make that line in the news. It had been the first to suffer a new attack. *Plaguewalkers* was the popular name; the popular image was dark men in chameleon camouflage walking slowly through the crops, hands outstretched as if to bless, but sowing disease and blight. It was a strategy of desperation—deny the separatists as much as they could—and was only ever partially effective; after the few first attacks plaguewalkers were shot on sight.

But they killed Ahraura, and when the last cow died and the wind whipped the crumbled leaves and the dust into yellow clouds, the people could put it off no longer. By car and pickup, *phatphat* and country bus, they went to the city; and though they had all sworn to hold together, family by family they drifted apart in Varanasi's ten million and Ahraura finally died.

Sanjeev's father rented an apartment on the top floor of a block on Umbrella Street and put his savings into a beer-and-pizza stall. Pizza pizza, that is what they want in the city, not samosas or tiddy-hoppers or *rasgullahs*. And beer, Kingfisher and Godfather and Bangla. Sanjeev's mother did light sewing and gave lessons in deportment and Sanskrit, for she had learned that language as part of her devotions. Grandmother Bharti and little sister Priya cleaned offices in the new shining Varanasi that rose in glass and chrome beyond the huddled peeling houses of old Kashi. Sanjeev helped out at the stall under the rows of tall neon umbrellas—useless against rain and sun both but magnetic to the party-people, the night-people, the *badmashes* and fashion-*girlis*—that gave the street its name. It was there that he had first seen the robotwallahs.

It had been love at first sight the night that Sanjeev saw them stepping down Umbrella Street in their slashy Ts and bare sexy arms with Krishna bangles and henna tats, cool boots with metal in all the hot places and hair spiked and gelled like one of those J-anime shows. The merchants of Umbrella Street edged away from them, turned a shoulder. They had a cruel reputation. Later Sanjeev was to see them overturn the stall of a pakora man who had irritated them, Eve-tease a woman in a business sari who had looked askance at them, smash up the phatphat of a taxi driver who had thrown them out for drunkenness; but that first night they were stardust, and he wanted to be them with a want so pure and aching and impossible it was tearful joy. They were soldiers, teen warriors, robotwallahs. Only the dumbest and cheapest machines could be trusted to run themselves; the big fighting bots carried human jockeys behind their aeai systems. Teenage boys possessed the best combination of reflex speed and viciousness, amped up with fistfuls of combat drugs.

"Pizza pizza pizza!" Sanjeev shouted, running up to them. "We got pizza every kind of pizza and beer, Kingfisher beer, Godfather beer, Bangla beer, all kinds of beer."

They stopped. They turned. They looked. Then they turned away. One looked back as his brothers moved. He was tall and very thin from the drugs, fidgety and scratchy, his bad skin ill-concealed with makeup. Sanjeev thought him a street-god.

"What kind of pizza?"

"Tikka tandoori murgh beef lamb kebab kofta tomato spinach."

"Let's see your kofta."

Sanjeev presented the drooping wedge of meatball-studded pizza in both hands. The robotwallah took a kofta between thumb and forefinger. It drew a sagging string of cheese to his mouth, which he deftly snapped.

"Yeah, that's all right. Give me four of those."

"We got beer we got Kingfisher beer we got Godfather beer we got Bangla beer—"

"Don't push it."

Now he ran up alongside the big slow-moving car they had bought as soon as they were old enough to drive. Sanjeev had never thought it incongruous that they could send battle robots racing across the country on scouting expeditions or marching behind heavy tanks but the law would not permit them so much as a moped on the public streets of Varanasi.

"So did you kill anyone today?" he called in through the open window, clinging on to the door handle as he jogged through the choked street.

"Kunda Khadar, down by the river, chasing out spies and surveyors," said bad-skin boy, the one who had first spoken to Sanjeev. He called himself Rai. They all had made-up J-anime names. "Someone's got to keep those bastard Awadhi dam-wallahs uncomfortable."

A black plastic Kali swung from the rearview mirror, red-tongued, yellow-eyed. The skulls garlanded around her neck had costume sapphires for eyes. Sanjeev took the order, sprinted back through the press to his father's clay *tandoor* oven. The order was ready by the time the Kali-hummer made its second cruise. Sanjeev slid the boxes to Rai. He slid back the filthy, wadded Government of Bharat scrip-rupees and, as Sanjeev fished out his change from his belt-bag, the tip: a little plastic zip-bag of battle-drugs. Sanjeev sold them in the galis and courtyards behind Umbrella Street. Schoolkids were his best customers; they went through them by the fistful when they were cramming for exams. Ahraura had been all the school Sanjeev ever wanted to see. Who needed it when you had the world and the web in your palmer? The little shining capsules in black and yellow, purple and sky blue, were the Rajghatta's respectability. The pills held them above the slum.

But this night Rai's hand shot out to seize Sanjeev's hand as it closed around the plastic bag.

"Hey, we've been thinking." The other robotwallahs, Suni and Ravana and Godspeed! and Big Baba nodded. "We're thinking we could use someone around the place, do odd jobs, clean a bit, keep stuff sweet, get us things. Would you like to do it? We'd pay—it'd be government scrip not dollars or euro. Do you want to work for us?"

He lied about it to his family: the glamour, the tech, the sexy spun-diamond headquarters and the chrome he brought up to dazzling shine by the old village trick of polishing it with toothpaste. Sanjeev lied from disappointment, but also from his own naïve overexpectation: too many nights filled with androgynous teenagers in spandex suits being clamshelled up inside block-killing battle machines. The robotwallahs of the 15th Light Armored and Recon Cavalry—*sowars* properly—worked out of a cheap pressed-aluminum go-down on a dusty commercial road at the back of the new railway station. They sent their wills over provinces and countries to fight for Bharat. Their talents were too rare to risk in Raytheon assault bots or Aiwa scout mecha. No robotwallah ever came back in a bodybag.

Sanjeev had scratched and kicked in the dust, squatting outside the shutter door, squinting in the early light. Surely the phatphat had brought him to the wrong address? Then Rai and Godspeed! had brought him inside and shown him how they made war inside a cheap go-down. Motion-capture harnesses hung from steadi-rigs like puppets from a hand. Black mirror-visored insect helmets—real J-anime helmets—trailed plaited cables. One wall of the go-down was racked up with the translucent blue domes of processor cores, the adjoining wall a massive video-silk screen flickering with the ten thousand dataflashes of the ongoing war: skirmishes, reconnaissances, air-strikes, infantry positions, minefields and slow-missile movements, heavy armor, and the mecha divisions. Orders came in on this screen from a woman *jemadar* at Divisional Headquarters. Sanjeev never saw her flesh. None of the robotwallahs had ever seen her flesh, though they joked about it every time she came on the screen to order them to a reconnaissance or a skirmish or a raid. Along the facing wall, behind the battle harnesses, were cracked leather sofas, sling chairs, a water cooler (full), a Coke machine (three-quarters empty). Gaming and *girli* mags were scattered like dead birds across the sneaker-scuffed concrete floor. A door led to a rec-room, with more sofas, a couple of folding beds, and a game console with three VR sets. Off the rec-room were a small kitchen area and a shower unit.

"Man, this place stinks," said Sanjeev.

By noon he had cleaned it front to back, top to bottom, magazines stacked in date of publication, shoes set together in pairs, lost clothes in a black plastic sack for the *dhobiwallah* to launder. He lit incense. He threw out the old bad milk and turning food in the refrigerator, returned the empty Coke bottles for their deposits—made *chai* and sneaked out to get *samosas* that he passed off as his own. He nervously watched Big Baba and Ravana step into their battle harnesses for a three-hour combat mission. So much he learned in that first morning. It was not one boy one bot; Level 1.2 aeais controlled most of the autonomous process like motion and perception, the pilots were more like officers, each commanding a bot platoon, their point of view switching from scout machine to assault bot to I-war drone. And they did not have their favorite old faithful combat machine, scarred with bullet holes and lovingly customized with hand-sprayed graffiti and *Desi*-metal demons. Machines went to war because they could take damage human flesh and families could not. The Kali Cavalry rotated between a dozen units a month as attrition and the *jemadar* dictated. It was not Japanese anime, but the Kali boys did look sexy dangerous cool in their gear even if they went home to their parents every night. And working for them—cleaning for them getting towels for them when they went sweating and stinking to the shower after a tour in the combat rig—was the maximum thing in Sanjeev's small life. They were his children, they were his boys; no girls allowed.

"Hanging round with those *badmashes* all day, never seeing a wink of sun, that's not good for you," his mother said, sweeping round the tiny top-floor living room before her next lesson. "Your dad needs the help more; he may have to hire a boy in. What kind of sense does that make, when he has a son of his own? They do not have a good reputation, those robot-boys."

Then Sanjeev showed her the money he had got for one day.

"Your mother worries about people taking advantage of you," Sanjeev's dad said, loading up the handcart with wood for the pizza oven. "You weren't born to this city. All I'd say is, don't love it too much; soldiers will let you down, they can't help it. All wars eventually end."

With what remained from his money when he had divided it between his mother and father and put some away in the credit union for Priya, Sanjeev went down to Tea Lane and stuck down the deposit and first payment on a pair of big metally leathery black-and-red and flame-pattern boots. He wore them proudly to work the next day, stuck out beside the driver of the *phat-phat* so everyone could see them and paid the owner of the Bata Boot and Shoe store assiduously every Friday. At the end of twelve weeks they were Sanjeev's entirely. In that time he had also bought the Ts, the fake-latex pants (real latex hot hot far too hot and sweaty for Varanasi, *baba*), the Kali bangles and necklaces, the hair gel and the eye kohl. But the boots first, the boots before all. Boots make the robotwallah.

"Do you fancy a go?"

It was one of those questions so simple and unexpected that Sanjeev's brain rolled straight over it and it was only when he was gathering up the fast food wrappers (messy messy boys) that it crept up and hit him over the head.

"What, you mean, that?" A nod of the head toward the harnesses hanging like flayed hides from the feedback rig.

"If you want; there's not much on."

There hadn't been much on for the better part of a month. The last excitement had been when some cracker in a similar go-down in Delhi had broken through the Kali Cav's aeai firewall with a spike of burnware. Big Baba had suddenly leaped up in his rig like a million billion volts had just shot through (which, Sanjeev discovered later, it kind of had) and next thing the biocontrol interlocks had blown (indoor fireworks, woo) and he was kicking on the floor like epilepsy. Sanjeev had been first to the red button, and a crash team had whisked Big Baba to the rich people's private hospital. The aeais had evolved a patch against the new burnware by the time Sanjeev went to get the lunch tins from the *dhabawallah*, and Big Baba was back on his corner of the sofa within three days suffering nothing more than a lingering migraine. *Jemadar*-woman sent a get well e-card.

So it was with excitement and wariness that Sanjeev let Rai help him into the rig. He knew all the snaps and grips—he had tightened the straps and pulled snug the motion sensors a hundred times—but Rai doing it made it special, made Sanjeev a robotwallah.

"You might find this a little freaky," Rai said as he settled the helmet over Sanjeev's head. For an instant it was blackout, deafness as the phonobuds sought out his eardrums. "They're working on this new thing, some kind of bone induction thing so they can send the pictures and sounds straight into your brain," he heard Rai's voice say on the com. "But I don't think we'll get it in time. Now, just stand there and don't shoot anything."

The warning was still echoing in Sanjeev's inner ear as he blinked and found himself standing outside a school compound in a village so like Ahraura that he instinctively looked for Mrs. Mawji and Shree the holy red calf. Then he saw that the school was deserted, its roof gone, replaced with military camouflage sheeting. The walls were pocked with bullets down to the brickwork. Siva and Krishna with his flute had been hastily painted on the intact mud plaster, and the words, *13th Mechanized Sowars: Section headquarters*. There were men in smart, tightly belted uniforms with mustaches and bamboo *lathis*. Women with brass water pots and men on bicycles passed the open gate. By stretching Sanjeev found he could elevate his sensory rig to crane over the wall. A village, an Ahraura, but too poor to even avoid war. On his left a robot stood under a dusty neem tree. *I must be one of those*, Sanjeev thought; a General Dynamics A8330 *Syce*; a mean, skeletal desert-rat of a thing on two vicious clawed feet, a heavy sensory crown and two gatling arms—fully interchangeable with gas shells or slime guns for policing work, he remembered from *War Mecha*'s October 2038 edition.

Sanjeev glanced down at his own feet. Icons opened across his field of vision like blossoming flowers: location elevation temperature, ammunition load-out, the level of methane in his fuel tanks, tactical and strategic satmaps—he seemed to be in southwest Bihar—but what fascinated Sanjeev was that if he formed a mental picture of lifting his Sanjeev-foot, his *Syce*-claw would lift from the dust.

Go on try it it's a quiet day you're on sentry duty in some cow-shit Bihar village.

Forward, he willed. The bot took one step two. *Walk,* Sanjeev commanded. *There.* The robot walked jauntily toward the gate. No one in the street of shattered houses looked twice as he stepped among them. *This is great!* Sanjeev thought as he strolled down the street, then, *This is like a game.* Doubt then: *So how do I even know this war is happening?* A step too far; the Syce froze a hundred meters from the Ganesh temple, turned and headed back to its sentry post. *What what what what what?* he yelled in his head.

"The onboard aeai took over," Rai said, his voice startling as a firecracker inside his helmet. Then the village went black and silent and Sanjeev was blinking in the ugly low-energy neons of the Kali Cavalry battle room, Rai gently unfastening the clips and snaps and strappings.

That evening, as he went home through the rush of people with his fist of rupees, Sanjeev realized two things; that most of war was boring, and that this boring war was over.

The war was over. The *jemadar* visited the video-silk wall three times, twice, once a week where in the heat and glory she would have given orders that many times a day. The Kali Cav lolled around on their sofas playing games, lying to their online fans about the cool exciting sexy things they were doing—though the fans never believed they ever really were robotwallahs—but mostly doing battle-drug combos that left them fidgety and aggressive.

Fights flared over a cigarette, a look, how a door was closed or left open. Sanjeev threw himself into the middle of a dozen robotwallah wars. But when the American Peacekeepers arrived, Sanjeev knew it truly was over because they only came in when there was absolutely no chance any of them would get killed. There was a flurry of car-bombings and I-war attacks and even a few suicide blasts, but everyone knew that that was just everyone who had a grudge against America and Americans in sacred Bharat. No, the war was over.

"What will you do?" Sanjeev's father asked, meaning, *What will I do when Umbrella Street becomes just another Asian ginza?*

"I've saved some money," Sanjeev said.

With the money he had saved, Godspeed! bought a robot. It was a Tata Industries D55, a small but nimble antipersonnel bot with detachable free-roaming sub-mechas, Level 0.8s, about as smart as a chicken, which they resembled. Even secondhand it must have cost much more than a teenage robotwallah heavily consuming games, online time, porn, and Sanjeev's dad's kofta pizza could ever save. "I got backers," Godspeed! said. "Funding. Hey, what do you think of this? I'm getting her pimped; this is the skin-job." When the paint dried, the robot would be road-freighted up to Varanasi.

"But what are you going to do with it?" Sanjeev asked.

"Private security. They're always going to need security drones."

Tidying the tiny living room that night for his mother's nine o'clock lesson, opening the windows to let out the smell of hot ghee though the stink of the street was little better, Sanjeev heard a new chord in the ceaseless song of Umbrella Street. He threw open the window shutters in time to see an object, close, fast as a dashing bird, dart past his face, swing along the powerline and down the festooned pylon. Glint of anodized alu-plastic: a boy raised on *Battlebots Top Trumps* could not fail to recognize a Tata surveillance mecha. Now the commotion at the end of Umbrella Street became clear: the hunched back of a battlebot was pushing between the cycle rickshaws and phatphats. Even before he could fully make out the customized god-demons of Mountain Buddhism on its carapace, Sanjeev knew the machine's make and model and who was flying it.

A *badmash* on an alco moto rode slowly in front of the ponderously stepping machine, relishing the way the street opened in front of him and the electric scent of heavy firepower at his back. Sanjeev saw the mech step up and squat down on its hydraulics before Jagmohan's greasy little pakora stand. The *badmash* skidded his moped to a stand and pushed up his shades.

They will always need security drones.

Sanjeev rattled down the many many flights of stairs of the patriotically renamed Diljit Rana Apartments, yelling and pushing and beating at the women and young men in very white shirts. The robot had already taken up its position in front of his father's big clay pizza oven. The carapace unfolded like insect wings into weapon mounts. *Badmash* was all teeth and grin in the anticipation of another commission. Sanjeev dashed between his father and the prying, insect sensory rig of the robot. Red demons and Sivas with fiery tridents looked down on him.

"Leave him alone, this is my dad, leave him be."

It seemed to Sanjeev that the whole of Umbrella Street, every vehicle upon it, every balcony and window that overlooked it, stopped to watch. With a whir the weapon pods retracted, the carapace clicked shut. The battle machine reared up on its legs as the surveillance drones came skittering between people's legs and over countertops, scurried up the machine and took their places on its shell mounts, like egrets on the back of a buffalo. Sanjeev stared the *badmash* down. He sneered, snapped down his cool sexy dangerous shades, and spun his moped away.

Two hours later, when all was safe and secure, a Peacekeeper unit passed up the street asking for information. Sanjeev shook his head and sucked on his asthma inhalers.

"Some machine, like."

Suni left the go-down. No word no note no clue, his family had called and called and called but no one knew. There had always been rumors of a man with money and prospects, who liked the robotwallah thing, but you do not tell those sorts of stories to mothers. Not at first asking. A week passed without the *jemadar* calling. It was over. So over. Rai had taken to squatting outside, squinting up through his cool sexy dangerous shades at the sun, watching for its burn on his pale arms, chain-smoking street-rolled *bidis*.

"Sanj." He smoked the cheap cigarette down to his gloved fingers and ground the stub out beneath the steel heel of his boot. "When it happens, when we can't use you anymore, have you something sorted? I was thinking, maybe you and I could do something together, go somewhere. Just have it like it was, just us. An idea, that's all."

The message came at 3 AM. *I'm outside.* Sanjeev tiptoed around the sleeping bodies to open the window. Umbrella Street was still busy; Umbrella Street had not slept for a thousand years. The big black Kali Cav Hummer was like a funeral moving through the late-night people of the new Varanasi. The door locks made too much noise, so Sanjeev exited through the window, climbing down the pipes like a Raytheon 8-8000 I-war infiltration bot. In Ahraura he would never have been able to do that.

"You drive," Rai said. From the moment the message came through, Sanjeev had known it would be him, and him alone.

"I can't drive."

"It drives itself. All you have to do is steer. It's not that different from the game. Swap over there."

Steering wheel pedal drive windshield display all suddenly looked very big to Sanjeev in the driver's seat. He touched his foot to the gas. Engines answered; the Hummer rolled; Umbrella Street parted before him. He steered around a wandering cow.

"Where do want me to go?"

"Somewhere, away. Out of Varanasi. Somewhere no one else would go." Rai bounced and fidgeted on the passenger seat. His hands were busy busy; his eyes were huge. He had done a lot of battle drugs. "They sent them back to school, man. To school, can you imagine that? Big Baba and Ravana. Said they needed real-world skills. I'm not going back, not never. Look!"

Sanjeev dared a glance at the treasure in Rai's palm: a curl of sculpted translucent pink plastic. Sanjeev thought of aborted goat fetuses, and the sex toys the girls had used in their favorite pornos. Rai tossed his head to sweep back his long, gelled hair and slid the device behind his ear. Sanjeev thought he saw something move against Rai's skin, seeking.

"I saved it all up and bought it. Remember, I said? It's new; no one else has one. All that gear, that's old, you can do everything with this, just in your head, in the pictures and words in your head." He gave a stoned grin and moved his hands in a dancer's *mudra*. "There."

240   **FAST FORWARD 1**

"What?"

"You'll see."

The Hummer was easy to drive: the in-car aeai had a flocking reflex that enabled it to navigate Varanasi's ever-swelling morning traffic, leaving little for Sanjeev to do other than blare the triple horns, which he enjoyed a lot. Somewhere he knew he should be afraid, should feel guilty at stealing away in the night without word or note, should stay *stop, whatever it is you are doing, it can come to nothing, it's just silliness, the war is over and we must think properly about what to do next.* But the brass sun was rising above the glass towers and spilling into the streets, and men in sharp white shirts and women in smart saris were going busy to their work, and he was free, driving a big smug car through them all and it was so good, even if just for a day.

He took the new bridge at Ramnagar, hooting in derision at the gaudy, lumbering trucks. The drivers blared back, shouting vile curses at the *girli*-looking robotwallahs. Off A-roads on to B-roads, then to tracks and then bare dirt, the dust flying up behind the Hummer's fat wheels. Rai itched in the passenger seat, grinning away to himself and moving his hands like butter-flies, muttering small words and occasionally sticking out of the window. His gelled hair was stiff with dust.

"What are you looking for?" Sanjeev demanded.

"It's coming," Rai said, bouncing on his seat. "Then we can go and do whatever we like."

From the word "drive," Sanjeev had known where he must go. Satnav and aeai did his remembering for him, but he still knew every turn and side road. Vora's Wood there, still stunted and gray; the ridge between the river and the fields from which all the men of the village had watched the battle and he had fallen in love with the robots. The robots had always been pure, had always been true. It was the boys who flew them who hurt and failed and disap-pointed. The fields were all dust, drifted and heaped against the lines of thorn fence. Nothing would grow here for a generation. The mud walls of the houses were crumbling, the school a roofless shell, the temple and tanks clogged with wind-blown dust. Dust, all dust. Bones cracked and went to powder beneath his all-wheel-drive. A few too desperate even for Varanasi were trying to scratch an existence in the ruins. Sanjeev saw wire-thin men and tired women, dust-smeared children crouched in front of their brick-and-plastic shelters. The poison deep within Ahraura would defeat them in the end.

Sanjeev brought the Hummer to a halt on the ridgetop. The light was yellow, the heat appalling. Rai stepped out to survey the terrain.

"What a shit-hole."

Sanjeev sat in the shade of the rear cabin watching Rai pace up and down, up and down, kicking up the dust of Ahraura with his big Desi-metal boots. *You didn't stop them, did you?* Sanjeev thought. *You didn't save us from the Plaguewalkers.* Rai suddenly leaped and punched the air.

"There, there, look!"

A storm of dust moved across the dead land. The high sun caught glints and gleams at its heart. Moving against the wind, the tornado bore down on Ahraura.

The robot came to a halt at the foot of the ridge where Sanjeev and Rai stood waiting. A Raytheon ACR, a heavy line-of-battle bot, it out-topped them by some meters. The wind carried away its cloak of dust. It stood silent, potential, heat shimmering from its armor. Sanjeev had never seen a thing so beautiful.

Rai raised his hand. The bot spun on its steel hooves. More guns than Sanjeev had ever seen in his life unfolded from its carapace. Rai clapped his hands and the bot opened up with all its armaments on Vora's Wood. Gatlings sent dry dead silvery wood flying up into powder; missiles streaked from its back-silos. The line of the wood erupted in a wall of flame. Rai separated his hands, and the roar of sustained fire ceased.

"It's got it all in here, everything that the old gear had, in here. Sanj, everyone will want us, we can go wherever we want, we can do whatever we want, we can be real anime heroes."

"You stole it."

"I had all the protocols. That's the system."

"You stole that robot."

Rai balled his fists, shook his head in exasperation.

"Sanj, it was always mine."

He opened his clenched fist. And the robot danced. Arms, feet, all the steps and the moves, the bends and head-nods, a proper Bollywood item-song dance. The dust flew up around the battle-bots feet. Sanjeev could feel the eyes of the squatters, wide and terrified in their hovels. *I am sorry we scared you.*

Rai brought the dance to an end.

"Anything I want, Sanj. Are you coming with us?"

Sanjeev's answer never came, for a sudden, shattering roar of engines and jet-blast from the river side of the ridge sent them reeling and choking in the swirling dust. Sanjeev fought out his inhalers: two puffs blue one puff brown and by the time they had worked their sweet way down into his lungs a tilt-jet with the Bharati Air Force's green, white, and orange roundels on its engine pods stood on the settling dust. The cargo ramp lowered; a woman in dust-war camo and a mirror-visored helmet came up the ridge toward them.

With a wordless shriek Rai slashed his hand through the air like a sword. The bot crouched; its carapace slid open in a dozen places, extruding weapons. Without breaking her purposeful stride the woman lifted her left hand. The weapons retracted, the hull ports closed, the war machine staggered as if confused and then sat down heavily in the dead field, head sagging, hands trailing in the dust. The woman removed her helmet. The cameras made the *jemadar* look five kilos heavier, but she had big hips. She tucked her helmet under her left arm, with her right swept back her hair to show the plastic fetus-sex-toy-thing coiled behind her ear.

"Come on now, Rai. It's over. Come on, we'll go back. Don't make a fuss. There's not really anything you can do. We all have to think what to do next, you know? We'll take you back in the plane, you'll like that." She looked Sanjeev up and down. "I suppose you could take the car back. Someone has to and it'll be cheaper than sending someone down from Divisional, it's cost enough already. I'll retask the aeai. And then we have to get that thing . . ." She shook her head, then beckoned to Rai. He went like a calf, quiet and meek down to the tiltjet. Black hopping crows settled on the robot, trying its crevices with their curious shiny-hungry beaks.

The Hummer ran out of gas twenty kays from Ramnagar. Sanjeev hitched home to Varanasi. The army never collected it, and as the new peace built, the local people took it away bit by bit.

With his war dividend Sanjeev bought a little alco-buggy and added a delivery service to his father's pizza business, specializing in the gap-year hostels that blossomed after the Peacekeepers left. He wore a polo shirt with a logo and a baseball cap and got a sensible haircut. He could not bring himself to sell his robotwallah gear, but it was a long time before he could look at it in the box without feeling embarrassed. The business grew fast and fat.

He often saw Rai down at the ghats or around the old town. They worked the same crowd: Rai dealt Nepalese *ganja* to tourists. *Robotwallah* was his street name. He kept the old look, and everyone knew him for it. It became first a novelty and then retro. It even became fashionable again, the spiked hair, the andro makeup, the slashed Ts and the latex and most of all the boots. It sold well and everyone wore it, for a season.

A SMALLER GOVERNMENT

Pamela Sargent

Nebula award–winning author Pamela Sargent is a considerably talented writer whose fiction always contains deft characterizations executed with an assured touch. She is also a consummate anthologist, renowned for her Women of Wonder series, which highlights science fiction stories "by women about women." Her Venusian trilogy— Venus of Dreams, Venus of Shadows, Child of Venus—*is a landmark tale of terraforming often compared to Kim Stanley Robinson's Mars trilogy, which it predates. Her novel* Earthseed *is recently out from Tor, along with a sequel,* Farseed. *She offers us a bit of satire here, emerging from sentiments that will be all too familiar to those of us troubled by our current times.*

> My goal is to cut government in half in twenty-five years, to get it down to the size where we can drown it in the bathtub.
>
> —Grover Norquist

Hector was sitting on his usual bench in Lafayette Park, across the street from the White House, freezing his ass off in the cold wintry air. On a bench nearby, the Homeless Lobbyist was consulting with the Homeless Philosopher. The Philosopher was expounding to the Lobbyist and anyone else within earshot about something he called the ethics bank and moral bankruptcy problem, although he wasn't being all that coherent. Now he was saying something about physical manifestations of moral lapses and chickens coming home to roost.

The mention of chickens reminded Hector that he hadn't chowed down in a while. He was thinking that maybe it was about time to head for the shelter when the night air rippled. Then there was a loud whooshing sound, followed by a thunderclap.

"Shee-it!" the Homeless Lobbyist exclaimed.

"What the hell?" the Homeless Philosopher asked. For a moment, Hector had wondered if the rippling air and the whooshing noise were only symptoms of some weird-assed case of the DTs, but the Lobbyist and the Philosopher had apparently seen and heard the same thing.

Then the bright lights across the way went out, and the White House disappeared.

"Shee-it!" the Homeless Lobbyist shouted again. He dropped his brown paper bag, and the bottle inside shattered.

Hector sat there, too surprised to move. After a few moments, the low rumble to Hector's right grew into a roar. A convoy of tanks rolled past the Eisenhower Executive Office Building and stopped in front of the park. A couple of soldiers climbed down from one of the tanks, while other members of the armed services fanned out across the park.

"Come on," the taller of the soldiers said as he approached. To Hector's left, the Lobbyist and the Philosopher were being dragged away by several other soldiers.

"What the hell's going on?" Hector asked. "Where'd the White House go?"

"Didn't go anywhere." The soldiers grabbed him by the arms.

"It disappeared, for Chrissake." He twisted in their grip. "Was sittin' right here, and it fuckin' disappeared!"

"Not exactly," the shorter soldier replied.

The Secretary of Commerce was with the Senator and the Congressman in a relatively comfy secure and undisclosed location. The Secret Service had brought in some snacks, plates of little puffed pastries with shrimp and crabmeat, diminutive tarts, and tiny cocktail wieners impaled on toothpicks. The

Secretary could have used a cocktail himself, but the only beverages in evidence were coffee, tea, bottled water, and assorted soft drinks.

He sat back with a cup of coffee, figuring he'd need the caffeine to stay awake throughout the State of the Union address. The President was not only long-winded, but also had a voice that had become noticeably whinier and more high-pitched since his inauguration a year ago. If he had sounded like that during the campaign, thought the Secretary, he would never have made it past the first primary. Then again, the President had a lot on his mind, enough to give anyone a whiny voice and rapidly graying hair. His predecessor had left him with cesspools on all fronts.

"Did he get Joey to polish the speech this time?" the Senator asked. She was an imposing woman from Connecticut who belonged to the other party.

"I dunno," the Secretary replied; he wasn't exactly in the inner circle and didn't even know who among the President's speechwriters had sketched out the first draft.

"Sure hope he did," the Congressman muttered; he was a barrel-chested man of the Secretary's own party from Illinois. "Or else we're in for a long fuckin' night."

On the large plasma screen, tuned to C-SPAN to spare the Secretary any media gasbagging from the major networks, the President was still glad-handing his way toward the dais, shaking hands and clutching shoulders. The Secretary had finished his coffee and was munching on a tiny cocktail frank by the time the President was handing copies of his address to the Vice President and the Speaker of the House.

The screen abruptly went blank.

"Fuckin' C-SPAN," the Congressman said. "If you ask me, they got too many damn glitches lately." The Secretary reached for the remote on the coffee table and switched to CNN.

". . . just disappeared." A blonde news babe was on the screen. She looked a bit green around the gills, but not because of any issues with the screen's color contrast controls. "And now a report's coming in from our White House correspondent. The White House is gone, too."

"Holy shit," the Congressman said.

In the corner of the room, two of the Secret Service agents were cupping their ears, clearly intent on whatever was coming in through their earpieces. The Secretary switched to Fox.

". . . reports from all over the city," the voice of a male correspondent intoned. The dark and murky image on the screen showed tanks rolling past Lafayette Park. The Secretary was seized by a powerful surge of emotion compounded of both ecstasy and terror. He, the Senator, and the Congressman—those chosen this time to be tucked away in the customary secure and undisclosed location while the rest of Washington's potentates were at the Capitol—might be all that was left of the government.

He tried for NBC but found himself back at C-SPAN. The President was still at the podium, with no words coming out of his mouth, while the look on his face was that of a man about to be arrested. A big bruiser wearing an earpiece was passing a piece of paper to him.

"I don't get it," the Congressman said.

Three of the Secret Service agents stepped in front of the screen, blocking the Secretary's view. "What's going on?" he asked.

The agent tapped his earpiece. "You're not going to believe this, Mr. Secretary," he began.

The Secret Service officer had performed some odd actions in the course of his duties. He had ridden in the freight elevators of hotels where the President was staying, the only elevators that could be truly secured, with himself and his fellow agents packed as tightly around their charge as passengers on a low-fare flight. He had rerouted traffic during rush hours to allow for the Presidential motorcade, closely observed annoyed chefs in restaurant kitchens, had forced the cancellation of long-held reservations at resorts where Air Force One was headed, and generally made an unholy nuisance of himself in the course of protecting the Commander in Chief. But looking out for the big guy during the State of the Union address was, generally speaking, a piece of cake, because security was so tight throughout the Capitol and in DC at that time.

But now, looking around at the assembled dignitaries in the House chamber, he could see that pretty much all of them suspected that something was up. One of his fellow agents had discreetly passed a note to the President just before he was to begin his opening remarks, and so far the President was doing a decent job of huddling with the Vice President and the Speaker as if he just had a few last-minute items to iron out, but the Supreme Court justices were definitely looking restless, while the Joint Chiefs of Staff looked like they had bigger than usual ramrods up their asses. Camera crews from the networks were still going about their business, and he wondered what the TV audience, that small percentage that even bothered to watch the State of the Union, was seeing.

"C-SPAN's just about to cut off its cameras," a voice said in his earpiece, answering his question, "and all the networks have gone to their anchors for special reports. We've got the Capitol and the White House surrounded, so nothing's going to get through." There was a pause. "Okay, guys, time to tell you just exactly what's going on, but brace yourselves."

Terrorists, the officer thought. They'd finally done it, struck at a time when the whole country, or at least that segment of it that wasn't in the middle of watching ESPN, HBO, or rented DVDs, would be transfixed with terror, glued to their screens the way they'd been during those dark days in September at the turn of the century. All of the Secret Service agents inside the chamber—those by the doorways, at the end of the aisles, in the balcony with the First Lady and honored guests, and standing near the President—stood at attention while continuing to scan the room, heads turning from side to side.

"It's like this," the voice in his ear continued. "The Capitol, like, suddenly got real small, and so did the White House. What happened was this weird rippling-in-the air kind of deal, and then suddenly stuff shrank. I'm talking about the White House, the Capitol, the House and Senate Office Buildings, and pretty much everything on either side of Pennsylvania Avenue. Basically, the White House is now about the size of Malibu Barbie's beach house, and the Capitol dome isn't much bigger than a goddamn teacup."

The Secret Service officer pondered this statement. If the Capitol was so tiny, how could all of them still be inside it? The answer came to him just before the voice provided further illumination.

"And it looks like all of you . . . us . . . shrank right along with every-thing else."

|| ||

Pennsylvania Avenue was still the same size, despite the shrunken size of the bordering real estate. Rows of troops, along with police called in from sur-rounding counties of Maryland and Virginia, had been stationed around the Capitol and were lined up on Constitution and Independence avenues, ready to protect the Lilliputians trapped inside the Capitol Building from any Brobdingnagian constituents seeking redress for real or imagined grievances. There was a rumor that some residents of Anacostia were preparing to con-verge on the Capitol.

They could stamp us all flat, the First Lady thought. She stared at her hands, which seemed the same size they had always been; but if everything here had shrunk proportionately, then everything should still look the same. If she went outside, she would notice the difference. Any eagle soaring over-head would probably look like an Airbus.

She sat in an office just outside the House chamber, along with the Pres-ident, the Vice President, the Vice President's wife, the National Security Advisor, the Domestic Policy Advisor, and several Secret Service agents, her jaws aching from the smile she had struggled to keep in place even after she had been led out of the chamber and ushered to this temporary sanctuary. Her husband, as usual when things got really heavy, had a bewildered expression on his face, as if hoping that, real soon now, somebody would tell him exactly what to do.

"So what the hell happens now?" the Vice President asked, looking even more morose than usual. "Can't park our asses here forever."

"True enough," the Domestic Policy Advisor muttered as he rubbed his bald pate, "but we're safer staying here for the moment. Easier to protect us."

The First Lady shuddered, then thought of all the time she had spent refurbishing the White House, rescuing it from the tacky excesses of her predecessor and restoring the residence to its former glory, only to have it all taken from her, reduced to the size of a dollhouse. But perhaps all of her efforts weren't necessarily wasted.

"Couldn't we all just go back to the White House?" she asked. Her husband gazed at her as if clutching a life preserver; the Vice President glowered at her as though wanting to push her overboard. "I mean, it's teeny now, but so are we, apparently, and I'm sure we could be just as well protected there." The staff had to be as tiny as they were, at least those who were still there attending to their nighttime duties, so life could go on, even if on a somewhat smaller scale.

"That's all well and good for you," the Vice President's wife murmured, "but where are we supposed to live? If we set foot inside our house, it's a toss-up which of our cats gobbles us up first." The Vice Presidential residence had apparently escaped shrinkage, along with most of Washington, but that was small consolation to the First Lady. The Rayburn, Longworth, and Cannon House Office Buildings, along with the Russell, Dirksen, and Hart Senate Office Buildings, were the size of a set of children's blocks, while the Supreme Court Building could now rest easily on scales held by any good-sized statue of Justice. She should be grateful that the FBI Building hadn't shrunk during the daytime, when many more people there would have been in their offices, and that the Pentagon and the CIA remained untouched, even though nobody there had been able to prevent what seemed a massive breach of national security.

"I have an idea," the Foreign Policy Advisor said. "Couldn't we just, well, like, go about our usual business?" She cast a wide-eyed glance around the room. "I mean, apparently the broadcast wasn't affected, at least not until the cameramen were told to shut it down, so wouldn't we still look the same on TV?"

"That won't do us any good the next time we hold a summit," the Vice President growled.

"Or a state dinner, for that matter," the First Lady said.

The Vice President frowned even more. "Some superpower we'd look like."

A door opened, and a man wearing the dark suit and earpiece of a Secret Service agent lunged into the room and slammed the door behind him. "Got some news," he said.

"Hope it's good news," the President said, looking a little less lost.

The Vice President scowled. "In this context, about the only thing that might count as good news is getting low bids from Mattel and Toys "R" Us for future government services."

"Better news than that," the agent replied.

‖

The House Sergeant at Arms made the discovery. He was standing in a doorway at the East Front of the Capitol because, after all the strangeness of the evening, he needed a smoke but also some fresh air, which would be unattainable in the smog of the Speakers' Lobby, already crowded with stressed-out smokers. Luckily, his cigarettes had shrunk along with him, while the few inches of snow that had been predicted for that evening had failed to materialize; he would not have wanted to confront a glacial mass in order to get some air.

He stood above the stairway, puffing away, until someone tapped him on the shoulder. He turned to find that the Mayor of Washington, DC, had also stepped out for a smoke. The two men smoked together in silence, gazing out at the mountainous dark forms of tanks and forests of trousered legs that surrounded the Capitol. Finally the Sergeant at Arms said, "Think I'll take a walk."

"Man, maybe that ain't such a good idea," the Mayor said, "you bein' sized so small as you are."

"I advise against it," a member of the Honor Guard said behind them. "You wouldn't want to get gooshed." Another serviceman nodded his head.

"Nobody's going to goosh me with all those tanks around, and my doc keeps telling me I need more exercise, what with my cholesterol and all," the Sergeant at Arms said.

"If you're worried about your cholesterol," another young military man muttered, "then you ought to quit smoking."

"Watch out for pigeons," the Mayor added.

The Sergeant at Arms descended the steps, breathing in the cold night air between drags, and wondered how that was possible; maybe the molecules of air around him had shrunk along with the Capitol. He dropped his butt, ground it out with his foot, and tried to recall what one of his high school science teachers had said about a square cube law or whatever it was. If people were the size of grasshoppers, they'd be able to hop around like grasshoppers.

He was envisioning tiny members of Congress leaping high in the air from the Capitol steps, flapping their arms to ward off flies that would be nearly half their size, when the air seemed to ripple around him. For a moment, as his body vibrated, he felt a not-unpleasant electrical sensation as the ground shifted under his feet.

Three uniformed policeman ran toward him, followed by a man in a long tweed coat, and then the Sergeant at Arms saw that the tanks, although still imposing, were now their normal size. The men coming toward him were of normal size, too; in fact, two of them were considerably shorter than he was.

"What the hell did you just do?" the man in the tweed coat asked.

"Came outside for a smoke and took a walk," the Sergeant at Arms replied.

"What you did," one of the cops said, "was just pop up out of nowhere. Maybe we better take you in for questioning." The policeman gestured toward the barricades and at the tiny Capitol dome inside them, which glowed under its small floodlights, its tiny flags on its east and west sides still proudly flying.

"I'm the House Sergeant at Arms; I can show you my ID." He was about to reach inside his jacket pocket before realizing that this might not be such a good idea with armed cops standing around.

"Wait a minute." The tweed-coated man scratched his head. "Maybe we'd better try an experiment." The man clapped a hand on the Sergeant at Arms's shoulder and shoved him toward the miniature Capitol. He felt the vibrations and then the prickly electrical sensations again as the Capitol abruptly loomed up before him in all of its majesty.

"So *that's* how it works," the man in tweed said softly.

The two tiny men turned around in unison to face six legs as big as sequoias. Far above them, a voice as loud as God's exclaimed: "Jesus H. Christ!"

They moved toward the policemen. This time, the Sergeant at Arms felt himself suddenly shooting up like Jack's beanstalk, or maybe Alice in Wonderland after eating that weird cookie in that Disney flick that was a favorite of his daughter's. He was again looking down at two cops who were shorter than he was.

"What now?" the Sergeant at Arms asked.

"Evacuate the Capitol," the man in the tweed coat said.

‖

It had taken a couple of weeks, but everything was almost back to normal, or at least as normal as anything could be under the circumstances. The President's Chief of Staff stood at his office window, gazing below at the cordon of tanks and soldiers around the tiny White House. He'd had to move himself and the rest of the staff over to the Eisenhower Executive Office Building, which had caused a fair amount of hard feeling. Those who had lost their cherished offices in the West Wing were not happy about their relocation to the EEOB, while those who had earlier been exiled to that Siberia resented having to move their operations to the New Executive Office Building, the State Department, and the campus of George Washington University, where some basement offices had been turned over to them.

His first trip down Pennsylvania Avenue, three days after everyone had been evacuated from all the shrunken buildings, had been a sobering experience. The reduction of the FBI Building had been almost as disturbing to see as the tiny Capitol. There had been talk of bringing out essential records, which would have restored them all to their normal size once they were carried outside the Peewee Zone, the appellation that had unfortunately adhered to the region of shrinkage. The problem was figuring out what was essential, since just about everything was considered essential by somebody in authority, and then finding places to store the whole shebang. In the meantime, FBI agents could no longer access their files and computers, Senators and Representatives were cut off from the tiny records in their offices, the Supreme Court justices could no longer peruse their now-minute law volumes, and documents in the National Archives and at the Federal Trade Commission were unreadable to anyone over three inches in height.

At least the Lincoln Memorial, the Smithsonian Institution, and other national treasures had escaped; he would not have been able to bear seeing the Washington Monument reduced to the size of a pencil. It was also their good fortune that the offices of the Internal Revenue Service, not far from the Zone, had not been affected. But to have so many sites of power reduced to the size of scattered toys had been a heavy blow. The Chief of Staff thought of his recent conversation with the Canadian Ambassador, whose embassy on Pennsylvania Avenue was one of the shrunken structures. "So now you know how we feel sometimes, eh?" the Ambassador had said in his bland voice.

The phone on the desk behind him beeped. He turned to pick up the receiver. "The First Lady's Chief of Staff is here," his receptionist's voice said.

"Send her in." The door opened; a tall and emaciated woman in a red suit strode inside and sat down in the worn leather chair on the other side of his desk. "How are things going over at Blair House?" he asked. The First Family was now in residence at the guest house across the street from the Eisenhower Executive Office Building.

"About as well as you'd expect," the First Lady's Chief of Staff replied. "In other words, they totally suck. Everybody's bitching. The First Lady still thinks that she and the President should have moved into the Vice President's residence."

"You know how the Vice President felt about that." Actually, it had been the Vice President's wife who had pitched a fit at that suggestion, but the Veep hadn't looked overjoyed at the idea of sharing their quarters with the First Family, either. "The setup we've got now is about the best we can do in the interim."

The interim, he thought; he was still imagining that the tiny buildings would somehow balloon to normal size. He wished that they'd appointed a real science advisor to the President's staff instead of that Bible college biologist who had been put in to appease the more rabid of their constituents. Maybe they should put out some feelers to some of those strange institutes of nanotechnology that were popping up around the country. He didn't know much about nanotechnology except that it had something to do with very tiny things.

"I suppose you're right," the First Lady's Chief of Staff murmured, "but after all the work we put in fixing up the White House—" She paused. "That's what I'm here about. The First Lady is getting very concerned about the condition of the furnishings there."

The Chief of Staff scowled at his colleague. "What can possibly happen to them now?"

"Tiny bits of dust. Tiny spiders weaving their webs. Teeny little moths, teeny little bacteria in the kitchens, eensy-weensy dust bunnies in the Lincoln Bedroom and the Oval Office and everywhere else—you name it." She sighed. "We want to send in a cleaning crew."

The Chief of Staff was suddenly wary. "We can't," he managed to say.

"Come on; we already know that people can shrink going into the Zone and expand on their way out. Just shrink 'em in and grow 'em out."

He wondered how she had found that out. The Secret Service had sent some agents into the FBI Building and both buildings of the National Gallery of Art under cover of night, making sure that they were unobserved by anyone except a few guards, and they had gone inside and emerged again with no apparent ill effects. "Who told you that?" he asked, vowing silently to punish the leaker. It occurred to him then that if they could ever find a way to control the shrinking process, tiny little buildings might make for very effective and easily guarded prisons. That would also settle the hash of any whistle-blowers who crept in to expose abuses in the system.

"Let's just say I have my sources, and this place leaks like a sieve." The First Lady's factotum leaned forward. "So whaddya say?"

"It's too risky. Maybe the next time somebody'll go in and stay tiny when they come out. Or maybe they'll suddenly blow up when they're inside and mess up the whole damned place."

"You don't have any reason to think that'll happen."

"I don't have any reason to think that it won't." He was silent for a bit. "Wait until we've run a few more tests."

His counterpart leaned back. "Okay, okay." She let out her breath. "But don't take too long. You have no idea how messy things can get when you haven't cleaned in a while."

She was worse than his mother.

‖

By cherry blossom time, it was clear that people could go into the shrunken artifacts and come out again, shrinking and then expanding, with no apparent problems. The Metro under the Zone was running again; as long as passengers boarded and exited the trains at stops outside the Zone, it didn't much matter if they shrank in the interim, and nobody noticed much difference during the ride anyway. By Memorial Day weekend, tourists were returning to visit all of the famous sites, including the cute little Capitol and diminutive White House, although no visitors were allowed inside while skeleton staffs of agents, law clerks, and Congressional aides scanned and photographed the most essential of the small documents inside the Zone and emailed copies to the larger world outside; wireless Internet access was apparently unaffected by the differences in scale.

Which was all very well, the Senator from Montana thought, but having to put up with a shit-hole of an office in the Ford House Office Building instead of her nicely appointed and roomy space inside the Hart Building was really getting on her nerves. That all of the Congresspeople were even more crowded in the offices over at the O'Neill House Office Building, since they had conceded one of their two remaining unshrunken buildings to the Senate, did nothing to assuage her annoyance.

One of her aides sat in a corner, pecking away at a laptop; another aide was pouring himself a cup of instant coffee at the counter near the microwave. "Pour me a cup of joe, too," the Senator said. The young man poured, stirred, and set the cup on her desk with a flourish.

The Senator looked around resentfully at her crowded domain. "I don't know how much longer I can take this," she added. "Got a good mind to announce I'm not running again and that I'm resigning from public service and hauling ass back to Butte."

"I thought you hated Butte," the young woman with the laptop said.

The Senator had made her remark about Butte only for rhetorical purposes, because it sounded better than saying that she was thinking of resigning and then getting into the lobbying racket. Fortunately, K Street lay well outside the Peewee Zone. "At least I'll have enough space to turn around in back home," the Senator replied. Using "home" as a synonym for "Montana" was another rhetorical flourish; she had been living quite contentedly in her house in Virginia's much tamer horse country for over a decade. "Look, the fact of the matter is that the rest of my staff inside Hart has a lot more room right now than we do."

"They should be done with copying and e-mailing everything we need pretty soon, Senator," the male aide said.

That was the problem, the Senator thought, gazing at the pillars of printouts still standing on her desk for lack of enough filing cabinets. They would finish retrieving everything she really had to have within a week or so, and then she would have the impossible task of finding space for those staffers here. "Somebody should do something," she muttered.

The female aide looked up from her laptop. "Why don't you introduce a resolution?" she asked.

"A resolution about what?"

"Resolved, that the Senate will return to its offices and chambers by Election Day in order to more effectively continue to serve the American people. I mean, if everybody's staff can go in and out and get bigger and smaller as needed, there's, like, no reason why the whole Senate can't do the same. And if you introduce a resolution, somebody in the House will probably introduce one, and then maybe everything can finally get back to normal."

There was some logic to that, but something inside her resisted the suggestion. "It's absurd," the Senator said. "We can't have little tiny Senators and Congresspeople debating and passing laws inside the Zone and having them signed by an itsy bitsy President. Who the hell would take us seriously?"

"What difference would it make?" the male aide asked. "There's nothing in the Constitution or the rules of the Senate that says you have to be a certain size to hold hearings and pass laws. Besides, everything would still look the same on TV."

Her aides had a point. The Senator finished her coffee, then said, "Maybe you could start drafting that resolution, but let's change the date. We'll be back to business as usual by the Fourth of July."

Shrinkage had done nothing to improve the slovenly ambiance of the White House Press Room. The same crappy chairs were still there, the White House Correspondent noticed as he filed in behind some other newsfolk, the same outdated equipment, the same wires all over the floor, even the same coffee and food stains on the tabletops, but the shabby familiarity of it all was oddly reassuring. The White House Correspondents' Dinner, even though postponed to a later date than usual, had been a reassuring affair this year as well, drawing nearly the same number of Hollywood celebrities as in the past. It had helped that the comedian providing the entertainment had been warned not to make any jokes about size or smallness unless he wanted everybody in the press corps and all of their famous friends to boycott his show permanently and also bring some pressure to bear on his bosses. The guy had been relying far too much on such humor for his program anyway.

The Correspondent, whose name everyone tended to forget more and more often since his network's ratings had tanked, had not been a happy camper when the head of the news department had told him in no uncertain terms that if getting tiny was what was needed to cover the President, then tiny was what he would get unless he preferred to lose his job. It wasn't as if he would have to stay tiny, except when he was inside the White House or doing stand-ups outside of it; the network had nixed any footage that showed any of their newspeople towering over either the official residence or the Capitol. And there was no danger that anybody going into the Zone wouldn't be able to get big again outside of it. The President had been living inside the White House for over a month now, and he was still able to resume his six feet of height for trips to Camp David.

There were also the Correspondent's home in Georgetown, his Manhattan digs, his son's tuition at William and Mary, and the financial arrangements with his first and second ex-wives to consider. Anyway, he told himself, everything was pretty much photo ops these days. As long as everything looked a certain way, people in front of their TVs would come away with the impression that nothing essential had changed. Eventually most of them might forget that any shrinkage at all had occurred.

He sat down in his usual seat in the front row as the camera crews finished setting up and his colleagues settled in around him. What mattered was acting as though everything was still the same, and now that he was here, it was easier to feel that way, especially since there were no windows in the Press Room to reveal the size of everything outside these tiny walls. They were all in this together, he and the President and everybody else in Washington who mattered; he had to look at it that way.

The President's Press Secretary entered the room, smiling as he approached the podium, then resumed his usual bland expression. "I have a few announcements to make," he began, "and then you can ask your questions."

The Correspondent already knew what those announcements would include. His sources had told him that in addition to the usual bromides about staying the newest course in the Middle East, the growing strength of the economy as indicated by the latest statistics, and more insistence that the investigation of the shrinkage incident was continuing to go forward, the President's staff had decided to have the British Prime Minister visit the President at his summer home instead of at the White House. Apparently even a close ally would not shrink in order to schmooze.

He settled back in his rickety chair; his spirits lifted just a bit. In spite of everything, the useless ritual of the White House daily briefing was comforting.

A small Congressional investigative committee, both in numbers and size, met to inquire into what had happened.

"Any ideas about who did this to us?" the Chairman asked. The eyes of his four fellow Senators and their five House colleagues remained devoid of inspirational sparks.

Moments passed. "A terrorist," the Senator from Maryland said at last. "Some joker of a tech-terrorist." He slapped the table with one meaty hand.

"Right," muttered the Congresswoman from Florida. "He's, like, riding around in some, uh, conveyance, picking on national symbols to shrink—er, diminish."

"Sure, like Captain Nemo sinking warships with his submarine." The

Chairman snorted. "If you ask me, maybe we'd better bring in some of those nano-whatever-they-are scientists. They might be able to tell us something."

"Or else they might be behind all of this," the Senator from Maryland muttered. "There's some mighty suspicious characters among scientists. A lot of them aren't even Americans."

"In terms of environmental impact," the Senator from Kentucky intoned, "we might leave a far less large footprint on the Earth if we remained at a smaller level. Perhaps we should be asking the EPA to address the environmental effects of shrinkage."

"We're here to figure out how to find the guys that did this," the Senator from Maryland said, "not to ride your hobbyhorse."

"We couldn't get shrunk any smaller, could we?" the Chairman asked. "I mean, we're already so small." He sighed. "We have to get to the bottom of this." He did not say that he suspected what the others were already thinking, that this might be only the beginning. There were a whole lot of places that the joker, or jokers, might be planning to reduce.

▌▌

Hector wasn't on his usual bench, and neither were the Homeless Lobbyist and the Homeless Philosopher. The benches where they usually sat were now behind a protective cordon of soldiers, and there were rumors that more of the park would be declared out-of-bounds. At this rate, he and the Lobbyist and the Philosopher would soon be living in the middle of H Street.

But Hector understood. The Secret Service had to think about security, and there had been stories going around about people who were angry enough over various issues to want to rush the place and stomp on everything, the White House and the Capitol. In a way, he couldn't really blame them for feeling that way, but if they had talked to the Homeless Philosopher, they would have realized that such hopes were futile.

"See, it's this way," the Philosopher had explained to him during a recent seminar and consultation over a pint of rye. "You got this here Zone where everything shrinks, so even if people got past them soldiers and the cops and the Secret Service and everybody else, they'd get small as soon as they got inside the Zone. So how the hell could they stomp anything? They'd just be milling around on the lawn until they got arrested. Jeez, they couldn't even lob a few big rocks at the place, 'cause the rocks'd shrink on their way in."

"So why are they beefing up security so much?" Hector had asked. "If there's anything to your goddamn premise, they could just station a few guys here and there and save some bucks. It's not like the deficit's gonna shrink."

"Oh, there's probably good reasons for all the protection," the Philosopher had replied. "You still gotta worry about terrorists. Teeny tiny terrorists could still do a hell of a lot of damage, 'specially if they're aiming at tiny targets. But if you ask me, I think they beefed up security out of habit. It's what they do, whatever the reason—anything happens, get more security, it doesn't matter what. More of the same. Problem solved. Makes 'em feel important." That had seemed like fallacious reasoning to Hector, but he had been too far in the bag by then to offer a convincing refutation.

The Homeless Philosopher suddenly stood up. Even in the evening light, Hector could see that the Homeless Lobbyist was trying to restrain the other man. The Philosopher knocked the Lobbyist's arms away, staggered toward the line of soldiers, then drew himself up. "Little bastards!" he yelled. "Little pricks! You're bigger than they are! Shit, *I'm* bigger than they are! So why don't you act like it?"

The soldiers were taking aim. Shut your piehole, Hector wanted to shout, but fear constricted his throat.

"Little bastards!" The Philosopher was not about to quit. "You were always small, goddamn it! You were always little guys. You didn't shrink, you diminished yourselves! You fucking did it to yourselves!"

Several soldiers were moving rapidly toward the Philosopher, but at least they had lowered their rifles. "You diminished yourselves!" the Philosopher cried as the soldiers dragged him away. In their boots and gear, they seemed so much bigger than his friend.

PRIDE

Mary A. Turzillo

Frequent Analog *contributor Mary A. Turzillo won a Nebula Award for best novelette for her wonderful "Mars Is No Place for Children." She returned to the Red Planet in the serialized novel* An Old-Fashioned Martian Girl. *Now, she stays terrestrial in a story about the unexpected joys and dangers of the husbandry of rare felines.*

The hot fur thing under Kevin's shirt clawed at his chest. *Nice going,* he thought. *First the bum rap for weed, and now if I don't get caught stealing lab animals, I'll get rabies from this freak.*

Frankenlab, at Franken U, AKA Franklin Agricultural College, was messing with animals, electrodes in their brains, cloning them like Dolly the Sheep, except not regular animals. Dead animals from frozen meat. And they were going to kill the animals.

He couldn't save them all. Those fuzzy orange-furred mice, most wouldn't make it. Those guys from Animals Our Brethren had pried open cages, and when the mice wouldn't come out, they shook them out, and when the mice squeed, cowering under lab tables, they kicked them until they ran into corners, and from there may God have mercy on their itty souls.

Kevin petted the little monster through his shirt, but it writhed around and gummed him. "I'm saving your life, dumb-ox!" He dashed out of the building minutes before alarms brought the fire department.

Kevin had been in trouble before. A year ago, his girlfriend's cousin Ed and he had been cruising around in Ed's van, which had expired plates. Kevin didn't know about the baggie of pot under the driver's seat. When the state patrol started following, Ed asked Kevin to switch places. His license, like the plates, was expired, he said. They switched, veering madly, on a lonely stretch of 422. When they finally stopped and the cops asked to search the van, Kevin shrugged and said okay.

"And whose is this?"

Ed said, not mine. Kevin was too surprised to look properly surprised, and this was a zero-tolerance state. So Ed got off with a warning, and Kevin, stuck with court-appointed counsel, served thirty days.

‖

Kevin had been looking for a job to pay for college when local papers broke the story that some thousand-odd animals (mostly, admittedly, mice) would be killed because their experiment was over. What was he thinking of? He wasn't an animal-rights kind of dude. Still, he felt panicked exultation fleeing the scene of the crime.

He struggled to control his Pinto while driving with the squirming thing scratching inside his shirt. He fumbled the back door key and pounded downstairs to the basement, where he pulled the light cord above the laundry tub and took the furball out of his shirt.

"Oh God, what have they done to you?" It was deformed: big head, chopped-off tail. Cat? Dog? A mix?

He deposited it in the laundry tub. Boggling at the size of its mouth, he realized it needed food. Now.

Forward pointing eyes. Meat-eater. He ran upstairs and grabbed a raw chicken breast from the fridge. He held it out to the cub.

The cub flopped down on its belly in the tub, and tried to howl. All that came out was a squeak.

He tried to stuff the meat into its mouth, but it flinched away and lay looking at him, sides heaving.

Maybe the mother chewed the food up for it. Mother? Not hardly. This thing didn't have a mother. It was fucking hatched in Frankenlab.

Raised in farm country, Kevin liked animals. He sometimes even petted Rosebud, the town pit bull, when Rosebud wasn't into tearing people's arms off. If his parents had been rich, he'd be pre-veterinary at FrankenU. Or a cattle rancher, or a discoverer of rare snakes.

He retrieved a knife from upstairs, hacked tidbits off the chicken breast, and put them in the cub's mouth. The cub sucked on them, famished. It got to its feet and seized Kevin's finger with its front paws. Head held sideways, it chomped down on his finger. It did have a few teeth, it seemed.

He jerked away. "Stop it, you little monster!" Then he realized he might wake his mother.

Kevin, it's a baby. Duh.

Where would he get a baby bottle?

He opened a can of condensed milk from the pantry, dipped a chicken chunk in it, and let the monster suck milk off the meat. Twenty minutes later it either got satisfied, or gave up. Its little belly looked marginally bigger, and the can was empty, mostly spilled on the laundry tub or his shirt.

It stretched and unsheathed claws way too big for a little guy the size of a raccoon.

Kevin thought, *It'll purr now.* Instead, it washed its face, running front paws over those deformed big jaws.

And then, just when Kevin decided it was almost cute, it reached out a claw and pricked his arm, not enough to hurt, just to say, *More?*

"You're beginning to tick me off," he said. The cub's gaze radiated adoration. It licked his hand, nearly rasping his skin off.

Its fur was golden retriever blond, its eyes the color of river moss. Green-eyed blonde, like Sara. Dappled coat, like freckles on Sara's sweet shoulders. Sara Jones: they were almost a couple before his arrest; now she acted distant.

The monster leapt out of the tub and landed on the floor. It shook itself, surprised at the fall.

He lay down and stared at it, eye to eye. "You need a name."

He was furious that they planned to kill it. It was harmless. Uh, maybe not harmless. Planning to get big, judging from those paws, each the size of cheeseburgers. But innocent.

"What the hell have I got myself into?" he asked it.

Its grotesque little face shone with trust.

With the knife he'd used to cut the chicken, and thinking of Sara Jones, he tapped the little monster on each shoulder, and said, "I dub thee Sir Jonesy."

For a week, he kept Jonesy locked in the root cellar. His mom either didn't know, or pretended not to. Rosebud, Mr. Trumbull's pit bull, kept getting off his chain and sneaking over to paw at the basement door. There was an article in the paper about the lab fire, but the lab animals were hardly mentioned.

The scientists downplayed it all. The animals had been slated for "sacrifice," Dr. Betty Hartley said. Federal regulations required that animals be euthanized at the end of an experiment, she said, plus the money had run out. Cold. "Sacrifice": nice euphemism. Like "put to sleep." Like anything ever woke up from that sleep. Sacrifice? What, were they going to dance around an altar and beg God to protect them from weird-ass animal zombies?

Dr. Hartley said she was sad that the animals had all died in the fire, but accidents will happen.

So now he couldn't let anybody in on his secret. It would be insane to let the scientists find the cub again and kill it. But Jonesy (the cub was female, he discovered) whined and shivered in the root cellar, so he brought it upstairs.

His mother was not pleased.

"Look, Mom. I know it's humongous for a kitten, but that's all it is. Pet it?"

She refused to touch it. "I don't care what it is, I don't want it in my house."

"Listen, they'll kill it if I take it back. It's cute, see?" He held it to his chest to minimize her view of the monstrous head. Its fur was rough, not silky like a kitten's. But it was warm and happy to snuggle.

"Cute? Kevin, I'll show you cute. I know you stole it from Frankenlab. It'll probably get up in the night and suck our blood."

"Shit, Mom. It eats milk, not blood. You can't just kick it out on the street like a—like a broken TV."

"Kevin, get a job. And get that thing out of my house."

But Kevin's mother was too tired to put her foot down.

▐▐

The cub's teeth started coming in. On a diet of ground meat that Kevin got from Dumpster-diving, it had loads of energy. It used the energy stalking Kevin and shredding everything in Kevin's room.

The eye teeth erupted. And erupted. And erupted. Not domestic cat teeth. Long as the fishing knife the cops had taken away from him when he was caught with the pot.

He woke up one morning to find the monster sitting on his chest, hungry or affectionate, as if you could tell even with a tame cat.

"Man," said Kevin, peering closer. "Your mom should have sued your orthodontist."

The cub did not laugh.

Not a vampire, but those sharp, sharp teeth—

And then his mind chewed through a bunch of information and farted out the truth. Rumors of ice age frozen flesh? Cloning? Bingo.

The damn thing, scrutinizing him with gold-green eyes, opening its huge mouth in a silent howl, was a saber-toothed tiger.

"Woo, dude. I thought you were trouble before."

It would need lots more meat.

At first he bought cheap cuts; then, when he realized his money from mowing lawns wasn't cutting it, he abstracted food from his own meals and from the refrigerator. And Dumpster-dove the local supermarket.

One day, he found his mother in the kitchen, her hand bandaged. He hoped the bite was from Rosebud, but if Rosebud had bitten her, she'd probably be a mangled corpse.

He sank into a chair while the saber-tooth attacked the stinky mess he'd brought home for it.

"That's it, Kevin. You're my only son, the light of my life, a good smart boy although way too trusting, but that cat is out by tonight or I call the cops." She blew her nose on a crumbled tissue. "I know where he came from."

Kevin didn't blame her. She was tired from overwork, just wanted to be left alone and sleep more than five hours at a time. They'd been moderately affluent before Kevin's dad left. But Dad had a really good lawyer. The measly child support had stopped when Kevin turned eighteen. Dad still sent birthday cards with a two-dollar bill in each.

"If the boy wants a college education, a job will make him appreciate it more."

Jobs, yeah, well. Jobs for twenty-one-year old guys who've done even a little time aren't easy to come by. Odd jobs, maybe shoveling walks in winter. Kevin wasn't a drinker, so he didn't have AA networking to fall back on.

Also, the damn cub was too mischievous to leave alone for long.

The week before the cat nipped Mom, Kevin had come home from helping a neighbor get her hay in and found the cub playing with a large rat. When the saber-tooth saw him, she grabbed the rat in her mouth and tried to run away. Thank God it had been a rat and not one of those ratty-looking poodles the Parks owned.

So Mom was right. The cat needed a home.

Sara. Their beginning romance had aborted, but he ran into her sometimes at the feed store. She'd understood Kevin didn't know about the pot. But she always said, "It's not a good time," if he wanted to come over to the farm, or ask her out—not that he had much money for dates.

Guess she didn't want to be with a loser.

But, hell, he could rise again. Many great men—millionaires, politicians—had a shady past.

Sara didn't hate him.

He put the cub in an appliance carton (it whimpered, but complied), wrapped it with pink and ivory paper and gold ribbon, and lugged it to the Pinto. The cub thrashed around inside the box on his front seat while he drove like a maniac to Sara's farm. Sara's parents hadn't really worked the family farm much since her granddad died, just kept geese and a big garden, and when they had moved south to escape the winters, Sara kept the farm. Kevin had used to help out, before he went to jail.

He lost his nerve and left the gyrating package on her paint-peeled porch.

The phone was ringing when he got back.

"Kevin, what is this? It nearly took my arm off."

He breathed slowly. He'd enrolled in an anger-management class while in jail—not because he had problems with anger, but because the textbook had looked interesting—and he found the breathing helped calm him. "Sara, it's a saber-toothed tiger."

"They're extinct."

"Yeah, yeah, yeah, so's the Bill of Rights. But this thing is a clone. From frozen meat."

"And this concerns me how?"

"It's, uh—"

"Look, Kevin, I remember the Maine Coon kittens you gave me. I love those cats. But this is different, no? You must have stolen this thing from the college. And that's not all. It's going to grow up and be really aggressive. And, well, also—"

"Sorry. I'll come and get her back. Don't let her out, though. I'm not sure she knows how to defend herself."

When he got to the farm, Sara acted nervous, but she kissed him, and they sat on the couch and talked, about Ed, about jail. They didn't have sex, but he got his hopes up they could reconnect. Jonesy, meantime, tried to shred everything in the living room. She had put out a bowl of hamburger; otherwise the cub might have started shredding their clothes.

"It's not exactly *cute*," she said.

Jonesy's whiskers were almost as amazing as her teeth. Long and delicate. She stalked everything in the room, even shadows.

Kevin watched. The cub would hunker down and wriggle her backside, then dart forward and roll upside down. The hunker/wriggle part looked like any cat, but he'd never seen an animal do a half roll while attacking. Did that have anything to do with the swordlike canines?

"Kevin, you know I love animals."

Kevin said nothing. Their shoulders touched, and he put his hand on hers.

She left it there. "Okay. Until you get a place of your own. Don't come visiting without calling, though." She withdrew her hand.

Somebody was living with her. Of course.

The arrangement lasted three weeks.

When he drove over in answer to her phone call, Sara was crying. Jonesy had killed one of her geese, a real achievement, since even Rosebud was loath to fool with the geese. But when Kevin opened the door, he boggled at how much the saber-tooth had grown. Jonesy had to weigh as much as Rosebud now.

Oops. What if Jonesy had attacked Sara?

"I let her run," she said. "You can't keep an animal like this cooped up. And it killed Emily Dickinson." Emily Dickinson was one of her geese. She named her geese after women poets.

"What have you been feeding her?" He felt shame that he hadn't offered to pay for Jonesy's food. As if he could. He had a sudden panic over the welfare of the two Maine Coon cats, but they were dozing on the sofa. The sofa was shredded, but the cats were fine.

"I feed her canned dog food, but she's always hungry. I haven't seen a raccoon in the neighborhood for two weeks. Kevin, I don't know where you can take her, but she can't stay here."

Was Jonesy grown enough to survive on her own, on garbage, raccoons, and people's geese? "How did she learn to eat the raccoons?"

"When I separated them, Emily kind of—split open, you know—and Jonesy stood over Emily, and then, as if she was sorry for the poor goose, she bent over and started licking her feathers, and she tasted the blood, and all of a sudden—"

Kevin had seen barn cats experience this epiphany. They discover their toy tastes good. Most learned from the mother cat, but get them hungry enough—

"She doesn't bother the geese anymore. They run away. But then there's the deer."

Kevin looked at his baby monster. "Jonesy couldn't take down a deer."

"Maybe not, but she sure knows how to chase them. And I worry about Mr. Trumbull's cows."

Kevin stood. "Thanks for taking care of her."

She took his hand, then moved closer. They gazed at each other. Could he kiss her?

She stepped back. "Take her somewhere. Hey, what about your dad's old trailer?"

The trailer featured scarcely more than a bed and a mini-dinette, abandoned on the lot near his mom's apartment. Roof leaked, plumbing wasn't connected. No trailer park would let him in with that wreck.

Nor with an "exotic animal." Even if he could pass Jonesy off as a rescued bobcat or lion cub.

"I'll call around." He had brought a collar and leash, and he snapped these on Jonesy. Jonesy had been on leash before and didn't like it, but she trusted Kevin enough not to fight.

Kevin was becoming an expert on *Smilodons*. They weren't even from the same branch of the Felida family as lions and tigers, but still might live in families. He must seem to Jonesy like her mother or the leader of her—what did they call lion families?—pride.

He smiled at Sara, eyes full of hope.

"Go!" she said, shoving him playfully. The saber-tooth bared huge teeth at Sara until she smoothed its back fur. "You can come back. Bring Jonesy if you can control her. Just call first."

He led the saber-tooth to his car. His mind roiled with possibility. *Ask her!* he thought. *She's got a new guy, or she doesn't. Ask!*

Too many secrets in Kevin's life: an animal he couldn't give up and couldn't keep, and a girl he wanted and whose life had become a mystery.

"Cat," he said. "We ain't neither of us got no pride."

Kevin's uncle owned some unworked farmland twenty miles out of town center. He got permission to park the trailer there, planning to haul water and use cartridges for gas heat. He bought a generator and parked the trailer well back from the road.

Odd jobs weren't enough. His mom's restaurant needed a dishwasher.

Since the owner knew him—and about the jail time—there was no back-ground check problem. Kevin bought a cell phone that didn't require a credit card, and the modern man out of his time and the Ice Age cat went there to live their hard life.

College plans receded into mist. Maybe someday Kevin could write a book about this. He bought a cheap digital camera and started a journal of the Jonesy's growth and behavior.

The saber-tooth soon learned to paw open the refrigerator. Kevin was forced to keep only vegetables in it. To supplement the dog food, he brought home a cut-up chicken or a chuck steak every night. Jonesy tore into these, sometimes before Kevin could get the wrapper off. Sometimes the wrapper would get impaled on the four-inch-long canines, and she would run around the room trying to scrape them off. Kevin fell down laughing the first time that happened.

Kevin's own meals were either vegetarian or eaten at the restaurant.

He bought a used copy of _Born Free_ at a yard sale. Jonesy wasn't any kind of modern cat, but it was a start. The librarian found him treatises on the _Smilodons_ of North America, though he wasn't even sure that's what Jonesy was. He had to play it cool when the librarian got nosy about his interest in cloning.

Jonesy shredded any book he brought home. To her, books, like every-thing else, were toys. So his reading was restricted to the library and their Internet computers, and since he didn't like leaving the cat alone when she was awake, he kept all his research in his head.

He couldn't keep the saber-tooth penned up, any more than Sara could. So after a few weeks, he let her off the long line he'd tied to the trailer, and watched her lope the perimeter of the mowed area, where the demolished farm-house had set. The line wouldn't hold her anyway, if she wanted to get away. She would chew through chain, though it might damage her beautiful teeth.

She stopped periodically to smell things, and her ears perked at the pas-sage of a bird.

Then she saw the fox, and he thought he'd have to change her name to Turbo.

Did she eat the fox? No doubt she'd caught it. No bloody carcass in the trampled-down area where the chase had ended. But for two days, Jonesy looked quite pleased with herself.

The rest of that summer, the winter, and spring. The saber-tooth grew sleek and menacing, muscles moving smoothly under short tawny fur. One of her magnificent eyeteeth loosened. When it fell out, she let Kevin feel inside her mouth, underneath where the tooth had been, and another one was coming in. Which grew and grew and grew. The other side did the same, and one morning he awoke to her heavy paws on his chest and opened his eyes to see her monstrous white glistening sabers new and sharp and creamy white, each as long as the knife they used in the restaurant kitchen to hack apart beef joints.

Her inscrutable face and hot moist breath made his heart jump with terror. But she was his companion; he had held her under his shirt. He had fed her milk.

He reached up and stroked her ears, which alone of her fur retained kittenish silkiness. Then, with the greatest caution, he touched her saber fangs. Smooth, like ivory knives. This meant she was—*Smilodon fatalis? Smilodon neogaeus?* Or the other genus—*Megantereon?* He couldn't tell: he was no paleontologist.

He called Sara, to share this experience. She picked up after two rings, and hung up. But not even Sara's rejection could spoil that moment.

He was the first man ever to touch a living *Smilodon*'s teeth, and survive.

Sara would call now and then to ask about Jonesy, or tell him about a job opening. He could leave the saber-tooth with her during the day, she said.

But when he called, employers always knew he was the kid who had gone to jail for drugs. Such is rural town gossip.

Jonesy and he walked the perimeter of the farm every night, out of sight of the road. He'd been four years out of high school. College seemed much further away now. He thought, *Some would say I have no life. A dumbass job. Had good grades, could have gone to college, married a beautiful woman who owned land. Lost all that because I trusted the wrong person, didn't fight the system hard enough. Could have done better. But I've touched the saber teeth of a* Smilodon, *and if no other gift is given me in this life, that might be enough.*

If Jonesy missed anything, she never said so.

Then Jonesy came into heat.

As she came insinuating up to him, dragging her butt against the floor, trying to hump the ragged sofa arm, beseeching him to do something, anything, he just said, "Kitten, I'd write you a personals ad, but your kind don't subscribe to the *Country Crier.*"

Spaying, but how the hell would he pass her off as anything but what she was? The vet would remember the incident at Frankenlab, and all would be up. Another jail sentence for Kevin. Worse for Jonesy: "sacrifice" at the hands of the scientists.

He tried penning her in the trailer while he slept in the Pinto, but she started chewing through the metal window frame. He let her out, and she howled to get inside with him.

Next night, his cell phone rang.

"Kevin, Keith, whatever your name is. People hear that howling, don't know what it is. But I do."

Kevin's heart lurched. Caller ID said: *B. Hartley.* The scientist. "Doctor Hartley. You plan to 'sacrifice' her now?"

"No, you dolt. Do I have to spell it out for you? I incited your stupid Animals Our Brethren people to start that fire so she'd get away."

He took it in. "She's in heat. What should—"

"She'll either go out of heat, or she'll attack somebody. She may even decide you're the lucky tom. Give her back to me."

"Was there another saber-tooth? A male?"

"Of course not, you idiot."

He snapped the cell phone shut and threw it against a wall.

Jonesy disappeared into the woods behind French Lick Creek.

A week later she slunk back. Kevin waited, but she was not knocked up. How could she be?

▌▐

He was pretty sure Jonesy was keeping down the deer and raccoon population, but nobody mentioned missing any dogs. Cats, maybe.

When he needed to go to work, he had to lock her in the trailer, and she gnawed at the door and chewed the knob. Thank God she didn't have opposable thumbs; she was smarter than most dogs and cats. And some people.

But heaven, even Kevin and Jonesy's twisted heaven, can never last.

He had to run an errand. The feed store, which closed in the evening, was the cheapest place to get her dog food.

How she got out and trailed him wasn't that hard to reconstruct. He'd been careless. As he walked out of the store, he nearly tripped over her sunning herself on the front steps.

And across the square was Rosebud. Rosebud wasn't supposed to be out, either, but Mr. Trumbull was pretty lax too.

Rosebud hated cats. And Jonesy smelled like a big, unspayed cat. Rosebud killed cats. Smart cat owners in French Creek Township kept their pets indoors. As to farm cats, thank God Rosebud couldn't climb trees.

Rosebud was across the square, urinating on a post. He stopped abruptly and put his leg down, tiny ears perked, nose twitching. Then he charged.

Halfway across the square, he suddenly changed his mind. Uncertain, he froze, then turned tail.

Jonesy wasn't a long-distance runner, but she was fast on a sprint.

What Kevin saw next was that weird *Smilodon* leap. Jonesy charged and without stopping, rolled to her back, hugged Rosebud's neck, then sank her saber teeth into the dog's throat. The dog heaved into the air, Jonesy rolled over on top of him, and the two struggled. Rosebud had no offensive weapons but his jaws, and he'd never had to defend himself before, so his struggles turned to spasms and in seconds, he lay still.

Jonesy straddled the dog and raised her bloodied jaws in a terrifying roar. Everybody ran out of the feed store, the diner, and the gift shop.

Jonesy lowered her jaws and began to tear pieces out of the dog's belly.

Kevin fought vertigo and nausea. Somebody yelled, "Anybody catch that on video?"

He charged across the square, screaming at Jonesy. Three guys tried to stop him, yelling, "It'll kill you!" but he slid to a stop by the scene of carnage and yanked on Jonesy's collar.

"He's crazy!" somebody yelled.

Kevin realized he *was* crazy. Jonesy weighed maybe five hundred pounds by now. He'd read plenty of accounts of people mauled by previously docile big cats. Why did he assume Jonesy was different?

But he had to get the cat away, before somebody with a gun thought to use it.

A small, strong hand gripped his wrist.

Sara. Sara had the rifle her grandfather always carried in her truck. It had been a fixture in the truck for so long he'd forgotten about it. Nor did he wonder why she happened to be in town that day.

She gave him a serious look, then handed him the rifle. "It's under control," she yelled at the gathering crowd. "Back off before somebody gets hurt."

The dog was mangled meat. Jonesy had ripped open its throat and its belly and was standing over it, sides heaving with desire, jaws quivering with hunger and triumph.

The crowd all took a step back.

"Get her in the truck," Sara said. "You can still control her, can't you?"

Jonesy roared again, a softer roar.

Very deliberately—he believed that crap about animals being able to sense fear, but also knew he could fake courage pretty well—he took a handful of the loose flesh at the back of Jonesy's neck and said in a low growl, "Into the truck, bad girl."

And it was over. Jonesy lowered her head and her stump of a tail and climbed into Sara's truck. Kevin slammed the door.

Which left Sara and Kevin standing outside.

Sara was shaking. She reached up and grabbed Kevin's ears and kissed him hard, tongue and all. Breaking loose, she said, "You're an idiot! But, God almighty, you've got guts!"

What now? Kevin couldn't leave Jonesy inside the truck; first, the saber-tooth would demolish the inside. Second, it was a nice spring day, sunny, and heat would eventually build up and kill her.

But he could no longer predict the cat's behavior. Jonesy's blood was up; she might boil over.

"We have to get her out of here before the cops come," said Kevin. He shrugged, grabbed Sara's keys, and sprang into the truck.

Jonesy didn't kill him. The rest of his life, he would wonder why. Because he was dominant? Because she loved him? Do top predators know love?

He let Jonesy out of the truck outside his trailer. She lingered, licking his hand and making begging grunts, so he opened one of the dog food cans. She took it away from him and rasped the horse meat out, then lay down in the grass.

He went inside and wept.

Yes, somebody had videotaped it. Not the two animals running toward each other, not Jonesy's karate-like attack, but the dog underneath Jonesy, thrashing, then still, and Jonesy pulling out intestines. The video played several times, always zooming on the dead pit bull, then panning to Kevin pulling the cat away. He lay on the bed staring at the ceiling.

Thank God the cat looked like a female lion in the video. Some bystanders remarked on its teeth, but nobody connected it with the break-in and fire at the lab a couple years previous.

In the evening, Sara brought his car back. He didn't know how she had started it, but she came in uninvited and lay beside him on the bed.

They kissed. She said, "Lock the door."

He did, obediently. "It won't stop Jonesy, if that's what you're thinking."

Hours later, they dressed and talked about hunting for Jonesy. Did anybody recognize them from the video? It was really jerky. Nobody was knocking on the door. But Kevin's mind roiled with possibilities: if somebody recognized Sara's truck, they'd go to her house, then figure she was here. They'd come with guns for Jonesy. Jonesy was tame; she wouldn't know to run.

Hellfire. Maybe Jonesy *should* be put down.

He said, "I always thought you still loved me a little. Unless this is just a stress reaction."

She leaned into him, then grabbed and shook him, hard enough that he thought, *She's going to slug me next.* She said, "I loved you, you jerk, but I couldn't keep on loving somebody who was stupid enough to go to jail for what he didn't do."

"Ed is your cousin. I couldn't rat out your cousin. And I never was sure the pot was his, anyway."

"Idiot!" And she did slap him, not enough to hurt, then turned away, hiding tears. "Ed is a goddamn jerk. He got you in trouble; you shielded him. He's my blood, but nobody I'd ever choose for family. Kevin, Kevin. I can't be with a man who spent time in jail and who—who lives with this monster."

"You like animals."

She sobered. "I do. I'm not sure what you should do with Jonesy. Maybe we could get rid of her somehow? Not kill her. Find somebody who would take her and keep her safe. Would you do that if I asked?"

"And we'd be like before?" He didn't say, *And you'll marry me?* but he hoped she'd know that's what he meant.

"We'd at least solve a problem. I have a friend who knows how to sell things on the Internet. Remember those people who tried to sell their kid on eBay?"

"They got caught."

"They were stupid. EBay's not the option I had in mind. Listen, Ed isn't the only shady character we know. Maybe we can find a place for her."

He was reluctant. "Sara, don't get her killed."

He stayed up drinking cola after she left, but fell asleep in his lounge chair and awoke to early light and his cell phone ringtone.

"It's happened," said Hartley.

"What?" He thought she was talking about the attack on Rosebud.

"Sara Jones, that's your girl, right? The cat's over at her farm."

"Yeah, but Sara will be okay. Jonesy loves Sara."

"Judas Priest, boy, that cat is a top predator. Her definition of love is different from yours and mine. Big cats seem okay for years, then go off like a bomb and eviscerate somebody for no reason. For hunger. For a mate. Because a fly bit them on the nose."

"She loves Sara—"

"Yeah, she loves you, too. And maybe she thinks Sara is a rival in love."

That sounded crazy. But Kevin pulled his clothes back on and ran to his car.

He beat the police cruisers to the farm.

Jonesy was bashing the front door, roaring her earsplitting roar, not the roar of triumph she'd roared over Rosebud, not the roar of desire she'd yowled in heat. This was rage. And she was destroying the door.

As the first cruiser threw open its door and a cop sprang out with weapon drawn, the door imploded and Jonesy bounded inside.

Why had he thought Sara was safe? For some reason—oh God maybe it *was* sexual rivalry—Jonesy was after her.

Kevin bolted out of his car and up the porch stairs.

Inside, he smelled the fury of big, enraged cat.

"I'm up here!" Sara screamed.

He pounded up the stairs three at a time.

Sara's voice came from the upstairs bedroom. Outside that closed door,

Jonesy reared on her back feet, head scraping the ceiling. She clawed at the doorknob, chewed at the door panels.

One door panel split and fell inward. Jonesy threw herself with renewed rage, and the door splintered.

"Here girl! Bad girl!" Why hadn't he thought of bringing meat?

No. Meat wouldn't work.

Sara was screaming, punching at the jammed window.

He raced up and grabbed the cat's collar, but she turned and knocked him flat.

As he lay gasping from the blow, Jonesy lunged for Sara.

He crawled, dizzy, trying to rise despite the agony in his chest. He had just reached the door when Jonesy rolled across the floor, sprang up, and sank her teeth into Sara's throat.

Sara's eyes went wide, green as Jonesy's eyes. Her head snapped back. The cat ripped out her flesh together with a piece of her T-shirt, then howled, head thrown back, whiskered black nose grazing the ceiling light fixture.

Then the cat leapt through the window, splintering the frame.

Kevin crawled over to Sara. Her head was nearly separated from her body, blood gushing everywhere, in her beautiful golden hair, on her torn shirt, the cracked linoleum floor. More blood than he had ever seen.

He buried his face in the hollow between her breasts and sobbed.

Then he rose and looked out the window. Jonesy was loping into the barn.

He felt his way down the stairs, shattered. Sara was so beautiful. And Jonesy, his charge, his responsibility, his pet, had killed her. Pet? Oh, no. Not a pet. No more than an astronaut would call the moon a pet. No more than a composer would call his greatest symphony a pet. No more than a mountain climber would call Everest a pet.

He stumbled out into the light. Five police cruisers ringed the house now, and a paramedic van. One of the paramedics had the rifle from Sara's truck.

"Cat still in there?" one cop yelled.

"Sara's upstairs. She's dead," Kevin said. He sank to his knees and sobbed.

Hartley appeared. "The cat ran into the barn. I saw it."

The paramedic raised the rifle, and another cop hauled open the barn door. He had a German shepherd with him on a short leash. Kevin pulled himself erect.

The dog strained forward, then turned to cower behind the cop. The cop broke into a run, at the same time trying to unholster his service revolver.

Jonesy exploded out of the barn. The cop with the dog fell down, and Jonesy vaulted over them.

Kevin heard the sound of the rifle being cocked.

Kevin screamed, "No!" He launched himself at the rifleman.

The rifleman stumbled and the shot went wild.

A tawny streak—Jonesy—broke into the woods behind the barn and coursed out of sight.

Hartley screamed, "Why did you do that?"

"Killing the cat won't make Sara be alive again."

"You're in denial! The *Smilodon* will kill again."

Kevin was silent. Hartley was right. He had no idea why he had pushed the rifleman. He felt his arms being jerked back; cuffs cut his wrists. But the saber-tooth, the miracle from another world, was free.

"You were involved with Sara Jones," Hartley said. "I thought you loved her."

"I did. Not what matters."

"This monster kills the woman you love, and you protect it?"

How could he explain?

Jonesy was never found, though attacks on domestic animals and deer increased in the county for a few weeks. Maybe the saber-tooth died; maybe she went north, where the woods were thicker and the game larger.

Kevin went to jail. He got most of a college degree in there, gratis the state. He wasn't street smart, that was obvious, but he had a talent for book learning.

His life had changed forever. He got out of jail, went to university, studied paleontology, but studiously avoided Franklin U and Hartley, though she begged him for his photos of the *Smilodon*.

He never married.

But he had companioned a *Smilodon*, brought back from the deeps of time. It had been like stepping on the moon. He had touched its white, saberlike teeth. And it made him immortal.

It was enough.

I CAUGHT INTELLIGENCE

Robyn Hitchcock

Elsewhere, Robyn Hitchcock opines that humanity is "an evolutionary leap that's probably not going to work, and unfortunately it knows it's not going to work. That's part of the appeal of the Frankenstein's monster. You know, the look in the monster's eyes— it knows it's this hideous deformed creature that's going to throw little girls in the river, but it would like to be something better. And that's pretty much us."

I caught intelligence today:
Different eyes from the others,
It thrashed in the sink and I called Renee.

"Hey, check this out."

"How do we handle it?"

"So it's comfortable and feels nothing when we drain its mind."

"Uh-huh"

So we lay it on the counter
And sliced into its hypothalamus

And for a moment it carried on staring as if at a distant timetable and
    then—it looked at us.

"Look at Renee," I willed it, being smart and cowardly.

It flapped its tail and looked at Renee to oblige me,
Like a saint under torture;
Then it reared up towards my face, for a kiss or a bite.

"Renee" I yelled. "It's moving. Do something now. Renee?"

But she looked at me with her eyes adjusted and did nothing.

So intelligence was inches from my face as its life ebbed on the enamel.
Its eyes reflected me pitifully, mercilessly:
A hairy boar with rodent snout and weak sad cruel mean eyes.
And I knew that only death would ever compensate for my humanity.

There is no forgiveness but oblivion, I realized:

Intelligence will change places with us one day and a miracle will occur,
But not in words that we can speak;
We are too lethal to resurrect
Too stupid to continue
Too dangerous to survive

And just intelligent enough to know that every word is true, Renee.

SETTLEMENTS

George Zebrowski

A worthy successor to the grand idea SF of Olaf Stapledon and the philosophically literate Stanislaw Lem, George Zebrowski writes with an uncompromising vision and a firm pen. His early masterpiece, Macrolife: A Mobile Utopia, *was included in the* Library Journal's *list of the best 100 SF novels of all time, while his newest novel,* Brute Orbits, *won the 1999 John W. Campbell Memorial Award. A tireless crusader for excellence in science fiction, George was quoted in* Science Fiction Weekly *as saying, "Be critical, give warning, but also show constructive possibility. Failures, of course, make for more drama. But the utopian/dystopian pendulum swing of SF since* Frankenstein *was published is the way to go. It's only when the pendulum stops that we should worry about the health of the field."*

> I sit on a man's back, choking him and making him carry me, and yet assure myself and others that I am very sorry for him and wish to ease his lot by all possible means—except by getting off his back.
>
> —Leo Tolstoy

Jefferson James sat with the small tactical nuke in his right leg, his mind settled and ready to make the final decision. A year after he had lost his leg to a terrorist bomb he had left field operations and returned to low-level diplomacy, where his leashed tongue was trusted by his superiors and his opposite numbers. It occurred to him as he waited that he was either a fool or the most important man in all history.

"This is what you get for serving your political criminals," his fiancée had said one day as she stared at the stump of his leg.

"Criminals?"

"Liar! The powerful steal from everyone—and we all connive with them to survive! You work for the thieves—from a desk. God knows what you did before!"

"It's the leg, isn't it?" he had said. "But I'll wear this dead one only until they grow my own."

"Sure they will. You'll never have a truthful leg to stand on until you get a new brain!" She had raged for a week and then left him. For a better thief. How could it be otherwise—if what she said was true?

Now, as he waited for the meeting to start, he felt unsuited to talk to the aliens. No one was and no one could be, and *the* impossible moment waited just up ahead in the orderly divisions of time, freeing him to say anything, constructive or not. Talk for effect, agree to nothing, he had been told.

He tried to believe that he was here on his own, free of the person in his files. It was the only way to care now for a world that was ready to go on without him. How much time did he have to care? He could choose any moment after the meeting started. It was the only freedom left to him outside his thoughts.

Waiting, he wondered if a sum ever came out differently without errors in the addition. Maybe there was something he had overlooked, that everyone had overlooked. A faraway hope whispered to him that he wanted to live and heal into the new leg grown out of his own cells. They had long delayed that miracle, because life spans doubled by perfect replacement parts would diminish the power of the topmost. A leg had waited for him instead of a bride—but in his present state of mind he would gladly take a leg instead of a bride, and success over his life. She had been right, of course, up to a point, but that was just the way things were, and it was difficult to see how else humankind might have risen out of the subsistence poverty of nature, which was content to let an organism become just healthy enough to reproduce before it died; no wonder that the first few to achieve a surplus made pigs of themselves. One day all the horror of that first human climb would have to be redeemed.

There, he told himself, that was settled, as he thought of 2029, the first year of his prosthetic, a number obscuring numberless and differently noted histories, as the many still struggled in the grip of the few (who had learned well from the insurgencies of the many), and the year in which the alien breadboxes had appeared. Three in North Africa, where they were taken for a new form of impregnable American base; one in Germany, whose zealots hailed it as the long-awaited return of the wonder-weaponed Fourth Reich and demanded the dissolution of the government; near Colorado's NORAD-Space Command, where they were declared to be inflatable confusions raised by protestors; three around Shanghai, where a bitter old architect insisted that they were his very own mental projections; three around Moscow, which wisely said nothing; and one in the Australian outback, to which frenzied citizens rushed with the hope of buying tickets to an apotheosis, or at least to an extravaganza of happy revelations.

White rectangular boxes a thousand meters long and half that across. No comings and goings. No communications, despite officious government lies about being "directly in touch," while people within a hundred kilometers or more insisted that they heard a soft starsong calling for them to "gather 'round."

"Once they get a toehold, we won't be able to drive them out," Jefferson was told.

"Can we now?" he asked. More of a foothold than a toehold, it was an insult to the power of the world's hierarchies, whose client states began to doubt their allegiances as they called their anxious masters on secure lines from undisclosed locations for their usual daily instructions and were told to do nothing. Bunkered high officials took their calls in panic and anger, but gave no advice except to wait. Were the major states ready to collaborate, even surrender if it meant retaining their positions? asked the lesser states. Ballets of fearful ifs danced through the houses of power, and the word came down that no collaboration would be tolerated.

Wounded but doggedly loyal, doubts had wandered into Jefferson James as climate change slowed, diseases died, sterile oceanic zones filled again with life, and a large asteroid missed the Earth. The sway of the fossil fuel families weakened as alternatives surged into a truly free market. Adam Smith and Karl Marx smiled in their graves as officialdom denied that the alien presence had anything to do with these long-planned improvements, but seized the various black boxes into which anything electrical might be plugged with no limits on amperage or voltage output—and found empty "quantum vacuum wells" that unnerved older physicists and happily awed younger ones. Several smaller nations claimed these innovations to be the result of their own secret efforts.

The topmost fewest whispered amongst themselves that they were no longer the masters of the many. Too much "peace and plenty" withered power. More for the many, less for the few undermined the very meanings of "more" or "less."

"We won't let it happen!" they had cried in secret conclave, trembling before the likely loss of domains so carefully interlocked with other top-mosts—and had declared the alien structures to be illegal settlements.

There was no choice left but to safely bomb from on high.

But the wondrous boxes were not breached by even the cleanest of clean bombs in the most acute angular strikes. The humiliation of the fewest fes-tered as their bottom-feeding clients awaited a new master. In desperation, the fewest of the few hand-carried a message to the domes on large posters, in every language:

CAN WE TALK?

"Of course," answered a female voice, heard everywhere. "Where?" asked the startled UN secretary-general, addressing the air in front of his newly renovated glass building. Buried strategists had pushed him forward to carry a sign for the planet. "Where?" he had asked again.

"Anywhere. All will hear."

"Couldn't we . . . keep this . . . private?"

"We are being heard everywhere in the world's commons. But if you like, come to the Central Park Zoo Cafeteria in New York City."

Three need-not-to-know delegates were sent with the nuke in Jefferson's leg. If you can't beat an enemy's weapons, you must defeat the occupiers face-to-face and not count the cost. We must do what they least expect, he was told as they readied him for this sacrifice of one for the many, including the top-most, however one felt about the mass of humankind, his lost bride included.

He looked up as four figures walked into the bright, windowed daylight of the cafeteria—tall, healthy-looking humanoids with olive skin and short brown hair, two men and two women, it seemed to Jefferson James. They glided in with an irritating arrogance, sat down on the other side of the large wooden picnic table, and smiled.

"Who are you?" he demanded.

"And by what right have you built . . . put these things on our homelands?" asked Hugo Herbert, the pale German at his right.

"Please realize," said John Ke, the tall Chinese delegate whom everyone also knew as an acceptable Russian double agent, "that we feel strongly about your uninvited presence."

"There was no need to use weapons against us," said one female, and they all smiled like sophisticated children.

We won't apologize for anything we do, Jefferson wanted to say but restrained himself. "Who are you?" he demanded again. "And where have you come from?"

The second, plainer-faced female said, "From here, half a million years ago."

"Impossible!" cried Hugo after a silence.

The Chinese speaker said, "*We* are the oldest."

"The evidence is beneath the domes," said one of the males. "But we offer our genome for examination, if you wish. We would not be able to converse easily if we were not from here."

Still startled, Jefferson asked, "But why would you want to come back?"

"Sentiment," said the second male.

"Our roots," said the first woman.

Jefferson labored to laugh. "With all your obvious advances, you are moved by . . . sentiment?"

The woman smiled and said, "Some of us, but sentiment and sympathy are *the* basis of ethics, as you may well know."

"Well, it's one theory," Jefferson said, and felt useless; the aliens had already enforced their will and were capable of much more even if a few of them died here.

"You have no rights here," he said calmly, wondering if his superiors would advise him through the implant or rely entirely on his judgment. The matter had been left open.

"How long will you stay?" asked Hugo.

"For as long," said the first male, "as the need sings within us."

"Sings?" asked Ke.

"Sings!" cried Hugo. "Who are you, really, and why did you leave, as you claim?"

"We were helped," said the first woman.

"And our ancestors were left behind?" said Ke.

"A small population at the time," she said.

So there are at least two humanities, Jefferson thought. Maybe more, if all this was true. "Who or what helped you?" he asked.

"We don't know much about them," the second woman said.

"Tell us what you do know," Jefferson said.

"Quantum-field trollers, you might call them," she said, "but they rarely interfere."

"More than enough," whispered Hugo.

Jefferson said, "And they . . . helped only a few?"

"Enough."

"*What* were they?" he asked.

"We never saw them."

"But why did they take you?"

She said, "To string intermediaries between emerging forms of intelligent life."

"And you're here to add us to the string?" Jefferson asked. Or reattach a lost piece, he thought.

"Perhaps."

So there was a purpose, an uncertain one, Jefferson thought as he scratched his phantom limb. The ghost behind the interim prosthetic had not visited him for some time. Cutting free an earlier sample of humankind was a survival strategy, but there might still be another motive beyond stringing neighborhoods across the cosmos.

"But this is absurd," he said. "Half a million years invalidates all rights of return."

The second man said, "You are getting much better at destroying yourselves."

"And you will save us?" Jefferson said.

"Do we ask permission to aid the injured?" asked the first woman.

"Please request our help," said the second man.

Jefferson looked blankly at him. Odd responses, misunderstanding, stupidity, or a hidden purpose?

"Request it," insisted the alien, and Jefferson felt that the powerful-powerless divide would not be bridged; each side could say anything, even nonsense, and it would not matter. Much worse, the help of these alleged cousins would change too much. Worse than any political redistricting in nation states.

Jefferson asked, "Are you suggesting that we need more help?"

"You need no help to destroy yourselves," the first woman said. "Assure us that you will not and we will leave."

Jefferson felt suddenly that he wanted them to go and also to stay.

"Shall we stay?" she asked with a show of sympathy.

His diplomatic training aimed at a familiar humanity that was not rational but rationalizing, not at beings who seemed to be either the reverse or powerful naifs.

"But you *want* to stay," he said, "to cleanse us of our devils."

"You know the need," she said.

They see monsters, Jefferson thought, and wondered how survivalist origins might ever be surpassed. Controlled, perhaps, never removed.

"We are not strangers, we *are* you," the second woman said, "and also struggle with ourselves."

"But not as badly as we do," Hugo said skeptically.

"Tell us more about *our* mutual past," Jefferson said, suddenly uncaring of who they were; right or wrong, helpful or harmful, they had no right here. Keep that in mind. A world, like a nation, must control its borders.

"We have come home," said the first man.

Jefferson asked, "Who among you are not . . . nostalgic? And where are they?"

"Out there," he said, glancing upward.

"Throughout the quantum field's endless histories," said the first woman.

Were they ghosts of some kind? Jefferson asked himself. Quantum spirits, or thoughts?

He stood up suddenly. "You are unjust!" he shouted, diplomacy be damned. "You can destroy us, but we can't touch you. That is no basis for negotiation."

"We will not destroy you," said the four in unison, and he thought of a porcupine, unapproachable and smug behind its quills.

"Why not?" he demanded, still standing and half believing that these hard-to-hate naifs might be turned away with words.

"We are good," they said in unison.

"What?" he asked.

"Surely you have felt . . . goodness?"

He sat down into a skewering silence, then said, "We don't want you here, and demand that you leave. You can't just come here and occupy us."

"An outrage," said Hugo. "Your very presence and your help will discourage us from developing as we would have on our own."

The first woman, whom Jefferson James had begun to think of as Eve, said, "No culture grows without intrusions and constraints."

"Even given your best intentions," said the Chinese-Russian double agent, "we will not be the light of our world. You will become that light. . . ."

"Take from us what you like," she said.

Light up and lighten up, went through Jefferson's head. "And if we don't?" he asked instead.

Eve said, "You will harm yourselves."

"So you *will* stay?" he asked, thinking of his unstaying bride.

"Yes," she sang to him, and he felt relimbed by the music of her voice.

"And imprison us in your shadow," he said. "Can you understand that?"

"Shadow?" she asked.

"Your . . . superiority," he said, avoiding her gaze.

"A few may feel humiliated," said the second woman. "Most will benefit."

"Oh, so you do understand the effect," Jefferson said.

"Learn from us," Eve said.

"We'll drive you out," he muttered as pride's vise took hold of him.

The first man said, "Note that you *are* speaking freely."

"Easy to be tolerant," Jefferson said, "since we cannot harm you."

"You do not speak to us as equals," said Hugo.

"That," said the first man, "will not affect our ways toward you."

"Heaven help us," Jefferson muttered, then saw that Eve was smiling at him, her large eyes unblinking in her unlined face.

"We have been here for some years now," the man continued, "and know that you are not a cowardly people."

Just thieves, he thought, as silence shouted the truth of inequality, and Jefferson felt the strain of his own leashed anger.

"But you do know," the man continued, "the difference between lesser and advanced states of mind, since you have treated many of your regions accordingly. Imperfectly, with gain in mind, but with the hope, in some of you, that your advancement would be of help, later."

Some of us, Jefferson thought.

"I know well," said Ke. "A wall . . . a line has to be drawn or all may be lost to the horde."

"That line will not be a wall between us," said the man. "Unavoidably, some may cross it sooner than others."

Jefferson's thoughts danced on slippery slopes. Tangled motives and confused treasons shouted at him from deep pits.

"Your climb," Eve said to him, "*will* be up to you."

The man continued, "Raise the many and remove the burdens of power from the few. Restraint of the many slows progress and also harms privilege. You destroy only to build up again, to keep the many down by busying them with rebuilding, recruiting a few for their ability. Wealth's power weakens you, passing to progeny like a disease. A disease to the many who cannot have it and a diseased fear in those who cling to it."

Jefferson had heard too much of this from thinkers with too many answers, and had grown immune to pointed arguments, living as he had among people who believed in their immunity and would have cast him out if he had spoken out. A raised bottom would do as well or badly as the topmost who had ever held power—that much was true, but not enough to say that there was no other way. Had not a desert god offered one?

"Distribute power's burden everywhere," the man from the stars continued, "but let backwardness run through its own fevers."

Jefferson gave him an amused look and asked, "Do you know how backward they are . . . below us?" It was a stupid question, he realized. Of course they knew.

Eve nodded at him. "But we hope, those of us who still feel for this place, or we would have let you fail."

They are fools, he told himself, *and fools can take them out. I can take them out.*

"You're interfering with our necessary fever," he said, turning their angelic logic against them. But what was logic and truth spoken to power? When had anything changed except under the pressure of catastrophe?

"So how shall we settle all this?" asked Hugo. "If we fail here, the world will become an endless insurgency, and we will have let it happen!"

"A patient must not be left to fall out of his bed," Eve said to Hugo's suddenly tearing eyes. "There is no freedom from merit and truth, and only slavery for those held back from decisions."

They *were* going to dictate, Jefferson realized, but would it be with Jove's thunderbolts or Jehovah's commandments?

"You will disarm," Eve said.

Jefferson thought of declawed cats and wondered whether there would be any body parts left after the incineration? His implant was silent.

"You will be inspected," Eve said.

"Or what?" he asked, seeing sides of beef hanging in a freezer.

"Better your world," she said. "Those of you who have the power to better it do not because you fear the rise of new powers. That is also why you have not opened the way to your sun system's resources."

He stood up and was unable to speak as he realized what he would have to do.

He sat down again and felt small.

"No need," the four said in unison, "to keep climbing over the deaths of generations, hating yourselves in a universe rich enough for all."

"But," he stammered, "you will . . . police us," racing with his fear, straining to hear what his implant would offer.

"Yes," said the foursome from the stars, and he knew that there would be those who would happily join the choir of the new hegemony, and sing as they had with the previous congregation before new masters, rejoicing that they were no longer alone, that kindred souls now sang with them in the big dark, that they were in fact not the universe's only children, even though he had sometimes wished it for himself when he had felt his brother's weight, to have been born alone; but there was a difference, he realized; solitary was not the same as alone in an empty universe. The quarantine of light-years bestowed a time to grow and learn, and should not be lifted too soon. . . .

He struggled past himself, recalling Arthur C. Clarke's claim that "if the decades and centuries pass, with no indication of intelligent life elsewhere . . . the long-term effects on human philosophy will be profound, and may be disastrous. Better to have neighbors we don't like than to be utterly alone."

Well, now we have them, he told himself, *invading our cradle, and we don't like them.* And he wished that this were a dream or a story, where nothing is proven—and he rebelled against the parenting universe that had brought these well-meaning, gently violent intruders to break a natural quarantine and crush human pride for its own good. They were the imaginary god of that Bronze Age tribal library called the Bible, tampering too effectively with human history. If somehow this was a story, then nothing could be learned from it, nothing decided; but it was not a story; it was a reality to be stopped because we "cannot bear too much reality," said the poet.

So invent your own and be damned. . . .

Self-hatred filled him, and rage at being found out and judged, exposed to the gaze of outsiders who claimed kinship, spoke plausible truths, and turned love on and off with a glance. Exposed also to his own gaze, as one who needed no instruction from strangers to know that there had never been a human day when someone was not bending a knee to power and receiving a medal for failure, being executed or quietly murdered in some dark place. In all of humankind's serial wars against itself, he thought, we have never defeated ourselves. . . .

Looking up, he gestured to the four and asked, "Is there a God?"

Eve said softly, "Not the extreme, eternal, all-powerful being above all others."

A Jesuit had once told him that faith's insistence was about something *else* that was yet to be understood—a state toward which humanity was striving, somewhere ahead in cosmic history's hyperpersonal noosphere.

"What do you mean?" he asked as his unfeeling leg longed for its ghost, still alive somewhere in the quantum dream, questioning his new leg inside his stem cells about whether he would live to knit back into himself. Would killing these four in the Central Park Zoo Cafeteria do anything but set back the clock?

What had they *not* told us?

They had been gone too long, his pride cried, past any historical rights of return. What else were they not telling? That maybe we weren't from here at all, but something like Plato's souls come from afar in a ten-thousand-year cycle of swirling reincarnation? What further humiliations awaited his kind?

He asked the question.

"Oh, no," Eve said. "You are from here. We all are."

"And God?" he asked her softly.

"God is the best in us," Eve said.

"No more?" he asked.

"What else do you need?" she answered.

"That . . . that God is *there*," he said, and can overpower us, he thought madly, exhausted at a picnic table by a struggle with angels!

"A principle *is* there," she said, "and has always existed because a true nothing, a zero-field, is impossible. Being is always full, always has been, and needs no beginning. That's just the way it is observed to be. You don't ask beginnings of a god, so why demand it of being? But that is all beside the point—because you don't need authority to choose right from wrong. A godless infinity leaves us responsible to one another, to choose our own way. Anything else would be a tyranny. Would you wish anything less than this freedom? It is the best possible universe, until we learn enough to make another. If anything made it, it was wise beyond imagination to have left us alone."

"So there is no God?" he said. *And we may do as we please*, he thought. Dostoyevsky's non sequitur still damned.

Eve said, "Do not succumb to confusions. Ideas coincide with experiences. Superstition arises from an experience hooked by imaginings, refuted only by evidence. Wishful insistence offers the invincible but false comfort of certainty in an uncertain quantum. Pascal's Wager, for example, was his superstition. He would have won his wager only if he had encountered his god after death—and never known if he had lost."

"And you approve of uncertainty?" he asked. All his old student fears and loves and longings lay nakedly answered.

As if binding a wound, she said to his dismay, "Faith is a brute alliance of culture and physiology to support needed ways, which are feared to be arbitrary if they can be chosen or rejected, and so have to be given a plausible pedigree. But right and wrong have their own authority, free of divine insistence."

"And you came here," Jefferson said, "to disabuse us of . . . faith?"

"No," she said, "faith's insistence flows harmlessly away when you see the needs it was meant to serve."

"Then why are you here?" he asked, holding his anger, praying for his implant to speak.

"There are those among us who know where intelligent life grows and perishes, and regret that some distant contribution might be lost."

"What contribution?" demanded Hugo. "You know too much to learn anything from us."

"A distant contribution," Eve repeated. "Insights still to come, about *what* it is that we find ourselves in, *where* we have come from, and *where* our creativity might take us. At the edge of knowledge waits a greater beyond."

"And your others," Jefferson said to her purblind hopes, "do they care?"

"They do not," she said. "That's what it's like out there. Freedom sometimes chooses not to care, even when answers are clear."

And suddenly he felt that all the gifts the visitors had brought and the harm humanity had done to itself was nothing before the need to resist being occupied and subsumed. He felt its nameless pull—the same immunity that rejected transplants but would embrace his own cells when his new leg was grown and he might not be here to claim it. His kind would go back to its fevered ways, free of strangers, he insisted to himself even as Eve's face revealed to him that they had come to tire humankind of its past. . . .

Wordlessly he said back to her, against all reason, that *here* is mine, my land, and no one will have it even if I have only one leg with which to stand on it, though God himself wanted it back from the creatures who had perished in evolution's slaughterhouse to make it their own. . . .

He glanced at his German and Chinese colleagues; mercifully, they did not know that he had come here to die for humankind, for the many *and* for the unjust masters of the Earth, by obliterating the topmost who had come to pale humankind. . . .

Might they also claim that humanity's time had been arranged a million years ago, that Clarke's mythic sowers in the field of stars were engaged in a patronizing dialogue with their harvest here at this table? That we would not be permitted to stumble into oblivion because intelligent life was too precious to let stumble, that there was no other way except to *lead it* past stumbling? He wanted to be ashamed of the bomb in his leg, of the hurting pride in his brain that might choose personal extinction to the humiliation of helpful occupation. Nature was survivalist, but its cruelty, bemoaned even by Darwin, would be bypassed—but not as a gift, he told himself, not as a gift. We won't deserve it unless we get there on our own, or not at all, the horror of the survivalist mill whispered to him. Natural selection or bust, even in the jungle of civilizations.

These visitors did as they pleased, he reminded himself, so why were they trying to convince us of anything? Maybe, despite all appearances, they were vulnerable, if only in their scruples, and naive enough to place themselves in his hands . . . because *things* from elsewhere had no right to his Earth. He lived *here*, irrational, heaving up from violent origins, uncaring of reason and knowledge, hateful but strong against strangers. . . .

He closed his eyes and drifted ahead of his own death, but hoping for a reprieve from his implant.

It spoke, saying, "Do it now."

His phantom limb lived as he sought the light of thunder—

—and the bomb did not go off.

He opened his eyes, trembling as he looked at his companions and wondered whether they had conspired to stop him. Maybe it was only a delay of some kind in the bomb's mechanism.

"Settle with yourselves," Eve said, "and we'll leave."

He took a deep breath.

But we won't settle, so they will never leave. Not anytime soon. They are us, he told himself. *That's why they came back. Do we need their tyranny, or that of a god, to cease being "wolves to one another," as Ben Franklin had put it, not as a question but as a principle stronger than any god?*

Older words had asked, "If not now, then when?"

"Another time," Eve said. She looked as if to ask him to tea, and for an instant he was startled by the sympathy in her gaze, and knew that it might all be settled. Only thunderbolts were to be preferred to artillery, and diplomacy to cannon, Napoleon had said, but not in his time, so he had never replaced his artillery.

"We came too early . . . ," Eve added.

"And your . . . settlements?" Jefferson asked, afraid of what else they could do, would do.

Eve said, "Accept them as embassies for wiser times."

THE HOUR OF THE SHEEP

Gene Wolfe

Science fiction author Michael Swanwick once said of Gene Wolfe that he was "the greatest writer in the English language alive today. Let me repeat that: Gene Wolfe is the greatest writer in the English language alive today! I mean it. Shakespeare was a better stylist, Melville was more important to American letters, and Charles Dickens had a defter hand at creating characters. But among living writers, there is nobody who can even approach Gene Wolfe for brilliance of prose, clarity of thought, and depth in meaning." A 1996 recipient of the World Fantasy Award for Lifetime Achievement, Wolfe was also a frequent contributor to Damon Knight's landmark Orbit anthology series, itself an inspiration for this volume. It is an honor to have him here.

Tiero eyed his vprint with disfavor, then shook his head. Talking into the vprint would indeed be faster. Much faster. It might even be less laborious, though Tiero was not a good talker and knew it; but the manuscript that would sprout from the vprint would be wordy. Diffuse. Difficult to follow, and perhaps impossible to follow.

No.

He took up his pen and the little ivory-handled pen knife Mother had given him in the year before her death. He would write his book—the book the President-Protector had suggested—with this. Reading what he had written into the vprint (no doubt with a few additions and corrections) would produce a decent manuscript that might be sent to a publisher.

For his book *would* be published. There could be not the slightest doubt of it. Any book suggested by the President-Protector would find an eager publisher. It would be published; and he—Tiero, now called the greatest swordsman alive—would look an arrant fool unless it were insightful and decently written.

Decent. Decent writing was the key. Decent must be his watchword. He was no literary artist! Any attempt at fine turns of phrase, at thrilling descriptions, would be—

It had been his father's story. How did it go?

"The temple in Attenis had a beautiful statue of the goddess, Tiero. Naked, not only her outstretched hands but her whole posture offered blessing and forgiveness to an erring humankind. The people loved her and wished to make her statue more beautiful still, so they covered her lovely body with a gown of purple silk and put polychrome beads around her neck. For a time her feet puzzled them, since they were one with the block of marble upon which she stood. At last they cut the soles from a pair of black leather pumps and cemented them to the feet of their image of the goddess. When they had added a brown hat with a long scarlet feather, they declared their work at an end. And every visitor to Attenis was shown their beautiful goddess."

Recalling his father, Tiero smiled down at the pen-point he was shaping. His father had been a schoolmaster, and a good one. A fine, fine man, who had taught him how to shape a pen—with ten thousand other things. How proud Father would have been to see his son at the President-Protector's court! His son conversing with the President-Protector himself!

"First tell them what you're going to tell them, Tiero. Then tell them. And when you've told them, tell them what you've told them. That is nine-tenths of teaching."

He read over his first, still incomplete, chapter before dipping his pen in the shining black ink his father had favored.

So it is that we must master the five hours of the sword if we are to be safe in the streets and to make the streets safe for others. Permit me to review them. The Hour of the Sheep is that of relaxation. We are not on guard, and should danger come, we will go down to death as a sheep to slaughter. The Hour of the Sheep we must leave behind before setting our hands upon the door-pull. It is the hour of sleep, and too often of walking sleep.

The Hour of the Lion is that of watchfulness. When we walk abroad, the lion must pace at our side, invisible but ever-present. We see no danger and have no reason to fear it, yet we look for it everywhere. Are the tall man before us and the small man behind us allied against us? We must consider this, and consider, too, the most effective means of resisting their alliance. Where is the light, and where the shadow? Have they a confederate in a dark doorway?

The Hour of the Tiger is that of heightened awareness. When it comes, we no longer face merely hypothetical foes. Some action of our foes has betrayed them. Three men, let us say, have crossed the street to intercept us. We have identified them. We are in a position to predict their weapons and tactics, and perhaps to identify their leader. Our hands seek our hilts, and our eyes protection for our backs.

Swift comes the Hour of the Bull, rushing upon us! Our foes have commenced their attack. Now their leader confronts us, the knife in his hand hidden by his coat. A henchman stands behind him, ready to support him. A second circles behind us. Our minds are our best weapons, always. A ready mind for a red blade! We are not sheep to stand empty-eyed, awaiting the blow.

At once: the Hour of the Wolf. They find themselves engaged. We ourselves fight them, wolflike snapping and thrusting, and wolflike slaying man after man. Behold the empty eyes of our foes, those who thought to surprise us, themselves surprised!

Tiero wiped the point of his pen with a scrap of flannel and cast his mind back to the table of contents he had planned and written with so much care. Best to begin the next chapter now, to get it well launched while he might still write by daylight.

THE FOE
HIS TACTICS AND WEAPONS

When we fight a duel, we are at pains to learn all we can about the man we are to engage. Has he fought on previous occasions? If so, what have witnesses to say about his skill, his methods, and his preferred attacks? Has he studied at a school of arms? If the answer is no, we will be prone to relax—perhaps to relax overmuch. If it is yes, what is it that school teaches?

Beyond those simple questions lie many another. Is he old or young? Is he lame? Short of breath? Courageous or cautious? And so on.

If we are to defend ourselves on the streets, still more if we are to render those streets safe for the defenseless, we must learn all we can about those who have made them dangerous.

Tiero paused to dip his pen, but did not dip it. How would it look, this book of his, when it was displayed in the bookshops? When it stood among the other books on his shelf? Would he, as its author, be consulted as to the style of the letters? The binding?

Yes, absolutely. He was writing it to please the President-Protector, and the publisher would surely know—would not publish the book unless he did, for that matter. Such an author would be asked, and his every suggestion followed. A plain typeface, in that case, neither florid nor feminine. (And he must be sure to dedicate the book to President-Protector, and make absolutely certain that his dedication was included.)

As for binding . . .

He let his eyes rove over his own books, bound for the most part in dark cloth or darker leather. Vellum! He had seen a vellum-bound book somewhere, surely. No doubt in a bookshop. A leather thin but tough—like a good swordsman—and tan in color, like the face of a man who spends the greater part of each day outdoors. That was it. The title gold-lettered on the spine: SWORDS FOR PEACE. Beneath it, in letters somewhat smaller, TIERO OF TRIN. Almost, it seemed that he could see it before him.

He dipped his pen.

We should learn something of their weapons as well. Few if any will have swords. Long knives are the weapons most favored, and thus a weapon we must understand best if we are to be prepared. Yet our foes wield another weapon more important still.

If our minds are our own best weapons—and they are, never doubt it—are not the minds of our foes their best weapons also? We may deride the foes we find in the streets as men of little education, but they too have learned. They know how and when and where robberies and murders are best carried out. And too often it is they who find us. Let us learn what they know.

Full of thought, Tiero wiped his pen and returned it to the cylindrical vase that held half a dozen others. When his book was printed and sold, would not he be asked, not once only but again and again, about his own encounters with thugs in the streets? Clearly, he would. It could not be otherwise.

Yet there had been none. For half a minute or more he reflected on his career. Lessons at the greatest of all schools, and assiduous practice. Three duels, all against famous opponents. Two score matches with foils and two score wins— after which he had been acclaimed everywhere as the greatest swordsman of all. Thus his interview with the President-Protector. Thus the President-Protector's suggestion. Three fights on the close-cropped greens of dueling grounds. Forty or more mock fights, always on the boards of some estrade.

And here he was, wielding the pen instead of the sword. Reciting, like any other student, his masters' secondhand opinions.

It would not do.

Rising, he drew his sword. Its dial showed it at full charge. The white ray-skin that would keep his hand from slipping, even if it were drenched with blood, remained tightly glued to the metal of the hilt. His thumb found the demon-stone, and his blade leaped forth, aglow with fell Tyrian energy in the dimming room. A meter. Two meters. Three. A meter and a half. Two.

Satisfied, he released the stone.

It would take him an hour or more to get from his own well-appointed and almost luxurious lodgings to that very quarter of the city he had scrupulously avoided all his life. By that time, day and even twilight would be of the past. But first—

A necklace, the largest he owned, with a tourmaline at its center that might be mistaken for almost any other jewel in a bad light. Rings for his left hand, where they would not interfere with his swordcraft. Earrings, too. Dangling earrings sparkling with small gems. Silver and brass, raked from a drawer and dumped into the soft leather bag dangling from his belt, provided the appearance of ready wealth.

It was called the Questing Quarter, that part of the city. Questing because it was (or had been) here that men went looking for women, and women for men. Because it was (or had been) here that people of every station came in search of strong drink. Because it was (or had been) here that gamblers came to lose the little wealth that remained to them or that they had been able to borrow. Fifty years before, it had been popular and fashionable. It was worn, hard, and a trifle dirty now. When it was frequented by persons of quality, as it sometimes was still, they were generally men who hoped that poverty and perversion might season lives grown stale.

Swaggering into a tavern, he ordered a double brandy. His eyes challenged every man there while he sipped it, and he left feeling certain that he would need his sword before he had gone another block.

Nothing of the sort occurred. For a time he wandered the streets of the quarter in search of the darkest and most deserted. All of them proved dark, and none were deserted. Once a drunken roisterer nearly vomited on his boots; he skipped quickly to one side and reflected that it was his closest approach to danger.

Half a dozen well-dressed men went into a house whose tightly drawn curtains leaked a pinkish light. He joined them, accepted another brandy, took a chair in what had once been a reception hall, and watched as nearly naked strumpets paraded one by one among the chairs and ottomans.

One was little more than a child.

One was fat.

One had red hair, and freckles half concealed by powder.

One had a scarred cheek.

One was ten years older than Tiero himself, if not more.

One had been struck in the left eye not long ago; the bruises had just begun to fade.

One was extremely tall, and thin to the point of emaciation.

One had long golden hair—darker toward its roots.

One was somewhat drunk. She was the last to be taken, leaving Tiero alone with the oldest, the thinnest, and the redhead, who said, "Me, right? Come on. I'll show you my room."

He shook his head and rose.

The oldest said, "It has to be one of us, unless you want to wait until one of your friends is through."

"None of you," Tiero told her, "nor will I wait."

The thinnest tapped the wall with her knuckles. A door opened at once, and a big man with a cudgel entered. Leveling his left forefinger at Tiero, he said, "I don't want no trouble with you."

Seeing that the big man was watching his right hand, Tiero drew his sword with his left, little handicapped by the rings that flashed from all four fingers. His thumb found the demon-stone, and the blazing energy of his blade severed the cudgel half a finger's width from the big man's hand.

"You shouldn't play with things like that," Tiero told him. "You might be hurt." The point of his blade nudged the fallen cudgel, which burst into flame.

Outside, he walked the street in the Hour of the Lion, letting himself lurch and stagger a trifle—something the brandy made easy—but always aware of his surroundings, and particularly aware of anyone walking behind him. Time passed. The moon rose, rendering the dark streets less dark. There were fewer walkers now, and far fewer jitney coaches threading their way among them.

He entered a gambling den, tired, not quite sober, and firmly resolved that this would be his final stop of the night. A few large bets—after which he would leave, still apparently rich and ripe for the picking.

He made two and won both, dumping the gold his bag could not contain carelessly into his pockets. If this would not do it, nothing would.

Nothing did, clearly. A block, two blocks, three, and he was forced to turn away from the hurrying traffic and honest commerce of Bargain Avenue.

A woman screamed and he whirled, not conscious of having drawn the blade that flamed in his grip. He had thought himself about to be attacked, supposing that the woman had screamed to warn him. In that, he had been wholly mistaken. A dozen doors behind him, the woman was struggling furiously in the hands of two burly men. A third held open the door of a black coach larger than any jitney. Tiero shouted something—or perhaps, nothing—and sprinted toward them.

A moment later, she was sprawling in the filth of the street, and swords burned in her captors' hands. Tiero parried a clumsy thrust, and severed the arm that had held the threatening blade.

His second antagonist proved a worthy opponent. For a full two seconds their blades flashed and clashed like the lightnings.

The second man fell, his wounds spurting blood. As he did the door of the black coach slammed shut. The driver's whip cracked and the coach rattled away, all four horses plunging forward under the lash—galloping before they had taken four strides.

Tiero sheathed his sword and helped the weeping woman to her feet. She kissed him, damping his face with her tears, and shook with sobs until the jitney he had flagged down for them had put the Questing Quarter behind them. At last she gasped, "I was so fr-fr-frightened! I st-still am."

"You're safe with me," Tiero told her. "Who is he?"

"A s-suitor. That's what he c-calls himself. I . . . I knew his first w-wife. Oh, you won't believe me! I know you won't!"

"Did he kill her?"

"Sh-she k-killed herself. It's what they s-say." The sobs broke out anew.

"He drove her to it?" Tiero had heard of such things.

"She—oh, I'm so g-glad we don't have a mirror. I'm a mess. I know it! Don't look at me."

"I've looked at you a great deal already," Tiero told her quite truthfully, "and you're the most beautiful woman I've ever seen. The man I saved you from wants you because any man would."

"You?" She turned toward him. Her upper lip still trembled, but she smiled; and Tiero, seeing that smile in the fitful light that found its way through the oiled-parchment windows of the jitney, felt that no honor the President-Protector might confer could be even half so great.

"I am a human man," he said. "You smiled just now. No man who'd seen your smile could ever dream of any other woman."

"Your tongue is as nimble as your blade. Has no woman ever told you how handsome you are?"

"Of course not. What woman would be fool enough to believe such a lie could pass for gold?"

"But you're married?"

Tiero shook his head. When she said nothing, he added. "Now you'll wonder whether I killed a wife, or drove one to suicide. I've never had one."

"I—you'll want to know my name . . ."

"I should have introduced myself some time ago. I apologize. My concern for you was such as to drive all considerations of mere politeness far from me. I'm Tiero of Trin."

"The swordsman! I should have guessed! They—those two men you killed. They were bravos. He hired them. You can't have known."

"I knew that they were abusing you. I needed to know nothing more than that."

She drew a deep breath. "Will—I keep jumping ahead. It's a terrible habit. My name is Corlane Ryki Marella, Chatelaine-minor di Mirbellos. It means my father—it means that he—"

"Is Lord of Mirbellos," Tiero finished for her, "and that you're his elder unwed daughter, My Lady Chatelaine."

She swallowed, the tiny sound lost in the rattling of the jitney. "His only daughter. His only child. I mean, it doesn't say that but it's the truth." Beneath his chin, her hand lifted the face he had averted until his eyes looked into her own. "I'd never lie to you, Tiero. Not after what you did. Never! And now you're getting all respectful, and My-Lady-Chatelaine-this and My-Lady-Chatelaine-that, and I don't want that. Call me Ryki. It's what all my friends call me, I assure you, and if you're not a friend, who is?"

Tiero smiled. "I'll try to remember, Ryki. Please don't be angry if I should slip up now and then."

"That man—his name's Mercus—will go to my father's townhouse. He'll bribe a servant to tell him whether I'm there, and where. Probably Aengius. Will you—will you please, Tiero darling—take me home with you? I'll be safe with you tonight, I know."

Scarcely able to speak, Tiero gave the jitney coachman new instructions.

||

"Though knives and cudgels are, as I have said, the weapons most liable to be wielded by thugs, there was one occasion in my own experience in which I was forced to engage three men with swords." Stretched lazily beside a sleeping Ryki, Tiero had begun a new chapter, whispering directly into his vprint. *"That such situations are ever fraught with danger, I need hardly say. When engagement cannot be*

avoided—as in my own case—the swordsman must above all know that he faces an additional foe: time. If he does not win quickly, he will not win at all. In my own case I parried the thrust of an attacker with ease, and dispatched the maker of it at once. The second died nearly as fast. The third—"

At this point, the door of Tiero's lodgings was kicked down by a red-faced Mercus. A moment later Mercus shouted, "Deceiver! Adulteress!"

He shouted those things indeed, and more; but being a man of some experience in these matters, he did not shout them until the point of his blade had found Tiero's throat.

SIDEWAYS FROM NOW

John Meaney

John Meaney has been called "one of the best authors of hard SF in the world" by SFX, *and Charles Stross proclaimed that his ambitious saga* Paradox, Context, *and* Resolution *(collectively known as the Nulapeiron Sequence) was a "glittering jewel in the new British space opera." His most recent novel,* Bone Song, *fuses elements of science fiction with gothic fantasy. The story that follows could almost be a slice from a third fictional universe, one that forms some interstitial border between his space opera and his goth opera, existing just around the corner, sideways from now.*

Soft lighting and polished granite define the subterranean cemetery. A cool draft washes over oval stones atop each grave; while in the shadows, sharp-edged and hard, the headstones' projected holos shine.

Oh, Yukiko. You can't be gone.

Yet a year has passed. Back then, as grief swirled through me, I knew it was a mistake to mark the headstone: *Yukiko O'Connell née Akazawa; born March 27, 1995; died Austin, TX, August 13, 2021.* But I had no energy to contest it. Instead, I allowed the funeral directors to label Yukiko's resting place—if you can call it that—with their own unthinking words.

I miss you so bloody much.

Other holos move as visitors stop by graves. At each mourner's left earlobe, a tiny embedded stone lights up, ruby and bright. No one notices—no one has ever noticed—that my ear is devoid of decoration, yet Yukiko's holographic image brightens into focus. The headstone registers my presence. It is the only sign I have that things are different with me.

With us.

Yukiko, my beautiful Yukiko, liked puzzles. She adored every paradox, if it was robust and challenging. And her portrait, somehow, is a moving holo that appears still. Perhaps it captured her in eyes-open meditation, enriching the universe, as she enhanced so many people's lives. Or is that a grieving man's illusion?

The headstone's words were a mistake because *Austin, August 2021* is a curse overloaded with anger, like Pearl Harbor or 9/11 in earlier decades.

To my left, a short man called Abraham, aged seventy-three, approaches with a bunch of soft orange wallflowers, scarcely scented, their dark green stems wrapped with a rubber band. Abraham pauses at Yukiko's grave, en route to Muriel, his buried wife who lies at the end of the row.

Abraham nods. I nod. It's not our wives but their rotted remains that lie here. You think Abraham and I fool ourselves about what we're visiting?

On the first occasion we met, Abraham murmured something about the Atlanta August Virus. My reply was a snarl: "She died of cancer."

And I wonder how many other grieving relatives, two decades back, felt cheated or confused or *something* because their loved ones died on September 11 here in New York, somewhere other than inside the towers. For their deaths hurt just the same. Last year in Atlanta, the chimera-plague terrorists were not the sole bringers of disaster.

I have long since apologized to Abraham for my angry words. Sometimes, after paying respect to our dead wives, Abraham and I adjourn to Doyle's Bar. There I can hear the accents of my native Dublin and scratch the weeping wound that is memory. But today, "I'm running late," murmurs Abraham, while my overlapping reply is: "I've got a meeting, sorry."

It's all right, because there will always be another day . . . or there won't, in which case one of us will have no worries. I consider this as I back away from the grave.

Enough.

Six paces, and Yukiko's portrait winks out.

Last night I dreamed about a prince who dreamed through the minds of others. Through a hundred . . . no, *two* hundred thousand others: sleeping inhabitants of the vast lumbering construct that is the Clanking City, engaged on an endless journey along a cylindrical world.

The sleeper's name was Prince Argul. Lying, he appeared tall. Certainly he was lean, his narrow face bearded. Prince Argul slept atop a couch furnished in silver, a detail I remembered as I fell awake, back into reality.

Inside the twenty-mile length of the Clanking City's steel-jointed carapace, articulated metal streets and cog-shaped inner buildings fitted together, sliding or turning in lubricated joints. But Prince Argul's mind was not constrained by the geographical engineering of his city.

Telepathy, I somehow knew, was characteristic of the ruling line. It also occurred randomly among the ordinary population; and whether this was caused by natural mutation or royal bastardy, only scurrilous scholars debated in whispers, far away from hard-eyed legal officials.

None of this could possibly be true.

As I sat up in bed, in a room filled with darkness, I remembered vividly the smile on Prince Argul's face as he slept. His chambers, I believe, had shielding capable of protecting him from his subjects' thoughts; but at night, the shields were open, not closed. The kaleidoscope of shifting, chaotic dreaming images and scents, the myriads of muscular sensations, of imagined voices, was not torture but soothing to Prince Argul.

He *bathed* in the minds of the dreaming populace.

Scarlet holographic digits hung near my pillow. The time was 3:07. Outside, featureless blackness hid the Connecticut forest. I supposed the place was filled with life, with millions of crawling organisms, hunting or sleeping or fleeing. Only my bedroom was empty.

"Why can't I dream of you, my love?"

I placed my palm on the side of the bed where Yukiko used to sleep.

II

I ascend from the cemetery via escalator, and come up blinking into the garish busyness of Sixth Avenue. Yellow mag-cabs hum; private cars mostly wait for the traffic to get moving. Crowds throng the sidewalks. Behind me in Central Park—I glance over my shoulder as always, and smile—rises the slow-morphing complexity of Grimwood Towers, foreshadowing a new Manhattan.

At the beginning of the 1960s, a visitor from the '30s would have thought New York unchanged; a few years later, his opinion would be radically different. Yukiko would love to have seen motile bioarchitecture change the city now. I remembered in Dublin—

Oh, my love.

—how Yukiko admired the new developments north of the River Liffey. "Creeping tenements" means something different since buildings gained the ability to grow and slowly move.

"Excuse me, pal."

A rotund man in a business suit pushes past, jostling a white-haired woman who stops in her tracks. The businessman crosses the street just as the holo stick-figure raises one hand, shifting hue to red. The old woman looks on stoically; but across the street, a dark-skinned youth with dreadlocks, rainbows shimmering across his eyes, frowns at the rudeness.

Reflections slide across the young man's silvered contacts; then the qPin in his left earlobe flares crimson and the signals change, stopping the traffic once more.

He crosses, purely so he can lead the woman back across the street. I watch, standing in place, while the rest of the crowd bustles into motion. As the young man accepts the woman's thanks with humble grace, I touch my eyebrow with a fingertip and salute him. He nods in return.

Nice work.

We didn't design the qPin to interface with public traffic systems. Neither did our competitors.

Two blocks at a slow walk, and I'm at the entranceway to our building. Inside, I wave at Martin, who remains sitting behind the security desk. He looks anorexic as always, his bulging eyes symptomatic of recurrent thyroid problems.

"Hey there, Ryan," he says. "How's it going?"

"Fantastic," I tell him. "How's the book getting on?"

"Put episode seventeen to bed last night." Martin shrugs. "Nearly a thousand folk have downloaded so far."

In the evenings I'm in town, if I stay late, I chat with Martin about relativity or reincarnation, prions or primal scream therapy. Most of the building's other visitors say nothing as they pass him en route to their office or back out to the street, as if Martin were part of the fittings.

"You're on fire, my friend."

"I hope so, Ryan. Um, you're up with the bigwigs on twenty-seven."

"Sounds good."

The elevator's door is polished and warm, somewhere between brass and gold. As I approach, the door slides open. Behind me, Martin says: "Hey . . . I meant you're with the *other* bigwigs, right?"

I give him a half-salute from inside the elevator.

"If you say so."

Ian comes out to greet me, then leads the way back to the boardroom as though I don't know where it is. It's been a while since I made the trek into Manhattan, and I'm not sure why I'm here. Something's going on, but I don't really care.

That's the real problem, isn't it?

Val, our new VP of marketing, is checking her presentation material. I look over at Ned, gray-haired engineer and true geek. When I raise one eyebrow, Ned grins: we are fellow nerds in the face of the marketroid invasion.

The presentation begins. After a while, I'm biting my lip, then sucking in quiet breaths, anything to stop falling asleep. Perhaps Ian notices, because he breaks in with, "Remember how we nearly ended up in the trash with the monthly rags?"

Beside me, Irina from R&D directs her gaze up to the ceiling, shaking her head.

"Point taken," I tell Ian.

The qPin in Val's ear flares scarlet, brighter than anyone else's. In the holovolume, her presentation freezes, then minimizes into a rotating cube.

"Something I should know about, guys?"

"Um . . . Before your time," mutters Ian.

"He's talking about *qPad*." Irina gestures at Ian. "That was the original branding for qPins. And this one"—she nods at me—"suggested we call the smallest model *femto*."

"Er . . ." Val frowns.

"Your predecessor," says Irina, "wanted to know whether we were launching a quantum interface or a feminine hygiene product."

Ned is beginning to blush. Last I heard, he was still—aged thirty-eight—honest-to-goodness living with his mother.

Val's shoulders begin to shake. I notice she has a large bosom that ripples when she laughs. Ian notices me noticing, so I have to shake my head, meaning: *Not interested.*

"You invented the q-pairing concept, Ryan," Val says to me. "Do I have that right?"

"I'm not sure 'invented' is the right—"

"He also," Ian breaks in, "came up with the slogan *Play Cupid with your qPin.* Marketing were smart enough to use it."

"Oh . . ." Now a small, warm blush is growing on Val's face. "My husband . . . We *met* because of that—well. All I can say is, Ryan, your own married life must be wonderful."

A dislocated silence slips across the table. Everyone's expression changes.

"I'm sorry . . ." Val realizes she's made a faux pas.

"She died." I keep my voice gentle. "That's all."

"Oh my God. You must . . . Oh, Ryan, how you must miss her."

I lower my head. Anger brightens in Irina's eyes, but it's misplaced. Val obviously understands everything about deep pairing. And I *can* talk about Yukiko's death. It's my colleagues who assume I can't.

"The agenda," murmurs Ian. "Perhaps we should move on?"

"Of course."

Val resumes the presentation, taking us through sales targets and marketing initiatives, and a product release schedule, with an aside to discuss the opening of the new plant in Greenland. None of it excites me. None of it requires my presence.

Every now and then, I catch Ian watching me. Each time, he looks away.

When we take a break, Irina and I stand together in the corner. She brings me up to date on her son's life, filled with small adventures that contrast with Irina's Lithuanian childhood.

"Sleepovers," she says. "He and his friends stay in each other's houses, building up a network of friends who can help each other as they grow older. Isn't it great?"

In the past, Irina's given me invaluable tips on how to bribe my way through officialdom, should I ever find myself in a country where corruption is a way of life.

"It's not like the Old Country," I tell her, unsure of whether I'm referring to Lithuania or Ireland. "How long have we lived here?"

Irina raises her eyebrows, understanding what I mean. You can live in a new culture for years and still be fascinated by life's small details. In Ireland, for instance, Yukiko would have been in the ground within two days of her death, but in New York we had to wait for the postmortem and then the—

"Looks like round two"—Irina gestures with her cup—"is starting. Glad you came?"

"I don't think," I murmur, "that this is the real meeting. Not for me."

"Ah."

Neither of us looks at Ian as we retake our seats.

Afterwards, we ride down to the first floor. The elevator is full, and while most of the people wear *qRious Minds, Inc.* IDs like Ian's and mine, some are visitors. So Ian confines his remarks to: "Have you ever wondered what would happen if terrorists released a coffee virus? I mean something that would wipe out coffee beans across the globe."

"Jesus," I murmur. "The world's economy . . . I'd never manage a stroke of work again."

My last comment is provocative. Both of us know that my contributions these days are nominal, meaning nonexistent-but-let's-not-discuss-it. Or not until now.

"Better drink some while you can."

"I could murder a cappuccino."

The other folk look puzzled. Did I just use a foreign idiom? But Ian knows what I mean. He grins in no particular direction, then looks up at the indicator holo. The elevator slows and my stomach tugs more than it should, vision blurring as—

Through a thousand, ten thousand miles of pipes and pistons, gaskets and manifolds, the Clanking City's motive power pulsed and thrummed and whooshed. From a distance, the city appeared to undulate, to flow, its articulated metal joints flexing as it crawled over ridges and through valleys.

Most recently, it had crossed a wide mesa, from whose flattened surface the horizon showed on either side, where the world dropped away, and to fore and rear, where the world simply arrowed onwards in perspective view, towards infinity. Scholars had long debated whether the world formed an *endlessly* long cylinder or one that was simply *unimaginably* long; but for practical purposes it extended forever.

And the City continued to clank onward or die.

—the elevator door slides open, revealing the bright, glass-walled foyer and beyond, the bright Avenue of the Americas, trapped in sunshine.

"You okay, Ryan?" Ian's hand grasps my arm.

"Why shouldn't I—"

The faintest of lines, some miles distant, traced the atmospheric perimeter. Between scouting teams and scholars, the Clanking City's academies maintained careful records of the great air bubble's estimated volume. It had shrunk at times during centuries past, always to expand again while traversing dark beds of certain minerals.

As the bubble continued its peregrination along the world, its speed remained approximately constant. Slow enough for the Clanking City to keep pace.

Devices of mirrors and lenses and flexible polished tubes watched from silvery balloons tethered to the city's upper carapace. The highest balloons floated above the breathable limit, within the caustic layer. What they revealed was unsettling.

Soon, the city would pass through an area of great outcrops from which round towers rose. But it was the most distant terrain that concerned the long-term planners.

Farther ahead, maybe two decades' traveling time into the future, lay an area of broken blue-and-red ground whose hues betrayed the presence of minerals no human scholar had examined . . . or at least, no scholar from *this* city.

Some observers thought they had observed a faint, dark outline of a crashed city far ahead. Others claimed it was merely a geological outcrop, sparking overactive imaginations.

Yet no one could deny the existence of broken human cities. Five were recorded in the Clanking City's archives. There were grizzled veterans still alive who had explored the ruins of Traction.

Whether it was mechanical breakdown, demonic artillery fire, or civil strife that had destroyed Traction, no one knew (though scholars fiercely and humorlessly maintained their differing interpretations).

And what if the minerals that lay ahead were injurious to the traveling atmosphere? But while scholars and planners worried about distant futures, the Observers Guild kept unstinting watch, their presence in the moment, alert for immediate and imminent dangers.

Rivet-encrusted armored steel formed the Clanking City's carapace. From slits in the major sections, most of them set two hundred feet above the ground, Observer teams, unstinting, scanned terrain and sky.

Inside one observation chamber, a junior observer early for duty was sketching with charcoal on a pad. The picture growing on the page was of jumbled towers that stood in place amid aeries and caves. Winged shapes moved among the towers.

"You've drawn it well, lad." The watch sergeant leaned over the young observer's shoulder. "Too bad you ain't captured the shitty color."

The young man stopped, then rubbed at a tower's outline with his fingertip. Ordinary folk might say he was drawing a nest, but observers knew that such places were towns or cities . . . of a sort. Cities that could never move.

This was the habitation they would soon bypass. The oxygen atmosphere would envelop most of the demonic city, maybe all of it.

"Is it true, Sergeant"—the young man tapped the sketch—"that demons fall asleep when real air passes over 'em?"

"Of course, lad. They seals themselves in, doesn't they?"

"Will we see any?"

The sergeant folded his hands above his convex belly. "You was thinking of a transfer to the Raiders, like?"

"Um . . . No, Sergeant. I prefer it here."

"Good lad."

Outside, a chitin-protected flitterbug thumped into the armored glass, bounced off, was gone.

"Sorry, Sergeant."

"And I'll have a cup of tea now, thank you, lad."

Deep inside the city was the Core Palace. Underneath the palace, three decks down, a sweating man in leather vest and grease-stained pants was lashed to a hot steel pipe, its diameter almost equal to the man's height. The man's shoulder bore the triple brand of a Senior Artificer, but neither his proud office nor the tallow stick clenched between his teeth could stop the whimpering.

Three men wearing purple headbands—a punishment detail—stood behind him. One of them held a seven-knotted whip.

"You failed to check the gasket."

"Mm-mmm."

"When it blew, it could have killed someone."

"Mmm . . ."

"It could've *stopped the city*."

The man with the whip raised his hand once more. The prisoner turned his head away, eyes shut, knowing there was no avoiding this.

"We are engineers. We live and breathe control systems. Consider this *feedback*."

The whip came down.

║║

Two miles farther aft and one deck higher, a slight girl, aged perhaps eight, was watching her master as he poured molten crystal—red-yellow and viscous—into steel molds. Around the chamber, clockwork devices clacked their incantations, controlling and measuring. A shaven-headed servant stood poised with a long-handled ladle. It was important to hold back the *aqua mementa* until the exact moment that—

"Now."

The servant poured. Steam hissed and puffed.

"Yes . . ."

Shivering into a web configuration, the crystal solidified and did not shatter. The new web looked clear and perfect as if it had always existed, and always would.

"You saw the hue, Shama? You felt the heat when the time was correct?"

"Yes, Master." The girl stared at the crystal. "When can I make one?"

The tiniest of flaws marked a spot near the dreamweb's center. Shama would not have dreamed of shaming her master by pointing this out.

"Not this year." A smile rippled the scar which streaked down Master Teldrasso's face. "Or the next. Ordinary baubles first. But then . . . Oh, and tomorrow, I'll let you work the bellows."

His left eye was cloudy, a reminder that molten crystal was dangerous stuff. Yet the webs and other artifacts he cast were wonderful: even with the so-tiny flaw, this new dreamweb was magnificent.

Disciplined expertise like her master's—that was what Shama, her skin child-soft and as yet unblemished, dreamed of attaining.

"Oh. Yes." Shama looked down at the steel deck. "Thank you."

Master Teldrasso sighed.

Lost in sleep-trance, near the Core Palace's heart, Prince Argul continued to share his subjects' dreams. His respiration was slow. His somnolent form looked *solid* atop the silver sleeping-couch.

Then the dreaming prince frowned. Perhaps a transient groan sounded.

But his eyelids failed to flutter, and in seconds his face was masklike, once more unmoving.

Prince Argul, like thousands of his subjects, slept on.

"—be okay?" I asked Ian.

"Um . . . If you say so." The worry clears from Ian's face, then returns. "If the qCafé is busy, we'll go somewhere else."

He means if any of our colleagues are around, we'll look for some privacy.

"All right," I tell him. Then: "Hey, Martin."

From the security desk, Martin says, "The café's pretty quiet right now."

Ian turns away and crosses the lobby. You can get into the qCafé from here or directly from the street. Beside the entrance, two young women are sitting on a dark green upholstered bench seat, staring into each other's eyes as their qPins blink a stroboscopic red.

Once inside the café proper, Ian stops in front of the holo menu—*qappuccini* and *brazilian roast qoffee*, honestly—pretending to read it, shaking his head. He disapproves of the women integrating their thought-images as the qPin processors attempt to classify neural patterns in terms of *qualia*, of world-perceptions, deciding which patterns to entangle.

"You didn't like San Francisco, did you, Ian?"

He lived there for two years. Now he says: "What do you mean?"

"Nothing. Never mind."

According to the menu notes, a *qappuccino* contains equal mixes of steamed milk and quantum foam. Don't ask me who dreams this stuff up.

I take a seat near the round inner doorway, the one painted as a giant white letter "Q": a bit of marketing I find amusing. Beside it, a small holo sign reads: *Follow the Quantum Tunnel.* And, in smaller floating blue script: *Free upgrades this week!*

The whole café setup is to entice consumers into the product test-room for market research. They get to play; our psych teams get to watch.

When Ian brings back the coffees and sits down, I remain still. After a moment, I take my cup, place it in front of me, and flick it with a fingernail. The sound is a half-musical *clink.*

"You're not drinking it? Janey mac, Ryan, are you feeling all right?"

Yukiko used to say that in a County Louth brogue. She was a great mimic. Ian isn't.

The Clanking City moved across the . . .

I blink away the vision. There's nothing wrong with daydreams. I hope the two young women outside manage to share theirs.

"Do you want my resignation?"

There. I've brought it out into the open.

"Jesus H. Christ, Ryan. I want you to pull your goddamn finger out. You remember *churning?*"

"Oh. Well, yeah . . ."

It was the old-time gospel according to a business guru called Kawasaki. In the old days, when Apple produced an initially superior product (a computer that used a mouse, if you can remember such a thing), a competitor called Microsoft brought out an inferior version. But Microsoft *churned*—Kawasaki's term—as they made major improvements, over and over, working to a timescale of months, not years. They buried the opposition.

I never was much of a history student.

"So we need to churn, my friend." Ian gets up, coffee in hand. "Come on, let's go see."

"I've seen it."

"Come on."

Ian walks through the giant Q. I can stay behind or follow. As Ian enters, the qPin in his left earlobe flashes briefly. The system must recognize him, or it would complain about the latte he's carrying: ordinary customers have to leave theirs in the café.

I take a sip of my cappuccino—sorry, *qappuccino*—and put it down. As I follow, I'm in the company of several youngsters whose qPins are strobing overtime. They look at me as if I'm weird . . . or rather, they stare at my bare, unadorned earlobe.

You ungrateful little snots, I want to say. *I developed telepathy. Doesn't mean I have to use it.*

Luckily they cannot read my thoughts.

At the Quantum Tunnel's far end, Ian sips his latte and waits for the young-sters to pass through the gateway.

"I'll get you authorized," he tells me, "in just a second."

I feel too tired to tell him it's pointless. Ian breathes in deeply, puffing his chest like some parody of a drill sergeant as he uses his qPin and struts inside. After a second, I follow along.

The youngsters pass straight through the hanging golden schematic and the blue holo text that proclaims *Persistent Entanglement Explained.* They're more interested in upgrading their implants than learning the principles. For God's sake, how many people think about the magical mystery behind even old-fashioned TV and cell phones?

I remember Yukiko, how she sat entirely still and focused on me as I talked about moving magnets to choreograph electrons dancing in a length of wire, so that other electrons *across the nation* dance in time along their own wires.

"You see the magic in everything, don't you, Ryan, my love?"

For sure, I remember Yukiko's magic. I ache with its absence now.

"Three out of every seven qPins in the world," murmurs Ian, gesturing at the product displays, "are ours. Two dozen competitors share the remaining market. But that could change in an instant."

The youngsters gaze enraptured as upgrade signals flow into their qPins.

"They're not interested"—I gesture at them—"in who they buy from."

"Right. Do *you* care?"

I allow a slow exhalation before answering. "You said you didn't want my resignation."

"Didn't I mention churning?"

My stomach rumbles at the word, and I start to smile, but Ian frowns. In the old days, he'd have laughed until he farted.

"You've changed, Ian."

"Yeah . . ." He looks at the youngsters, rather than at me.

Knock, knock.

I hear the invitation as a sound inside my skull. I shake my head. Luckily Ian doesn't notice.

And then I surprise myself. Perhaps my unconscious has noticed the tension in Ian's shoulders as he comes to some decision about me.

"I'm working on something new," I tell him. "Kind of a story, kind of a fantasy game, and it's all nebulous so don't ask me too much yet. And it's a shared quest."

Ian stares. Slowly blinks.

"You mean . . . a three-user sharecast? An *n-user* 'cast?"

So he's not forgotten his nerd roots. N-user, where *n* is any number greater than three.

A prince who dreamed, bathing in the thoughts of thousands *of his subjects . . .*

"Could be."

With a step backwards, Ian says, "You fancy the Four Seasons tonight? I promised Jacqui and the kids, but you're welcome to join us. We haven't hung together for . . . too long."

"It is too long," I tell him. "But tonight, I'd rather just go home."

Ian looks for a place to dump his latte, but there's nowhere. He says, "Home alone in Stephen King country? Don't you get . . . tired of it?"

He'd been going to ask whether I got *lonely.*

"I've got a new product to work on, remember?"

"Well . . . Yes. All right, buddy."

Ian claps me on the shoulder, and we leave side by side. But our footsteps are out of sync, and when we shake hands in the foyer, there's something awkward about the gesture.

When I rode the subway this morning, the car was hot inside although it's only March. I was pleased by the notion that we're beginning to share each other's thoughts, but can't keep subway cars cool. I'm staying aboveground now as I reach Grand Central . . . and carry on walking.

"I'd rather just go home," I told Ian; but I can be alone anywhere. I notice a diner I've not used before. I slip inside and order a bagel and espresso.

"Take a seat, pal. Be a minute."

"Yeah. Thanks."

The small round tables are bunched close together. I lean on my table, chin on hand.

The royal court, vast and hollow, formed of dark gray metal, was dominated by a construct formed of crystalline webs. Overall, the webs formed a bulging cylinder perhaps a hundred feet wide, while inside the cylinder a shadowy horizontal form floated.

A sword lay lengthwise along his body, the hilt clasped in his gauntlet-covered hands, like a statue of some dead knight except that this was no ordinary death, this was the Sleeping King who—

"Coffee. Bagel."

The waitress thumps them down on the table.

Jesus, Mary, and Joseph.

My subconscious swears using Grandfather Jack's voice. It always has.

I eat half the bagel and drink all of the coffee. Afterward, in the bathroom, I splash water on my face, although what comes out of both taps—I still don't use the word *faucet* in my thoughts—is lukewarm. Then I leave, not sure where I'm going, walking approximately south among commuter crowds.

In Washington Square, I buy a bag of honey-roasted peanuts from a vendor. A handful of stalls stand in an arc close to the outdoor chess tables. Chewing the sweet nuts, I watch a young woman relieve a bespectacled, gray-bearded tourist of his cash, using a checkmate that comes from nowhere.

Smiling, I turn away and stop. One of the stalls features hanging dream-catchers, woven constructs with dangling feathers, supposed to capture wandering dreams. The tan-skinned man behind the stall wears jewelry of silver and turquoise. His right eye is opaque with cataracts. He taps a sand painting, multihued layers trapped between glass, and looks at me.

What does he expect me to say?

Shama looked up at Master Teldrasso's face, no longer seeing the milky left eye, and waited for his nod before beginning to work the bellows that—

Shivering, I break eye contact. Then I walk away fast, past the penned-in area where dog owners exercise their pets. I'm hurrying, not knowing why.

Close to its original location, an old haunt waits. The KGB Bar's claustrophobic rooms remain dark red; old photos of Beria and his cohorts still hang upon the walls. The literary crowd is absent, which means there's room to sit.

I take a rum and Coke to a corner table, and sit without drinking. Then I carry the glass back to the counter and ask for Coke, no rum, assuring the barkeep that she didn't mishear: I've changed my mind.

To form the new game story, I need to allow the daydreams to come. Drunkenness is not creative.

Yukiko and I, along with Ian and others, used stories—we called them telemetaphors—to lead people into calibration-hallucinations for the early qPins.

In the first stage, we simply scanned the about-to-be-paired individuals as they watched the same pictures in reality, to the same soundtrack, smelling the same scents. But telemetaphors drove the second stage, as users attempted to create similar pictures in their minds—pictures they might eventually both see—and to hear the same imaginary sounds, feel the same feelings.

And how's this for internal dialog? Am I crazy?

I drink three Cokes in quick succession, trying not to think.

Martin is still on duty. He gets up from behind the desktop monitors, looking surprised.

"I thought you'd be in Stratford by now."

"Got something to do. Work."

"Well." The qPin in Martin's left ear blinks scarlet. "Good."

"Um . . . I don't suppose I could get into the café first?"

"No, you couldn't."

"Oh."

"But I could. Hang on." His qPin flares.

The door marked *qCafé* slides open.

"Thanks a million."

In the darkened café, lights begin to flicker and the cappuccino machine boots up, or whatever the things do. I ask for a *qappuccino massimo.* When it arrives, I carry the mug through the Q-shaped doorway and follow the Quantum Tunnel to the far end, to the closed door.

Dark crimson shifts within the sensor plates.

Ian believed he had to authorize my entry here. Martin must think I'm in the café, prevented by the building's control systems from venturing further. After all, my earlobes are bare and no, I don't have a qPin inserted through some other part of my anatomy, though I've heard stories of—

The door slides back.

The product cave is only half-lit, reminding me of the subterranean cemetery that shelters Yukiko's remains.

(And I know there's only thing that prevents me from stepping off every high place I visit, from falling into the void. For I have seen myself through Yukiko's eyes, and felt *everything* she felt for me, how precious she thought I was. I cannot destroy a thing that mattered to her, even myself.)

Oh, my dearest, dearest love.

The universe has ripped her from me: my lover, my soul, everything that was good in my world.

Knock, knock. The invitation sounds.

Ian doesn't know. No one knows; although sometimes, Irina stares thoughtfully at me. She might suspect that Yukiko and I led the way, and wonder why we never claimed public credit.

Because Yukiko and I shared thoughts.

We were the first in the world.

The invitation repeats inside my head: *Knock, knock.* As a holding action, I sip my cappuccino, hot espresso bitterness beneath creamy foam. To my right, the holo brightens into sapphire blue: *Free upgrades.*

You have no idea how upgrade-capable I am. But the building system knows.

"All right," I say aloud. "I accept."

Ian and Martin know . . . hell, *everybody* knows I have no implant. What they don't realize is—

Pulses of red and white race across the walls, quickening and brightening, as a low bass thrum slowly builds, louder and louder, until the carpet vibrates beneath my feet.

—my entire body is a qPin.

Nova-light slams into me.

‖

I am incandescent. I *burn* as quantum op-codes pour through me, particles reset, and a thousand giant fists hammer me out of the universe. I flare and the world snaps down to point-size . . .

Yukiko.

. . . is gone.

Sideways-on, with the carpet pressed against my cheek, I watch a cleansebot work, cleaning up dried foam. I can smell the old coffee, though the mug has rolled out of sight.

Dropped it as I fell.

So I'm awake enough to appreciate the obvious. I turn sideways, then push myself up, reach a kneeling position. I get to my feet.

"Thanks. I suppose."

There is no reply from the building system. Every display is dark. The power hum has stopped.

"Ah, ya gobshite . . ."

The front of my pants is stained dark, and I don't think it's coffee.

"Scared the piss out of me."

Floor-level lights wink once, then nothing. So that's my answer.

I snag a barista's black apron from behind the counter, and I'm wearing it as I pass through the foyer. Martin stares but merely says goodnight as I leave fast, out into the street, looking for a department store.

It's getting late but this is Manhattan, with everything available. In fifteen minutes I'm wearing a new tracksuit, with the whiffy pants and the barista's apron zapped in a flash-trash, gone.

From the balcony inside Grand Central, I sip a strawberry-and-banana smoothie and watch passengers move about on the concourse. Then I close my eyes, wondering if visions of the Clanking City will come to visit; but all I see is the orange of my eyelids; what I hear is a chaotic babble around me.

There are no green uniforms. Eyes closed, I think about what I've just seen beneath the balcony. The military guard of the past decades has gone from the station.

There . . .

I can feel the sensor strips like a distant itch. I can hear the near-silent movement of hidden AI guns, swiveling inside black glass casings.

Putting down my unfinished drink, I descend the steps to the concourse, checking the departure boards that most qPin-wearing travelers ignore. I love the poetic rhythm of the names. Poughkeepsie. New Haven.

My first experience of the States was Richmond, VA, when I was on sabbatical from Imperial College. I found the Virginians friendly, open to strangers, just as I'd grown used to in Ireland then failed to find in London. But in Connecticut I discovered a basic law that applies everywhere: commuters are miserable.

Traveling back on the train, I close my eyes again, allowing my head to sway, sensing no trace of the Clanking City.

I expected intense visions. Since the upgrade, I've felt nothing.

As the train slides into my station, I catch the fading end of a dream: Yukiko standing before a polished brass sphere that is taller than a man. And her voice: "Get away, ya blaggarts."

The sculpture was in Trinity College, set back from the gray cobblestone courtyard. The words, in a perfect Louth accent, came from Yukiko's mouth, shooing away well-fed youngsters who were begging for money.

It was my first glimpse of Yukiko.

As the youngsters left, she murmured: "Ya wee skitters." Yet the manga book she was holding was Japanese.

Then she caught my eye, and I had to reply: "*Konnichi-wa.*" We both laughed; and that was our beginning. As we walked to the refectory that first time, Yukiko said little. Such moments of moving stillness are what I most remember.

Yukiko was already set to transfer to London the following September. I was still trying to decide whether I wanted to carry on to PhD. I was broke, tired of lodgings with damp-smelling carpets, fed up of eating takeout curries.

But University College, London, was exploring new directions in neuroscience that fascinated Yukiko. By the fall we were there, Yukiko at UCL and me at Imperial College, sharing an apartment in Kilburn.

In Grandfather Jack's day, in the 1950s when he lived in London, Kilburn was the Irish ghetto. Boardinghouses everywhere bore signs that read NO IRISH OR DOGS.

Now I'm here in Connecticut, another emigrant from the Old Country. Diaspora is a national tradition.

Through coalescing darkness, I drive into the forest, and finally up the long stony track to home. I park the car, and jack it in to recharge. Then I walk away from the house.

At the forest's edge, everything is quiet. A dark shadow flits overhead, near-invisible against the night. For a moment I think of demons gliding among strange towers that cannot exist.

Hands in pockets, I head home. Lights shine amber as the system registers my approach.

For a moment I can pretend that Yukiko is inside, waiting for me.

As I lie back, my head seems to continue backwards and down into the pillow, falling into dreams. My last thought is, *Back to the Clanking City.*

But that is not what I experience.

I'm drunk, pissing up a white-painted wall in moonlight. Six of my comrades are doing the same.

"Come on, Jack." Rory is zipping up his uniform shorts. "Man with the smallest dick buys, right?"

"But I'm *always* paying for the drinks," I tell him.

There's laughter as we stumble back across the well-kept lawn. The scent of rhododendron is strong in the night. Gordon, weaving, shushes us with one finger to his lips, then giggles. Finally we're past the gateway pillars and out onto the road.

Looking back I see the brass plate, silver-white beneath the moon, clear enough to read the words RAFFLES HOTEL.

Beside me, Zenon throws a salute. I can even read the motto on his winged insignia: *per ardua ad astra*. The Royal Air Force, shooting for the sky.

"Why are you saluting?" I ask.

"It's famous, innit?" Zenon comes from Warsaw. Drunk, he sounds like a Londoner. "The hotel."

"Bleeding hell," mutters Fred. "If the MPs catch us, we're in the clink."

We weave along the road on foot. After some time—God knows how long—we come across a group of local Malays, standing by a drainage hole, pointing down and muttering.

"What are they on about, Jack?"

I rub my face, wishing the world would steady. "Dunno."

"Come on, Paddy," says Gordon, who's incapable of calling me Jack. "You've picked up the lingo."

"Only a little."

"I'll buy you a whiskey, a wee drop of the . . . What do you call it?"

"The craythur," I tell him. "All right."

I do my best to form the question, but the reply comes rattling back too fast to follow. So I try again, slower, and the Malay uses simple words this time.

"Big snake," I tell Gordon. "Boa."

"Down the drain?"

"Yep."

"Well," mutters Fred. "Boas. Big buggers."

"Got just the thing for 'em." Gordon, swaying, digs through his pockets. "Anyone like pineapples?"

Zenon shakes his head. Fred stares at him. "What, you don't—?"

But the pineapples that Gordon's pulling out have pins and three-second fuses.

"Oh, sweet Jesus—"

Down the opening they sail, and then there's a massive *crump* and a silvery cloud of moonlit dust, and I'm on my hands and knees on the road, laughing and cursing with the rest.

For a moment I groan awake, in my silver-gray room hours before dawn. Then I let my head roll to one side, sliding back down to sleep.

The Malays are running away down the road.

"What got into them?" asks Rory, picking debris from his hair.

"God's sake," mutters Gordon. "We liberated Singapore, didn't we? Bloody *Changi*. We're heroes of the whatsit. Hour."

"Right," says Rory.

"Deserve bloody medals, don't we?"

"But you can't drink a medal," says Fred.

For a moment we all stop. Fred may have hit on a profound truth. But I wish Gordon hadn't mentioned Changi.

We were the second team into the prison camp, to see near-skeletal bodies, to move through the stench of dysentery and death. One of the ex-prisoners, somehow, persuaded Gordon to hand over his Webley. I guess Gordon wanted to see if the man would head for the Japanese guards, now under our watch, and pick out a particular guard or just try to wipe out the lot.

But the man with shaking sticks for arms turned the revolver to his own head. Gordon was only just in time to swipe the weapon away from him.

A medic caught the man before he fell, fainting.

"Should do the Japs our bloody selves," the medic said. "Saw off their heads with their own bastard swords."

I could have stayed in Dungarvan, rode out the war—Ireland is neutral, after all—working in the leather factory, reading my library books in the pub every night. I didn't have to come into hell.

"Come on." I clap Gordon on the shoulder. "A wee drop of the craythur, right?"

"You're a hero, Paddy."

"Grand man yourself, Gordon."

We head back towards the barracks.

▌▌

It's 3:07 AM by the clock when I haul myself from bed. Outside, the forest remains black beneath darkness. Did I wake because of my dreams, or because something in the real world—?

There.

Twin points of scarlet, glowing in the night.

"Home alone in Stephen King country," wasn't that what Ian said?

I wait. The scarlet lights remain still. Finally I call, "Patio lights. On."

Magnesium-white beams flood the exterior.

"Jesus, Mary, and Joseph."

The two cats blink but stay sitting. One is a silver tabby, the other calico. They stare at me for a long time. Then they look at each other, their implants strobing scarlet.

And the patio lights go out, though I did not command this.

Sweet bleeding hell.

Shadows slip gracefully among shadows. I think they're heading for the forest.

"Kitchen. Make coffee."

No more sleep tonight.

I almost drop my coffee when the doorbell sounds. The sun is painting amber-gold above the treetops now, and I'm getting set for a quiet, exhausted day. But through the door-screen I can see a brown uniform, and the package in the courier's hands. Perhaps Irina has sent me new hardware from the labs.

"Morning, sir."

"Hi." I slide the door open. "Do I need to sign?"

"Yeah, could you—?" The courier holds up a qNote then falters, noting the absence of a qPin in my ear. "Oh. Just a minute."

He starts to unclip a light-pen from his pocket, but I'm ahead of him. The qNote beeps.

"Um. . . . How did you . . . ?"

"Next year's model." I take the package from his hands. "I'm trying it out."

"So where . . . ? Wow. I mean, *wow.*"

And he walks back towards his chocolate-brown truck shaking his head. I could do with solitude today, but I'd better open the package. Irina only sends me stuff when it's—but it's not from her.

My cousin Deirdre, in County Clare, has sent me—as I find, cutting open the envelope—a red diary marked 1943, and a small cardboard box.

Inside the box is a metal button with embossed initials, RAF, and the motto: *per ardua ad astra.* And there's a brownish photograph—not just 2-D, but monochrome—of military officers atop white stone steps, while massed troops at parade-ground attention form the backdrop. On the back of the photograph is scrawled: *Surrender of Singapore by the Japanese Imperial Army, 1943.*

When I open the diary, I read the owner's name: *Jack O'Connell.* Tucked inside is a covering note from Deirdre, explaining that she found these old things that belonged to Grandpa Jack. She thought I might like them.

I put everything inside a drawer.

Then I carry my coffee outside to the patio, and stare at the forest while the drink grows cold.

Much later, on the couch, feeling washed out, I finally lean back, closing my sore eyelids—

Three large-limbed men, wearing grease-stained tunics that were originally orange-and-burgundy, sat around a small portable stove, sipping hot tea from tin cups. Black oil streaked the steel wall. Overhead, a concertina joint in the corridor ceiling was leaking.

To the Clanking City, such malfunctions were like microscopic cuts or infections. Maintenance crews were the city's antibodies.

A slender man of medium height, wrapped in a black cloak, was waiting in an iron alcove farther down the corridor. Several times, he consulted a small bead in his palm. Eventually he shook his head, and wandered over to the maintenance crew, who were finishing up their break, wiping out their tin mugs with gray rags.

The dark-cloaked man stared at them, then: "Didn't I see you around here a tenday ago?"

A bulky engineer wiped a greasy hand across his stubbled pate. "It's our corridor, ain't it?"

"You mean you live here?"

"Nah." One of the others spat into his cup, then continued polishing. "He means we work it. Corridor twenty-nine, deck five, fore to aft."

"But"—the cloaked man looked along the corridor, to where it bent out of sight, then back the other way—"that's twenty miles long."

"Takes a couple o' years. Then we starts all over again."

"There's other jobs that are urgent, like," volunteers the smallest man. "Iffen the emergency crews can't get there, we lend a hand."

"Good for you. And you get to see the entire City. Amazing."

"Yeah?" The team chief shakes his head. "Don't go up nor down nor sideways. Just the one corridor, ain't it?"

"All the same, you must meet interesting people."

The three engineers stare at each other, then their chief harrumphs. "I s'pose you could say that."

As the floor lurched—"That's an awkward step, then"—the men automatically adjusted their footing to accommodate the City's gait. From around the corner came a muttered "*Bugger.*"

A stocky figure clad mostly in green was approaching. His grin was cheery, his shock of copper-red hair half hidden by his hood.

"At last," muttered the dark-cloaked man. To the engineers, he added, "Be seeing you."

He strode off to meet his red-haired friend.

The chief grinned and said, "Thinks we don't know who he is, don't he?"

"Yeah," said the second engineer.

"So who is he?" asked the smallest after a moment.

"Well I don't know his *name*, do I?"

"Oh." The small man thought about this. "Who is he, then?"

"He's a noble, ain't he? They wrap themselves up in old cloaks and think that makes 'em one of us."

The second engineer stared down the corridor at the two cloaked figures. "Wonder what they're up to."

Then the two men turned and took a starboard corridor, and were gone from sight.

"Boozin' and whorin'," said the chief. "They're headed to the Busted Star, ain't they? Lucky bastards."

"Yeah."

After a minute, the smallest man said, "So where are *we* goin', at shift's end?"

"Dunno about you," answered the chief, "but I'm going to the Busted Star."

The second engineer paused, spat into his cup once more, and resumed polishing.

—and I wake, smiling, from my doze. What an odd dream. Perhaps I should take notes.

But my head lolls back and the couch is so comfortable.

Peetro, the dark-haired man, placed one hand on his friend's shoulder. "I don't really like this, Hoj. It isn't the old days. Argul's the responsible leader now. We aren't kids together anymore."

"I know." Hoj ran his fingers back through his untidy copper hair. "But I'm serious tonight." With a grin: "Or as close as I can manage."

"Shadroth," muttered Peetro, in a blasphemous invocation of the TriGods' first name. "So what is it? You really think Vul is a psychopath?"

"What, you reckon our beloved Viceroy is normal?"

"Hmm." Peetro looked around the dim-lit corridor. A burned-oil smell rose from somewhere. "I think *all* the High Council treat people like pawns."

"Not Argul."

They continued to walk, slowly. After a moment, Peetro said: "I hope not. I hope he's still our friend, particularly if you're trying your hand at scheming."

"You think everything will *be* all right if Vul gets his Internal Watch formed? And him at the head of it?"

"Argul won't appoint Vul as chief."

"What if the only candidates available are Vul's puppets?"

Peetro stopped. "You're sure of that?"

"I think so." Hoj shrugged. "The bastard's got to General Lanishen. I'm sure of it."

"Bilkroth," said Peetro, "and bleeding Vikridor."

"What kind of language is that?"

"Who cares? Vul's going to turn us into another Broken City."

Hoj gave another grin, but his gaze was serious. "That's what I've been telling you, isn't it?"

Broken City. Twisted City. Traction. All were names (the last favored by scholars) for the same corrupt, decaying wreckage. Forty years earlier, the Drive Guild had edged the Clanking City close to the atmosphere-bubble's edge, where the foundered wreck lay.

And Hoj had shared an evening recently, buying many rounds of drinks, with two palsied veterans of High Observer teams who had been inside the Broken City. Dressed in clumsy environment suits, they had brought back corroded relics that had endured two centuries of acidic, alien winds.

The men described the myriad motive wheels, wrapped within steel tracks, that had borne the dead city across the terrain, following its own great bubble of oxygenated atmosphere until the disaster. Burn marks and scores, ripped armor plating and torn bulkheads told a confusing story.

Perhaps internal war had—suicidally—destroyed Traction's ability to move. Perhaps catastrophic mechanical failure occurred first, while desperate engineers worked to fix the broken city before the air moved on.

"And the winds"—hand shaking, the old veteran had reached for his drink—"just moaned."

They'd had precious little to say beyond that, though Hoj had plied them with more drinks until they'd made their staggering way to bed. Hoj appreciated once more the imperative that lay beneath every law and custom of the Clanking City: *the city must move.*

Now, Hoj muttered: "I could do with a drink."

"Yeah, me too." Peetro pulled his heavy cape around himself, though the corridor was warm. "Ah . . . Balls."

Ahead of them, above a well-oiled armored door, hung a grime-encrusted star-shaped symbol that might have been brass. From inside, discordant cheering echoed. But beneath the raucous sound, a soft scrape insinuated itself.

Peetro drew out a long dagger.

"What?" Hoj fumbled at his belt, though he knew he had left his dirk at home.

Off to the left, beyond an iron threshold, stood a junk chamber filled with broken iron spars and ceramic joints, discarded bric-a-brac waiting for the Reclamation Artificers. Amid the detritus, metal moved.

"Could just be a rat," said Hoj. "Or two."

Peetro edged towards the doorway, crouching low, transferring his dagger to his left hand and keeping it close to his ribs. Stretching out his right hand as if to feel the darkness, he advanced with crosswise steps into the junk chamber.

"Oh, darn . . ." It was a child's voice, a girl's. Junk scraped and tumbled. "Got it."

Turning his right shoulder forward, hiding his weapon, Peetro straightened up. "Will you come out of there?"

"Oh! Sorry." Something fell. "I'm coming, sir."

Out scrambled a young girl, holding what looked like a broken glass brick, covered in dirt. She blinked her orange eyes.

"How old are you?" said Peetro. "What's your name?"

"Um, eight and a half, sir. I'm Shama."

Behind Peetro, Hoj crossed his arms and smiled. "We're pleased to meet you, Shama."

"What?" Peetro looked back at him. "We're what? Pleased to meet a criminal. Eh?"

"Sir . . ." Shama's lip trembled.

Hoj said, "You might explain what you're up to, young Shama. Shouldn't you be at home in bed?"

"Yes, sir. But . . . Look." Shama held up the large, broken translucent shard. "Sir, my master threw it out. It's his, really."

"In a city junk chamber?" muttered Peetro. "It's municipal property."

"Really?" Shama let her hand drop, and bowed her head to mumble: "I can pay, noble sirs. I have twelve pennies saved."

Hoj laughed, and clapped Peetro on the shoulder. "This is a thief with a sense of fairness, wouldn't you say?"

"I'm not a thief! My master discarded the crystal."

Hunkering down, Hoj asked, "So who is your master, child? And why would he discard something, unless it were worthless?"

Peetro slid his dagger back into its sheath. Hoj glanced up at him, then back at Shama.

"Lintral Teldrasso is my master." Shama clutched the shard. "He's a web-maker, sir."

"Never heard of him," muttered Peetro.

"He's apprenticed to Master A'Queran, who—"

"Rultin A'Queran, I know of." Hoj touched the grimy shard with a fore-finger. "Tell me about this, young Shama."

"There's a bad flaw." Shama held up the crystal, angling it so the dark-ened area was obvious. "My master threw it out."

"So you said. And why"—Hoj looked up and winked at Peetro, who shook his head—"would you seek to retrieve it?"

"Because the rest of it is beautiful! Can't you see?"

What Hoj and Peetro could see in her hands was a grimy, dirt-caked shard; but what they saw in Shama's orange eyes was the light of inspired pas-sion. Hoj reached inside his tunic, and drew out a half coin.

"As a city councilor," he said, "I'm paying you to take this crystal away from the chamber. I trust you'll dispose of it properly."

"Oh." Shama blinked. "Sir, I'll make the best web you've ever seen, I promise. I really promise."

"I know you do. Here, take the coin."

Shama hesitated, then took the money, and backed away from Hoj. Then she curtsied, first to Hoj and then to Peetro. "Thank you."

"Go on. Get home."

"Yes . . ."

"Go on."

Shama turned and scampered off.

"TriGods' Blood," breathed Peetro. "I thought we were worried about saving the city."

"We did." Hoj raised himself to his feet. "In a tiny way, we just did."

I rub my face, and stretch on the sofa. I've designed games before, and they never proceeded so vividly in my daydreams. Whatever the upgrades did for me, they've changed the way I slip into trance, the way I dream.

It's too late to worry about screwing up my mind.

I look around the too-clean lounge. When Yukiko was alive, our few arguments revolved around my messiness. Since her death, I've kept everything polished and lined up.

Suddenly, I want to be among other people.

As I haul myself up from the sofa, I think about the reams of notes I would normally keep about a game scenario, as I dream it up.

Are you kidding?

The internal door to the garage slides open.

You think this is a game?

As I unjack the Bronco and command it to start, I realize that I'm operating devices in a new way. I stare at the outer door and it rises up.

I drive into town along the main drag. There, the traffic thickens, and soon I'm waiting at stop lights. Off to my right, in a strip mall dojo with a holo proclaiming KICKIN' KARATE, young kids in white pajamas leap energetically, ineffectually around.

Behind me, a horn sounds.

I wave sorry. The lights are green, and there's a long gap in front of me. I drive on, take the next turn, and continue to the bookstore, where I park. Inside, I pick up two thin hardcopy books, Funakoshi's *My Karate* and Bronowski's *Science and the Imagination*, and carry them into the coffee shop.

Sometime later, I put the Bronowski down, staring into space with espresso in hand, considering telepathy. In reading, I've just shared insightful thoughts of a man who no longer lives.

I place the book facedown.

It was a cold January morning, with gray mist pressing against the windows, when I went to UCL to talk to Yukiko's fellow grad students. They were neuroscientists with AI experience, so I used concepts from software design to explain the new physics.

"All right," I said to the group. "Everyone whip out their mobiles."

After a moment, they grinned and took out their cell phones.

"Now imagine," I continued, "that we're all software objects. Bear with me, this'll be painless."

"You sure about that?" asked a slight woman.

"Positive. Now, the thing about objects in software is that you can only send them text messages, using their reference or pointer. It's their address in computer memory, like a phone number. Got it?"

"Er . . ." One of the researchers raised her hand. "Isn't object orientation a bit old-fashioned? I mean, I've been hearing about coevolutionary skeletons that—"

"Yeah," I said, "but this is for the purposes of illustration. We're really here to talk *quantum*, right?"

"Oh. Okay."

Yukiko rolled her eyes. Someone snorted.

"Let's pretend"—I cleared my throat, then nodded toward Yukiko—"that she's a software object representing, uh, let's say an airplane in the real world. So she's got properties like a certain speed, altitude, direction—"

"Color," said Yukiko. "Am I a pretty color?"

"Of course."

"Hey, nice properties," muttered a bearded guy. Then he looked at me. "Sorry."

"This is going to be a long morning," I said. "Okay, if you have Yukiko's phone number, you can text her a message. You can only ask certain questions, like what height she's at, and send certain commands, like change heading."

A couple of them were nodding. All you can do with an object is invoke its defined functions. Its internal data remains hidden.

"You and you"—I pointed—"are two controller objects. So if you have Yukiko's number, you can send her messages. Otherwise, you don't even know she exists."

A big woman called Evelyn laughed. "Yukiko's got *your* number, sonny boy."

"Okay." I decided to go along with this. "And if you don't know my number and want it, darling, you could ask Yukiko for my identity, and Yukiko could send it to you. Just my phone number, not the real me."

Evelyn nodded. "The map is not the territory. The object's address is not the object."

"You've got it."

"So what," Evelyn asked, "has this got to do with *quantum?*"

"When two particles are entangled"—my skin prickled as everyone's attention zeroed in—"they appear to change properties instantaneously, no light-speed limitations, no matter how far apart they are."

This time only a couple of people nodded.

"But if you tell Yukiko to change speed"—I pointed—"and then two people ask her new speed, they'll get the same answer, because they've texted to the same telephone number, right?"

"Wait a minute. You're saying that electrons and photons and shit aren't *real*? Two entangled electrons are actually one thing?"

"That," I said, "is exactly right."

"Then . . ."

"Djikstra said you can solve every problem in software engineering by introducing an extra layer of indirection." I spread my hands. "It works in quantum physics, too. Particles are pointers to an underlying ur-stuff, somewhere we can't get hold of. Reality is *encapsulated.*"

"Like parallel universes?" said Evelyn.

"No," I told her. "That's not . . . Well. Actually. There's no reason the ur-stuff couldn't support other continua at the same time."

Evelyn looked from me to Yukiko and back.

"Did I just say something clever?"

"I think so." I kissed Evelyn on the cheek, and Yukiko grinned. "I think you did."

Movement snaps me back into the moment. A lithe, blonde-haired woman is pointing to the other chair at my table.

"Is it taken?"

"Um, no." I glance down at the Bronowski book, then around me. Several tables are completely vacant.

"I'm glad." She sits down, and briefly touches the book. "I loved *The Ascent of Man*, didn't you? My father used to own it."

"Right." I get to my feet, and slide the book towards her. "Enjoy."

I leave without looking back, wondering when it was that bookstores morphed into singles bars. Or perhaps I misunderstood.

Outside, I climb into the Bronco and then I do look back. Inside, the pretty woman is bent over the table, reading something that might be the Bronowski.

I miss you, Yukiko.

There's nothing to do but put the truck into drive and head home.

The next evening, after a shorter than usual working day, Lintral Teldrasso escorted his young servant back to her quarters. Stopping outside the door, he listened to the trilling, burbling notes from inside.

"You're looking after your moth well, Shama. It sings prettily."

Shama's face dimpled in a smile. "Yes, Master."

"Now you'll be fine overnight. If you need anything, call Mistress Dilva in the kitchen."

"Yes, M—"

"Or Kigfan, he can help. And make sure Mistress Dilva gives you supper." Teldrasso mussed Shama's white-blonde hair. "And study hard tomorrow. I'll be back the day after. You never know, I might test you."

Shama nodded.

"Good. You will be fine." It was almost a question.

"I'm eight and a *half*, Master."

"Yes. I keep forgetting. Take care of the place for me." Teldrasso sighed.

Then he turned and walked away to his own chambers, running through a mental checklist of things to pack for the overnight stay in House Sildrov, on the seventh deck. Tomorrow he would accompany Master A'Queran, discussing new commissions.

Shama waited until Master Teldrasso was out of sight before opening the concertina door to her chamber. She slipped inside. The purple-winged dodecamoth fluttered in the center of the room, making no attempt to escape.

"Wait," Shama said. "Just wait."

She locked the door from inside, then dug in her tunic pocket and pulled out a handful of twisted black slivers: crushed *parma* leaves, the moth's favorite delicacy. Shama spread the leaves on the old tabletop, then stood back to watch as the moth descended, folding up its twelve-sided wings. It hummed as it fed.

The sound dipped in tone as Shama reached towards a built-in cupboard.

"Hush," said Shama. "I'm just checking."

She peeked inside. All three cocoons were soft, furry, yellow, and intact. With a serious, adult expression, Shama nodded to herself and closed the door.

"It's fine," she told the moth. "Everything's fine."

The musical burbling resumed as the moth bent back to its meal of black leaves.

"Yes, everything *is* fine." Opening another cupboard, Shama folded back her spare work tunic, revealing the heavy crystal shard she had recovered.

Most of the grime was gone now, the flaw more obvious. But the rest of the crystal was sublime. And Shama had learned, observing Master Teldrasso, how to shear fragments.

Shard in hand, Shama clambered onto her bed and sat cross-legged. She opened her orange eyes wider, then closed them, controlling her breathing. Her mental picture sharpened in focus: picturing her goal before she got to work.

The best dreamweb, she promised for her master's sake, *that anyone has ever seen.*

Back at the house, I open my eyes to see that late afternoon is rendering the pale walls gold. How long have I been daydreaming?

From my study I fetch pastels and sketchpad, and a portable *makiwara* pad. With everything under my arm, I walk out of the house and across the grass to the forest's edge.

"Jaysus, sure isn't that old-fashioned?" Yukiko had said when I told her about my karate, learned from a traditional sensei called Conan O'Brian in County Clare.

None of Yukiko's friends in Tokyo had trained in such quaint disciplines. Martial arts were approximately as cool as Irish dancing: something your grandparents might have done.

(And the strip mall dojo karate *looked* like dancing. That's why I train alone.)

I fasten the brick-sized *makiwara* pad to a birch tree and begin to punch. Soon I am movement, rhythm without thought, clothes soaked in sweat as I strike. I'll stop only after a thousand thrusts with each hand.

Afterwards, sweat cooling, I sit on a laser-cut tree stump and stare at the tree line, and begin to sketch. But I am tired, and the day seems to drift away from me. . . .

Oh, Yukiko.

. . . until the sun is molten gold behind silhouetted trees, and I take deep breaths of the evening air then stop, seeing the strange web I have drawn on the sketchpad. A translucent web, shimmering with strangeness, in which nonshapes swim.

You still think this is a game?

We were holed up in a basement of Imperial College, where Yukiko and her neuroscientist colleagues were making use of physics lab facilities. The persistent entanglement kit was a mess of chaotic innards, made tidy by stuffing the lot inside an old fridge casing. Most physicists don't care what their labs look like, but their test subjects are electrons and the like. Ours were people.

I was the first to go under the particle spray, closing my eyes against the warm mist enveloping my head. Something smelled faintly of oranges.

After a time, Yukiko and a small woman named Maria worked the console, and Yukiko said, "Tell me what you see."

I closed my eyes.

"A wire," I said. "Hundreds of glowing, fuzzy green electrons sliding through a lattice—"

There were sounds of controls adjusting. "Go on."

"—speeding as they're pushed closer together."

"And you see this in color?"

"Vividly, and all around me"—I gestured, eyes still shut—"I feel the inverse square law compensating wherever the wire narrows. Over there"—pointing—"is a glowing yellow equation, $I = dq/dt$. Current is the rate of charge flow . . ."

Part of me realizes they're not physicists. They can't appreciate that I'm simply describing ordinary electric current.

"And does this equation move?"

"Well, yeah. . . . It kind of pulses."

"And do you hear any sounds?"

"I'm not sure. . . ."

And so on, with Yukiko continuing the questions until she had a full description to correlate with the equipment's readings. Finally she closed the session down.

"Well," said Yukiko.

I rubbed my eyes, opened them. Maria was smiling.

"What?"

"Come on, Ryan." Maria spread her hands palm-up. "Is that really what the inside of your head looks like?"

"Um, yeah. . . ."

And Yukiko said, "But you never hear music? Doesn't everyone hear music in their mind, changing mood as the day goes on?"

Maria and I both looked at her.

Evelyn came in later to go through the lab results. While Yukiko and the others were discussing how everyone is unique, Evelyn remained quiet.

"What are you thinking?" I asked eventually.

"You know, every human being is different, but nearly any man and any woman, darling"—Evelyn winked at Yukiko—"can collaborate to build another human being, right?"

"So we're not doomed to failure?"

"I'd say we're guaranteed to succeed." Evelyn looked around the group. "Listen, I go to a slightly weird pub called the Crescent Moon. Bit of a New Age crowd."

"Uh-huh . . ."

"You mind," Evelyn asked, "if I bring in a couple of new test subjects tomorrow?"

"All right."

The next day, she introduced us to Jade and Helen, professional mediums—"Shouldn't that be *media*, plural?" Maria said later—who agreed to be scanned in turn.

To demonstrate the harmless nature of the scan, I went first—again— and described my vision of photons flying across the room, and the magic that lets me see someone in front of me, while people to either side of me can see each other, via crisscrossing light without interference.

"Bloody hell," said Jade afterwards. "I'm glad I'm not inside your head. You're scary."

"Um . . ." I looked into her shining green eyes. "*You* see dead people, and you think *I'm* scary?"

"God, if I could see them, I'd be petrified."

"Then . . . ?"

"I hear the voices." Jade pointed to her own head. "In there."

"That's very—"

"Oh, but *I* can see dead folk," said Helen. "All the time. Really vivid."

I avoided Yukiko's glance. "So how," I asked, "do you know they're not real?"

"You mean not *alive*?"

"I suppose—"

"Because the colors are really, really bright. Oh, and . . . I see them through my eyelids. When I've shut my eyes, I mean."

Yukiko gave a peaceful Zen smile.

"That'll be a clue," she said.

Persistent entangled tomography revealed no difference between Helen's visions and my own, in terms of neural activity. Yukiko asked me what I made of that.

I had no answer.

Leaning against the kitchen wall, flash-heating a coffee, I microsleep, coming back to awareness with a fading vision of a shadowed chamber where a big electric oven glowed orange-red. Beside it, Shama knelt, waiting for the moment, for the exact conditions when she could plunge the crystal shard inside.

The best web—her thoughts or mine?—*that anyone has ever seen.*

Soon she would begin to form the dreamweb.

My parents worked all hours, as teachers and devout churchgoers who spent a lot of time in charitable work and not so much at home. Grandfather Jack, self-taught, was the one who took me through integral calculus when my schoolmates were solving simple quadratics.

Mum wanted me to be a writer or a poet. Dad saw a future in civil service, something respectable. But Grandfather Jack showed me that magic resides everywhere, that new theories and theorems come from lightning inspiration no different than a poet's, while linear logical proof forms a reality test, confirming intuition. At the same time, he taught me to question everything. I never stepped inside a church after my fourteenth birthday.

I was the only member of the family to attend his funeral, in pouring rain on a Wicklow hillside in coldest November.

We went cycling on the Thames. Evelyn rented float-bikes with pink stabilizers. Seven of us set out, cycling along the placid waves, close to the Embankment. Evelyn's boyfriend Colin was beside me, puffing with effort, when a pink float sheared off his bike.

As Colin tipped, the safety shield snapped into place. Faceted, domelike, and formed of glass, it would keep him breathing as he bobbed helplessly on the water. His mouth opened and I had to laugh, along with the others. Evelyn was laughing so hard I thought she'd be the next to fall in.

Then I realized the glass shield was cracked.

Water swirled inside, surrounding Colin, and his face was pale as I tried to grip the wet glass, my fingers slipping off. I tried again.

"Help me!" I called.

Colin's voice joined in, muffled and dead inside the filling shield.

Soon Yukiko was with me, then the others, as we tugged and rolled the sinking cycle closer to the stone wall of the Embankment. A ring-shaped life-saver came sailing down from above. Some twelve or fifteen feet overhead, atop the wall, passersby were staring down.

The lifesaver had a rope attached, its other end fastened somewhere up above.

"What's the point of that?" muttered someone, but Yukiko was already moving.

She slipped off her bike, took hold of the rope, and dived beneath Colin's sinking bike. I leaned over, thinking to tie a loop, then saw I could fit the lifesaver ring around the broken float shaft.

Soon, with help from the people above, we were pushing and hauling the water-filled shield and bike onto an abbreviated jetty, clear of the water.

Except that Colin was trapped inside a water-filled glass bubble. There was air at the top, but he had already slipped under, his hair waving like fronds. He was no longer breathing.

"Shit shit shit."

Yukiko tried to work the safety release. Nothing. Behind Yukiko, her face pale as death, Evelyn stumbled onto the jetty, unable to speak.

I sank into a deep stance, my spine vertical, and did what Sensei O'Brian had taught me, so much easier now, since I had played awareness games inside the lab. I placed my consciousness metaphorically in my body's core, at the *tanden*, the center of gravity. I breathed in, allowing the world to slow.

"Colin—" Evelyn, finding her voice.

Slowing.

And when I exhaled, my hand slammed forward, heel of palm first, aiming three inches *inside* the glass. I struck. The facet shattered, a spiderweb of cracks tearing open as water poured out.

I stepped back as the others took over, kicking at the shattered shield, tipping it to empty out the water. Finally they broke internal catches so the shield collapsed in shards across the unconscious Colin.

An air ambulance descended, its rotors beating the air, vibrations thrumming subsonically through my guts as it hung above the water. Then it touched down on its floats.

Colin was safe.

They worked on my broken wrist in the Accident & Emergency Room. Colin was fine, they told me (truthfully) as the technician injected me with amber fluid. Then he sat me down before a cylindrical scanner, and I placed my hand inside.

Yukiko was fascinated by the holo display that sprang up, showing the bones of hand and wrist as silvery translucent shapes, and the bright threads of the femtocyte load as injected particles spread around my bones and got to work.

"The femtoscopic carriers," Yukiko said, "transport the healing femtocytes into place, is that right?"

"Um, yeah. Sure." The technician kept his attention focused on the console.

I was pretty sure his concentration was a good thing. Why would Yukiko want to distract him?

"So the carriers," she continued. "Could they take any femtoscopic load into place? Anything at all?"

The technician shrugged. "Why not?"

"Anything?" I said.

"Er . . . Yeah." The technician looked at us. "What are you thinking of?"

"Where can we buy," asked Yukiko, "equipment like this?"

But the technician's phone chimed just then. He listened for a moment, then said, "I'll be right there." To Yukiko and me he added, "Sorry, guys. I'll be back in ten. Just keep your hand in place."

"No worries," I told him.

After the technician had left, Yukiko said, "It can carry anything. Including pets."

She didn't mean cats or dogs. Yukiko meant *pets*: persistently entangled twins. Twin particles. Injecting lone particles into one person, and as for their entangled twins . . .

"We've already talked," Yukiko said, "about using the nozzle spray that way. Entangling you"—her smile was Zen-serene and sensuous at the same time—"with me, not some old console."

It was unreal. Feasible now, yet still unreal.

Yukiko reached out and touched my shoulder.

"Are you thinking what I'm thinking?"

I stared at her. She was perfect. I had done nothing to deserve her, or the possibility of such an amazing future.

"Not yet," I said. "But I will be."

Shama stood as Master Teldrasso had taught her, ready with the platinum axe she had to hold two-handed. Then she breathed, remembering the silent chant.

I am the crystal.

And she swung, striking pure. The blackened area snapped off. What remained was perfect, a crystal shard aching to be reworked. Now the oven glowed the exact scarlet-and-gold required, smelled of that hot ceramic tang. This was the moment.

Shama used tongs to place the shard just right. As she concentrated, the tip of her tongue showed between her teeth. Then she sat back on her heels and watched.

Inside the oven, the crystal grew yellow then orange, starting to spread into the convoluted mold, ready to reshape, yet retaining essential wholeness.

The crystal is me.

I'm tired now. In need of unbroken sleep.

On his silver-chased couch, Prince Argul grew very still, statuelike, as his mind spread farther and wider than ever before. His lean, bearded face held a static smile: like a statue, but a happy one.

Yet somewhere on the edge of his dream-awareness, as he bathed in the refreshing thousands of sleeping minds, the men and women and children of the city currently dreaming, something new shone. A different kind of possibility, something that resonated, drew him . . .

A web, of such perfection.

In the sleeping chamber, there was no one to see as the smile faded from the somnolent prince's face. Perhaps some part of his dreaming unconscious knew the danger even then.

Mothlike, Prince Argul responded to the power, to the attraction of a superbly resonant web.

The *inescapable* attraction.

A soft moan sounded from the prince.

I gasp, come awake in what must be the tag-end of a dream: silver web-lines glowing on my naked skin. They shine in the night-dark bedroom. Then they waver, grow translucent.

And are gone.

I drop back onto the bed.

Inside heavy purple robes, the viceroy's thin body trembled. Or perhaps it was just his stomach churning. The viceroy, known as Vul, sat at the narrow end of his black glass oval-shaped conference table. Halfway along the right-hand side, General Lanishen leaned his elbows on the polished black tabletop and stared at Vul.

For Vul—whose real name, mostly forgotten, was Triklan Vulkishan—this was a turning point, a moment when Lanishen became ally or enemy. Vul breathed out and focused, using peripheral vision to pick up every nuance of the general's body language, sensitizing his hearing to stresses in the general's voice.

They were alone in the steel conference chamber. The only sound was a soft pneumatic hiss; the only movement, background swirls in pale-amber globes: observation globes that ringed the chamber.

Various toxin-spewing devices were hidden in the bulkheads and furniture, their existence theoretically secret, but surely suspected by General Lanishen. His tone was polite.

"My tactical developers' brief," the general told Vul, "includes investigating the possibility of new weapons. The city must remain safe."

"And so it must, General."

Vul waited a moment, analyzing. His natural empathy was almost zero; but his parents had been teachers who worked down in deck two, and at home they had taught Vul ways of observation, to intellectually deduce the thought processes of others. Those skills, now superlative, had taken time to learn. At school the kids called him Vul the Fool.

And now he was their viceroy.

Vul added: "A *working* Void Egg might be considered going beyond the bounds of your brief, might it not?"

General Lanishen placed his hands palm-down on the black glass table. "You're implying two things. A fully developed weapon and my part in . . ."

The general paused. Perhaps he could read Vul's body language, just as Vul could read his.

". . . its development. Of course your agents, Viceroy, are highly trained."

"Yes."

Neither man mentioned the forthcoming discussion in the royal court, when Prince Argul was expected to rule in favor of Vul's new policing agency. But the agency, without royal charter, was already in clandestine operation.

Behind General Lanishen, an amber globe changed hue.

"Then we should drop it," said Vul.

"What? The program has lasted years. So I admit it. To cancel at this stage would mean—"

"I mean drop the bomb."

Silence rocked through the chamber. Then: "You can't mean that."

"We lay the egg," Vul nodded as he spoke, a movement designed to influence the general's subconscious, "as we pass the next demon city. We leave the Void Egg as close to the tri-damned demons as we can. Set it to detonate when the air bubble has passed on . . . just afterwards. The demons will still be waking up."

General Lanishen shook his head. "There's no strategic value in destroying the next demon city."

He called it city, not nest, upgrading its status in his mind to honorable enemy. It took a moment for Vul to work this out.

"Twelve years ago," said Vul, "a nest of demon commandos came at the

Clanking City, when we passed into their territory. They weren't asleep in their own towers or aeries. They attacked us."

"That's well known, sir."

"Yes, General, and you're going to argue that it was a different demon city. That there is no evidence to suggest that demons communicate across different regions. But there's no evidence against it, either."

General Lanishen tensed in his chair. He did not like Vul trying to deduce his thoughts. And that, Vul realized, was a dislike that could be used against Lanishen.

"Why would you want demons to fear us, Viceroy? That can work two ways. They might leave us alone, or plan further attacks in the future."

"Demonic commandos," said Vul. "Have you ever read the reports of that operation?"

"No . . . I was a lieutenant then, in charge of—"

"The defenders failed to find any hidden bivouacs." Vul pointed at a convoluted brown-and-white sculpturelike object on a shelf. "What they did find was a collection of ceramic devices that trapped air. I mean demonic air, not ours. They had their own little bubble of acidic vapor in place, allowing them to breathe when the real atmosphere passed over their land."

General Lanishen pushed himself back from the table, but remained sitting.

"I fail to see where this discussion is leading. If you have charges to make, sir, then please to do so now."

"I'm not playing games, General. My theories indicate that our air might not continue to travel in the same direction forever. And can any city maintain motive power without *ever* failing?"

"It's been centuries—"

"And do we not plan for the far future? If we force the demons to provide devices that can hold our atmosphere in place, we can settle down."

"You mean live like demons?" General Lanishen half stood. "In one place like *vermin*?"

"In the future, perhaps. Not in our lifetimes."

It was enough to calm the general, enough for him to sit back down. He had reservations about working with Vul. But Vul had revealed plans and intentions as treasonous as General Lanishen's own.

"How many scholars," said the general, "share your theory, Viceroy?"

Vul shook his head.

"Unimportant. What's important is that we work together."

Over General Lanishen's shoulder, Vul could see the observation globe that had changed color earlier. Something shifted inside. It fractionally darkened.

"Prince Argul," said the general, "will not approve of such actions."

At the mention of the prince, Vul felt that same old feeling. "Oh, Prince Argul. We'll create some kind of story for him."

There was a theory that creating a Void Egg (long speculated on by scholars) could break open the world, shearing the infinite cylinder into two. As a thought experiment, scholars liked to use such a catastrophe to teach the arithmetic of infinities: both remaining halves of the world would (if current cosmological theories were correct) be infinitely long cylinders.

Neither Vul nor Lanishen believed that theory.

"Even you," said General Lanishen, "cannot shield against a psych inquisitor."

"My concerns are for the city, nothing more."

The general gave a tiny shake of the head, relaxing, allowing more of his hidden thoughts to reveal themselves in his body language. He had heard the overtones in Vul's voice when Vul mentioned Prince Argul.

And Vul was thinking, even now: *Argul, so beautiful . . .*

Vul's suppressed desires for the prince, even as thoughts, were illegal and punishable by death; and Vul realized he might have betrayed himself.

How subtle this game had become!

Should Vul acknowledge the general's deduction, cementing their alliance yet revealing a mortal weakness? Or should he convince the general that he was mistaken?

The metal deck shifted as the city missed a step. Both men waited. The deck leveled itself, and the Clanking City continued as always.

"That globe—" Vul pointed behind the general.

"What is it?"

"More than you think." Vul got up from his seat and walked to the amber globe. "This maps Prince Argul's mind. Topography, not geometry."

"What does that mean?"

Vul decided to use the truth. "It means we're seeing pictures of Argul's mind"—he deliberately dropped the royal title—"and it seems our ruler is lost in dreams."

General Lanishen rose, glanced at the globe, then stared at Vul. "So he's asleep. I don't need your arcane devices to tell me a man can sleep."

"No." Vul pointed. "I mean *lost*. In dreams."

"Explain."

"That bright spot? It's a form of trap, for certain gifted people. Something attractive they can't get away from."

General Lanishen's hand moved toward his hip. He wore no obvious weapons. The gesture was unconscious.

"I mean it," Vul continued. "Argul is losing his mind."

The general stood very still.

"You mean that?"

"More literally than you imagine, General."

"Then a power vacuum is approaching."

"Yes."

After a moment, General Lanishen said, "Good."

We were naked in the lab at night when we performed the injection sequence. As our particles entangled, I entered Yukiko, and we made love as our nerves resonated in a mystical experience that was ours alone.

You think we would dream of publishing results like that? Describing to others the mystical feedback of loving someone who loves you, who loves you loving them, becoming one person, experiencing infinite, burning, nova-bright recursion?

Afterwards, in our everyday lives, it took time to manifest a shared imagined vision, of a red apple or a black cat with bright green eyes, but over time we managed it. And our nights were wonderful. I learned to hear the music playing in Yukiko's mind.

Then, two months into our joining, I felt the difference in Yukiko compared to myself, the strangeness of feeling in certain locations. We went together to the hospital, and I waited outside while they performed the scans; but we knew the results before they started.

What we had yet to find out was the way that the cancer would fight back, resisting treatment, metastasizing with an aggression the medics had never encountered. Soon we would learn that death was coming.

In Shama's cupboard, movement occurred inside the three cocoons. The mother, the purple dodecamoth, began to croon and warble.

At around the same time, Peetro and Hoj were pressed back inside an alcove, observing a half-lit corridor down which three soldiers were dragging a beaten prisoner. Peetro never drank alcohol; Hoj was sobering up fast. This was serious, and dangerous: following soldiers from the Viceroy's Own Guards.

"Could it be Argul?" whispered Hoj.

"No." Peetro continued to watch. "Maybe."

He drew back. If the soldiers spotted them . . .

But the injured prisoner *might* have been Prince Argul. It was someone slightly built and dark-haired.

"Not even Vul would dare . . ."

"Yeah?" Hoj started to raise his voice, then lowered it. "Argul failed to turn up to committee meetings, is what I heard. Not like him."

Since taking over after his father's death, Argul had changed. Prince Sardal, his father, had been a strong and meticulous leader, yet a scarcely functional telepath. Argul, a dreamer, raised by his talented but directionless uncle, Count Hamel, had been different. In his late teens, he had even gone off the rails somewhat, along with his youthful noble friends, Hoj and Peetro.

Hoj liked to think of himself as a calming influence in the old days. Peetro kept his opinions to himself.

But Argul, since his elevation to power, had done his best for the city. His face nowadays, it seemed to Peetro, was perpetually tight with stress.

"TriGods damn it," Peetro muttered now. "I really don't want to follow them."

The soldiers had dragged the prisoner away from Vul's chambers. A general and Vul himself had looked on, while Peetro and Hoj, skulking, had observed from a distance.

"So what," said Hoj, "are we going to do?"

"Follow them. What else?"

"But you said—"

"If it *is* Argul, could we ever forgive ourselves?"

Hoj rubbed his coppery hair. "Well eventually, I suppose we—"

"Come on."

As members of the Median (though not High) Council, Hoj and Peetro were aware of certain security codes. Spinning the combination locks of two sets of armored hatches got them close to the three guards and their prisoner.

But the metal cell where the guards finally incarcerated the man lay beyond a large reinforced hold. Other guards, stationed in the corridor outside, kept watch. It was only as the trio led the prisoner inside that surveillance relaxed for a moment. Peetro leaned around a steel buttress, seeing the strange sapphire glow that shone inside the hold. Hoj looked also, then pulled himself back into hiding.

"Oh, shit," muttered Peetro.

Guards swung the hold's big door. It sounded a dull bong as it shut.

"Did you see the prisoner's face?" said Hoj.

"No . . ."

"So maybe it wasn't Argul."

"Shadroth, Bilkroth"—Peetro stared at Hoj—"and bleeding Vikridor."

Hoj recoiled, unused to such blasphemy from Peetro. "What is it?"

"That shade of blue . . ."

"You mean the light?"

"It's a, er, transition frequency. I remember the tutorial, and Academician Tiklov telling us about—"

"A what frequency?"

"Listen." Peetro grabbed Hoj's shoulders. "Vul's insane. That blue glow means there's a Void Egg inside the hold."

"You can't be . . ." Hoj's voice trailed off.

"Yes, I bloody can."

In the evening, I go for a walk in the forest. Yukiko is with me, holding my hand, but only in my mind.

I miss you so much, my love.

She told me once that walking like this in forest air was a medical treatment in Japan. Proper doctors prescribed it.

"Oh, really," I told her.

"Don't be cynical, darling." Yukiko pressed my arm. I remember the feeling. "Healthy organic molecules are making their way through your lung tissue, your skin, right this moment."

She was right. I inhale pine scents, remembering that Yukiko was always right.

Oh, my love . . .

When I finally return to the house, the kitchen automatically lights up and starts the coffee, but there's something different. It takes me a moment, but—

In one corner of the ceiling, a yellowish cocoon is fastened.

A *moving* cocoon.

They were in a back room of the Busted Star. Peetro, holding a mug of cold purple tea, watched as Hoj downed a fire-brandy.

"I don't think the prisoner was Argul."

"Then where is he?" Hoj put down the brandy glass, and rubbed his nose. "Anyway, did you see the brass flanges?"

"Excuse me?"

"In the hold ceiling. Folded-up grab claws. Some holds, you can lower things right down through the lower hull. Or raise things up, but that's not what Vul's going to do, is it?"

"You can't mean Vul's going to lay the Void Egg. But where? Why?"

"We're in the Clanking City," said Hoj. "And what do we clank over? Neutral ground or demon land. Only two choices."

"Oh. But . . . Demons haven't attacked for ten years, must be."

"Twelve." Hoj raised his glass, drank the last of the brandy, and shuddered. "And that was different demons, thousands of leagues back. But to bigots, all demons are the same."

"Vul's no bigot," muttered Peetro. He put his purple tea down untouched.

"He isn't?"

"No, he's bloody insane. Bigotry and fear are his tools."

"Ah. Good idea." Hoj picked up Peetro's cup, took a sip, and made a disgusted face. "Oh, TriGods. You got to stop drinking this stuff."

"I just did. What do you mean, good idea?"

"Don't look so worried."

"The last time you had a good idea—"

"Yeah, yeah. What I mean is, we're not sure about the prisoner, and we daren't go accusing Vul . . ."

"I know that, Hoj."

". . . but I *did* recognize one of the guards. I've just realized." Hoj tapped his empty brandy glass. "Mostly 'cause I've usually had a few of these when I've seen the bugger. His name is Riktor."

"Oh."

"And I know where he lives." Hoj grinned, and his green eyes were bright and entirely sober. "You coming?"

"I don't—"

"And I also thought"—Hoj gestured to the closed door that led to the Busted Star's main bar, where raucous laughter sounded even at this late hour—"we might invite some of our rougher friends along."

"Ah. Right."

Three months after Yukiko's funeral, I roused myself from apathy long enough to book a flight to London.

There, I spent a morose evening in the Crescent Moon with Evelyn, trying to remember the good times but crying instead. I asked Evelyn whether I could see her medium friends, Jade and Helen. She said they'd not been around much, but gave me their numbers.

The next day, jet-lagged and feeling awful, I met Jade in a Camden coffee shop called Bug-Eyed and Sleepless. Over triple espressos Jada told me that she no longer did "that kind of thing."

"But my singing career"—she smiled—"is taking off. I mean, what I always dreamed of. It's happening."

"Oh. Good."

"Ever since I went under your machine in the lab, my life just kept getting better. *Is* getting better."

"Well . . . I'm really glad, Jade."

It just wasn't what I'd flown to London to hear.

I'd left a vmail for Jade's friend Helen, gotten a text-only reply: an invitation to Helen's home in Swiss Cottage. The next morning, I turned up at ten.

It was a basement flat with a passageway, secured with a wrought-iron gate, that led through to a surprising, peaceful garden out back. There, sipping pineapple juice on the tiny patio while an orange cat watched with yellow-green eyes, Helen and I looked at each other for a long time.

Then I had to ask: "Is Yukiko there? In the spirit world?"

I was irrational. I was desperate to know.

Helen shook her head.

"Oh," I said. "I . . . Oh."

Then Helen reached over and touched my forehead.

"You'll see, Ryan."

"What do you mean?"

But Helen shook her head, and I understood it was time for me to leave.

Inside the hold, the Void Egg pulsed sapphire blue. A platoon of the Viceroy's Own Guards kept watch. None of them looked up into the shadows cloaking the high metal ceiling, or noticed the small yellow cross-slitted eye that regarded the Void Egg, and slowly blinked.

After a long time, the small creature decided it had seen enough.

It scuttled upside-down across the ceiling, stopped before a metal grill, then spat hydrofluoric acid. In moments the metal was dissolving and the creature scrabbled through.

The tiny creature moved along the hollow duct, heading for the city's hull, where it could leave and make the journey back to its masters. They would be waiting for its report.

I wake up in the forest, thinking they're going to die. I mean the whole Clanking City.

But it's just a dream.

I'm sitting on a damp fallen log.

A dream. Oh, really?

The log is patched with silvery algae and dark green moss. Everywhere, life grows. And before my eyes, fading now, is a remembered dream of a yellow-eyed creature with cross-slit eyes, bred by demon masters, ready to strike against those who plan to drop the Void Egg.

None of this can possibly be real.

The whole city . . .

Somehow I know about demon warriors and specially bred attack-lizards, their ultra-high-pressure sacs filled with hydrofluoric acid, incarcerated for the Poison Time, ready to awaken, to strike if humankind threatens them.

They'll destroy the Clanking City.

It's imaginary. It must be.

How can I warn the people about Vul's disastrous plans?

Taking a sabbatical from qRious Minds, I visited a series of quacks and spirit healers. With every new meeting, I wandered farther from rational pathways. I was so desperate for the touch of Yukiko's lips, just to hear her voice—

In the Sonoran Desert, or rather in Guru Gabriel's air-conditioned house, I sat with twelve fellow seekers on a wooden floor that smelled of beeswax-and-lemon polish. We each held a violet crystal while the guru told us to stare at the crystalline flaws, breathing slowly.

New Age music softly played.

"And it is no matter whether you see the flaw open now or in a moment as it forms a gap between the worlds. . . ."

Suddenly Yukiko's features moved inside the crystal.

Ryan, this is wrong.

I blinked, dropping out of trance. The others remained unmoving. The guru continued intoning, watching me as I rose to my feet and backed out of the room.

Yukiko. You exist.

Dazed, I stumbled to the rental car, a silver WhisperGlide whose batteries thrummed as the gull-door rose and I climbed inside.

Somehow. You . . .

Did I pass out? Sob? Stare at the hot desert without thought?

Whatever happened, the car's onboard system detected vital signs beyond normal parameters. When I woke, two nurses were helping me out of the car, carrying me into a medical center.

"What happened to you?" asked a bright-faced young man called Dr. Davies, a few minutes later.

I surprised myself by telling Dr. Davies everything, starting with Yukiko's death, telling him we were deeply entangled, deeper than anyone else. He raised an eyebrow at that.

"I'm a researcher," I told him, "for qRious Minds."

"Ah." And after a moment: "I think I see. And you know about trance states, neurochemically speaking?"

"Um, kind of."

"So let me tell you about hypnotic inductions, how I use them for medical treatment . . . and how Guru Gabriel's words can lead people into seeing whatever they want to see."

"Oh," I said.

Dr. Davies remained silent, allowing me to think.

"Oh, shit," I added.

"Precisely. Now you need to relax, Ryan, so I want you to close your eyes. . . ."

Two days later I was back in New York, down in the lab, getting some kind of work done. The New Age quest was history.

In the back room of the Busted Star, Riktor sat on a hard-backed chair, his guard's uniform undone, blinking at Hoj and the hard-faced men behind him.

"Is a disgrace," said Riktor. "Wot they're doin' to the prisoner."

On a plain table stood a black bottle. Hoj passed it to Riktor.

"Thanks." Riktor took a swig. "Ah—"

It was not Riktor's first bottle of the evening. He'd already reached this state before Hoj's friends took him back here.

Riktor burped.

"Gassy. Sorry."

"This prisoner." Hoj's copper hair fell over his eyes as he leaned forward. "Tell me more."

"V-Vul." Riktor took another swallow. "Bypass . . . bypassing *procedures.* Bastard."

"Correct procedures are important, are they?"

"Damn straight."

"So this prisoner . . ."

"Jolrood. Academ—Academician Jolrood. Poor bugger."

Hoj frowned. Just then a tap sounded, and the metal door swung inwards. Hands moved towards sheathed knives, stopping as Peetro entered.

"Well met, my friends. What's happening?"

"You . . . ?" Riktor blinked. "You his mates, is that it? Jolrood's mates?"

Peetro took a deep breath, biting his lip as if unsure he should remain. Riktor's glance slid to the hard men behind Hoj. Their hooked belt-knives were in plain view.

It seemed to Peetro that Riktor was more sober than he seemed, or at least more aware of danger.

"I could"—Riktor paused, then looked straight at Hoj—"get you in there, iffen you want."

"When?"

"Er . . . Now?"

"*Shadroth,*" muttered Peetro.

"Let's go," said Hoj.

I waken in darkness, check the floating red digits—01:27—and mumble, "Oh, Shadroth," rubbing my face. I sit up on the edge of the bed, wondering why, if I'm so tired, I'm not still sleeping.

A faint trill sounds from somewhere.

Maybe a bird?

Somewhere inside the house.

Oh, for God's sake.

I stand up fast, feeling my muscles loosen, and the carpet is warm beneath my feet as I pad out to the kitchen, wondering whether I need a towel to wrap up a young bird that's fallen from its nest, or a knife to defend myself from—

The yellowish cocoon is split open, abandoned. I'd left it alone earlier, without quite knowing why.

By the TriGods . . .

"No. Stop that."

My voice bounces harshly off the walls. Dreams and wakefulness are separate things. Only delusional schizophrenics merge the two.

Outside, the patio lights snap on, painfully white, and a small purple shape flits, startled, out of the light and into darkness. The moth, if that's what it is, moves fast.

Twelve-sided wings.

This cannot happen.

You saw it.

Impossible.

I spend a long time spent staring outside, then ask myself: What can I do? I drink some water and return to bed.

As the small party moved along grease-stained, rust-patched corridors that were overdue for maintenance, Peetro hung back to exchange muttered words with Hoj.

"Why are we doing this?"

"It was your idea, wasn't it?"

Ahead of them, Riktor was scarcely visible, ringed by eight toughs from the Busted Star.

"I don't know," murmured Peetro. "But it doesn't—"

"We decided together."

"When we thought *Argul* was the prisoner."

The others were climbing over a mass of discarded pipes and broken flanges. Hoj pushed his copper hair back and said, "Oh."

"Who is this guy we're breaking out?"

"Some academician. Jolrool or something."

Hoj started to climb the pile of junk, but Peetro's fingers fastened on his sleeve. "We're sneaking into a cell to reach a prisoner under armed guard, and you're not even certain of his *name*?"

"Yeah." Hoj looked down at the half-shattered pipe he was standing on, then grinned up at Peetro, his green eyes bright. "Bloody excellent, isn't it? Just like the old days."

Shama opened the cupboard, smiling, then suddenly serious.

"What have you babies done?"

Inside the cupboard, over a pile of tasty black leaves, a pair of tiny dode-camoths warbled. From the room behind Shama, the mother dodecamoth sang back at her young.

There were *two* young moths. Not three.

"Oh . . ."

Blinking against tears, Shama saw yet scarcely processed the sight of the open cocoons that remained inside the cupboard, fastened against the ceiling.

The two cocoons that remained.

In a semidream state, I experience my moonlit bedroom as a misty chamber, the walls distant on every side, though it is a room of ordinary size.

I remember a yellow-eyed demon-creature, sneaking out of the city to inform its masters of the danger. And I hear the trill of a young dodecamoth, and realize it is back inside the house.

None of this makes any—

Vul's guards had chosen a location well away from the military holds that Core Palace officers, loyal to Prince Argul rather than Vul, might have inspected without warning.

But Hoj's cronies had decades-long experience of sneaking through rusty conduits to unlikely parts of the Clanking City. It took the best part of three hours to reach the corridor they needed, using a maintenance duct to bypass the hold proper, and reach the cell's rust-patched door.

"Ready, men," said Hoj.

The regulars from the Busted Star arranged themselves at either end of the short corridor, drew weapons, then crouched or went down on one knee to present low targets.

"Shadroth." Peetro shook his head. "I don't like this."

"Afraid of some hard work?" Hoj put his hands on the wheel. There was no combination lock, because the corridor itself was sealed by bolted hatches that led to the hold they'd managed to bypass. The hold where Peetro was sure a Void Egg shone.

"I wish we'd brought some oil."

But the wheel turned easily. Peetro and Hoj swung the door inwards.

"No . . ." On the solitary steel bunk, a thin man flinched. "Please."

"Why are you here?" asked Hoj.

"I—I don't know what you want me to say."

"You're Jolroon, is that right?" asked Peetro. "A scholar."

"Er, if you . . . I'm Belik Jolrood."

"And why in all the tri-damned hells are you locked in here?"

"Because . . . Because Vul disagreed with me . . ."

"He bloody disagrees with me," muttered Hoj. "Like raw rat stew."

". . . about the Void Egg."

"Oh, bugger," said Peetro. "He really is planning to—"

"Drop the Egg, and break the world in two."

Shama knew she ought to wait one more night before the final annealing. But Master Teldrasso was due back in the morning, and besides . . . this was a perfect crystal. It was pure and strong enough to handle any shock, including the forced transition to its new state, locking in the patterns it must already have trapped.

She readied the platinum-coated tongs, set the harmonic plates into vibration, and—reaching on tiptoe from a stool—tugged down a heavy-handled switch. White beams shone from spherical lenses in every corner of the room—

The best crystal ever, Master.

—focusing on the crystal at the room's heart.

The crystal began to moan.

Something tugs at me; then a *million* things, a million barbed hooks, drag at my nerves, hauling me into agonized wakefulness.

"No . . ."

Yet I still hear strange harmonies, knowing that—

On his silver couch, Prince Argul's orange eyes snapped open. He shuddered, opened his mouth . . . and then his head lolled to one side, eyelids sliding shut.

—the danger is growing as I roll off the bed, onto the floor on my hands and knees. A silver web of pain and light is drawn across my skin as I pull myself upright and stagger to the bathroom.

The light comes on automatically. In front of the mirror, I blink hard against the brightness.

Blink my *orange* eyes.

Shama returned back to her room, full of elated knowledge, a feeling of power at her new understanding and ability. She was ready to face anything.

Even the sudden appearance of *three* baby dodecamoths inside the cupboard. The trio of abandoned, split cocoons hung in place. Their mother floated in circles around the room, gliding on her silklike purple twelve-edged wings, her high-pitched song of triumph made discordant by overtones of worry.

Shama forgot about the perfect crystal still shining in the casting chamber.

She held out her hands. The baby moths alighted on her fingers.

Inside his chambers, Vul wept. An amber surveillance globe swirled, its arcane network of silver lines forming a diagrammatic language only Vul could understand.

"I should have . . . calibrated." Vul rubbed his face, then sobbed again. "To physical . . . location. Or sent the patrols out sooner."

Because there was no way to backtrack. Somewhere in the Clanking City an annealed crystal had wholly trapped Prince Argul's mind. No power that Vul knew of could drag the prince back into conscious wakefulness while the crystal remained intact.

And if the crystal were simply to crack or shatter, so would the thoughts and memories that formed Prince Argul's identity.

Yesterday, Vul had assigned teams to check the quarters of every dreamweb maker and glassharp player in the city. Still there were jewelers and antique dealers who might have some artifact that bore such power . . . but Vul did not have enough men to check everywhere.

Now, it was too late.

Vul had never seen the need to correlate this scanner's measurements with physical location. He had never expected that such a crystal would appear, or that he would want to know exactly where it was.

Where his beloved Argul's mind was trapped.

For Vul adored Argul in a way he could never declare, even as he recognized that Argul was the barrier to all the power that he needed.

Finally, Vul wiped away his tears.

Oh, my darling Argul.

And shut down the amber globe display.

Thank you for giving me your city.

And I stumble out into the night, towards the dark forest, knowing the baby dodecamoth has gone back to the world it came from, safe from Connecticut owls and bats. But more . . .

Something is missing. Perhaps I know the truth.

Oh, God. Oh, God.

Know it, and fear to recognize it.

It's insane.

None of this can be true.

The emptiness, the new void inside me—

Very early, Shama came awake, sitting up as she heard Master Teldrasso's voice outside. He was back! Wait till she showed him the—

Other men were talking, growling commands. Then a thud sounded.

Master Teldrasso was silent.

Shama blinked away acid-hot tears, knowing straightaway that bad men had her master. Scared, she looked for the dodecamoth whose trills might attract the men. But the moth was in the cupboard with her three offspring, warbling subsonic warnings to hush them.

After a time, she heard the men leave. Trembling, Shama padded across the floor, then opened the door. Nothing outside.

She slipped out.

At the first intersection, she nearly ran into the men. Master Teldrasso, conscious once more, was surrounded by four guards.

"—to know the legal charges."

"You've a damned cheek. With a dangerous resonant crystal like that."

"That's not . . ." Master Teldrasso fell silent.

"What? You didn't make it?"

"It's a dreamweb. It's what I do."

Shama bit her fist. Had she done something wrong? And had Master Teldrasso realized it? Was he covering for her, paying for her sin, whatever it was?

One of the guards held up a fine platinum fork, vibrating so fast it blurred.

"You ain't heard o' safety protocols, then?"

"Nor," muttered another guard, "what happens to them what ignores them, eh?"

After a moment, Master Teldrasso straightened up, and adjusted his tunic. From her vantage point, Shama could see bloodstains on the fabric.

"Do whatever you're going to do."

"Damn bloody right we will."

Shama turned away when the guard's fist swung towards Master Teldrasso's head.

My fault. I'm sorry!

Afterwards, when they hauled her unconscious master along still-deserted corridors, Shama followed.

In Ireland we'd call it a forest dell, except the cup-shaped depression is huge. The drop—invisible in the darkness—is like a cliff. Enough of a drop to end it all.

Yukiko is truly gone.

Oh, my darling. My love.

Even at her grave, even in the subterranean cemetery, I have never felt this hollow. I am torn open and emptied. I don't even understand why. Why now.

Yes, I do.

But I cannot face this reality.

The mother dodecamoth trilled and warbled urgently, from subsonics to human-audible range.

Two of her offspring had folded up their wings as commanded, and were hidden inside the cupboard. But the third young dodecamoth was flitting around the chamber, searching for some trail in the air . . .

Found it.

In seconds, the young moth was out in the corridor, leaving the distraught mother to flap her wings inside the chamber, unwilling to abandon her two quiescent offspring for the sake of a renegade.

The lone youngster flew faster now, following Shama's scent.

At the moonlit edge, where I can step off so easily. Less than two seconds until impact. The emptiness will be gone—

The four guards and Master Teldrasso were close to the Busted Star, by coincidence, when they suddenly stopped. Ranged in front of them was a group of ten—no, eleven men.

Some of them Shama recognized as cutthroat regulars from the Busted Star. Scarred yet sentimental for the most part, they would often buy her a cup of sweet juice to drink.

And there were two other men, the nobles she had seen on the night she retrieved the crystal—

They can help!

But fear held Shama back. The men who had taken her master were armed and in uniform.

"Gentlemen." It was Peetro who spoke. "I am a city councilor, and this is my sigil." He showed a small silver artifact. "And these are deputized men."

Behind him, the Busted Star regulars shifted. They bore spiked chains and hooked knives, and their gazes were flat, used to violence. And they were, to a man, patriots.

Vul's men did not move.

"The thing is"—Hoj stepped forward, raising his own sigil of office—"treason has been committed this night. But not by this man."

"I . . ." Master Teldrasso stopped.

"We know who you are, good master," said Peetro. "Well met, sir."

Hoj pointed at the cloth-wrapped dreamweb that one of the guards held. "And what is that?"

"This, councilor, is evidence of what we call a criminal offense. As is stopping officers in the course of—"

Shama stepped forward.

No. I'm too scared—

But her voice worked by itself: "It's the *best dreamweb ever* and I made it and I'm sorry, Master, and I'll never do it again. . . ."

"By the TriGods—"

"Shadroth, Bilkroth, and Vilkridor."

And Master Teldrasso said, "A dreamweb with no safety flaws," just as Peetro added, "Has this got anything to do with Prince Argul's disappearance?"

Silence struck the two opposing groups of men.

The leader of Vul's guards swallowed.

I'm doing it. I'm really taking the step that ends it all . . .

Yukiko.

. . . when scarlet lights flare in the darkness, and silver tracery lights up across my skin in answer. It is cold and alien, the sensation that spins through me. I am one with creatures unlike myself, whose extended predatory senses are so fine that I am in awe.

Then the cats turn away and are one with the shadows once more.

My love?

But she's been truly gone, ever since the young dodecamoth—

Yukiko?

—flew onwards, following Shama's trail.

The standoff repeated itself an hour later, but with a difference. This time, Hoj and Peetro were backed up by nearly two hundred men and hard-faced women, regulars of the Busted Star and neighboring decks, bristling with knives and fighting-poles, barbed chains and razorglass maces.

In front of them stood a thirty-strong squadron of guards who wore the purple that identified them as Vul's own.

They were in a curved, high corridor whose walls were of intricately patterned silver and whose floor was gleaming obsidian. Beyond the uniformed guards stood embossed polished doors leading to the royal sleeping chamber.

Peetro had made his points coldly; Hoj had allowed his anger to show. But the guards' captain was either loyal to Vul or more scared of Vul than of a larger (but undisciplined) fighting force.

Finally Vul came striding into view, with only two more guards trailing him. He held a small dark blue globe in each hand.

"So. Peetro and Hoj. One might have known."

Peetro gave a bow, equal-to-equal. "Viceroy, under article two-twelve of the Breakdown Regulations, a councilor is entitled to—"

But Hoj said, "You bloody bastard, Vul. Are you insane?" He held up the dreamweb. "To trap Prince Argul in *this*?"

The blood swept from Vul's face, and he took two stumbling steps back. "Argul . . ." Vul swallowed. "*No.* Not here."

Peetro's eyebrows raised. His linguistics tutor had taught him much about reading undertones in voices. It wasn't just that Vul had not expected to find the dreamweb containing Prince Argul's mind . . . It was the feelings that Vul bore for Argul.

"Stand aside," Peetro said, using Vul's tonality to command Vul's own guards.

The men moved apart fractionally, just enough for Hoj to recognize the opportunity and sprint forward, dreamweb in hand. They grabbed for him, but he was through, slamming the heel of his palm against the heavy doors—

"Look out!" yelled Peetro.

—that swung open, massive but finely balanced on silent hinges, to reveal the sleeping chamber, and Prince Argul atop his silver couch.

That was when the vicious fighting started.

I back away from the edge, half daring to understand, to believe that everything might be all right. I've lost her once . . .

Shama hung well back as the fighters swung bloody weapons, yelling with pain and fear. Neither she nor the guards nor the Busted Star regulars noticed the small, purple shape with tiny twelve-sided wings flitting overhead, into Prince Argul's chamber.

On the silver couch, the prince remained in coma.

"You're insane!" Hoj's voice rose above the melee. "Vul's planning to drop a Void—" Swirling violence enclosed him.

At the sleeping chamber's far wall, the young dodecamoth hovered before a particularly intricate decoration formed of diamond. The diamond flared with blue light.

And the wall split apart into shards and fragments that slowly lowered into the floor.

"Hey—"

"Stop!"

"Lay down arms . . ."

Beyond the sleeping prince, now revealed, was the Core Court, huge and echoing, where a vast crystalline lattice stood. Inside the great construct floated the refracted, broken, horizontal image of the Sleeping King, Prince Argul's ancestor.

An image that spoke, for the first time in three centuries.

I weep oil, my subjects. I bleed rust. Did you not know this?

The words sounded inside people's minds, not in their ears.

They called me King Nirgultal, in the days of my ascension—

And the guards and civilians alike slowly lowered their arms. One by one, they genuflected in the archaic fashion, down on one knee and bowing their heads.

—though I was president before that, and once I was plain Nirgul Talonsen, in days that scholars no longer remember.

Vul gasped, from the shock of the royal words in his mind, and from the sight of Hoj, who held the dreamweb in his hands.

For the dreamweb was glowing white.

Glowing brighter by the second.

I dream in the pipes, I haunt the pistons, and my joints ache as I clank forever, and you can never realize how lonely it can . . . Did you know, for a time, they called me the Laughing King?

A series of hollow, overlapping, echoing laughs sounded in the Core Court. Shama shivered.

So many dead generations ago . . .

Hoj was stumbling now, towards the sleeping Prince Argul's body, while the dreamweb that had trapped the prince's mind flared white-hot. Hoj whimpered as his hands burned. Still he advanced, his carefree features lined with agony.

"By the TriGods," muttered Vul.

Then Vul regarded the dark blue spheres he held in each hand, and remembered the Void Egg he had been planning to deploy. Perhaps the void was where the answers lay.

Where *his* answers lay.

As Hoj reached the prince, Vul could stand no more. He crushed the two spheres against his own chest and screamed.

"No . . ." This was Peetro. It was not Vul he was concerned with. "Hoj, for the TriGods' sake, *let go!*"

Vul's suicide was irrelevant now.

Peetro moved fast, pushing himself through the kneeling men and women, ignoring the powerful words that slammed through his brain.

Strange visitors awaken me, and I am in no state to cope, and what will happen to the city when I am confused and—?

A stench of burning meat was rising from Hoj. His tears glistened as he laid the dreamweb on Prince Argul's chest. Finally, Hoj could let go and slump back on the floor, gasping.

His hands, when Peetro reached him, were red-black glistening ruins.

"Save . . . Argul," Hoj gasped.

Peetro clasped Hoj, saying nothing. Vul, the knowledgeable bastard, was dead. But Peetro knew enough to realize that breaking the dreamweb would shatter Argul's mind. As for how to actually save Argul—

Do I need to rule again? I have scattered my being among motive parts for so long . . .

Master Teldrasso, kneeling, raised his head.

"Sire? My pardon, but your descendant is trapped in a dreamweb that no human can undo. I would beseech you—"

No. Not for you.

Some of the guards glanced at each other. Did anyone understand what was happening here?

But I am so in need of company, just to visit for a while, perhaps a century or two. And your world, dear visitor, is interesting.

Now Peetro could see the purple dodecamoth hovering just before the crystal lattice. So, too, could Shama.

My fault . . .

Oh, no, young Shama. The Sleeping King's words roared only in her brain. **You will be the greatest webmaker of them all.**

"Sire . . ." she gasped out loud.

Peetro looked at her.

I have company in my dreams; therefore the city needs Argul. You may have him back.

Master Teldrasso blinked. Hoj whimpered and passed out.

And as my descendant awakes—the Sleeping King's words seemed stronger and deeper as Prince Argul's orange eyes fluttered and the dreamweb began to melt *into* his body without harm—**I welcome Yukiko, my otherworldly visitor.**

I scream. I sob. I weep.

Oh, Yukiko.

Was I right? Will she be okay?

Wait for me. . . .

❙❙

The purple moth slipped inside the lattice, and was lost from sight.

You're safe, Yukiko. And you, my friend who observes from her realm.

I'm present in the Core Court.

When the time comes, you will be welcome, too.

And now I'm not.

Gone. This is my world, though the Sleeping King's words promised a certain future.

Next morning, I open a holo display. Inside the cubic space, an image of Ian's head and shoulders sharpens. Behind him I see a partially rendered backdrop: Sixth Avenue.

"Sorry," I tell him. "But I'm resigning."

"No. Don't. Look, Ryan, if I've been too heavy-handed then I apol—"

"You were right, my friend. I just don't want to do this anymore."

Ian stares at me from the display.

"Come and talk. Come to dinner with the family."

And I surprise myself by saying, "I'd love to. You can help me plan my trip."

"Trip?"

"To Japan. There are places to visit."

Places I can remember, though this physical body has never been there.

"Um, okay . . ."

"I'll call you back later."

"Do that. Er . . . Nice lenses. Weird, but . . . Good to see you make a change."

"Thanks, Ian."

"Though you might have just settled for a haircut."

And another surprise: I actually laugh.

"Yeah," I tell him. "I probably should have. Take it easy, old pal."

"Hang loose, buddy."

I close the call.

I remember, in retrospect, the dream fading. Deep in the crystal lattice, two shapes moved: a regal waving figure, and the one who smiled, that familiar mixture of Zen calm and sensuous love, eyes filled with stillness and movement at the same time.

A good dream.

As I leave the house, I wink at myself in the hallway mirror, and the orange-eyed reflection winks back. The air is pure and clear as I make my through the forest and stop at the edge of the depression where I nearly stepped into space, when I thought I had to end it all.

Keep well, Yukiko.

I am alone. I am empty. But I can go on—

I love you.

—because I know that somewhere, elsewhen, sideways from now, she waits inside a web of crystal and dreams, waiting for the day when we are joined once more.

WIKIWORLD

Paul Di Filippo

Paul Di Filippo manages the nigh-impossible task of being a unique voice in a field of unique voices. He has been a finalist for the Hugo, Nebula, BSFA, Philip K. Dick, Wired Magazine, and World Fantasy awards. He is a trendsetter, a fearless explorer, a charter of hitherto unknown territories, and a laugh-out-loud riot. One can always count on Paul to be plugged into whatever the current cultural zeitgeist is, though his writings leap from the unclassifiably mind-bending and absurd to examinations of plausible futures lurking just around the corner from today. His writing is always sexy, funny, relevant, and now, and his latest is a perfect concluding tale for this book of future fiction in an accelerated age.

1. Meet Russ Reynolds

Russ Reynolds, that's me. You probably remember my name from when I ran the country for three days. Wasn't that a wild time? I'm sorry I started a trade war with several countries around the globe. I bet you're all grateful things didn't ramp up to the shooting stage. I know I am. And the UWA came out ahead in the end, right? No harm, no foul. Thanks for being so understanding and forgiving. I assure you that my motives throughout the whole affair, although somewhat selfish, were not ignoble.

And now that things have quieted down, I figured people would be calm enough to want to listen to the whole story behind those frighteningly exciting events.

So here it is.

2. Mr. Wiki Builds My Dream House

It all started, really, the day when several wikis where I had simoleons banked got together to build me a house. Not only did I meet my best friend Foolty Fontal that day, but I also hooked up with Cherimoya Espiritu. It's hard now, a few years later, to say which one of those outrageous personages gave me the wildest ride. But it's certain that without their aiding and abetting, plotting and encouraging, I would never have become the jimmywhale of the UWA, and done what I did.

The site for my new house was a tiny island about half an acre in extent. This dry land represented all that was left of what used to be Hyannis, Massachusetts, since Cape Cod became an archipelago. Even now, during big storms, the island is frequently overwashed, so I had picked up the title to it for a song, when I got tired of living on my boat, the *Gogo Goggins*.

Of course the value of coastal land everywhere had plunged steadily in the three decades since the destruction of New Orleans. People just got tired of seeing their homes and businesses destroyed on a regular basis by superstorms and rising sea levels. Suddenly Nebraska and Montana and the Dakotas looked like beckoning havens of safety, especially with their ameliorated climates, and the population decline experienced for a century by the Great Plains states reversed itself dramatically, lofting the region into a new cultural hot zone. I had heard lately that Fargo had spawned yet another musical movement, something called "cornhüsker dü," although I hadn't yet listened to any samples of it off the ubik.

Anyway, this little islet would serve me well, I figured, as both home and base for my job—assuming I could erect a good solid comfortable structure here. Realizing that such a task was beyond my own capabilities, I called in my wikis.

The Dark Galactics. The PEP Boyz. The Chindogurus. Mother Hitton's

Littul Kittons. The Bishojos. The Glamazons. The Provincetown Pickers. And several more. All of them owed me simoleons for the usual—goods received, or time and expertise invested—and now they'd be eager to balance the accounts.

The day construction was scheduled to start, I anchored the *Gogo Goggins* on the western side of my island, facing the mainland. The June air was warm on my bare arms, and freighted with delicious salt scents. Gulls swooped low over my boat, expecting the usual handouts. The sun was a golden English muffin in the sky. (Maybe I should have had some breakfast, but I had been too excited to prepare any that morning.) Visibility was great. I could see drowned church spires and dead cell-phone towers closer to the shore. Through this slalom a small fleet of variegated ships sailed, converging on my island.

The shadow of one of the high unmanned aerostats that maintained the ubik passed over me, the same moment I used that medium to call up IDs on the fleet. In my vision, translucent tags overlaid each ship, labeling their owners, crew, and contents. I was able to call up real-time magnified images of the ships as well, shot from the aerostats and tiny random entomopter cams. I saw every kind of vessel imaginable: sleek catamarans, old lobster boats, inflatables, decommissioned Coast Guard cutters . . . And all of them carrying my friends—some of whom I had met face-to-face, some of whom I hadn't—coming to help build my house.

I hopped out of my boat onto dry land. My island was covered with salt-tolerant scrub plants and the occasional beach rose. No trees to clear. Construction could begin immediately.

As I awaited my friends, I got several prompts displayed across my left eye, notifying me of four or five immediate ubik developments in areas of interest to me. I had the threshold of my attention-filter set fairly high, so I knew I should attend to whatever had made it over that hurdle. For speed's sake, I kept the messages text-only, suppressing the full audio-video presentations.

The first development concerned an adjustment to the local property-tax rates. "Glamorous Glynnis" had just amended the current rate structure to penalize any residence over 15,000 square feet that failed to feed power back to the grid. Sixty-five other people had endorsed the change. I added my own vote to theirs, and tacked on a clause to exempt group homes.

Next came a modification to the rules of the nonvirtual marketplace back on the mainland, where I sold many of my salvaged goods in person. "Jingle-horse" wanted to extend the hours of operation on holidays. Competitively speaking, I'd feel compelled to be there if the booths were open extra. And since I liked my downtime, I voted no.

Items three and four involved decriminalizing a newly designed recreational drug named "arp," and increasing our region's freshwater exports. I didn't know enough about arp, so I got a search going for documents on the drug. I'd try to go through them tonight, and vote tomorrow. And even though I felt bad for the drought-sufferers down south, I didn't want to encourage continued habitation in a zone plainly unsuited for its current population densities, so I voted no.

The last item concerned a Wikitustional Amendment. National stuff. This new clause had been in play for six months now without getting at least provisionally locked down, approaching a record length of revision time. The amendment mandated regular wiki participation as a prerequisite for full enfranchisement in the UWA. "Uncle Sham" had just stuck in a clause exempting people older than sixty-five. I wasn't sure what I thought about that, so I pushed the matter back in the queue.

By the time I had attended to these issues, the first of my visitors had arrived: a lone man on a small vessel named *The Smiling Dictator*. The craft crunched onto the beach, and the guy jumped out.

"Hey, Russ! Nice day for a house-raising."

Jack Cortez—"Cortez the Queller" in the ubik—resembled a racing greyhound in slimness and coiled energy. He wore a fisherman's vest over bare chest, a pair of denim cutoffs bleached white, and boat shoes. His SCURF showed as a dark green eagle across a swath of his chest.

"Ahimsa, Jack! I really appreciate you showing up."

"No problem. The Church still owes you for retrieving that Madonna. But you gotta do *some* work nonetheless! Come on and give me a hand."

I went over to the *Dictator* and helped Jack wrestle some foam-encased objects big as coffee-table-tops out of the boat. When we had the half dozen objects stacked on land, he flaked off some of the protective foam and revealed the corner of a window frame.

"Six smart windows. Variable opacity, self-cleaning, rated to withstand Category Four storms. Fully spimed, natch. One of our coreligionists is a contractor, and these were left over from a recent job."

"Pluricious!"

By then, the rest of the boats had arrived. A perfect storm of unloading and greeting swept over my little domain. Crates and girders and pre-formed pilings and lumber and shingles and equipment accumulated in heaps, while bottled drinks made the rounds, to fortify and replenish. The wiki known as the Shewookies had brought not materials nor power tools but food. They began to set up a veritable banquet on folding tables, in anticipation of snacking and lunching.

A guy I didn't recognize came up to me, hand extended. His SCURF formed orange tiger stripes on his cheeks and down his jaws. Before I could bring up his tag, he introduced himself.

"Hi, Russ. Bob Graubauskas—'Grabass' to you. Jimmywhale for the Sunflower Slowdrags. So, you got any solid preferences for your house?"

"No, not really. Just so long as it's strong and spacious and not too ugly."

"Can do."

Grabass began to issue silent orders to his wiki, a ubik stream he cued me in on. But then a big woman wearing overalls intervened.

"Margalit Bayless, with the Mollicutes. 'Large Marge.' You truly gonna let the Slowdrags design this structure all by themselves?"

"Well, no. . . ."

"That's good. Because my people have some neat ideas too—"

I left Large Marge and Grabass noisily debating the merits of their various plans while I snagged an egg salad sandwich and a coffee. By the time I had swallowed the last bite, both the Mollicutes and the Sunflower Slowdrags had begun construction. The only thing was, the two teams were starting at opposite ends of a staked-off area and working toward the common middle. And their initial scaffolding and foundations looked utterly incompatible. And some of the other wikis seemed ready to add wings to the nascent building regardless of either main team.

As spimed materials churned under supervision like a nest of snakes or a pit of chunky lava or a scrum of rugby robots in directed self-assembly—boring into the soil and stretching up toward the sky—I watched with growing alarm, wondering if this had been the smartest idea. What kind of miscegenational mansion was I going to end up with?

That's when Foolty Fontal showed up to save the day.

He arrived in a one-person sea-kayak, of all things, paddling like a lunatic, face covered with sweat. So typical of the man, I would discover, choosing not to claim primary allegiance with any wiki, so he could belong to all.

I tried to tag him, but got a privacy denial.

Having beached his craft and ditched his paddle, Foolty levered himself out with agility. I saw a beanpole well over six feet tall, with glossy skin the color of black-bean dip. Stubby dreadlocks like breakfast sausages capped his head. Ivory SCURF curlicued up his dark bare arms like automobile detailing.

Foolty, I later learned, claimed mixed Ethiopian, Jamaican, and Gullah heritage, as well as snippets of mestizo. It made for a hybrid genome as unique as his brain.

Spotting me by the food tables, Foolty lanked over.

"Russ Reynolds, tagged. Loved your contributions to *Naomi Instanton*."

Foolty was referring to a crowd-sourced sitcom I had helped to co-script. "Well, thanks, man."

"Name's Foolty Fontal—'FooDog.'"

"No shit!"

FooDog was legendary across the ubik. He could have been the jimmy-whale of a hundred wikis, but had declined all such positions. His talents were many and magnificent, his ego reputedly restrained, and his presence at any nonvirtual event a legend in the making.

Now FooDog nodded his head toward the construction site. A small autonomous backhoe was wrestling with a walking tripodal hod full of bricks while members of competing wikis cheered on the opponents.

"Interesting project. Caught my eye this morning. Lots of challenges. But it looks like you're heading for disaster, unless you get some coordination. Mind if I butt in?"

"Are you kidding? I'd be honored. Go for it!"

FooDog ambled over to the workers, both human and cybernetic, streaming ubik instructions with high-priority tags attached faster than I could follow. A galvanic charge seemed to run through people as they realized who walked among them. FooDog accepted the homage with humble grace. And suddenly the whole site was transformed from a chaotic competition to a patterned dance of flesh and materials.

That's the greatest thing about wikis: they combine the best features of democracy and autocracy. Everybody has an equal say. But some got bigger says than others.

Over the next dozen hours, I watched in amazement as my house grew almost organically. By the time dusk was settling in, the place was nearly done. Raised high above sea level against any potential flooding, on deep-sunk cement piles, spired, curve-walled, airy yet massive, it still showed hallmarks of rival philosophies of design. But somehow the efforts of the various factions ultimately harmonized instead of bickered, thanks to FooDog's overseeing of the assorted worldviews.

One of the best features of my new house, a place where I could see myself spending many happy idle hours, was a large wooden deck that projected out well over the water, where it was supported by pressure-treated and tarred wooden pillars, big as antique telephone poles, plunging into the sea.

Three or four heaps of wooden construction waste and combustible sea-wrack had been arranged as pyres against the dusk, and they were now ignited. Live music flared up with the flames, and more food and drink was laid on. While a few machines and people continued to add some last-minute details to my house, illuminated by electrical lights running off the newly installed power system (combined wave motion and ocean temperature differential), the majority of the folks began to celebrate a job well done.

I was heading to join them when I noticed a new arrival sailing in out of the dusk: a rather disreputable-looking workhorse of a fishing sloop. I pinged the craft, but got no response. Not a privacy denial, but a dead silence.

This ship and its owner were running off the ubik, un-SCURFED.

Intrigued, I advanced toward the boat. I kicked up my night vision. Its bow bore the name *Soft Grind*. From out of the pilothouse emerged the presumptive captain. In the ancient firelight, I saw one of the most beautiful women I had ever beheld: skin the color of teak, long wavy black hair, a killer figure. She wore a faded hemp shirt tied under her breasts to expose her midriff; baggy men's surfer trunks; and a distressed pair of gumboots.

She leaped over the gunwales and off the boat with pantherish flair moderated only slightly by her clunky footwear.

"Hey," she said. "Looks like a party. Mind if I crash it?"

"No, sure, of course not."

She grinned, exposing perfect teeth.

"I'm Cherry. One of the Oyster Pirates."

And that was how I met Cherimoya Espiritu.

3. In Love with an Oyster Pirate

Gaia giveth even as she taketh away.

The warming of the global climate over the past century had melted permafrost and glaciers, shifted rainfall patterns, altered animal migratory routes, disrupted agriculture, drowned cities, and similarly necessitated a thousand thousand adjustments, recalibrations, and hasty retreats. But humanity's unintentional experiment with the biosphere had also brought some benefits.

Now we could grow oysters in New England.

Six hundred years ago, oysters had flourished as far north as the Hudson. Native Americans had accumulated vast middens of shells on the shores of what would become Manhattan. Then, prior to the industrial age, there was a small climate shift, and oysters vanished from those waters.

Now, however, the tasty bivalves were back, their range extending almost to Maine.

The commercial beds of the Cape Cod Archipelago produced shellfish as good as any from the heyday of Chesapeake Bay. Several large wikis maintained, regulated, and harvested these beds, constituting a large share of the local economy.

But as anyone might have predicted, wherever a natural resource existed, sprawling and hard of defense, poachers would be found.

Cherimoya Espiritu hailed from a long line of fisherfolks operating for generations out of nearby New Bedford. Cape Verdean by remotest ancestry, her family had suffered in the collapse of conventional fisheries off the Georges Bank. They had failed to appreciate the new industry until it was too late for them to join one of the legal oyster wikis. (Membership had been closed at a number determined by complicated sustainability formulae.) Consequently, they turned pirate to survive in the only arena they knew.

Cherimoya and her extensive kin had divested themselves of their SCURF: no subcutaneous ubik arfids for them, to register their presence minute-to-minute to nosy authorities and jealous oyster owners. The pirates relied instead on the doddering network of GPS satellites for navigation, and primitive cell phones for communication. Operating at night, they boasted gear to interfere with entomopter cams and infrared scans. They were not above discouraging pursuers with pulsed-energy projectile guns (purchased from the PEP Boyz). After escaping with their illicit catches, they sold the fruit of the sea to individual restaurants and unscrupulous wholesalers. They took payment either in goods, or in isk, simoleons and lindens that friends would bank for them in the ubik.

Most of the oyster pirates lived on their ships, to avoid contact with perhaps overly inquisitive mainland security wikis such as the Boston Badgers and the Stingers. Just like me prior to my island-buying—except that my motivation for a life afloat didn't involve anything illicit.

Bits and pieces of information about this subculture I knew just from growing up in the Archipelago. And the rest I learned from Cherry over the first few months of our relationship.

But that night of my house-raising, all I knew was that a gorgeous woman, rough-edged and authentic as one of the oyster shells she daily handled, wanted to hang out on my tiny island and have some fun.

That her accidental presence here would lead to our becoming long-term lovers, I never dared hope.

But sure enough, that's what happened.

Following Cherry's introduction, I shook her hand and gave my own name. Daring to take her by the elbow—and receiving no rebuke—I steered her across the flame-lit, shadowy sands towards the nearest gaggle of revelers around their pyre.

"So," I asked, "how come you're not working tonight?"

"Oh, I don't work every night. Just often enough to keep myself in provisions and fuel. Why should I knock myself out just to earn money and pile up *things*? I'm more interested in enjoying life. Staying free, not being tied down."

"Well, you know, I think that's, um—just great! That's how I feel too!" I silently cursed my new status as a landowner and house-dweller.

We came out of the darkness and into the sight of my friends. Guitars, drums, and gravicords chanced to fall silent just then, and I got pinged with the planned playlist, and a chance to submit any requests.

"Hey, Russ, congratulations!" "Great day!" "House looks totally flexy!" "You're gonna really enjoy it!"

Cherry turned to regard me with a wide grin. "So—gotta stay footloose, huh?"

To cover my chagrin, I fetched drinks for Cherry and myself while I tried to think of something to say in defense of my new householder lifestyle. That damn sexy grin of hers didn't help my concentration.

Cherry took a beer from me. I said, "Listen, it's not like I'm buying into some paranoid gatecom. This place—totally transient. It's nothing more than a beach shack, somewhere to hang my clothes. I'm on the water most of every day—"

Waving a hand to dismiss my excuses, Cherry said, "Just funning with you, Russ. Actually, I think this place is pretty hyphy. Much as I love *Soft Grind*, I get tired of being so cramped all the time. Being able to stretch in your bunk without whacking your knuckles would be a treat. So—do I get a tour?"

"Yeah, absolutely!"

We headed toward the staircase leading up to my deck. Her sight unamped, Cherry stumbled over a tussock of grass, and I took her hand to guide her. And even when we got within the house's sphere of radiance, she didn't let go.

Up on the deck, Foolty was supervising a few machines working atop the roof. Spotting me, he called out, "Hey, nephew! Just tying in the rainwater-collection system to the desalinization plant."

"Swell. FooDog, I'd like you to meet—"

"No, don't tell me the name of this sweet niece. Let me find out on my own."

Cherry snorted. "Good luck! Far as the ubik knows, I'm not even part of this brane. And that's how I like it."

FooDog's eyes went unfocused, and he began to make strangled yips like a mutt barking in its sleep. After about ninety seconds of this, during which time Cherry and I admired a rising quarter moon, FooDog emerged from his trawl of the ubik.

"Cherimoya Espiritu," he said. "Born 2015. Father's name João, mother's name Graca. Younger brother nicknamed the Dolphin. Member of the Oyster Pirates—"

Cherry's face registered mixed irritation, admiration, and fright. "How—how'd you find all that out?"

FooDog winked broadly. "Magic."

"No, c'mon, tell me!"

"All right, all right. The first part was easy. I cheated. I teasled into Russ's friends list. He added you as soon as you met, and that's how I got your name and occupation. My SCURF isn't off the shelf. It picked up molecules of your breath, did an instant signature on four hundred organic compounds, and found probable family matches with your parents, whose genomes are on file. And your brother's got a record with the Boston Badgers for a ruckus at a bar in Fall River."

Now I felt offended. "You teasled into my friends list? You got big ones, FooDog."

"Well, thanks! That's how I got where I am today. And besides, I discovered my name there too, so I figured it was okay."

I couldn't find it in myself to be angry with this genial ubik-trickster. Cherry seemed willing to extend him the same leniency.

"No need to worry about anyone else learning this stuff. While I was in there, I beefed up all your security, nephew."

"Well—thanks, I guess."

"No thanks necessary." FooDog turned back to the bots on the roof. "Hey, Blue Droid! You call that a watertight seam!"

Cherry and I went through the sliding glass door that led off the deck and inside.

I made an inspection of my new home for the first time with Cherry in tow. The place was perfect: roomy yet cozy, easy to maintain, lots of comforts.

The wikis had even provided some rudimentary furniture, including a couple of inflatable adaptive chairs. We positioned them in front of a window that commanded a view of the ocean and the Moon. I went to a small humming fridge and found it full of beer. I took two bottles back to the seats.

Cherry and I talked until the Moon escaped our view. I opaqued all the glass in the house. We merged the MEMS skins of the chairs, fashioning them into a single bed. Then we had sex and fell asleep.

In the morning, Cherry said, "Yeah, I think I could get used to living here real fast."

4. Mucho Mongo

My dad was a garbageman.

Okay, so not really. He didn't wear overalls or hang from the back of a truck or heft dripping sacks of coffee grounds and banana peels. Dad's job was strictly white-collar. His fingers were more often found on a keyboard than a trash compactor. He was in charge of the Barnstable Transfer Station, a seventy-acre "disposium" where recyclables were lifted from the waste-stream, and whatever couldn't be commercially repurposed was neatly and sterilely buried. But I like to tell people he was a garbageman just to get their instant, unschooled reactions. If they turn up their noses, chances are they won't make it onto my friends list.

I remember Dad taking me to work once in a while on Saturdays. He proudly showed off the dump's little store, stocked with the prize items his workers had rescued.

"Look at this, Russ. A first edition Jack London. *Tales of the Fish Patrol.* Can you believe it?"

I was five years old, and had just gotten my first pair of spex, providing rudimentary access to what passed for the ubik back then. I wasn't impressed.

"I can read that right now, Dad, if I wanted to."

Dad looked crestfallen. "That digital text is just information, Son. This is a *book*! And best of all, it's *mongo*."

I tried to look up mongo in the ubik, like I had been taught, but couldn't find it in my dictionary. "What's mongo, Dad?"

"A moment of grace. A small victory over entropy."

"Huh?"

"It's any treasure you reclaim from the edge of destruction, Russ. There's no thrill like making a mongo strike."

I looked at the book with new eyes. And that's when I got hooked.

From then on, mongo became my life.

That initial epiphany occurred over twenty years ago. Barnstable is long drowned, fish swimming through the barnacled timbers of the disposium store, and my folks live in Helena now. But I haven't forgotten the lessons my Dad taught me.

The *Gogo Goggins* has strong winches for hauling really big finds up into the air. But mostly I deal in small yet valuable stuff. With strap-on gills, a smartskin suit, MEMS flippers, and a MHD underwater sled packing ten-thousand candlepower of searchlights, I pick through the drowned world of the Cape Cod Archipelago and vicinity.

The coastal regions of the world now host the largest caches of treasure the world has ever seen. Entire cities whose contents could not be entirely rescued in advance of the encroaching waters. All there as salvage for the taking, pursuant to many, many post-flood legal rulings.

Once I'm under the water, my contact with the ubik cut off. Relying just on the processing power in my SCURF, I'm alone with my thoughts and the sensations of the dive. The romance of treasure-hunting takes over. Who knows what I might find? Jewelry, monogrammed plates from a famous restaurant, statues, coins—whatever I bring up, I generally sell with no problems, either over the ubik or at the old-fashioned marketplace on the mainland.

It's a weird way of earning your living, I know. Some people might find it morbid, spending so much time amid these ghostly drowned ruins. (And to answer the first question anyone asks: yes, I've encountered skeletons, but none of them have shown the slightest inclination to attack.)

But I don't find my job morbid at all.

I'm under the spell of mongo.

One of the first outings Cherry and I went on, after she moved in with me, was down to undersea Provincetown. It's an easy dive. Practically nothing to find there, since amateurs have picked it clean. But by the same token, all the hazards are well charted.

Cherry seemed to enjoy the expedition, spending hours slipping through the aquatic streets with wide eyes behind her mask. Once back aboard the *Gogo Goggins*, drying her thick hair with a towel, she said, "That was stringy, Russ! Lots of fun."

"You think you might like tossing in with me? You know, becoming business partners? We'd make good isk. Not that we need to earn much, like you said. And you could give up the illegal stuff—"

"Give up the Oyster Pirates? Never! That's my heritage! And to be honest with you, babe, there's just not enough thrills in your line of work."

Just as I was addicted to mongo, Cherry was hooked on plundering the shellfish farms, outwitting the guards and owners and escaping with her booty. Myself, I knew I'd be a nervous wreck doing that for a living. (She took me out one night on a raid; when the PEP discharges started sizzling through the air close to my head, I dropped to the deck of *Soft Grind* [which possessed a lot of speed belied by its appearance] and didn't stand up again till we reached home. Meanwhile, Cherry was alternately shouting curses at our pursuers and emitting bloodthirsty laughs.)

Luckily, we were able to reconcile our different lifestyles quite nicely. I simply switched to night work. Once I was deep enough below the surface, I had to rely on artificial lights even during the daytime anyhow.

Several nights each week, you'd find us motoring off side by side in our respective boats. Eventually our paths would diverge, signaled by a dangerous kiss across the narrow gap between our bobbing boats. As I headed toward whatever nexus of sunken loot I had charted, I'd catch up on ubik matters, writing dialogue for *One Step Closer to Nowhere*, the sitcom that had replaced *Naomi Instanton*, or monitoring border crossings for an hourly rate for the Minute Men.

Cherry and I would meet back home on my little island, which Cherry had christened "Sandybump." We'd sleep till noon or later, then have fun during the day.

A lot of that fun seemed to involve Foolty "FooDog" Fontal.

5. A Portrait of the Con Artist as a Young FooDog

During all the years we hung out together, we never learned where FooDog actually lived. He seemed reluctant to divulge the location of his digs, protective of his security and privacy even with his friends. (And recalling how easily he had stolen Cherry's identity from my friends list, who could blame him at worrying about unintentional data-sharing?) FooDog's various business, recreational, and hobbyist pursuits had involved him with lots of shady characters and inequitable dealings, and he existed, I soon realized, just one step ahead—or perhaps laterally abaft—of various grudge-holders.

I should hasten to say that FooDog's dealings were never—or seldom— truly unethical or self-serving. It's just that his wide-ranging enthusiasms respected no borders, sacred cows, or intellectual property rights.

But despite his lack of a public meatspace address, FooDog could always be contacted through the ubik, and Cherry and I would often meet him somewhere for what invariably turned out to be an adventure of the most hyphy dimensions.

I remember one day in November . . .

We grabbed a zipcar, FooDog slung several duffels in the interior storage space, and we headed north to New Hampshire. FooDog refused to tell us where we were heading till it was too late to turn back.

"We're going to climb Mount Washington? Are you nuts?" I picked up the feed from the weather observatory atop the peak. "There's a blizzard going on right now!"

"Precisely the conditions I need for my experiment."

The normal daily high temperature atop the peak at this time of the year was thirteen degrees Fahrenheit. The record low was minus twenty. In 1934, the observatory had recorded the biggest wind ever experienced on the planet: 231 MPH. There were taller places and colder places and windier places and places with worse weather. But Mount Washington managed to combine generous slices of all these pies into a unique killer confection.

Cherry said, "C'mon, Russ, trust the Dog."

I grumbled, but went along.

We made it by car up the access road to 4,300 vertical feet, leaving only

2,000 feet to ascend on foot. With many contortions, we managed to dress in the car in the smartsuits FooDog had provided. When we stepped outside, we were smitten with what felt like a battering ram made of ice. We sealed up our micropore facemasks and snugged our adaptive goggles more firmly into place. Cherry had a headset that provided a two-way audio feed to the ubik. We donned our snowshoes, grabbed our alpenstocks, and began the ascent, following the buried road that was painted by our ubik vision to resemble the Golden Brick path to Oz. FooDog carried a box strapped to his back, the object of our whole folly.

I won't belabor you with the journey, which resembled in its particulars any number of other crazed climbs atop forbidding peaks. Let's just say the trek was the hardest thing I've ever done.

We never even made it to the top. Around 5,500 feet, FooDog declared that he could conduct his experiment at that altitude, with the storm raging slightly less virulently around us. He doffed his box, unfolded its tripod legs, spiked it into the snow, and began sending an encrypted command stream to the gadget over the ubik.

"Can we know now what we risked our lives for?" I asked.

"Sure thing, nephew. This gadget messes with the quantum bonds between the hydrogen atoms in water molecules, via a directional electrostatic field. I've got it pointed upward now. Good thing, or we'd all be puddles of slop."

I took a nervous step or three away from the machine, unsure if FooDog was kidding or not. But I should have trusted him not to endanger us—at least via technology.

I looked toward Cherry, to make sure she was okay. She gave an exclamation of awe. I looked back toward the machine.

There was an expanding hemisphere of atmospheric inactivity above the gadget. It grew and grew, providing an umbrella of calm. Some snow still pelted us from the side, but none reached us from above.

FooDog's box was quelling the blizzard.

FooDog undid his mask. His black face, wreathed in a wide grin, stood out amidst all the white like the dot of a giant exclamation point.

"Hyphy!" he exclaimed.

The ubik was already going insane. Weather-watcher wikis frantically sought to dispatch entomopter cams to our location, to supplement the reports of the fixed sensors located at some distance, but were frustrated by the surrounding storm, still in full force. But I suspected that if FooDog's bubble continued to expand, sooner or later a cam would get through and ID us.

Evidently, FooDog had the same realization. He said, "Brace yourself," then shut off his machine.

The blizzard socked us with renewed vigor—although I seemed to sense in the storm a kind of almost-human shock, as if it had been alarmed by its interruption.

FooDog resealed his mask, and we headed down.

"Aren't you worried we'll be ID'd on the way down the mountain?"

"I hired the zipcar under a spoofed name, then despimed it. Cherry's untouchable, and you and I have our denial flags on. Once we get down the mountain, anyone who manages to get near us in meatspace will have to distinguish us from a hundred other identical cars on the road. We're as invisible as anyone gets these days."

"So your little invention is safe from greedy and irresponsible hands."

"Sure. Unless I decide to open-source it."

"You're kidding, right?"

But the Dog replied not.

So that's what the average outing with Foolty Fontal was like.

Of course, I had certain thrills in my own line of work.

One day my not-inconsiderable rep as a salvage expert attracted an offer from the Noakhali Nagas, a wiki from Bangladesh. That unfortunate country had suffered perhaps more than any, due to oceanic incursions. The creeping Bay of Bengal had submerged thousands of shrines. Rescuing deities would provide me with a significant chunk of lindens. And the challenge of new territory—the Cape Archipelago was starting to bore me a little after so many years—was a plus as well.

I sat with Cherry on our favorite spot, the deck of our house on Sandybump. It was late afternoon, our "morning" time, and we were enjoying brunch and watching the sun go down. I explained about the offer I had received.

"So—you mind if I take this job?"

"How could I? Go for it, babe! I'll be fine here alone till you get back."

I emerged from the warm waters of the Bay of Bengal on a Tuesday afternoon two months later to find a high-priority news item, culled from the ubik by one of my agents, banging at the doors of my atmosphere-restored connection.

Cherimoya Espiritu was in Mass General Hospital in Boston, suffering from various broken limbs and bruised organs, but in no mortal danger.

I blew every isk I had earned in Bangladesh plus more on a scramjet flight back to the UWA. Four hours later I was hustling through the doors of MGH.

Cherry smiled ruefully as I entered her room. Vast bruises, already fading from subcutaneous silicrobes, splotched her sweet face. Various casts obscured her lovely limbs. Wires from speed-healing machines tethered her down.

"Damn, Russ," Cherry exclaimed when she saw me, "I am so sorry about the house!"

6. Wormholes and Loopholes

Looking back at this narrative so far, I see that maybe right here is where my story actually begins, or should've begun. After all, it was Cherry's accident that precipitated my run for jimmywhale of the UWA, and the subsequent trade war, and that's when I entered the history books, even as a footnote. And that's what most people are interested in, right?

Except that how could I possibly have jumped into the tale right here? None of it would've made any sense, without knowing about my backstory and FooDog's and Cherry's. I would've had to be constantly interrupting myself to backfill.

And besides, aren't most people nowadays habituated to ruckerian metanovels, with their infinite resortability and indrajal links? Even though I chose to compose this account in a linear fashion, you're probably bopping through it in a quirky personalized path anyhow, while simultaneously offering planting advice to a golden-rice grower in Bantul, contributing a few bars to an electrosoul composer in Los Angeles, and tweaking the specs of some creature's synthetic metabolism with an a-lifer in Loshan.

So:

I rushed to Cherry's side and grabbed her hand.

"Ouch! Watch my IV!"

"Oh, babe, what happened? Are you gonna be okay?"

"Yeah, I'll be fine. It was just a stupid accident. But it wasn't really my fault. . . ."

Cherry had been sunning herself on the deck yesterday, half asleep. As the sun moved, she got up to shift her chair closer to the deck's edge. The next thing she knew, she was lying in the shallow waters surrounding Sandy-bump, buried under the timbers and pilings of the deck. Her head projected from the waters, allowing her to breathe painfully around her busted ribs. But lacking personal ubik access to summon help, she surely would've died in a short time from the shock of her injuries.

Luckily, the house itself knew to call one of the 911 wikis. Within minutes, an ambulance service run by the Organ Printers had her safely stabilized and on her way to MGH.

"The deck just collapsed, Russ! Honest. I didn't do anything to it!"

My concern for Cherry's health and safety began to segue to anger. Which wiki had built the deck? I started to rummage through the house's construction records, at the same time pulling up real-time images of my dwelling. The tearing-off of the deck had pulled away a portion of the exterior wall, opening our beloved house to the elements.

The Fatburgers. They were the wiki who had built my deck. Bastards! I was in the middle of composing a formal challenge suit against them, prior to filing it with a judicial wiki, when FooDog contacted me.

"You're back stateside, nephew! Great! But there's information you need to know before you rush into anything. Drop on by my offices."

"Can't you just tell me over the ubik?"

"Nah-huh. C'mon over."

I gingerly kissed Cherry good-bye, and left.

I pooled my public-transit request with those of a few dozen other riders heading in my direction, and I was over the Charles River in no time.

Foolty Fontal maintained an occasional physical presence in a building on Mass Avenue in Cambridge owned by the Gerontion wiki, whose focus was life-extension technology. Jealous of their potentially lucrative research, the Gerontions had equipped the building with massive security, both virtual and analogue, the latter including several lethal features. Thus FooDog felt moderately safe in using their premises.

But the building knew to let me in, and I followed a glowing trail of virtual footprints blazoned with my name to a lab on the third floor.

FooDog stood by a table on which rested a dissection tray. Coming up to his side, I looked down at the tray's contents.

I saw a splayed-open rust-colored worm about twenty inches long.

"Eeyeuw! What's that?"

"That and its cousins are what brought down your deck. Shipworms. *Teredo navalis.* Molluscs, actually. But not native ones, and not unmodified. This particularly nasty critter was created in a Caracas biolab. They were used in the hostilities against Brazil ten years ago. They'll even eat some plastics! Supposedly wiped out in the aftermath—extinct. But obviously not."

I poked the rubbery worm with a finger. "How'd they get up north and into my deck pilings? Is this some kind of terrorist assault?"

"I don't think so. Now that we know what to look for, I've done a little data-mining. I've found uncoordinated, overlooked reports of these buggers— enough to chart the current geographical dispersion of the worms and back-track to a single point of origin. I believe that a small number of these worms came accidentally to our region in the bilge water of a fully automated container vessel, the *Romulo Gallegos.* Looks like purely unintentional contamination. But until I know for sure, I didn't want to broadcast anything over the ubik and alert people to cover their tracks. Or rouse false alarms of an assault."

"Okay. I can think of at least three entities we can nail for this, and get some damages and satisfaction. The owner of the ship, the traders who employed him, and the jerks who created the worms in the first place."

"Don't forget our own coastal biosphere guardians, wikis like the Junior Nemos and the Aquamen. They should have caught this outbreak before it spread."

"Right! Let's go get them!"

"The conference room is down this way."

Ten empty chairs surrounded a large conference table formed from a single huge vat-grown burl. FooDog and I settled down in two seats, and then we called the offending parties to our meeting.

My SCURF painted onto my visual field the fully dimensional real-time avatars of our interlocutors sitting in the other chairs, so that it looked as if the room had suddenly filled with people in the flesh. Men and women scattered around the planet saw FooDog and me similarly in their native contexts.

Most of the avatars seemed to represent the baseline looks of the participants, but a few were downright disconcerting. I couldn't help staring at a topless mermaid, one of the Aquamen, no doubt.

FooDog smiled in welcoming fashion. "All right, ladies and gentlemen, allow me to introduce myself. . . ."

Everyone nowadays claims that instant idiomatic translation of any language into any other tongue is one of the things that has ushered in a new era of understanding, empathy, and comity. Maybe so. But not judging from my experiences that day, once FooDog had spread out his evidence and accusations to the mainly South American audience. We were met with stonewalling, denials, patriotic vituperations, countercharges and ad hominem insults. And that was from our English-speaking compatriots in the UWA! The Latinos reacted even more harshly.

Finally, the meeting dissolved in a welter of ill-will and refusal of anyone to take legal or even nominal responsibility for the collapse of my deck and the injuries suffered by poor Cherry.

I turned despondently to FooDog, once we were alone again. "Looks like we're boned, right? All our evidence is circumstantial. There's no way we can redress this through the system. I mean, aside from convincing any wikis I'm personally involved in to boycott these buggers, what else can I do?"

FooDog, good friend that he was, had taken my dilemma to heart.

"Damn! It's just not right that they should be allowed to get away with hurting you and Cherry like this."

He pondered my fix for another minute or so before speaking.

"Seems to me our problem is this: You got no throw-weight here, nephew. You're only one aggrieved individual. Your affiliate wikis are irrelevant to the cause. But if we could get the whole country behind you, that'd be a different story."

"And how do we do that?"

"Well, we could mount a big sob campaign. Get all the oprahs and augenblickers talking about you. Make you and Cherry into Victims of the Week."

"Oh, man, I don't know if I want to go that route. There's no guarantee we wouldn't come out of it looking like jerks anyway."

"Right, right. Well, I guess that leaves only one option—"

"What's that?"

FooDog grinned with the nearly obscene delight he always expressed when tackling a task deemed impossible by lesser mortals.

"If we want satisfaction, we'll just have to take over the UWA."

7. Starting at the Top

I had always steered clear of politics. Which is not to say I had neglected any of my civic duties: Voting on thousands of day-to-day decisions about how to run my neighborhood, my city, my state, my bioregion, and the UWA as a whole. Debating and parsing Wikitustional Amendments. Helping to formulate taxes, tariffs, and trade agreements. Drafting criminal penalties. Just like any good citizen, I had done my minute-to-minute share of steering the country down a righteous path.

But I had never once felt any desire to formally join one of the wikis that actually performed the drudgery of implementing the consensus-determined policies and legislation.

The Georgetown Girls. The Slick Willy Wonkettes. The Hamilfranksonians. The Founding Flavors. The Rowdy Rodhamites. The Roosevelvet Underground. The Cabal of Interns. The Technocratic Dreamers. The Loyal Superstition. The Satin Stalins. The Amateur Gods. The Boss Hawgs. The Red Greens. The Rapporteurs. The Harmbudsmen. The Shadow Cabinet. The Gang of Four on the Floor. The Winston Smiths. The Over-the-Churchills.

Maybe, if you're like me, you never realized how many such groups existed, or how they actually coordinated.

By current ubik count, well over five hundred political wikis were tasked with some portion of running the UWA on nonlocal levels, each of them occupying some slice of the political/ideological/intellectual spectrum and performing one or another "governmental" function.

Each political wiki was invested with a certain share of proportional power based on the number of citizens who formally subscribed to its philosophy. The jimmywhales of each wiki formed the next higher level of coordination. From their ranks, after much traditional politicking and alliance building, they elected one jimmywhale to Rule Them All.

This individual came as close to being the president of our country as anyone could nowadays.

Until deposed, he had the power to order certain consequential actions across his sphere of influence by fiat; to countermand bad decisions; to embark on new projects without prior approval: the traditional role of any jimmywhale. But in this case, his sphere of influence included the entire country.

Currently this office was held by Ivo Praed of the Libertinearians.

FooDog set out to put me in Ivo Praed's seat.

"The first thing we have to do," Foolty Fontal said, "is to register our wiki."

The three of us—myself, a fully recovered Cherry, and the Dog—were sitting on the restored deck of the Sandybump house, enjoying drinks and snacks under a clear sunny sky. (This time, concrete pilings upheld the porch.)

"What should we call it?" I asked.

Cherry jumped right in. "How about the Phantom Blots?"

FooDog laughed. I pulled up the reference on the ubik, and I laughed too.

"Okay, we're registered," said FooDog.

"Now what? How do we draw people to our cause? I don't know anything about politics."

"You don't have to. It would take too long to play by the rules, with no guarantees of success. So we're going to cheat. I'm going to accrue power to the Phantom Blots by stealing microvotes from every citizen. Just like the old scam of grifting a penny apiece from a million bank accounts."

"And no one's going to notice?"

"Oh, yeah, in about a week, I figure. But by then we'll have gotten our revenge."

"And what'll happen when everyone finds out how we played them?"

"Oh, nothing, probably. They'll just seal up the back door I took advantage of, and reboot their foolish little parliament."

"You really think so?"

"I do. Now, let me get busy. I've got to write our platform first—"

FooDog fugued out. Cherry got up, angled an umbrella across the abstracted black man to provide some shade, and then signaled me to step inside the house.

Out of earshot of our pal, she said, "Russ, why is FooDog going to all this trouble for us?"

"Well, let's see. Because we're buddies, and because he can't resist monkey-wrenching the system just for kicks. That about covers it."

"So you don't think he's looking to get something personal out of all this?"

"No. Well, maybe. FooDog always operates on multiple levels. But so long as he helps us get revenge—"

Cherry's expression darkened. "That's another thing I don't like. All this talk of 'revenge.' We shouldn't be focused on the past, holding a grudge. We came out of this accident okay. I'm healthy again, and the house is fixed. No one was even really to blame. It's like when those two species of transgenic flies unpredictably mated in the wild, and the new hybrid wiped out California's wine grapes. Just an act of God. . . ."

In all the years Cherry and I had been together, we had seldom disagreed about anything. But this was one matter I wouldn't relent on. "No! When I think about how you nearly died . . . Someone's got to pay!"

Shaking her head ruefully, Cherry said, "Okay, I can see it's a point of honor with you, like if one of the Oyster Pirates ratted out another. I'll help all I can. If I'm in, I'm in. I just hope we're not bringing down heavy shit on our heads."

The door to the deck slid open, admitting a blast of hot air, and FooDog entered, grinning face glistening with sweat.

"Okay, nephew and niece, we're up and running. Even as we speak, thousands and thousands of microvotes are accumulating to the wiki of the Phantom Blots every hour, seemingly from citizens newly entranced by our kickass platform. You should read the plank about turning Moonbase Armstrong into the world's first offworld hydroponic ganja farm! Anyhow, I figure that over the next forty-eight hours, the Blots will rise steadily through the ranks of the politco-wikis, until our leader is ready to challenge Praed for head jimmywhale."

Suddenly I got butterflies in my stomach. "Uh, FooDog, maybe you'd like to be the one to run the UWA. . . ."

"No way, padre. The Dog's gotta keep a low profile, remember? The farther away I can get from people, the happier I am. Nope, the honor is all yours."

"Okay. Thanks—I guess."

FooDog's calculations were a little off. It only took thirty-six hours before the Phantom Blots knocked the Libertinearians out as most influential politco-wiki, pushing Ivo Praed from his role as "president" of the UWA, and elevating me to that honor.

Sandybump, a speck of land off the New England coast, was now the White House. (Not the current museum, but last century's nexus of hyperpower.) I was ruler of the nation—insofar as it consented to be ruled. Cherry was my First Lady. And FooDog was my Cabinet.

Time to get some satisfaction.

8. Wikiwar

The day after my political ascension, we reconvened the meeting we had conducted at Gerontion, this time at Sandybump. All the same participants were there, with the addition of Cherry.

(Lots of other important national matters were continually arising to demand my attention, in my new role as head jimmywhale, but I just ignored them, stuffing them in a queue, preferring not to mess with stuff that I, for one, did not understand. This abdication of my duties would surely cause our charade to be exposed soon, but hopefully not before we had accomplished our goals.)

FooDog and I restated our grievances to the South Americans, but now formulated as a matter of gravest international diplomacy. (Foolty showed me the avatar he was presenting to the South Americans and our coastal management wikis, and of course it looked nothing like the real Dog.) This time, with the weight of the whole UWA behind our complaints, we received less harsh verbal treatment from the foreigners. And our compatriots caved right away, acknowledging that they had been negligent in not protecting our waterways from shipworm incursion. When FooDog and I announced a broad range of penalties against them, the mermaid shimmered and reverted to a weepy young teenaged boy.

But the South Americans, although polite, still refused to admit any responsibility for the Great Teredo Invasion.

"You realize, of course," said FooDog, "that you leave us no recourse but to initiate a trade war."

One of the Latinos, who was presenting as Che Guevara, sneered and said, "Do your worst. We will see who has the greater balance of trade." He stood up and bowed to Cherry. "Madam, I am sorry these outrageous demands cannot be met. But believe me when I say I am gratified to see you well and suffering no permanent harm from your unfortunate accident."

Then he vanished, along with the others.

Cherry, still un-SCURFED, had been wearing an antique pair of spex to participate in the conference. Now she doffed them and said, "Rebels are so sexy! Can't we cut them some slack?"

"No! It's time to kick some arrogant Venezuelan tail!"

"I got the list of our exports right here, nephew."

From the ubik, I studied the roster of products that the UAW sold to Venezuela, and picked one.

"Okay, let's start small. Shut off their housebots."

After hostilities were all over and I wasn't head jimmywhale anymore, I had time to read up about old-fashioned trade wars. It seems the tactics used to consist of drying up the actual flow of unshipped goods between nations. But with spimed products, such in-the-future actions were dilatory, crude, and unnecessary.

Everything the UWA had ever sold to the Venezuelans became an instant weapon in our hands.

Through the ubik, we sent commands to every UWA-manufactured Venezuelan housebot to shut down. The commands were highest override priority and unstoppable. You couldn't isolate a spimed object from the ubik to protect it, for it would cease to function.

Across an entire nation, every household lost its domestic cyber-servants.

"Let's see how they like washing their own stinking windows and emptying their own cat litter!" I said. "They'll probably come begging for relief within the hour."

FooDog had pulled up another roster, this one of products the Venezuelans sold us. "I don't know, nephew. I think we might take a few hits first. I'm guessing—"

Even as FooDog spoke, we learned that every hospital in the UWA had just seen its t-ray imagers go down.

"Who the hell knew that the Venezuelans had a lock on selling us terahertz scanners?" I said.

FooDog's face wore a look of chagrin. "Well, actually—"

"Okay, we've got to ramp up. Turn off all their wind turbines."

All across Venezuela, atmospheric power plants fell still and silent.

The response from the southerners was not long in coming. Thirty percent of the UWA's automobiles—the Venezuelan market share—ground to a halt.

FooDog sounded a little nervous when next he spoke. "Several adjacent countries derived electricity from the Venezuelan grid, and now they're demanding we restore the wind turbines. They threaten to join in the trade war if we don't comply."

I felt nervous too. But I was damned if I'd relent yet. "Screw them! It's time for the big guns. Bring down their planes."

Made-in-the-UWA airliners around the globe running under the Venezuelan flag managed controlled descents to the nearest airports.

That's when the Venezuelans decided to shut down the half of our oil-refining capacity that they had built for us. True, oil didn't play the role it once did in the last century, but that blow still hurt.

Then the Brazilians spimed *their* autos off, and the nation lost another forty percent of its personal transport capabilities.

Over the next eight hours, the trade war raged, cascading across several allied countries. (Canada staunchly stood by the UWA, I was happy to report, incensed at the disruption of deliveries from the Athabasca Oil Sands to our defunct refineries. But the only weapon they could turn against the southerners was a fleet of Zamboni machines at Latin American ice rinks.) Back and forth the sniping went, like two knights hacking each other's limbs off in some antique Monty Python farce.

With each blow, disruptions spread farther, wider, and deeper across all the countries involved.

The ubik was aflame with citizen complaints and challenges, as well as with a wave of emergency countermeasures to meet the dismantling of the infrastructure and deactivation of consumer goods and appliances and vehicles. The poltico-wikis were convulsing, trying to depose me and the Phantom Blots. But FooDog managed to hold them at bay as Cherry rummaged through the tiniest line items in our export list, looking for ways to strike back.

By the time the Venezuelans took our squirm futons offline, and we shut down all their sex toys, the trade war had devolved into a dangerous farce.

I was exhausted, physically and mentally. The weight of what Cherry, FooDog, and I had done rested on my shoulders like a lead cape. Finally I had to ask myself if what I had engineered was worth it.

I stepped out on the deck to get some fresh air and clear my head. Cherry followed. The sun was sinking with fantastically colorful effects, and gentle waves were lapping at Sandybump's beach. You'd never know that several large economies were going down the toilet at that very moment.

I hugged Cherry and she hugged me back. "Well, babe, I did my best. But it looks like our revenge is moot."

"Oh, Russ, that's okay. I never wanted—"

The assault came in fast and low. Four armored and be-weaponed guys riding ILVs. Each Individual Lifting Vehicle resembled a skirt-wearing grasshopper. Before either Cherry or I could react, the chuffing ILVs were hovering autonomously at the edge of our deck, and the assailants had jumped off and were approaching us with weapons drawn.

With cool menace one guy said, "Okay, don't put up a fight and you won't get hurt."

I did the only thing I could think of. I yelled for help.

"FooDog! Save us!"

And he did.

SCURF mediates between your senses and the ubik. Normally the

SCURF-wearer is in control, of course. But when someone breaks down your security and overrides your inputs, there's no predicting what he can feed you.

FooDog sent satellite close-ups of recent solar flares to the vision of our would-be-kidnappers, and the latest sludge-metal hit, amped up to eleven, to their ears.

All four went down screaming.

Cherry erased any remnants of resistance with a flurry of kicks and punches, no doubt learned from her bar-brawling brother Dolphin.

When we had finished tying up our commando friends, and FooDog had shut off the assault on their senses, I said, "Okay, nothing's worth risking any of us getting hurt. I'm going to surrender now."

Just as I was getting ready to call somebody in Venezuela, Che Guevara returned. He looked morose.

"All right, you bastard, you win! Let's talk."

I smiled as big as I could. "Tell me first, what was the final straw? It was the sex toys, wasn't it?"

He wouldn't answer, but I knew I was right.

9. Free to Be You and Me

So that's the story of how I ran the country for three days. One day of political honeymoon, one day of trade war, and one day to clean up as best we could before stepping down.

As FooDog had predicted, there were minimal personal repercussions from our teasling of the political system. Loopholes were closed, consensus values reaffirmed, and a steady hand held the tiller of the ship of state once again.

We never did learn who sent the commandos against us. I think they were jointly hired by nativist factions in league with the Venezuelans. Both the UWA and the South Americans wanted the war over with fast. But since our assailants never went on trial after their surgery to give them new eyes and eardrums, the secret never came out.

Cherry and I got enough simoleons out of the settlement with the Venezuelans to insure that we'd never have to work for the rest of our lives.

But she still goes out with the Oyster Pirates from time to time, and I still can't resist the call of mongo.

We still live on Sandybump, but the house is bigger now, thanks to a new wing for the kids.

As for FooDog—well, I guess he did have ulterior motives in helping us. We don't see him much anymore in the flesh, since he relocated to his ideal safe haven.

Running that ganja plantation on the moon as his personal fiefdom takes pretty much all his time.

ABOUT THE EDITOR

LOU ANDERS is an editor, author, and journalist. He is the editorial director of Prometheus Books's science fiction imprint, Pyr, as well as editor of the anthologies *Outside the Box* (Wildside Press, January 2001), *Live without a Net* (Roc, July 2003), *Projections: Science Fiction in Literature & Film* (MonkeyBrain, December 2004), and *FutureShocks* (Roc, Janurary 2005). He is the author of *The Making of Star Trek: First Contact* (Titan Books, 1996) and has published over five hundred articles in such magazines as *Publishers Weekly, The Believer, Dreamwatch, Star Trek Monthly, Star Wars Monthly, Babylon 5 Magazine, Sci Fi Universe, Doctor Who Magazine,* and *Manga Max,* as well as in several volumes of BenBella Books's SmartPop series. His articles and stories have been translated into German, French, Dutch, Italian, and Greek, and have appeared online at Believermag.com, SFSite.com, RevolutionSF.com, and InfinityPlus.co.uk. Visit him on the Web at www.louanders.com.